Pyromancer

Soul of the Witch Saga - Book 2
C. Marie Bowen

Pixler Publications

Pyromancer
Soul of the Witch Saga – Book 2
by C. Marie Bowen
Copyright © 2021 C. Marie Bowen

This book was previously published as *Coven Moon, Book 2*.
ISBN-13: 978-1-945215-148 – Paperback

ISBN-13: 978-1-945215-155 – EPUB

Edited by Liette Bougie

Cover Design by C. Marie Bowen

Published by Pixler Publications

Discover other titles by C. Marie Bowen at www.cmariebowen.com

Contents

1. Chapter 1   1

2. Chapter 2   9

3. Chapter 3   15

4. Chapter 4   21

5. Chapter 5   25

6. Chapter 6   29

7. Chapter 7   35

8. Chapter 8   42

9. Chapter 9   46

10. Chapter 10   54

11. Chapter 11   59

12. Chapter 12   64

13. Chapter 13   69

14. Chapter 14   76

15. Chapter 15   83

16. Chapter 16   90

17. Chapter 17   95

18. Chapter 18   100

19. Chapter 19   104

20.	Chapter 20	111
21.	Chapter 21	120
22.	Chapter 22	128
23.	Chapter 23	137
24.	Chapter 24	149
25.	Chapter 25	161
26.	Chapter 26	171
27.	Chapter 27	180
28.	Chapter 28	188
29.	Chapter 29	198
30.	Chapter 30	212
31.	Chapter 31	222
32.	Chapter 32	232
33.	Chapter 33	247
34.	Chapter 34	255
35.	Chapter 35	264
36.	Chapter 36	273
	A Sneak Peek at Passage	282
	Also by	299
	About the Author	300

Chapter 1

Ayden MacKenna

—

March 1869—Rajputana, India

Ayden bowed his respect to the fiery brazier perched on the stone altar and pulled a white linen cloth over the pan of ash in his hands. He backed away from the raised dais beside the sacred pool. The clear water reflected burning torches along the far wall and the Zoroastrian altar's holy flame.

He pivoted at the door and stepped from the tiled temple floor to the dirt of a large public square. A sprinkling of sand blew across the empty stone benches surrounding the community well. The women had returned home at nightfall with the children to share supper and evening prayers with their husbands.

The vast sky stretched from lingering day to the oncoming night. The last glimmer of sunlight colored the western horizon while stars emerged, bright and close in the warm, dry air to the east. Outside the compound of clay homes and thatched roofs, the desolate sand filled the Thar Desert and stretched as far as the eye could see.

Silence held the village except for the shuffle of livestock, anxious for Ayden's evening visit. Feeding the camels and horses would be his final task before finding rest in his room at the back of the temple.

Without warning, nameless anticipation filled his chest, and Ayden hesitated. He turned on his heel, casting an anxious glance around the deserted square. A dim but steady glow along the eastern horizon outlined the hills and attracted his attention. His breath caught as the slender curve of a full moon inched above the mountains and cast its thin white light across the desert.

The spasm that passed through his chest took him by surprise. A strong current of ancient magic lifted the hair on his forearms and the nape of his neck. His limbs shuddered, and he lost all strength. The bin of ashes tumbled from his hand as he sank to his knees.

What's happening?

A gasp escaped his parched throat when the sorcerous shackles which bound him to Magi Rakesh shattered. The sudden and unexpected release from those invisible chains burned like wildfire. His fingers curled into the dirt of the village square. In the darkness, a red glow outlined his hands. The illumination lasted until the magical tie severed completely.

He'd been unconscious when the enchantment that imprisoned him stole his life. He'd awakened days later aboard a ship destined for India, compelled to serve the Magi Rakesh and forbidden to use magic to free himself. If the spell cast to bind him had been this painful, he couldn't remember it.

Since his capture, he'd traveled across the seas to India, the servant of Great Magi Rakesh. Their journey took them from Bombay to the Himalayas to the Gulf of Mannar at the tip of India. Eventually, Rakesh settled in this small Zoroastrian village east of the city of Bilara.

How long had he been enslaved? Fifteen years? Twenty?

His rare ability to read future events in fire made him valuable to the magi. At twenty-one, he'd been knocked unconscious in Boston Harbor and given to Rakesh because of his pyromancy skill. At least, that is what Rakesh believed.

Ayden thought otherwise.

He'd recognized his assailants in those desperate moments before he lost consciousness—trusted men—brothers to the young woman he loved.

A raised voice from the village's far side broke the silence, and Ayden lifted his head.

Rakesh felt the bond break as well. He'll seek to enslave me again—or kill me.

Although he'd learned much of the magi's Eastern magic, Rakesh's *elemental-animations* would be difficult, if not impossible, for Ayden to counter alone.

I've but one choice.

Escape.

Another shout from Rakesh spurred Ayden to his feet, and he raced around the temple into his small room near the animal enclosure. He snatched up a woven bag and stuffed his other set of clothes inside, along with the black robe he'd purchased from an Arab trader the year before, and pulled the pack onto his back.

Ayden picked up the amulet given to him by Gravâratav, the local priest he'd worked with since coming to this village. Rakesh had been furious with Tav for offering such a valuable gift to a servant.

He grinned at the memory, pulled the chain over his neck, tucked the red stone amulet into his kurta, and then ran from the room.

He vaulted the low stone wall of the corral with one hand and landed effortlessly amidst the animals.

Familiar with his scent, the camels and horses either nudged him for dinner or stepped aside.

Camel or horse?

A camel would afford him the greater distance, but longevity wouldn't be the problem if he couldn't outpace Rakesh.

A sprinter then, one that can climb hills.

He slipped a rope halter over the dappled gray gelding, tossed a blanket across the animal's back, and was out of time.

"Ayden-Mac!" Rakesh stood on the far side of the open square, torch in hand. "Do not attempt to flee, or you shall suffer the full weight of my wrath!"

Ayden leapt onto the gelding's back and glanced toward the magi. "You'll have to catch me, you bastard," he muttered.

Rakesh raised the torch to the night sky, threw back his head, and mumbled the incantation that would give life to one of his *elementals*.

He knows better than to use fire against me, and water would be too weak in the desert. He'll create an earth- or wind-animation.

Ayden gripped the reins as he leaned over the horse's neck and pressed soft leather boots into the animal's sides. "Yah!"

The gray took two long strides across the enclosure then cleared the corral wall with grace. They gained speed on the eastern road as the ground shook beneath them. At this pace, if the gelding tripped, the fall would kill them both.

A quarter-mile later, Ayden risked a glance over his shoulder.

An *earth-animation* followed them. The large lumbering *elemental*, raised from stone and sand, moved swifter than Ayden would have thought possible. The *animation* held the shape of a wide-chested, headless man. No fingers to grasp, its boulder-sized fists were designed to crush its prey rather than capture.

A zigzagging crack in the ground shot ahead of the monstrosity and cleaved the road, eager to catch and trip the horse.

He couldn't escape without a fight.

The only elements available for Ayden to manipulate in the empty desert were *Earth* and *Air*.

Earth was Rakesh's strongest element.

Something unexpected then.

He wrapped the leather reins around one hand, pulled the amulet from his shirt, and gripped the red stone with the other. "Caz, come forth and do my bidding."

The spark of fire within the stone flashed through Ayden's fingers and clung to the golden chain singeing his shirt. The tiny *elemental* waited near Ayden's hand for his master's command.

"Share your flame with me, Caz." Ayden opened his hand.

Fire flowed from the *elemental*, creating a blaze which Ayden rolled in his open palm. When the whirling flame filled his hand from the wrist to fingers, he hurled the tightly wound fireball at the stone golem, striking the monster in the chest.

The fireball clung to the stone and caused the beast to stumble. But it regained its footing and forged ahead. The remaining fire bled off the living rock like water.

Undeterred, Ayden threw three more orbs of fire in quick succession, but they had no more effect than the first.

The only element left to me is air.

"Caz, return."

The tiny *fire-elemental* slid into the stone, pulsating red on Ayden's chest.

In desperation, he raised his hand, pulling the dry, static heat that rose from the desert into his grip. Then he twisted his hand, casting his invocation at the *elemental* behind him.

A whirlwind lifted from the dusty road around the golem's feet as static-spawned lightning impaled the monster again and again.

The flashes blinded Ayden, and he turned away, blinking to clear his vision.

They'd come far enough from the village that the east road had made its long sweeping curve south to parallel the mountains.

British regiments often camp in these hills.

Ayden yanked the reins and directed his tiring horse into the scrub alongside the road, then up the hillside. As they crested the first low rise, he looked back.

Where Ayden's lightning found its target, large chunks of rock had split from the massive, *animated-elemental*. Thrown back at the monster by the whirling wind, the beast swatted at pieces of himself, its original objective forgotten. As Rakesh's magic failed, one of the giant's legs crumbled. The dying *animation* fell and thrashed in the road.

Dust from Ayden's windstorm filled his horse's tracks and concealed the point where they left the road.

Now to find a British camp.

It was early in the season for regiments to seek shelter from the heat in the mountains, but not impossible. If Ayden had to, he'd ride to Ajmer-Merwara and claim sanctuary as an American citizen.

He rode down a small embankment, then up a larger hill. The Aravallis were old mountains, rounded and filled with foliage as he climbed higher out of the desert. A stone cliff barred their way, and he rode south until they could ascend again.

At the top of the next rise, he drew rein and viewed the desert below.

Lights from the fires in his village remained visible to the northwest. He didn't see any *animated-elementals* on the moonlit hills behind him, but he didn't care to linger and find out.

He slid from the tired horse and walked beside the animal up the next hill. To his left, on the far side of the ridge, a campfire lit the night.

"Halt!" A command made in the Hindi language.

Ayden raised his hands.

Of course, the British army would post guards.

Why had he imagined he'd ride unchallenged into their camp?

"I'm American," he spoke English rather than Hindi. "I seek asylum."

"Asylum?" The question came from the darkness behind him in heavily accented English.

"Yes. I was held captive and only just escaped."

"Drop the reins. Are you armed?"

"I have no weapons." Ayden let the rope slip through his fingers and thought momentarily about his magic and the amulet around his neck. "I only wish to return home."

A match struck, a bright flare in the night. "And where is that?" A dark-skinned soldier in a British uniform and turban lifted a torch.

A second guard held a rifle but lowered the barrel as he studied Ayden.

"Boston. It's a city in the State of Massachus—"

"I know where Boston is." The man with the torch gripped his arm. "You can explain to the captain."

The guard with the rifle took the reins from the ground and followed.

Ayden's hair, grown long and streaked with gray over the years, had come unbound from his topknot during the race to escape Rakesh. Dressed in a hip-length collarless kurta and worn work pyjamas, with his skin tanned dark, he appeared more native than Bostonian. When searched, they'd find similar clothing in the pack along with the Arabian robe. The only thing of value he carried was the amulet—a red stone on a worn metal chain.

They'll not know its value even without mind-magic.

He'd watched Rakesh wield subtle *earth-based mind-magic* for many years. The Indian magi used a type of sorcery his family would never have considered possible. Although confident he could imitate his former master, if necessary, he had never attempted the use of that intrusive *mind-magic* but would if it helped him get home.

Home.

He never thought to return to Boston—never imagined the magical enslavement had an end. Rakesh made him believe his service would be for life, and Ayden found no reason to think otherwise.

Until the coven-moon rose tonight.

He glanced up at the glowing orb as the guards escorted him into camp.

Eight tents faced a central campfire. The largest boasted a commander's badge beside the closed flap.

"The horse needs care," the soldier holding the gray's reins told his watch partner.

The man who gripped Ayden's arm nodded. "See to it. I'll speak with the captain."

They waited in silence near the fire until the flap over the large tent opened, and three men ducked through the passage.

"With the full moon to light our path, we can leave right away." A turbaned cavalry officer indicated the golden globe in the sky then straightened his uniform.

"Good. That will see you well on your way to the gulf by morning." The captain's gaze caught Ayden's, and he held up a hand of dismissal to the cavalry officer. "Who is this, private?"

"We found him near the camp perimeter. He claims to be American."

"I *am* American." Ayden straightened his shoulders and stared at the officer. "I seek aid to return home."

The commander stepped close and narrowed his eyes. "You don't look American."

"I've been in India for twenty years."

"He said he was a prisoner," the private added. "He wants asylum."

"Asylum?"

"Safety from the man who kept me prisoner, yes—but above all else, I wish to return home."

The officer studied Ayden for several moments and then tipped his head. "There's a cavalry unit leaving now. If you like, you may accompany them."

Ayden's chest relaxed as he exhaled. "I have a gelding—"

"His horse is being cared for by Private Syed," the guard said. "He had no saddle."

"Have Private Syed provision the horse. There are old saddles in the tack house."

"Yes, Sir." The private departed at a brisk pace.

"Thank you, sir. I was afraid you would deny my request."

"I would have except for one thing." The captain smiled. "I have a cousin who has lived in Boston most of his life. Two summers ago, we spent time together at our late grandmother's estate in London." He chuckled and grinned again at Ayden. "I teased him mercilessly over the way he spoke. I can hear him in your words. You are, indeed, an American." He gestured to the pot hanging above the fire. "If you're hungry, you should eat now."

Ayden took advantage of the offer, filling one of the stacked metal bowls with stew. "Where is the cavalry heading?"

"The Gulf of Cambay. You should be able to find a ship going around the horn, or better yet, an overland passage across Egypt to the Mediterranean."

"I have no money to purchase passage either way."

The commander shrugged as Private Syed returned with the gray. "I have a feeling you'll be able to manage. Find work on a merchant ship or in the harbor."

Ayden put his empty bowl with the others and offered the man his hand. "Again, you have my thanks. If you ever visit your cousin in Boston, be sure to look for Ayden MacKenna."

The captain took his hand. "I will, Mr. MacKenna. I wish you the best of luck."

Ayden mounted the gray, now fitted with a worn leather saddle.

Several riders passed the tents on their way down the trail on the far side of the camp.

The cavalry officer wearing the turban rode between the tents and reined in beside the commander. "A not so young recruit?" he asked as he watched Ayden mount.

"An American citizen under our protection, Lieutenant Wells. He wishes to return home."

Chapter 2

Ayden MacKenna

—

October 2, 1872 – North Atlantic near Boston harbor

The lookout called the sight of land as Ayden came on deck; his black robe flapped furiously in the wind. A steady breeze filled the sails and sent a fine ocean spray over the rail to cool Ayden's face and hands. He'd cut his hair and trimmed his beard, even purchased trousers and a frock coat in London, but he'd kept the robe. And the amulet.

"We've made good time this trip." Captain Meadows stopped at the rail beside Ayden.

"What do they say? Fair winds?"

"Aye, and following seas. This voyage has been all of that, especially for this time of year." The captain puffed his pipe and returned to his duties. He paused and remarked over his shoulder, "Highly unusual. A blessing indeed."

Ayden nodded and looked up at the full sails.

My fair wind. My following sea. You're welcome, Captain.

Hours spent watching the watery horizon had darkened Ayden's already tanned face and hands. Although, at times, it seemed his skin had permanently browned from the many years in the Indian desert.

Ahead, the glittering midday sun sparkled across the water, and he squinted at the harbor in the distance.

Almost home.

He'd scarce allowed himself to dream of this. Over twenty years had passed since he'd last seen this harbor. Cudgeled by the two cowardly James brothers, he'd been thrown into the hold of a foreign ship and right into the clutches of Magi Rakesh.

The journey from the British camp in the Aravalli Mountains had been a long one. Longer than he had anticipated.

The cavalry unit he traveled with made good time to the Gulf of Cambay. In the city of Surat, near the mouth of the Tapti River, he and the British had parted ways. The merchant vessels belonging to the British India Company were happy to take their brethren aboard. Not so with a penniless American.

He slept in alleyways and worked odd jobs, saving what little he earned. After a year, he was fortunate to find a working berth in the galley on a passenger vessel bound for Cyprus via the newly opened Suez Canal. From there, he worked his way as a galley man across the Mediterranean Sea to Algiers, then through the straits of Gibraltar to Lisbon. After that, he traveled by merchant's vessel to Portsmouth, England.

In Portsmouth, he worked as a bartender near the harbor. It was there he met Captain Meadows and negotiated a passenger's berth on Meadow's ship, scheduled to set sail for Boston within the next fortnight.

Another shout from the crow's nest drew him from his reverie, and he pushed the hood from his head and stared at the harbor as it drew nearer.

Many times, during his captivity, he'd tried to read his lover's fate in a fire. But visions of her ceased the day her brothers had trundled him like a pig and sold him to the dark-skinned magi.

Perhaps his vision couldn't span the ocean.

She'll be gone. Even if she remains in Boston, she'll have made a new life without me.

A woman as beautiful and talented as Margaret James would have had no difficulty finding another to replace him. He couldn't return with false hope, set on revenge, and expect to make a life for himself. Besides, there were other people he needed to find.

Like my parents and baby brother, Melvyn.

Whatever these years had bestowed upon the James brothers and his lovely Margaret, they would have to wait. He needed to find his family.

Gods, give me the strength to bind the vicious wound within my soul and leave it be.

As the ship sailed into the harbor, Ayden withdrew to the small cabin he shared with three other men. He removed and folded away his comfortable robes and pyjamas and dressed in the only western clothes he owned, a simple pair of slacks, a collarless cotton shirt, and a brown frock coat. He packed his few remaining items into his used carpetbag, tucked the amulet into his shirt, and returned to the deck.

Once the ship was tied off and the gangway secured, a port official came aboard to speak with the captain. He held the vessel's manifest while one of the young cabin boys brought a small writing desk and chair. After he seated himself at the top of the gangway, he began to process the passengers.

The port official glanced up from his record book. "Your name and place of birth, sir."

"Ayden MacKenna, born in New Haven, Connecticut. Returning home to Massachusetts."

"Welcome home, Mr. MacKenna. Next."

With a flick of his wrist, the official placed a check beside Ayden's name, and the pyromancer proceeded down the gangway to shore.

There were several things Ayden needed to do, too many for the time left in the day.

The pier seemed to rock beneath his feet as he dodged through sailors and merchants, holding tight to his bag.

A busy drinking establishment caught his eye. Revere's Tavern looked like an ideal place to seek employment if the patronage gave any indication. Surely, they needed someone who could pour a drink or sweep the floor.

He stepped inside and paused beside the entrance to allow his eyes to adjust to the shaded interior. A sparkling chandelier from a high ceiling filled the room with a dim but steady light. Men relaxed at the tables, some enjoying a meal and a few drinking and gambling.

The decorative rail from the staircase extended across the second-floor balcony above the bar. Women in various stages of undress lounged there, peering down onto the tavern floor. A thin redhead wiggled her fingers at him.

Ayden lowered his chin and made his way to the bar.

"What'll you have?" the white-shirted bartender asked as he wiped the counter with a towel.

"I'm looking for work." Ayden pointed to the dusty floor and several empty tables covered with dirty dishes. "I could keep this place tidy, the floor swept, and the tables clean."

The barkeep, shorter than Ayden, with a shiny bald pate and a thick handlebar mustache, narrowed his eyes and considered him. "I have a girl who cleans up." He scanned the bar, then shook his head and tossed the bar rag under the counter. "No telling where she's gotten off to—or with whom."

"I could start now."

The older gentleman considered Ayden's carpetbag, then tipped his head as if considering him. "You're no youngster. By the look of you, I'd say you've seen forty years or better. Just off a ship?"

"Yes, to both." Ayden set his bag down and leaned his elbows against the bar. "Boston is home—or was." He took a breath and smiled. "I've been away."

"And now you're back hoping for a fresh start."

"You're very perceptive."

"I've been tending bar a long time. You get that way." He lifted the hinged counter, stepped from behind the bar, and nodded to a younger man serving drinks from behind the counter. "My son," he said by way of explanation and extended his arm. "Let's talk." He pointed to an empty table and chair beside the bar then held out his hand. "Marion Tull."

Ayden took his hand in a firm grip. "Ayden MacKenna."

Marion took a seat as Ayden pushed his bag out of the way and sat across from him.

The bald man considered Ayden for several moments before he spoke. "It's not easy to start over." He raised his hand to forestall Ayden's comment. "And I do need someone trustworthy, older than my boy, who can take orders when we're busy, clean tables, and sweep up when we're slow."

"I can do all that. *Trust me.*" Desperate to land this opportunity, Ayden shaded his words with *earth-skill* like he'd observed Rakesh use for so many years.

"Do you have a place to stay?"

"Not yet."

You're fortunate to have met me.

Ayden placed the mental suggestion with *mind-magic* and promised himself Marion Tull would never regret this decision.

Marion ran a hand over his hairless head and watched two men enter the establishment. "I happen to have a room in the back. It used to be an office before I bought the upper floors from the landlord." He raised a bushy eyebrow at Ayden. "After you clean it out, you are welcome to stay there until you find something better."

Ayden smiled. "When do I start?"

"Clean out the room first, then come see me for the outside key. Take today and get your bearings. Have a bath and get cleaned up. You'll start tomorrow. We open at noon."

Their chairs scraped across the wooden floor as they came to their feet.

"Follow me, and I'll show you the room. Then I need to get back to work." Marion entered the back room and wound his way through stacked liquor crates, grain bags, and canned goods. "The kitchen is over there." He waved at the far side of the room. "You can find a meal there when you need one. Introduce yourself to Qiang first. Let him know you're a new hire."

Marion opened a wooden door and stepped back.

The ten by twelve rectangular room had a door and a dirty window that looked onto an alleyway. Empty pallets covered the floor.

"I appreciate the work and the room. I won't let you down." Ayden set his bag inside the dusty room and then shook Marion's hand again.

"It is my good fortune to have met you." Marion nodded as he stepped back. "Stack those pallets over there." He pointed to an empty corner of the stock room. "I need to get back to the bar. My young Harry can get overwhelmed when he's by himself. I'll have the key to that outside door when you're done."

Ayden watched his new employer hurry through the back room, then walked to the window and wiped a portion clean with the edge of an empty potato sack.

A coal stove stood in one corner, along with an empty coal bin.

It's not much, but it's a start.

Ayden had a lot to do before noon tomorrow. He needed a new suit of clothes or two. One set, appropriate for work, like the wool slacks and white cotton shirts Marion wore, the other town clothes, a winter jacket, and a hat. He lifted a corner of the nearest pallet and pulled it through the door into the stockroom.

He'd also find a bathhouse, a barber, and a used furniture dealer. After he accomplished what he needed to do today, he'd settle back in his new room and build a small fire.

He needed to stare into the flames and find out what he could see.

Chapter 3

Jason Harris

—

October 17, 1872 —Boston, Massachusetts

Jason stepped from Revere's Tavern much later than usual. He inhaled the heavy mist that had rolled in from the harbor and cloaked the empty waterfront in dense fog. Instead of clearing his head of cheap perfume, the air reeked of dead fish, coal smoke, and oil.

He scanned the street from left to right. Along the wharf, silence held the night. No hansom cabbie called out to him to earn a late-night fare.

Already regretting tomorrow's early start, Jason held his walking stick beneath his arm as he tugged on his gloves and adjusted his top hat.

No help for it. I'll have to walk home.

The cobblestone pavement glistened with moisture under the cloud-diffused light of the streetlamp as he made his way to High Street. His usual companion, Otis Pierce, had picked up their tab and left the bar hours earlier after Jason had come to an agreeable price with a whore named Molly. He'd bedded Molly before, but she'd since raised her rates. Eventually, he'd met her price, as she'd known he would.

That's something else that must end.

Jason swore under his breath at his own stupidity. Not only was his purse lighter by a substantial sum, but he'd also have to go without a decent night's rest. Then his mouth twitched with amusement remembering his evening in

Molly's arms. As much as he enjoyed her stamina and expertise, he would have to find a less expensive partner next time.

He paused beneath the corner light to check his pocket watch.

Footfalls behind him continued for a moment and then ceased.

The hair on the back of Jason's neck lifted and he snapped the watch cover closed. The time forgotten, his ears strained into the darkness along the un-lighted diagonal cross street.

Someone follows and wishes to remain out of sight—for now.

He moved away from the pool of light and made his way up the thorough-fare. Too early for newspaper and milk delivery and too late for commerce, the downtown streets carried the sound of his muffled steps through the stillness.

The area near the wharf wasn't the best part of town, but he and Otis always hailed a cab from the tavern. They'd never had any trouble. Not that footpads were unheard of, but they tended to prey on solitary individuals late at night.

He scoffed at himself.

Here I am, their perfect target.

Jason's heart rate quickened. He set a brisk pace for another block, well into the business district, then abruptly turned the corner and pressed his back against the granite building. Steam from his breath added to the foggy night as he slid the épée from his carved walking stick. Not the fine dueling rapier he'd learned to use during his tour of France, the deadly three-sided blade would fend off a thug with a blackjack well enough.

Muffled footsteps stopped before the stalker reached the corner.

Jason waited for several moments, then clenched his teeth and spun around the corner of the building, épée in one hand and the wooden cane in the other.

The man stood at the corner of the cross street. The streetlight illuminated his back and cast his face in shadow. Taller than Jason, his pursuer wore a gentleman's greatcoat, collar up, with a top hat pulled low over his forehead.

Jason took a step forward. "I am no easy mark, sir. State your business or be on your way."

The man hesitated as though he were about to speak, then without uttering a word, turned and ran down the side street.

Jason held his stance and listened to the footfalls fade, senses alert to the night.

A foghorn sounded in the harbor, and the slow clip-clop of hoofbeats spoke of dawn and the merchants who would soon claim the streets.

Finally, feeling rather foolish, he slid the épée into his cane, straightened his coat and hat, and headed for his father's home on Beacon Hill.

The next morning, Jason woke later than usual and hurried through his morning routine. He had experienced only a few moments of restlessness after falling into bed last night, thinking about the footpad before sleep had finally claimed him.

He bit into a crisp apple as he descended the curved staircase. The freshly oiled banister sparkled like glass over the cherry wood. He paused in the foyer to check his neckerchief in the mirror beside the morning room door.

"I spoke with Bethany Dunham," his mother said. Her voice reached him through the open door. "She and I believe her daughter would be perfect for our Jason. Donetta is a tiny bit of a thing—blonde, biddable, and a perfect match for our son. They could announce their engagement at the masquerade."

Jason choked slightly on the piece of apple in his mouth, chewed swiftly, and swallowed.

What is this?

Tie forgotten—he leaned closer to the open door to hear his father's reply.

"As long as the girl's dowry is sufficient, I see no problem. Oh, by the by, I've invited a shipping merchant to your masked soirée. If he and I can reach an agreement, it will broaden our portfolio to include a steady flow of merchandise from the Orient."

"Oh Spencer, that's marvelous!" his mother gushed.

"Now, if only I could convince our son to give up that foolishness about becoming a barrister and agree to work for me."

Jason's lips pressed thin as he straightened and turned the corner into the sunlit morning room.

This nonsense had to stop.

His parents sat in their usual places. His father, Spencer, at the head of the table, and his mother, Rose, dressed in her morning gown, beside him.

Patrick, one of the new house servants, lowered a silver tray to allow his mother to take a pat of butter. The three paused as Jason crossed the room to the table, taking a second bite of the apple.

"Put the fruit down, dear." His mother indicated the clean plate, silver, and glassware across from her. "We've set a place for you."

Jason chewed and swallowed before he spoke. "I can't. Nathan is expecting me. I promised to meet him first thing this morning. His father won a large contract from Majestic Freight, and we must put their books in order immediately."

Rose's shoulders slumped, and air whooshed out, seeming to deflate her large bosoms. "But we have news, and I'd hoped to discuss several things with you this morning." She tapped his plate with the edge of her butter knife. "Sit down."

Jason glanced at his father.

Spencer ruled his home with a tyrannical fist, which may have been one reason Uncle Quincy chose to seek his fortune out west rather than live under his brother's thumb in Boston.

Nichole and her mother left Boston last summer, taking the train to join Uncle Quincy in Denver. Although Nichole arrived safely, Quincy's wife had not. Aunt Emily died unexpectedly on the train before reaching Colorado. His cousin remained devastated and often wrote to Jason.

"Hush, Rose. Give him the gist of your news and let him run along and play with his friend."

Heat inched up beneath Jason's collar, and he cleared his throat. "I'm not a child and working with Nathan is not a game. His father owns Dunham Accounting." He gave his father a slight smile. "I'm learning the accounting trade."

"I thought you had apprenticed to that barrister—what was his name? Hall?—because you were so anxious to become an attorney." Spencer's face darkened with ire.

"I am, and I do. I file and transcribe notes for Barrister Hall in the evenings, as you know quite well. The intricacies of law fascinate me. But my apprenticeship for Mr. Hall is performed without payment. The work I do for Mr. Dunham earns a wage."

"You should work for me." Spencer raised an eyebrow and pierced his son with an ice-blue glare. Once golden-haired like Jason, his father's thick curls had softened to silver.

Jason could hardly remember his Uncle Quincy, although he assumed the brothers looked much alike since Jason and his cousin, Nichole, had often been mistaken for siblings. Their golden curls and light blue eyes were striking individually. Together, they often caused strangers to stop and stare.

He tossed the apple core onto his empty plate and straightened his shoulders. "We've had this conversation before. We'll not have it again, especially this morning. As I said, I'm in a rush."

"At least listen to what your mother has to say before you go." Spencer turned back to his plate, his disappointment in his son palpable in the air between them.

Rose perked up and smiled as Jason turned his attention to her. "I want to remind you about our yearly masquerade on All Hallows' Eve. You'll need to be in attendance."

Jason closed his eyes and tipped his head back. "Mother, I don't have time—"

"I need you here," Rose spoke sharply, then ducked her head as her gaze darted to Spencer. Her voice softened, "I require your help hosting the guests. Your father may be otherwise occupied with a new business venture." Rose lifted one shoulder and pushed a piece of sausage across her plate. "Besides, it would be a perfect opportunity to announce an engagement. Do you remember little Donetta Dunham?"

The heat edging up his collar infused Jason's face, and his teeth ground together.

This is why I work two jobs. The quicker to be on my own and away from here.

Between his mother and his father, Jason would never be allowed to be his own man or make his own decisions. "Mother—"

"Leave off, Rose. You've embarrassed the boy. Look at his face." Spencer smirked and pointed his fork at the flaming skin on Jason's neck and cheeks. "He wants to sow his oats a while longer."

"This isn't embarrassment. This is anger." Jason pushed back his jacket, resting one hand on his belt as he leaned over the table, and punctuated his words with his finger on the table. "Mother, you need to understand. I do not intend to marry Donetta Dunham. Nor will I announce an engagement to suit your fancy or provide drama for your party."

"But Jason, the girl is perfect for you." Rose smiled hesitantly at her husband for confirmation. "You work for her father. You're friends with her brother. Her mother and I are the best of friends. Besides, her dowry would set you both up quite nicely."

"You could use her dowry to buy into the bank as a partner," Spencer proclaimed.

"For the last time—no! An engagement with Donetta is not open for discussion. I won't marry her." Jason buttoned his jacket and stepped back from the table. "And I won't be at dinner tonight. I have other plans."

"Stay away from that Pierce boy." Spencer dabbed his napkin to his lips while he eyed his son. "The apple doesn't fall far from the tree with that one. His father's business is highly questionable. Unscrupulous. Money should be invested wisely, for long-term growth, not used for speculation and chanceful gains in an unstable market."

"P&P Investments is a respected firm. Otis works for his father in the same way that Nathan works for his—"

"As you should work for me," Spencer declared and then sipped a freshly filled cup of tea.

Patrick stepped back from the table, holding the silver teapot with a clean linen draped over one arm. The wealthy could hire Irish immigrants for a fraction of what their Negro servants would demand. It seemed to Jason the entire household staff changed color overnight.

Jason met Patrick's gaze, and for a moment, the two men shared an unspoken understanding.

"Oh, and Saturday," his mother continued, "I'll need you to accompany me on my errands in preparation for the ball. Please make yourself available." Rose's smile did not reach her eyes as she sliced a small piece of sausage.

"As you wish, Mother." Without another word, Jason turned on his heel and left the morning room. He nodded his thanks to the new light-skinned maid as she offered him his top hat and cane. Before his father could call him back for another round of browbeating, he fled out the front door.

Whatever it takes, I must find a way to get away from this house.

Chapter 4

Amy Prescott

—

Amy scooped up the injured dove that struggled beside the back step. The bird quieted as she tucked it in the crook of her arm and covered the poor thing with her shawl. She considered the fleeting sky and the wind-blown clouds reflected in the upper story windows.

It must have flown into the glass and broken its wing—poor thing.

She glanced over her shoulder at the back door as she carried the bird across the narrow strip of lawn and peeked inside the carriage house. Assured the small building was empty, she slipped inside the unlatched door with a final guarded look toward the house. She'd learned to be cautious when she planned to use magic.

With the bird cradled close to her chest, she edged toward the workbench and knelt in the corner away from the door. The bird remained motionless in her warm hand, its damaged wing bent and extended.

Amy took a deep, cleansing breath and closed her eyes. Perhaps her previous attempts to heal injured animals had failed due to her lack of ceremony.

Mama would know the proper prayers.

But her mother, Margaret Prescott, had turned away from magic years ago, teaching her daughter only enough to instill in Amy a deep abiding fear.

Fear of mistakes. Fear of discovery.

Although that didn't stop Amy from using her magic, it did force her to hide her attempts.

She whispered in the darkened work area, asked the Goddess to bless her purpose, and then called the four elements to join and ward her task.

Her hands, clasped around the injured bird, warmed with a golden light. Eyes closed, her inner sight pushed down into the bird, past the feathers and skin. The tiny heart fluttered. Her *earth-vision* moved through the small body to the broken wing.

The smaller bones in the appendage were sound, but the larger bone, the humerus, had fractured. The ability to see the injury would be of no help. The skill to knit bone would take a type of magic she'd been born without—*Fire*.

"Amy?" Her mother called from the back door.

Startled, Amy released the dove. It hopped, broken limb extended, from her hand and disappeared behind a pile of leather scraps.

"Are you in here?"

"Yes, Mama." Amy stood and brushed at her skirt. She stepped around a saddle stand as her mother peered from the doorway into the darkened interior of the carriage house. "I'm here."

Her mother, Margaret, stood shorter than Amy by a hand's width and had grown soft and rounder over the years.

"Dear heart, what are you doing?" Margaret held an open envelope in her hands and had a suspicious look in her eye.

"I found an injured bird by the step—" Amy began.

"Shh!" Her mother edged into the carriage house, drawing Amy back into the darkness, and lowered her voice. "Do not even speak of it." She glanced back at the house. "There are things your father must never know. That no one can know."

"I understand. But you see—"

Her mother's voice dropped even lower, "Amy. You do not have the skill to heal. You never will. Healing requires the highest level of both *earth-* and *fire-magic*. You have no *fire-magic* within you. Not a drop." Margaret hesitated, then shook her head. "Even as I am blessed with all four elements, I cannot heal."

"You don't use your magic. Perhaps if you did—"

"I choose not to, Amylia. These gifts are dangerous. I've tried to show you enough to understand and appreciate your skills, along with the wisdom to be circumspect." Margaret reached up and touched Amy's face. "Keep to your herbs and flowers, dear heart. Those are the skills you have."

"*Earth* and *Water*." Amy took her mother's hand.

"Darling, wort-cunning is not considered a crime against the church. Your salves and ointments are miraculous enough."

"What's in the envelope?" Amy asked to change the subject. She stepped from the shadow of the workroom, drawing her mother with her. Sunlight danced along the streaks of gray in her mother's dark hair, piled in a loose bun atop her head.

Margaret took Amy's arm and led her toward the back of the house. "Your father has met with a potential investor. Spencer Harris has inquired about sponsoring a shipment of silk and spices from the Orient. If the voyage proves profitable, there could be an opportunity for expansion."

"All of that is in that small envelope?" Amy smiled at her mother's excitement. They stepped into the kitchen and continued into the dining room.

"Of course not." Margaret laughed. "Mr. Harris and his wife are having a masquerade ball on All Hallows' Eve—your birthday. This is an invitation for the three of us to attend."

"Mama, you know I don't enjoy—"

"But it wouldn't hurt you to support your father." Her mother's tone left no room for argument.

"Masquerade, not costume?" Amy grinned at her mother.

Margaret laughed and shook her head. "A mask and gown to match, sweetling. This will not be your opportunity to dress as a witch."

"I have gowns I've yet to wear even once." Amy sighed with resignation. "I'll want nothing new. I'll choose from what I have."

"Do not think to dress in black." Margaret's brow rose. "A lovely pastel, perhaps. You can take samples of our dress fabrics to the milliner on Saturday. He's been retained by Mrs. Harris and is said to make fine quality items. You can choose a mask and give him our swatches." Margaret placed the envelope on the calling table. "Take tonight and decide which gown you will wear. The soirée will be fun."

Wonderful.

Amy forced a smile and a nod for her mother, then climbed the stairs to her room.

"Oh, and Amy, the Harris's have a son close to your age."

Amy cringed. At twenty-two, she considered herself a confirmed spinster, as did other women her age who were married and had children. She had never been a popular debutante and never tried to fit in. Simpers and giggles were not part of her personality, and above all, her dark and dangerous secret made it difficult to share interests with friends.

Besides, to hide her true magical nature from a husband—as her mother did—would be preposterous.

Why marry at all?

"I hear he's quite handsome." Her mother called up the stairs.

Chapter 5

Ayden MacKenna

—

Ayden rested on his small cot, his head propped in one hand as he stared at the fire through the open door of the coal stove. The glow of the charcoal embers and movement of the flame spoke to him of times past and times yet to come. He let the half-vision, half-memory play across his tired sight as exhaustion lowered his eyelids.

The last two weeks had flown by in a blur of work schedules and errands for Mr. Tull. Each morning, Ayden would drop into bed after sweeping the barroom floor and awaken with only enough time to wash, dress, and open the tavern.

As a master pyromancer, he'd been forced to devote half his life reading futures for another. This morning, he intended to catch up—if he could stay awake enough to direct his vision.

He rubbed his eyes and blinked at the flames.

Let's start with the past.

Shadows moved within the flames and resolved into children. A group of boys, ragged in their play clothes, ran through the street and down to the pier.

His friends, Ross, and Freckles were regular, unskilled kids, running fast and looking for treasure along the waterline. Older and bigger, Emery decided who could play with them and who couldn't. A bully to the younger boys, Emery reminded Ayden of a couple of the coven children he'd known.

He hadn't thought of them in years.

The image in the flame changed as years passed. No longer a child and tall for his age, he saw himself, a serious young man with dark hair, initiated into the coven—pride and love shown from his parents' faces that night.

Across the room, he glimpsed the matriarch of the James family.

Chantal James.

She was a hard woman, especially after the death of her husband. She blamed Ayden for not seeing enough of the tragedy in the flames to prevent it. Chantal had gathered her family, the twins, and her daughter to leave the Samhain Celebration early. As she left the barn, she'd turned and looked directly at him, her glare filled with disgust and reproach.

Margaret James.

Even now, through the flames of time, he could feel the emotion that wove through his chest when Margaret James ran across the wide yard and smiled at him. That she could smile at all, with the strange and obsessive family she belonged to, astounded him.

Gods, how I loved her.

To know what became of her, he would have to skip forward too far, and he desperately wanted to remember her kiss, one more time, even if the visions were distorted by fire and tears.

Their coven assembled monthly, by the light of the coven moon, but Margaret had not been allowed to attend after her father's death. Instead, he met Margaret as often as they could in a hideaway near her home. She'd been seventeen and Ayden nineteen the first time passion swept them away, and they consummated their love for one another. The power of that shared melding of flesh and magic bound them.

At least, I thought it had.

Ayden observed in the flames as he and Margaret made their vows of love to each other, and as he watched, rage at her family filled him. At what they'd done to him—*to them*—for the sake of their mother's insane prophecy and petty revenge.

He rolled from his narrow bed and stood facing the wall. A man of forty-four had no business filling himself with the passion and fury of a twenty-year-old. He'd been so young then.

So naive.

There had been other witch children in the coven besides him and the James family. Of course, his little brother Melvyn would have been too young to attend those gatherings, but Ayden could only remember two other names, Gordon Carmichael and Milton Kohler. Tough and proud of their skills, they terrorized the youngest in the group with their threats of curses and disfigurement. He'd been wary of those two, but he had overlooked the ones closest to him, Margaret's brothers—the twins.

He scrubbed his hand across his face and moved to the window, pushing the heavy curtain wide and filling his tiny room with light. The alleyway was empty, and the morning light splashed across the adjacent building.

The embers' glow behind him reflected in the glass, and the outline of his silhouette stared back at him. Those twenty years in India had aged him. He still had the same thick curls, only now they were sprinkled with silver across his head and white at his temples. His beard, when he allowed it to grow, would be laced with silver.

No longer the sinewy lad he'd been at nineteen. His years of enforced magic and hard labor had filled out his arms and chest, hardening him both physically and mentally.

But it was his emotions that were raw and open—stinging blisters that shed bitter tears.

That will have to change.

He sniffed and wiped his eyes. With deliberation, he closed the curtains and returned to stir the coals with a poker. When the flames settled to a low burn, he resumed his seat on the cot.

The last twenty years—show me what I've missed.

From Gujarat Province in India, he had tried to see home countless times in the flame, but he never could.

It must have been the ocean. That great swath of water blocked my visions.

No matter how hard or how often he strained to see, he was unable to find a glimpse of home or his family.

Or Margaret.

Rumors had reached him, of course. British travelers bearing news of the States and tales of war, but that seemed impossible—his country torn apart and at war with itself.

Now he viewed the devastation first-hand.

Ross, the gentle playmate who ran down the beach beside Ayden, had caught a bullet at the Battle of Hatcher's Run. Ayden watched his troop bury him near Dabney's Mill.

Freckles fared better than Ross and came home from the war. He became a fisherman, like his father.

Emery also came home from the war, but he left his leg at Appomattox. He turned to his father's trade as well, a blacksmith near the pier they used to run along.

Of the coven children, there was no glimpse. His pyromancy skills were exceptional, and still, he could only direct his vision in general, not specifically. Having desired to see the children he grew up with, the fire had shown him the human children, but the magical children remained shrouded.

Ayden rubbed his eyes. He'd seen enough death and destruction. He blinked and focused his concentration on now.

Melvyn. Where are you?

Beyond hope, he tried to find his brother. He'd been only three when the James brothers snatched Ayden off the street and tossed him in the hold of that ship bound for India. That had been nearly a decade before the Civil War started—a lifetime ago.

He stared at the empty flames for nearly an hour before he gave up and shut the door to the stove.

With a wave of his hand, the lantern extinguished, and he rolled onto his back, staring at the ceiling.

I'll search again after work tonight. And if I'm brave enough, I'll look for Margaret.

Perhaps those with magic, including his brother and Margaret, were warded to escape prying eyes like his.

I'll look anyway. What can it hurt?

Chapter 6

Jason Harris

—

Jason tallied the column of numbers before him, double-checked the pile of receipts, and then entered the total into the accounting ledger.

Seated at the desk beside him, Nathan Dunham bent over his work. The tap-tap-tap of his pencil spoke of his friend's aggravation as he reconciled his own accounting assignment.

That afternoon, three new hires worked at desks across from Mr. Dunham. Another man, older than the rest, balanced ledgers near the office door.

Mr. Dunham's massive roll-top bureau claimed most of the space at the front of the room.

Jason sat in the fifth and last row beside Nathan. His satisfaction in balancing an accounting book, and his enjoyment of mathematics in general, were undoubtedly inherited from his father, along with the Harris legendary good looks.

Never shy about using his physical beauty to further his agenda, Jason's father had encouraged both Jason and his younger cousin, Nichole, to take advantage of the golden Harris attractiveness.

"You can get whatever you want, anytime you want it," his father had grinned. He had whispered to Jason and winked, "I've never had a woman turn me down yet."

Jason pulled another envelope from the leather satchel and spread the receipts across the top of his desk. He jotted down the total from each ticket, double-checked his accuracy, and then began to tally the column.

Behind Mr. Dunham's big desk, the long clock chimed three.

"You should come with us tonight," Nathan whispered without looking up.

"I can't," Jason whispered back. "I'm working for the barrister this evening."

"You should tell him you're ill. A few of us will gather at the Bisby house around ten. George's parents are visiting friends on Cape Cod." Nathan chuckled. "We're going to have a viewing."

"A what?" Jason glanced at Nathan. His gaze shifted momentarily to Nathan's father at the front of the room, then back to his friend.

Nathan grinned. "A few months back, George bragged he'd had a bit of horizontal refreshment with Mary Nash if you know what I mean. He even said she rode him like St. George." Nathan scoffed. "Of course, we all called him a liar, so he said he'd prove it."

"Mary Nash?" Jason watched as Mr. Dunham stood and exited the workroom toward the privy.

Nathan dropped his pencil in the open ledger and turned to face Jason. He leaned forward and lowered his voice even more. "Georgie cut little slots in his bedroom wall through to the deep linen closet in the hallway. The man's a mad genius."

"*George* Bisby?" Jason ran a hand through his hair. Images of dark-haired Mary, naked and astraddle little George Bisby befuddled his thoughts. He blinked and refocused on Nathan's urgent words.

"...so, after Georgie proved his claim about Mary, John Davis offered to show us Rachel Miller's sweet backside."

"Excuse me?" Jason's breath caught involuntarily, and he shook his head. "Georgie proved his claim—about Mary, and you—watched?" Jason tossed his pencil onto the desk and raked both hands through his hair. "You're all insane."

Nathan glanced at the door his father had exited as he laughed. "Maybe, but it will give you a cock-stand to think about it." Nathan snatched at Jason's crotch.

Jason batted his hand away and glared at his friend in disgust.

Nathan snickered. "Say you'll come to watch Rachel and John." His grin widened as he studied Jason up and down. "I say it's time you put those looks of yours to work. You could get anyone—two girls at the same time perhaps." He laughed again with his eyes on Jason's face. "I know you could get my sister. She's dotty over you." His words rose in a falsetto voice, and his hand flopped down as he batted his eyelashes. "Oh, Jason Harris is *sooo* handsome. I would do anything for Jason. I *loooove* Jason Harris."

"Enough." Appalled by Nathan's words, Jason's tone sharpened, "Donetta's your sister. You degenerate."

"But you're practically engaged. Our mums have it all but settled." Nathan shrugged. "If you don't fancy displaying your future wife to the boys, get some other puss to bed. One of your whores would do. Our friends aren't particular."

Jason's lip curled as though Nathan's suggestions carried a foul stench. Before he could reply, the door at the front of the room slammed shut.

Mr. Dunham stood staring at Jason and his son.

Nathan busied himself at his ledger.

Jason dropped his eyes and swallowed. A knot of hot bile sat uneasily at the top of his stomach. He knew Mary and Rachel—had danced with and spoken to them at various social functions since his return from France. They were trusting, young society debutantes who deserved better than to become a spectacle in this vulgar fashion, their reputations ruined by Nathan and his friends.

My friends as well, or so I thought.

He stared at the numbers on the ledger page and couldn't remember if he'd finished transferring the totals from the receipts to his tally sheet. His shoulders lifted and fell with a sigh of resignation as he gathered the tickets and started through them again.

Jason finished compiling last month's expenses by five o'clock and applied the totals to the balance sheet. He closed the ledger and raised his head.

The three young men in the front row were gone, along with the older man who sat to the side.

Mr. Dunham nodded to Jason and glanced at the clock. "If you're done, put the ledger in this pile. I'll check your tallies in the morning."

Jason added his log to the stack on Mr. Dunham's desk and retrieved his top hat, cane, and coat from the wardrobe near the door.

"Don't forget your wages, Mr. Harris." Nathan's father withdrew an envelope from the desk drawer and held it up.

Jason took the packet and slipped it into his vest pocket. "Thank you, sir."

"Have a nice weekend, son."

As Jason pushed open the door, Nathan called from the back of the room, "See you tonight then?"

Jason shook his head as he mouthed, "No," and stepped outside.

The setting sun hung low in the sky and would ease past the horizon within the hour. A chill breeze blew down into his face as he turned on Summer Street and headed west to Barrister Hall's office.

Jason dipped his hat to the wind and held the brim with chilled fingers while he adjusted his scarf, his cane clasped tight under his arm. He'd picked the wrong day to rush from the house without gloves. He hoped tonight's assignment would be limited since Otis would be around to find him for their usual Friday along the waterfront.

Jason shoved open the door beneath the Barrister's shingle, and a bell above his head tinkled. Warmth and the scent of pipe tobacco engulfed him as he pushed the door closed, shutting out the wind.

"I'm in the back," the attorney called from the file room, where Jason spent much of his time filing and retrieving case files for Mr. Hall.

Jason hung his overcoat, walking stick, and hat on the pegs beside the door and rounded the desk that divided the room. Keith Hall's pipe rested on its side in the small metal tray, the source of the aromatic scent.

A long table piled with law books and case files sagged beneath the weight along the back wall. Across from the table, the file room door had been blocked open with a short stack of books. Inside, movement between the tightly lined racks of shelves drew Jason's attention.

Tall and long of limb, Barrister Hall's shocking white thatch of hair gleamed as he bent and stood, shuffling along the towering rows of books.

"Do you need help?" Jason called as he made his way to the long table. "What would you like me to do?"

"Nothing. Stay there." Keith Hall edged around the end of an unsteady aisle, his arms laden with several hefty tomes. "I've found what I need."

The barrister carried the books to his desk. "There's not much for you to do tonight. A bit of filing that can wait." He sorted the books, then turned to Jason. "You could read more of Blackstone's Commentaries, but that's the best I can offer. I need to build my argument for Benton versus Orland. Proceedings begin next week."

"I understand." Jason tidied several of the piles of paper and books across the long table, uncovering Blackstone's. He carried the reading material to the chair at the end of the table, took a seat, and opened the tome.

"You would get a better education in law if you attended a law school. Columbia offers an outstanding education for a young man with your intelligence. Why, under Theodore Dwight's guidance, you'd pass the bar in no time."

"Thank you, sir, but I couldn't afford Columbia. I'd have to move to New York—find a place to live...." Jason shook his head.

"You're right, of course." Barrister Hall considered him for several moments as though he wanted to speak, then turned to his books. "It's likely you're knowledgeable enough to pass the examination." He turned his back and flipped open the publication on the top of the stack. "I noticed they posted new examination dates at the courthouse today."

"It sounds as though you're trying to get rid of me," Jason chuckled.

Barrister Hall glanced over his shoulder and smiled easily at Jason. "Not at all. But you've been my apprentice for more than two years. I'm sure you could quote Blackstone's front to back." He turned back to his investigation. "There's no doubt in my mind you could obtain your license."

"I appreciate your confidence, sir."

Conversation ceased as both men turned to their tasks.

Well after sunset, the bell above the door jingled, and Otis Pierce hurried inside along with a gust of wind.

Barrister Hall slapped his hand down on a stack of papers threatened by the breeze. He spoke without looking up from his notes, "Good evening, Mr. Pierce."

"And to you, Mr. Hall." Otis grinned at Jason and mouthed, "Can you leave?"

Jason suppressed a smile as he closed Blackstone's and gazed at the attorney. "With your permission, I'll go now."

The barrister waved his fingers. "You don't require my permission, Mr. Harris." He looked up as Jason straightened his jacket and reached for his overcoat. "Don't forget what I said. Examination times have been posted."

"Yes, sir." Jason grabbed his hat and cane and followed Otis out the door. "Thank you, sir."

Outside, Jason settled the top hat on his head and fell into step beside his friend.

"Revere's?" Otis asked, a skip in his step.

"Of course!" The night promised to be cold, and Jason shoved his hands deep in his pocket for the walk to the docks. "I have to tell you what happened after you left last night. Oh, and wait until you hear what that nitwit Nathan is up to now."

Chapter 7

Ayden MacKenna

—

Ayden cleared and wiped down another table, then carried the metal tub full of dirty dishes to the kitchen. If he kept his hands and mind busy, he couldn't dwell on his visions in the fire—or lack of them.

Although Marion Tull had hired a dishwasher, the youngster only came to work half the time. The other half, Ayden picked up his duties. This evening, the young man washed and rinsed the afternoon's dirty plates and glassware as though his job depended on it.

Ayden set the tub beside the sink and took off his apron.

Harry had looked as though he could use some help behind the counter as the evening crowd came in.

Without pause, Ayden slipped on the brown tweed work vest, which hung on a peg beside the kitchen door. He straightened his floppy black bow tie and ran a hand through his hair to tidy the curls.

He ducked under the hinged bar top, shared an understanding glimpse with Harry, and then filled several drink orders for the women who served the tables. Whiskey. Vodka. Beer. An occasional glass of water, and of course, hot coffee and tea.

The tavern filled with patrons. Mostly men who worked along the dock, sailors in port, and a scattering of nearby residents, several of whom he'd begun to recognize as regular customers.

One of the girls who rented a room upstairs, Molly wove between tables to reach two new arrivals—the broad-shouldered blond and the thin dark-haired man. Both young and both regulars at Revere's.

Ayden lost track of Molly and the young men while he completed several drink orders for the table servers and passed written food orders to Qiang through the service opening to the kitchen. An hour later, the rush had slowed, and several empty tables required cleaning.

"Harry," Ayden called to catch the other bartender's attention. "I'm going to clean the tables."

Harry nodded and turned back to the man at the bar who received another whiskey.

Ayden glanced at the older gentleman, and their gazes locked.

The dock worker's head jerked up, and his mouth fell open. The drink in his hand hovered several inches above the bar as he stared at Ayden with wide eyes.

The moment held for less than a heartbeat before Ayden bent beneath the counter. Uneasiness settled across his shoulders as he hurried into the back room to exchange his server's vest for the long apron. He picked up the empty tub then hesitated before he returned to the front. It unsettled him to be recognized, especially since he couldn't put a name to the man Harry served.

But he does seem familiar. I must have known him years ago.

He kept his head lowered as he cleared and wiped down the closest table. When he scanned the bar, the man had gone. He cleaned two more tables and lifted the full tub to return to the dish sink when one of the regulars waved him over to their table.

"Could you see if Molly is available?" The dark-haired man chuckled and cast an amused grin at his friend.

"Enough, Otis," the blond gentleman ordered. Heat clipped his words, and he stared hard at his drinking companion.

Ayden looked between the two men then glanced around the room. "She'd be down here if she weren't otherwise engaged, I'm sure." He rested the tub on the nearby table and wiped his hands. "Wasn't she at your table earlier?"

The dark-haired man howled with laughter.

The blond heaved a sigh at his friend, then stood and offered his hand. "Jason Harris. This cocky, ne'er-do-well is my former friend, Otis Pierce."

"Otis Junior." Otis took Ayden's hand as Jason returned to his chair. "Never confuse Otis Sr. with me."

Ayden smiled at the friends. Both were a bit unsteady on their feet. "I'm Ayden MacKenna. You should consider ordering dinner instead of another drink." He picked up his metal tub of dishes. "If Molly has disappeared, she's probably occupied for the evening."

"I should call it a night and head home," Jason muttered. "I'd hail a cab, but they're like hen's teeth these days."

"You'd rent a cab if you weren't so tight with your money." Otis laughed.

"Money has nothing to do with the lack of cabbies," Jason said.

"He's right. It's the horse influenza," Ayden informed them. "It has spread like wildfire."

"I read about the illness." Jason turned and squinted at Ayden. "I thought only the animals in New York were affected."

"No. It's here as well," Ayden said over his shoulder. "You'll likely have to walk home, regardless of the fare."

Ayden paused at the bar before taking the tub to the kitchen. "Harry."

The bartender finished pouring a drink, then walked to Ayden. "Need a hand?"

"No, but I wanted to ask if you knew the man who sat at the end of the bar earlier—if you know his name."

Harry chuckled. "Do you know how many men sat at the end of the bar this evening?"

Ayden laughed. "Too many to guess who I'm asking about."

Harry's eyes widened, and he shook a finger. "There was a fellow who asked about you. Big guy, older? He said you looked familiar and wanted to know your name."

"Do you know him?"

"No." Harry cleaned his hands with a bar towel and tipped his head to the customer who called for him. "He's been in the tavern before, but I never learned his name." Young Tull turned to the customer with a smile.

Ayden nodded at Harry's back and carried the tub to the kitchen, setting the tub near the young dishwasher. When he checked the tavern an hour later, the young men he'd spoken to were gone.

When the last patron left the tavern, Ayden walked Harry outside, bid him goodnight, and locked the double doors. He wiped down all the tables and swept the floor.

The new dishwasher had left a sink full of dirty plates and bowls when he departed. With a sigh, Ayden washed, dried, and put them away. The mindless work allowed troubling questions to sneak into his thoughts.

Who is the dockworker who asked my name?

What might Margaret be doing tonight? Did she ever wonder about me?

He dried his hands, tossed the dishtowel into the empty tub, and made his way to his small room at the far end of the storage area.

A chill permeated his room. He stacked coal on the grate in his stove, then passed a tiny flame from his lantern to the fuel with a thought. He shrugged into his overcoat and rubbed his hands while the stove built up heat.

I'm too restless to wait for the room to warm.

He snatched his hat from the bureau on his way out and locked the door behind him. His breath hung in the still night air as he adjusted the black felt derby on his head and gazed at the stars. In the silence, he could hear the water lap against the pier a block away.

The clear and cold night chilled him, and he shoved his hands deep into his overcoat's pockets as he paced along the dock. So much in Boston had changed. The city had grown beyond all recognition.

Across the channel, cranes stood abandoned amid the new construction, waiting for the morning crew to arrive.

Further down the street, movement caught his attention. A man stepped into the halo of a streetlamp and stopped. He faced the waterway for a heartbeat and then looked Ayden's way.

A watchman?

Ayden strolled toward the man in the light. There was no sense in avoiding the individual.

As he drew near, the man flicked the remains of his cigarette into the water. "I knew you'd come."

Ayden recognized the voice, the low, raspy whisper that haunted his childhood. "Gordy." He didn't realize he remembered the man's name until he spoke it.

"Little Ayden MacKenna."

Face-to-face, Ayden stood taller than the bully, and Gordy had grown plump. None of that mattered. Gordon Carmichael had been a strong witch as a teenager and the bane of anyone weaker than he.

Older than Ayden by three years, Gordon was closer in age to the James brothers. He hadn't been friends with the twins, though. As Ayden remembered, the twins kept to themselves. Gordy had run with the Kohler boy more than anyone.

Milton.

The silence between them stretched. Finally, Gordon shuffled his feet and peered back at the buildings.

Ayden slid his gaze over the shadows along the warehouses and storefronts.

More than Gordon, then.

"Is Milton with you?" Ayden guessed.

The hefty witch tipped his head toward the buildings. "He is. And a few others."

Ayden widened his stance. An attack appeared imminent.

But why?

"What do you want, Gordy?"

Gordon pulled a matchstick from his pocket and bit down on the wooden stick. "Once the barkeep told me your name, I knew there'd be trouble."

Ayden's gut tightened. "What trouble? I didn't know you were still in Boston. Nor do I care."

"That's the thing, Mac. My friends and I consider your presence a danger to us all. Your being here could bring the James family back. And no one wants that."

"They're gone?" Ayden scanned the buildings where several figures edged away from the shadows. Gordon wasn't taking any chances.

"Yeah, they're gone, and good riddance. The old lady left with her boys not long after your family ran off. The James girl, what was her name? Mary? She renounced her magic and married outside of our community if you know what I mean. She has a human daughter and husband now and no contact with her mother or brothers." The matchstick moved to the other side of Gordon's mouth, and he grinned. "And now you show up."

"What happened to my family?" Ayden edged closer.

Gordon backed away and chuckled uneasily. "You mean you don't know? You and your family challenged the old witch and her lot. When you lost, the MacKennas had to leave town." He glanced over his shoulder and took another step back.

Ayden reached out and gripped Gordon's jacket. He pulled him close, knocking the smaller man's hat to the ground. Ayden stared down into Gordon's upturned face, aware his men moved toward them. "Where are they—my parents—my brother? Where are they now?"

"Release me, or they'll kill you." Panic blanched Gordon's features. He gripped Ayden's wrists, attempting to dislodge the larger man.

"I don't frighten so easily anymore, Gordy." With a quick jerk of his head, a ward of *earth-magic* glistened around them for the blink of an eye, then faded into invisibility. When the first magical missiles struck from the shadows, they rebounded harmlessly away, skidding across the cobblestones.

Ayden dragged Gordon toward the waterfront.

A fireball landed against Ayden's shield and burst into ash, falling into the water. "Call them off, or you drown." With a thought, he shifted a mouthful of the lapping surf into Gordon's throat. A *water-magic* spell he'd learned from Rakesh.

Gordon choked and coughed up water, soaking the front of his jacket.

"I'm not a kid anymore to be frightened by you or your friends." Anger colored Ayden's words.

A thump jarred his *earth-shield,* and Ayden lifted Gordon into the air. "Call them off. Now!"

Another gush of water colored Gordon's jacket. "I will," Gordon choked. "Please—stop. I can't breathe."

Ayden released the bully, and he fell to the ground.

Gordon held up one hand toward his men as he coughed seawater from his lungs and gasped for air.

"My family." Ayden loomed over the man. "Talk."

"I don't know much—we were young." Gordon gulped and swallowed, then waved his coven back. "There was a falling out between your families. That's all I heard. You left first, then your parents with your brother. Less than a year later, the James family was gone. Except for Mary, like I said."

"Margaret."

"What?" Gordon struggled to his feet.

"Margaret James."

"Yeah, yeah. Margaret." Gordon brushed off his coat and picked up his hat. "We don't want either family back here. Troublemakers, the lot of you."

"You're the one who came looking for trouble tonight."

The cowed bully backed away until his friends surrounded him. "If you're smart, you'll pack up and go back to where you've been," he shouted across the street, bravado restored.

Ayden counted three men and two women in Gordy's group. Perhaps he should feel honored by the caution of their numbers. Instead, constant anger coursed through his veins.

"Leave me be, Gordon. I want nothing to do with you or your friends."

One by one, the group faded into the night until Gordon stood alone once more near the buildings. "I've warned you," he called in a threatening tone, no longer fearful of Ayden's magic.

He should be.

Ayden might have been the only pyromancer in northern India, but he was certainly not the only magic-user. He'd learned to defend himself against formidable witches and magical beings until, in the end, he was one of the strongest—he and Rakesh.

As he walked back to his room, he set wards in his mind against any subtle magical suggestions, like the ones Rakesh had used to manipulate the weak-minded, and resolved to wary of walking into another ambush.

Inside, he locked his door and shed his hat and jacket. He opened the stove with the poker and sat on his cot before the fire.

Show me.

He'd learned more from Gordon tonight than from his inconsistent fire visions. But the answers he sought still burned there. Although senseless at times and open to interpretation, his need for information would keep the flame stoked all night.

There were too many unanswered questions. Where had Ayden's family gone? Who did Margaret marry?

He stared into the flames until sunrise, waiting for visions that never materialized, then he closed the stove and fell asleep.

Chapter 8

Amy Prescott

—

Amy lay across her bed propped on her elbows, pencil in hand and sketchpad open. With a steady stroke, she shaded the curve of the blood vessel as it extended along the bird's tendon toward the tip of the wing.

The pencil waggled between her fingers while she reviewed her work. She paged back one sheet to the muscle diagram—one more page to the skeleton. And again, to the first page of the series, which detailed the feathered wing, spread as if in flight.

"Hmm." The tip of her tongue moistened her lips as she studied her drawings with a critical eye. She flipped back to the skeletal wing and reviewed the break, adding contrast for depth.

Amy held the pencil between her teeth as she reached under her bed and withdrew another sketchpad. This one detailed the inner working and bone structure of a cat.

"Sweetheart? Are you still up here?" Her mother's voice echoed up the staircase, followed by her footsteps.

Both animal sketchpads disappeared beneath the bed, and after a brief scramble to find the third, her sketchbook of botany and still life was beneath her hand.

"Ah, I suspected you were drawing." Her mother eased open the door and smiled. "Did you choose a gown for the masquerade?"

Amy closed the pad, leaving the pencil to hold her place. She shrugged one shoulder. "I confess, I have not. Are you certain I must attend?"

"Yes, of course." Margaret marched across the room to the wardrobe. "Your father has already spoken for the three of us, sweetheart. We don't want to disappoint him." She pulled a dark red gown from the closet. "What about this?"

"That color gives my skin a greenish pallor. It's why I've never worn the gown."

Undeterred, her mother pulled another from the tall case. "This one is lovely."

"If I was a bride, perhaps. The white frock and light blue skirt are so... so...."

"Virginal?"

"Mother!"

"These are debutante colors and certainly appropriate for you to wear."

"If it were springtime."

"With the jacket on and your hair trailing over one shoulder, you would look very appealing." Margaret grinned and wiggled one eyebrow.

Amy's annoyance fled, and she laughed with her mother. "I shall wear that gown then. A virginal sacrifice must be appealing."

Margaret hung the dress on a hook on the side of the armoire. "I have material samples for all our gowns. I will leave them on the front table if you agree to take them to the hatter in the morning."

"I would be glad to."

"Oh, and one more thing." Margaret paused in the doorway and scanned the hall to the stairs. She lowered her voice. "Would you try a divination? This evening perhaps, after the sun sets. The partnership your father is considering would mean a new ship, which is good. But I worry he may be tempted to sail to the new markets. His safety—"

"I understand, Mama. I will certainly try, although I haven't had any prescient dreams or visions of importance in quite some time. Perhaps the second sight has left me."

"Oh, posh. Gifts like that never go, no matter how much we pray to the Goddess to take them away."

After Amy changed her gown, she made her way downstairs for dinner. The unusual sound of raised voices made her pause momentarily outside the family's small dining room.

"It's the opportunity of a lifetime, Margaret. Think of it—the Orient!" her father proclaimed. "Silk and spices. A single good trip could set us right for the rest of our lives." He pointed to Amy as she entered the room. "My darling girl, wouldn't you enjoy having exotic silk for new dresses, a rare spice for your tea?"

"I'm not sure." Amy glanced at her mother, but Margaret had turned toward the window. "I believe I have everything I need. I certainly require no new dresses. Why?"

"All those things are fine, Robert, but why would *you* have to go?" Margaret turned back to the table. "We need you here. What if something should happen? I have to know you're safe."

"I will run my business as I see fit, without your interference," her father's voice held a sharpness Amy rarely heard.

The maid waited at the kitchen door, serving tray in hand. She glanced between Amy and her father through the open dining room door, uncertainty in her eyes.

Amy crossed the dining room and lifted the platter from her arms. "This looks wonderful, Peg. Could you check if there is butter for the dinner rolls?"

Peg backed away when Amy lifted her burden. "Of course."

"Thank you." Amy forced a smile as she carried the tray to the table. "Peg has certainly outdone herself tonight."

She set the tray holding a basket of soft rolls and covered dish on the edge of the table.

"Where's Peg? She has an apron. You'll soil your gown," her mother complained.

"I sent her back to the kitchen for butter." Amy lifted the lid and sniffed the steam from the creamy chicken casserole. Peas and mushrooms peeked through the white sauce.

"Take your seat," Margaret instructed. "Peg will serve when she returns."

Their conversation at dinner remained sparse throughout the meal. The argument Amy interrupted between her parents must have run deeper than her father's potential absence.

Perhaps my divination this evening will shed light on what's amiss.

Before her parents finished dinner, Amy excused herself from the table and returned to her room.

She locked her door and drew the curtains closed to the moonless night. Although she preferred moonlight or a single candle to reflect in the water for her readings, the colorful coal flame in the fireplace would be enough.

From the bottom drawer of her bureau, she withdrew a silver bowl and placed it on the hearth near the flame. Using the fresh water from her washstand, she filled the basin until the water seemed to stand above the rim, then she turned the knob to lower the light at her bedside until the flame flickered out.

She set a pillow for her comfort near the bowl. Then she lowered herself cross-legged to the cushion, careful to hold her gown out of the way and avoid brushing the water. Amy's lashes fluttered closed, and she inhaled a deep breath to settle her mind, another for her heart, and the last one for her soul. When her eyes opened, the reflection of the fire danced across the still water giving it the illusion of movement.

"Blessed Goddess, help me see," Amy murmured. She concentrated her sight on a point above the water, blurring the familiar reflection of the flame and still allowing the flickering motion. She thought on her mother's concern, her father's ships, but instead of the flowing movement of a trading vessel on the ocean, her vision tunneled through narrow streets lined with brick and stone buildings.

"Curious." Blinking dry eyes, she looked away from the flame on the water and watched the shadowy images dance across her wall. Another deep breath and request to the Goddess for clarity, and she turned back to her divination.

After an hour, she gave up. No matter how many times she divined her father's future, she only received impressions of the city. Familiar shapes, resembling nothing so much as portions of the buildings along Summer Street, not far from the Harbor. Her father's office was nearby, close to his warehouses and ships, as well as the financial district.

She sank into bed that night with the memory of the firelight reflected in the storefront windows, which became a mausoleum in her dreams.

Chapter 9

Ayden MacKenna

—

Ayden sipped a cup of coffee at a table near the front window. Harry and Marion had yet to arrive to open the tavern, but Li Qiang had rattled the front door an hour ago and now banged around in the kitchen.

Down the wharf, two men in long dark coats loitered, waiting for Revere's to open.

Gordon's witch friends.

At least one of Gordon's friends followed Ayden each time he left the bar. They never attempted stealth; in fact, they made sure he knew they were there. It didn't matter where he went—a witch followed him.

Ayden took another taste of the bitter brew and checked his watch. Mr. Tull would arrive soon and unlock the doors to begin the day.

Then one of the dark-coats would come inside to sit in the corner and watch me.

Sometimes two would linger in the tavern. Although bold enough to make the horned-hand gesture meant to ward off evil at Ayden, they never approached him. At least they were wise enough to keep their distance.

Why did they watch him?

If they feared Ayden's presence would draw the James family—or his own—back to Boston as Gordon claimed, their concern was misplaced. Had he any idea where his parents had gone, he would pull up stakes tomorrow and leave to find them. With Margaret happily married, and his loved ones absent, he sometimes questioned his reasons for remaining in the harbor town.

Then I remember.

Until he could see Margaret's happiness with his own eyes, perhaps even speak with her—make her understand he hadn't abandoned her—he couldn't leave.

But that's only a partial truth.

The ugly reality of his past burned with memories of being told what to do for so long, it stuck in his craw to leave Boston after Gordon Carmichael ordered him to do so. Gordy, the bully, hadn't changed. Both a tyrant and a coward, he expected Ayden to be intimidated enough to leave. Ayden chuckled to himself and finished the last drop of coffee in his cup.

Little Gordy doesn't know me anymore.

His dark thoughts evaporated as the front doors opened.

Marion Tull stood in the opening. He spoke to a man wearing an expensive caped overcoat and top hat. "Thank you, Archie. I'll have my man come by your place this morning to be measured."

Marion closed the door and smiled at Ayden as he rose from the table. "I have a surprise for you, young man."

"A surprise?" Ayden wiped the coffee ring with the table rag in his apron and carried his empty cup as he followed Marion toward the long bar at the back of the room.

"Yes. You've been opening and closing the tavern for three weeks now. You've kept the tables clean, the floors swept, and stepped up to help Harry behind the counter whenever he needed help."

"You're paying me with my room and board as well as a wage. It's the least I can do."

"I'd have you do more."

Ayden crossed his arms and rested his hip against the bar. "What more is there?"

"I'd have you manage Revere's for me."

"But Harry—"

"I've spoken with my son. He has no interest in taking over this responsibility. He's happy with his current position, but I'm an old man. I need someone in charge who can handle day-to-day operations, keeping Li Qiang supplied and happy, hiring a new dishwasher, one who'll show up for work, and another lad who can clear and sweep in front." He stopped before Ayden and squinted up at him over his lenses. "In addition, you'll need to show a profit and provide me with a reckoning each week."

"Sir, I'm honored, I truly am, but you don't know me well enough—"

Again, the tavern owner cut him off. "Perhaps not, but I have a good gut. I know when I can trust someone."

Ayden grinned and shook his head. "You really don't."

"Enough of that. You already manage the front-end during business hours. I need only turn over the ledgers. Say you'll try it, at least for a few months. My wife, Dolly, wants to see her sister in Charlotte over the holiday season, and I need someone I trust to watch over the place. When I return, if this isn't the job for you, then you can keep the suit and coat."

"Suit and coat?"

"Archie Thatcher—the tailor who just left. You have a fitting appointment with him for two new suits, a proper overcoat, and a fine pair of shoes. Across from Archie's is a milliner. They'll have your ties, undergarments, and a topper. I have accounts at both, and Archie will make sure the milliner is aware you're to be taken care of."

"Sir—I don't know what to say."

Marion patted Ayden's shoulder. "Say you'll be back in time for the dinner rush."

Ayden nodded, speechless, then went to his room for his coat. He stepped into the alley and locked his door. As he turned onto the street, the two men across the road turned to stare.

"We're going shopping, boys," Ayden called.

One of the men hurried in the opposite direction, while the other followed Ayden down the street.

Ayden found Thatcher's Tailoring and introduced himself to Archie, who turned him over to a man to be measured. With a tape measure draped around his neck, the clerk led him behind a privacy curtain and took his measurements. When they finished, the clerk directed him across the street to the millinery shop.

The bell above the door rang as he entered, and an older gentleman waved from behind the counter. "Mr. MacKenna?"

"Yes." Ayden glanced out the front window through the hat display and watched his follower check his watch and lean against the lamp pole.

"The men's display is around the corner of the aisle," the clerk directed as the bell above the door sounded again.

Two women entered as Ayden rounded the aisle.

Against the far wall were several men's toppers, both high hats and bowlers. His second-hand derby looked worn indeed compared to these. He plucked a high-top hat from the rack and placed it on his head, then grinned foolishly at his reflection in the mirror. He tried a shorter top hat and then a bowler. He froze in place when he heard a woman's familiar voice.

Cautiously, he leaned around the aisle and watched the older store clerk assist a young woman.

Although her back faced Ayden, the set of her shoulders and the tone of her voice captured his breath.

If only I could see her face.

The familiarity and the longing to see and speak to her choked him, and he turned away. Too much time had passed, and this young woman could not be who she seemed to be.

He listened to her conversation with the clerk as she made her purchase, then looked around the end of the aisle as the bell rang over the door, and she left the shop.

***

Amy Prescott

—

Amy opened the door, and a delightful warm breeze proclaimed a welcome change from October's dreary cold weather. It would be a beautiful day for a stroll. Amy tucked the address of the hatter into her reticule along with the dress samples her mother had set out.

As she selected a parasol from the stand near the entrance, her mother hurried down the stairs. "How did your efforts turn out last evening," Margaret whispered as she tucked a stray strand of hair behind Amy's ear.

"Were I to interpret the divination, I would speculate father will not be sailing."

"Shh!" her mother cautioned and glanced over her shoulder. "Please be more discreet in how you respond." She brushed at her skirt and grinned at her daughter. "And you're right. I should practice patience when asking questions."

"I understand. You're concerned about Papa, but you shouldn't be." She hooked the parasol over her forearm as she pulled on her gloves.

"Should I have Wrigley bring 'round the carriage?"

"No, Mama. It's a lovely morning for a walk." On the front stoop, she opened her parasol, wiggled her gloved fingers goodbye to her mother, and continued down the walk to the cobbled street.

The trees in the park had burst into their fall colors a week earlier, and the sky was a deep, cloudless azure. Leaves rustled past her ankle boots on a fragrant autumn breeze. The cold wind from the last week had moved out, and Indian summer spread its glorious mantle before her.

After a half-mile, the pedestrian traffic along the street increased as other shoppers took advantage of the brief return of mild weather. On the block that housed many of the town's dressmakers, tailors, and milliners, Amy paused to read the address from the card and then studied the shop signs. She passed three hatmakers before she found the numbers written on the invitation.

The bell above the door rang as she entered. An older gentleman and a younger man waited on separate women while another customer browsed the material samples.

The older man smiled at her as she continued into the shop. "I'll be with you in a moment, miss."

Amy nodded to the milliner, then looked around his store. Various hat styles, for both men and women, decorated the walls along with drawings of hats and masks. Many of the depictions were sketched with charcoal and etched with skill. Each illustration included incredible attention to detail. She'd never considered using her drawing talent for clothing or hats. Whoever had drawn these had a marvelous eye for fashion.

The shop bell rang as two of the women departed.

The tall older gentleman with an olive complexion and mustache came around the counter. "May I help you?" His dark, friendly eyes creased at the corners when he smiled.

Amy returned his smile. "Yes, you may. My family will attend the Harris masquerade at the end of the month, and we obtained your name from the hostess. I need to procure masks to match our attire." Amy withdrew the fabric samples from her clutch and handed them to the milliner.

"Come to the counter. I have sketchbooks and examples."

In less than an hour, she had rearranged and discarded several styles. She chose a tie-on mask without feathers for herself, and a disguise attached to an ornamental handle for her mother. The fabric and beadwork the milliner recommended would be a perfect match for their dresses. Her father requested a plain black cover, the style preferred by most gentlemen.

She stepped from the milliner's door as she slipped her samples and receipt for three masks into her purse.

***

Jason Harris

—

Jason Harris reined the horse, guiding his mother's two-wheeled covered carriage to a halt in front of the milliner's. Although he'd agreed to escort her while she ran several errands, the pleasant weather seemed to have encouraged half the city's population into town. Fair-weather shoppers packed the streets.

Thank goodness, this will be our final stop.

Jason tied off the reins and stepped from the chaise onto the walkway. He turned to face his mother and bent to offer her a hand. As he reached for her fingers, a bump from behind jostled him forward.

He turned at the feminine exclamation in time to grasp the young woman's shoulders as she stumbled away. Her samples and receipt fell to the ground and skittered down the walkway.

"My most humble apologies, miss." Jason held her upper arms to steady her and stared down into the most wondrous eyes. Wide, brown with long dark lashes, he could not look away.

The young woman smelled of summer flowers, and her thick russet-colored hair, the same color as her eyes, was pinned in a loose bun.

A perfect pearl among these city pebbles.

"My receipt—" She reached down to grab the slip of paper, but it blew away from her hand.

"I'll get it." Jason reluctantly released the woman and caught the receipt beneath his boot. He retrieved the paper, along with the samples, and presented them to the lovely stranger.

Her face flushed as she took them from his hand. "Thank you." Her dark-eyed glance darted to his for a moment, and then she tucked her chin and hurried down the walk clutching her items and parasol.

Jason shoved his hair from his eyes and realized his hat had been knocked from his head. He turned from the departing woman to his mother. "Do you recognize her? I don't think I've met her before."

Rose Harris handed her son his top hat. "No, I doubt you would. She doesn't socialize anymore, the poor dear."

"Who is she then?" He slipped the hat onto his head then helped his mother descend from the carriage.

"That's the Prescott girl, I believe. Robert Prescott's daughter."

"Prescott? The shipowner Father spoke of?" He opened the milliner's door for his mother.

"The merchant, yes. Your father invited them to the masquerade. That must be why she's here."

"So...I shall see her again," Jason whispered. His stare rested on the sway of the beauty's hips as she retreated down the street.

The young woman paused at the corner. She looked back and caught his gaze for a moment, then disappeared down the side street.

Jason drew a breath and considered his mother's amused face. "What's her name?"

"Her name is Amylia." Rose smiled at her son. "I remember because her mother always corrected everyone's spelling of her name. She spelled it with a 'y' instead of an 'e', the poor child."

"Amylia," Jason repeated, then followed his mother inside the shop.

Chapter 10

Amy Prescott

—

Amy glanced back at the blond-haired gentleman before she turned the corner. He still watched her from the stoop in front of the shop. She tucked her head and hurried past the church.

How could I be so clumsy?

She still clutched the swatches and receipt in her hand. Flustered, she moved to the side of the walkway and shoved them in her handbag. Her pulse raced as she leaned against a building and took a deep breath to slow its pace and cool her warm face.

Oh, for heaven's sake! He wasn't that handsome.

An older gentleman tipped his top hat to her and stared with one eyebrow raised.

Amy nodded with what she hoped was a pleasant expression on her face. After he passed, she opened her parasol and hurried home. The beautiful fall day, all but forgotten, she barely retained enough presence of mind to step around people along the walk.

The warmth of his hands where he'd held her shoulders tingled with a curious sensation when she thought of him. His curly blond hair had fallen across his forehead as he bent to retrieve her items, and his light blue eyes sparkled when he smiled and handed her the samples.

This is ridiculous!

She'd grown up around the social elite of Boston. After her debut at seventeen, she'd been courted and sought after by a handful of men, anxious to tie their name to her father's. None of them appealed to her. To her mother's dismay, she preferred to sit in the garden or sketch in her book.

Eventually, the calling cards and the invitations to social functions ceased. Society viewed her as an odd young woman with unbecoming interests. Amy didn't mind. The contrived interaction between men and women at group affairs repelled her. Pretentious posturing and stilted conversations left her cold. Besides, debuts and dances served one purpose.

Matrimony.

An institution she could ill afford if she were to continue her pursuit of healing magic.

Her mother had been deeply disappointed with Amy's decision to withdraw from society. She didn't have the heart to explain to her mother her reasons or confess it was the dishonesty in her parents' marriage that proved her point. That form of bondage did not appeal to her.

I wonder who he is?

***

Ayden MacKenna

—

With his arms filled with boxes containing everything from shoes to undergarments and a top hat, Ayden wished he could ask his coven escort to help lighten his load. He chuckled at the thought and glanced back at the whiskered man keeping pace behind him. What a dreary duty that would be. He could only imagine what horrible threat Gordon used to force the man to spend his day mirroring the steps of a stranger.

As he'd left the tailor's, Archie told him his new suits would be ready for fitting the next week.

Back in his small room Ayden stacked the unopened boxes in the corner, hung his overcoat and derby on hooks, and then hurried to the front of the tavern. His morning errands had taken longer than he anticipated. Harry could be overwhelmed.

The woman's voice stayed with him. Her words forgotten, only the timbre of her responses to the clerk remained. And although he tried to remember, he couldn't be sure if it had been his mother's tone he heard or Margaret's. The years had merged the sound of the two women's words into a single voice in his dreams, the mother he missed and the woman he loved. Both now belonged to the girl with auburn hair and a trim waist.

I wonder who the young woman was.

He waved to Li Qiang as he passed the kitchen, but Qiang ignored him, as usual.

Ayden slipped on the apron from beside the stockroom door and entered the tavern.

Harry placed a whiskey in front of a customer seated at the bar and grinned at Ayden. "Mr. Tull said you might be late."

"You call your father, Mr. Tull?" Ayden rested his elbows on the hinged bar top.

Harry nodded. "I do." He wiped spots from a drinking glass and moved to the next. "Da began calling me Mr. Tull when I started to work for him. At dinner with Ma, he calls me Harry."

The lunch rush had ended. Only a scattering of customers remained in the tavern.

The bearded follower from the morning's errand entered the bar, stopped, stared at Ayden and Harry, then ducked his head and seated himself at the corner table.

"A friend of yours?" Harry asked softly.

"No." Ayden lifted the broom. "Do you know him?"

"Only that he's become a regular since you arrived."

Ayden grunted his understanding and began to sweep, cleaning around the tables and moving chairs. He worked his way across the tavern and stopped behind the bearded stranger. "What does Gordy have on you to make you waste your day following me?"

The man must have been dozing. The moment Ayden spoke, the stranger startled and came to his feet, spinning to face Ayden. His face was white with terror.

Ayden rested his palms on the end of the broom and smiled. "I've no quarrel with you. I don't even know your name." He held out his hand. "I'm Ayden MacKenna."

The stranger swallowed. Instead of taking Ayden's hand, he stepped back. "I know who ye are." His brogue stretched the words.

"No, you don't. Not really. You only know what Gordon's told you."

"Aye, and that's enough, to be sure. Ye bear watching, and if I have to dance with the devil to keep my family safe, so be it." As he spoke, he leaned forward, anger coloring his face.

Two men entered and went straight to the bar.

The chill from outside followed them in, and the stranger with the Irish brogue visibly shivered.

Ayden lowered his voice, "I'm no devil, and I mean you and your family no harm. I don't know you—or them. I came home to Boston to find my family. That's all."

"So that the feud between the MacKenna family and the James family can begin again?"

"What feud?" Ayden straightened. "What happened after I left?"

The man shook his head and took a step back. "I wasn't to speak to ya, and this is why." He edged around the table, never turning his back to Ayden. When he reached the door, he paused. "I've passed along word that you threatened the James daughter so badly she rushed from the shop and collided with a young man." He opened the door. "This won't end well, Mr. MacKenna." The door slammed shut.

No one else from Gordon's coven came to sit in the tavern that night.

After Harry had left and the tavern was tidy and locked up, Ayden retired to his room and built a fire in the stove.

He checked his sudden urge to step outside and instead secured the lock on his outside door. After that, he sat in his old coat and watched the flames dance across the coals. He could see his breath as he waited for the room to warm.

As soon as the Irishman had said he'd threatened the James daughter, he knew. It had been Margaret's voice he heard in the milliner's shop.

Do they believe I would threaten Margaret's child to draw her brothers back?

The flames in his stove burned brightly, and the chill in the room lessened. The tingling sensation of foretelling tightened his scalp. "Show me Margaret's child."

The shadows between the flames whirled and dipped as they flickered across the coals in time with a silent rhythm.

Then she stood before him in the fire, on a grand staircase.

Ayden groaned, and his soul chipped a tiny bit more. She looked like the memory of Margaret he had carried in his mind—in his heart—for so long.

The young woman's fingers played nervously with the string ties of a beaded mask.

A blond-haired man stepped into the vision. He took her hand and bent to whisper in her hair.

Ayden slammed the door to the stove shut and covered his face as his shoulders shook.

Loss filled his heart, and he battled with hatred and resentment. They'd taken so damned much from him. For so long he had begged to see visions of home, tidings of the ones he'd been forced to leave behind, and now that he had—now that a face had formed in the fire, showing him the child that could have been his had he been allowed to stay, he could hardly bear it.

He pushed the tears from his lashes and shook his head.

The fire had given him two faces tonight. One he recognized—the blond lad that came in regularly to bed Molly. He rolled his eyes and lay back on his bed.

What had been the boy's name?

Ah yes, Jason Harris.

Chapter 11

Amy Prescott

—

Amy rolled over in bed and stared at the ceiling. Sleep wouldn't come. Tomorrow evening her family would attend the masquerade. Preparing for the ball would make for a long day, and the night—*ugh*—the night would be—*appalling*.

She covered her face with a pillow.

I need to rest.

Amy kicked free from the sheet tangled around her legs and crawled from beneath the covers, intent on straightening her bedding. After she shook out the blankets and bedspread, her gaze lifted to the window to find the position of the moon. Judging by the sky, night had slipped into morning.

A sigh mourning her lost sleep escaped as she rested her elbow on the windowsill. Once again, she recalled her first trip to the milliner's shop and the man she bumped into on the street.

He continued to stalk her thoughts.

The remembered touch of his hand sent a delicate sensation across her skin, and she shut her eyes. Whoever he was, he'd been going to the hatmaker's shop that day.

Perhaps he will attend the masquerade.

His unmistakable mop of golden curls would make him easily recognizable.

Not that it matters.

With a last glance at the fading stars, she slid under the thick down cover and closed her eyes, determined to find sleep.

Amy knew the precise moment her dream transformed into a vision.

In an ordinary dream, she viewed herself as a participant, observed from above or from across the way. She thought of this as the dreamer's perspective.

Nothing more than a dream.

But when her third eye opened, her point of view changed. She experienced the foretelling firsthand, through her own eyes.

Prescience came into her young life the same year her menses began. Even now, a strong vision during the daytime could unsettle her for hours. But when foretelling flowed from dreams, fantasy and memories mixed strangely with precognition. At times it became impossible to know where the dream ended and when prescience began.

Not this time.

She saw herself from above and behind in her dream, immobile with anxiety, inside her old schoolroom.

The stiff-backed schoolmarm marched before the chalkboard, slapping a thin wooden dowel against the palm of her hand. The remembered strike of that rod lodged a silent sob in Amy's throat.

The students in the chairs around her were young, perhaps twelve or thirteen. Their faces expressed indifference toward the teacher. Amy towered above them, an adult bent and stuffed into a child's desk.

From the next row, two seats nearer the front of the class, Donetta Dunham tossed her blonde curls and looked over her shoulder at Amy with narrowed eyes. "Everyone knows you're a witch," Donetta hissed, loud enough for the entire class to hear.

The room filled with childish laughter as a wad of spit-soaked paper smacked the back of Amy's head.

"Enough, Amylia! Where is your lesson?" Mrs. Soderstein's rod slapped the top of her desk with a loud crack as the bright flash of lightning blazed across the classroom.

Startled, Amy turned to the window.

Without transition, she stood in front of a long-paned window, her own eyes reflected in the rain-streaked glass.

No longer in school.

No longer a dream.

The anxious pressure in her chest lifted.

A vision then, simpler perhaps than a child's painful and distorted memory.

Concealed within imagery, the meaning of her premonitions always hid in muddled and vague symbolism. Awake inside the vision, she tried to remember every detail to puzzle out later.

Movement behind her reflected in the glass caught her attention. A man's strong hand caressed her bare arm as warm lips touched the soft indentation where her shoulder met her neck.

His voice murmured low in her ear, "Don't I know you?"

She couldn't turn to see his face. Her third eye focused on the raindrops sliding down the glass, locking her in place.

In the reflection beyond the man, dancers bowed and circled in time with happy music.

"Miss Prescott. Your attention, please." *Smack!* The rod slapped down on the desk.

Amy gasped in surprise and sat up in bed. Outside her window, the pre-dawn sun colored the early morning sky.

***

Jason Harris

—

Jason rubbed the Macassar oil between his palms and raked his fingers through unruly golden curls. He disdained the use of the men's hair tonic, but for the masquerade, it would tame his locks and darken their luster. He stepped back from the mirror and viewed his work, turning his head from side to side.

"No." His oiled hair glittered wetly in the light from the nearby window. "This can't be right." A drop of tonic tickled his temple as it ran from his hairline.

"I could help you with that, sir." Patrick placed a fresh stack of towels on the foot of the bed.

"You are familiar with this...elixir?" Jason handed the servant the bottle of his father's hair oil.

"Yes, sir." He offered Jason a towel for his hands. "If you'll take a seat, I'll set you right for your mam's party."

Jason lowered into the straight-back bedroom chair and watched the manservant refold the towel and move to stand behind him. Their gaze met in the mirror.

"If you'd close your eyes, sir, I'm going to remove some of the oil."

Jason complied and relaxed.

Patrick's strong fingers worked the towel around Jason's head.

"I must have used too much." Jason's voice sounded dreamy in his own ears. Patrick's massage relieved his tension.

"Yes, sir. A small amount of this tonic does the trick."

Jason opened one eye and peeked into the mirror, then chuckled at his reflection. His once golden curls stood straight out in oily brown clumps.

Patrick began to massage his head again. Starting at the forehead, he worked his way back, rubbing the oil into the hair and transferring most of the fragrant product onto the towel. After he finished the second wipe down, he took up Jason's brush and ran the bristles across his hair, smoothing the curls to lay flat on his head. "Do you prefer a left or right part, sir?"

"Will it lay straight back?" Both Nathan and Otis parted their hair far to one side.

"Your hair wants to part a bit to one side. Is this acceptable?"

"Yes." He studied Patrick's handwork in the mirror as he rose. Some of the golden color had returned, but his riot of curls remained tame. His hair was far too thick to lie flat as Nathan's and Otis's hair, but the Macassar oil changed its texture and color significantly. "This will do nicely."

"Your jacket, sir." Patrick helped him into his formal dress coat, sliding it up his arms. He straightened the material across Jason's shoulders, adjusted his neckerchief, and handed Jason his black satin mask from the desk. "I believe your mother awaits you downstairs."

"Have any of the guests arrived?"

"Only a few, sir. Would you like me to tie on your mask?"

"Thank you, Patrick. We don't want anyone suspecting my identity until midnight."

As Jason moved down the curved staircase into the main foyer, he couldn't help but think of his cousin, Nichole. She would have loved this masquerade—been in her element, in fact.

I miss her. I wonder how she's enjoying life on her father's cattle ranch.

Another woman came to mind as he crossed the foyer to the ballroom.

Amylia Prescott.

His father had mentioned that the Prescott family would attend tonight's festivities and that he hoped Jason would make every effort to bestow a good impression on his future business partner.

His father needn't have worried.

Jason intended to make every effort, indeed.

Chapter 12

Amy Prescott

—

One of the few private residences on Beacon Hill to have a full yard and cobblestone driveway, the Harris household set itself apart from the other Boston Brahmins' South Slope homes. Lights blazed, both inside the elegant house and out, while torches lined the drive.

A tall man in a red jacket greeted her father and directed the driver to circle to the side entrance. "Although no debutantes will be presented tonight, your host has asked that all eligible ladies descend the grand staircase," the valet explained with a nod to Amy.

"I don't want to do this," Amy whispered to her parents as their coachman turned the two-horse vehicle toward the side entrance. "It's beyond humiliating."

"Nonsense. Your dress is lovely." Her mother patted her hand. "Go inside and come down the stairs with the other ladies. We'll be waiting."

"It wouldn't hurt to make a few friends," her father grumbled as Wrigley pulled the team to a halt adjacent to the lighted side door.

"I'll be friendly and chat with the young girls," Amy complained as a valet helped her from the carriage. She peered at her parents through the coach window. "But they'll still find me odd."

Her father chuckled while her mother gave an understanding look. "We'll see you downstairs," Margaret called out as the carriage pulled away.

Amy ground her teeth and prayed the Goddess would give her patience and a calm spirit. She took a deep breath and smiled at the worried valet. "Thank you," she murmured.

He escorted her to the side entrance and held the door as another carriage rounded the drive to drop off two girls. Much younger than Amy, the pair giggled with excitement, clutching their masks.

Amy stepped inside the door to find a steep servant stair. Taking her skirt in both hands, she started up toward the sound of adolescent chatter.

I don't belong here.

At the top of the staircase, two young women blocked her path. As Amy approached, they inched back to allow her to pass. The red-haired girl covered her mouth with a fan to hide her amusement while the dark-haired child grinned openly. "Donetta told us you might be here tonight."

"Do I know you?" Amy studied both young women but didn't recognize them.

These are children, seventeen years at the most.

"It's doubtful." Red giggled from behind her fan.

"You're the Spinster Prescott," the dark-haired girl smirked. "I'm surprised they let you upstairs."

"No more surprised than I am, I'm sure," Amy replied as she searched the room beyond the two faces before her. Half-a-dozen young women in ball gowns groomed each other's hair and adjusted their gloves and masks. A harried maidservant in a light-gray dress straightened the bows on a yellow and white satin skirt.

"Excuse me," Amy raised her voice to catch the maid's attention. The chatter subsided, and half of the young women in the room turned to study her. "Could you direct me to the staircase?"

"Oh my," the maid muttered. She straightened and looked Amy up and down. "You've come in the wrong entrance, missus."

A group of girls near the servant erupted with laughter.

Amy ground her teeth and felt her face flush.

A thin blonde-haired girl in pink with dark adolescent spots on her face waved her hand for Amy to come forward. "The stairs are down the hall." The youngster opened a door and pointed.

"They're both so pathetic." Donetta Dunham rounded the maid and smirked at Amy. "Neither of you should have been allowed to share the debutantes' room with us."

Amy stared at Donetta. She hadn't seen the spoiled little shrew since they attended school together. Two years younger than Amy, the tiny Dunham girl only measured to Amy's shoulders and wore her mousy blonde hair in ringlets down her back.

Amy leaned toward the pimpled-faced adolescent beside the door. "You don't have to stay here with them. You're welcome to come downstairs with me."

The youngster shook her head and backed away.

"As you wish. I do thank you for your help." Amy turned one more time to face the young women in the room. She consigned their dresses to memory, so she'd know them when masked.

I must remember they are children. Vile and spoiled, but children, nonetheless.

She closed the door to escape their mocking laughter. Nothing had changed in the years she shunned society.

In the sudden silence of the hallway, the strains of a waltz floated up the staircase.

She tied the black satin ribbons of her mask behind her head and straightened her blue and white dress. Her disguise glittered with the black beaded design she had ordered to offset her virginal gown.

Her gloved fingers trailed along the glossy banister rail while her other hand held her skirt away from her feet. As she descended the curved staircase, the opulent marble foyer came into view. Liveried servants ushered a steady flow of masked attendees from the entrance to the double doors that stood open to the ballroom. No one noticed her as she hesitated on the stair.

Beyond the double doors, two elderly couples moved across the dance floor to the music. Other guests, all part of the Boston Brahmins, conversed in small groups along the edge of the large room. The musicians remained out of sight, as did her parents. She skimmed the crowd of covered faces with a sinking feeling.

When they unmask, I still won't know these people.

Even the young women upstairs, children from her tormented school years, were strangers. Their older siblings her age had long since married and borne children of their own.

At least there's no herald to stop me from slipping in unnoticed.

***

Jason Harris

——

A doorman directed arriving guests to the morning room left of the entrance hall, where another liveried attendant divested the partygoers of their overcoats and hats. The masked visitors then went to the large dining room, which served as the ballroom for this evening's event.

Jason placed his empty glass on a passing waiter's tray and took a full champagne flute. He sipped as he surveyed the momentarily empty foyer.

His mother had stationed him near the double doors to greet her guests and direct them to the refreshment table. Several of his parents' Brahmin friends had greeted him by name.

So much for my mysterious identity.

The doorman opened the front door, and the Dunham family entered. Jason's employer and his wife were followed into the foyer by their oldest child, Nathan. Donetta, of course, would be upstairs primping with the other eligible young ladies.

"Mr. Dunham." Jason shook Calvary Dunham's hand and tipped his head to his wife, Bethany.

"Jason," Calvary said as he surveyed the room. "We must be early."

"No, sir. You are right on time. The musicians are about to begin."

Various discordant notes drifted from across the room as the musicians tuned. The long dining table had been removed, leaving an elongated dance floor with chairs along the wall. On the far side of the room, glass doors allowed a view of the autumn garden. Colorful leaves and hearty pansies reflected their colors in the glow of small foot lamps placed along the stone pathway which wound beneath arched decorative arbors.

"Mrs. Dunham," Jason greeted his mother's friend.

She smiled and followed her husband into the ballroom.

"Nice disguise," Nathan quipped as he passed. "If you weren't playing host, I wouldn't have known it was you. What's this in your hair?" He touched Jason's glossy locks and sniffed his fingers.

"Macassar oil."

"Nasty stuff." Nathan cleaned his fingers on his handkerchief. "Donetta should be down shortly." He smirked at Jason as he strolled away.

"Mr. Prescott!" Jason's father sidestepped Nathan and offered his hand to a new arrival.

Of average height but athletically built, Robert Prescott took Spencer Harris's hand and smiled. "Mr. Harris. Good to see you again. May I present my wife, Margaret."

"Mrs. Prescott."

"How do you do, Mr. Harris."

"I'd like you both to call me Spencer." Jason's father held out his arm, indicating the far side of the room where the buffet table stood. "Slip on your masks and come with me. I want to introduce you to my wife." He steered his would-be business partner away without introducing his son.

Jason watched his father maneuver the Prescotts through the moderately crowded room toward his mother. When he turned back to the foyer, he saw her on the staircase.

She stood on the third or fourth stair, her hand on the banister rail, as though unsure if she should step down or turn back. She glanced briefly at the front door, perhaps thinking to escape the soirée before it began.

Even with her mask in place, Jason recognized her. The dark hair and delicate chin were seared into his brain, and he knew the color and shape of her eyes. Jason had spent too many restless nights reliving their brief encounter to allow her to escape him now. Without taking his gaze from her, he hurried toward the beautiful Amylia Prescott.

Chapter 13

Amy Prescott

—

Amy moved down another stair and gripped the stair rail. She'd lost the opportunity to sneak in unnoticed.

A gentleman approached across the elegant foyer from the ballroom as though he'd waited for her to appear. The tails of his black cut-away dress coat swayed with his quick stride. The black satin of his mask matched that of his lapel, the dark material stark against his crisp white shirt and raised collar.

He paused at the base of the staircase and smiled at her. "Good evening, my lady."

"Good evening." Amy continued her descent to the marble entry tile and offered the masked gentleman a cautious smile. "I decided to join the gathering early rather than wait for the—" she glanced up the staircase "—younger ladies. I hope that isn't a problem."

"Never a problem. More of a fortunate occurrence, at least for me." He offered her his arm. "May I escort you into the ballroom?"

"Thank you." Amy laid her gloved hand on his raised forearm and walked beside him through the open double doors.

The room's dimensions were smaller than she had imagined. A string quintet provided music from an alcove near the refreshment table at the other end of the room. Cushioned velvet chairs waited for future dancers to catch their breath. Across the dance floor, three pairs of glass doors displayed a small patio that led down to a garden.

"Would you like a glass of champagne, or perhaps you'd prefer to dance." The gentleman stopped at the edge of the sparsely filled dance floor and grinned at her.

Struck by his warm familiarity, the words from her vision last night echoed back to her as she murmured, "Don't I know you?"

Dimples creased his face, and he chuckled. "Perhaps we are acquainted after all. Then again, that is the mystery and intrigue of the masquerade." He held out his hand toward the couples turning on the floor. "Shall we dance?"

Thankful the quintet played the slower Boston Waltz rather than the galop, Amy placed her right hand in his and settled her left on his shoulder.

He rocked in place for a moment, allowing her to find the rhythm of the music. He dipped his chin as their eyes met and whirled her onto the dance floor.

His firm, steady hands guided her through the turns, and he matched his stride to her shorter step. They moved together effortlessly when he turned her beneath his arm, then fell into step with him once more.

"You're an excellent dancer," she confided with honesty. "Skilled enough for the both of us, which is quite fortunate." Amy tipped her head back to try to see his eyes again.

They sparkled with a haunting familiarity. "I am forever at your service, mademoiselle." He turned her with the music—his arms strong and supportive.

Over his shoulder, a ribbon of flame ran up the wall and across the refreshment table. Amy blinked and stumbled. Supported by the strength and skill of her partner, she regained her footing.

It would be impossible for the other guests not to notice the fire. It spread across the ceiling and swirled around the dancers.

Amy swallowed and blinked as the room disappeared into an ash-strewn inferno. Her breath rushed out, and she gripped his hand, searching the vision for a landmark in the desolate fire-ravaged street behind him.

I've seen this before, in the divination for father.

"Are you well, my lady?" her escort asked, concern coloring his voice.

Amy had stopped dancing and stood rooted as the vision roared around them. She could neither smell the ash nor feel the heat. The premonition affected only one of her senses, her eyes.

With a self-conscious laugh, she uttered, "I'm sorry," and offered him a strained smile. "I suppose I'm not used to dancing."

He guided her gloved hand to the crook of his arm. "Then would you care for some refreshments?"

"Thank you."

He escorted her across a rubble-scattered street as fire and ash twisted into the sky. The vision shredded bit by bit when they reached the refreshments, exposing the table and retreating from the floor. Pieces of reality wove through the image of flames as the ballroom returned around her.

"Champagne, wine, or my mother's special punch?"

"The punch, please."

"I won't deceive you. The punch is rather potent." He poured the red liquid from the dipper into a ceramic cup and handed it to her on a matching saucer. "But tasty. Do be cautious."

Amy sipped at the punch as the flames fragmented upward, revealing the dancers and seated guests. Uneasiness churned in her stomach, and she took another sip, surrounded by masked strangers.

The ash and flame of her vision swirled upward and disappeared as though down a drain in the middle of the ceiling.

She tore her attention from the departing flames and studied her escort.

He stood several inches taller than her five foot and six inches but would not have been considered an exceptionally tall man. His hair had been oiled into place and could be dark blond or brown. The mask shaded his eyes enough to disguise their color. Long dimples extended down both sides of his face from beneath his satin visor.

Although she found her companion somewhat attractive, he was no match to the gentleman at the milliner's shop. The golden hair and his light blue eyes would be a giveaway. If he were here, she could find him.

A hush spread across the room as giggles and squeals of juvenile excitement echoed from the entryway. The young women from upstairs were about to make their appearance.

"Wonderful," her companion muttered, then downed his champagne. Light blue eyes, suddenly visible behind the black mask, moved from the entrance to her. "Another dance, milady?" He set his fluted glass on the table and took the punch from her hand.

"I'm not sure we should." She glanced around, but no one was paying any attention to them.

Dancing twice in a row with the same man would be scandalous, according to her mother.

"Nothing too demanding, I promise. It's another waltz." He took her hand and led her to the center of the room, then his arm was on her waist, and he moved in time with the music. "Did your father never waltz you around the parlor when you were a child?"

The last of the hot ash sprinkled down from the draining flames above their heads, the only part of the vision that remained. She followed the ash down as heat infused her face behind the mask. "He may have. I can't seem to recall just now."

"I shall take that as a compliment."

Amy dropped her regard from the floating cinders to his eyes.

So blue.

Despite the fiery vortex above their heads, she smiled.

"There it is." He grinned. "That lovely smile."

The last of the vision blew away, and the chandelier became visible once more. "I am no better at flirtation than I am at the waltz, sir." Her view dropped to his broad smile.

Beautiful.

"I think, perhaps, we've met before," she suggested.

"Not formally, but we shall. Masks are removed at midnight before we dine."

"Well then, until we are formally introduced, please call me Amy."

"Amy," he repeated, his voice as soft as his smile. "My name is Jason."

She forgot to count her steps, but it didn't matter.

Jason's gentle lead moved her effortlessly around the floor in time with the music.

Each time her gaze dropped from his eyes to his lips, his grin grew—as though he could read her mind.

Their circular route took them back toward the entrance. Near the door, a group of young women watched the dancers.

As they waltzed past, the dark-haired girl standing beside Donetta hissed, "He only danced with her because he doesn't know who she is."

Jason looked over Amy's head and noted the girl who spoke. "Not a friend of yours, I take it."

"No. Not really. They're all very young, and I...well, I rarely attend social functions."

"Hmm. I'm not as fortunate." He glanced at the young girls clustered around the door then into Amy's eyes. "Or perhaps I am very fortunate indeed."

Amy's pulse quickened, and she tucked her chin to hide her grin.

They circled the floor another time, then slowed near the back of the dance floor. The room had become heated with the crowd, and the garden doors opened to the cool night air.

"Would you care to step outside? The garden is small but lovely, even at this time of year."

"Thank you, but I should say hello to my parents and introduce myself to our host."

"You're sure?" Jason scanned the flock of frilly-dressed girls who advanced toward them. "I believe I shall step out for a breath of air myself then."

Delight bubbled unexpectedly from the butterflies in her chest. "You're being chased outside by a pack of little girls." She looked from the youngsters to Jason and laughed with delight.

He performed a short bow and edged toward the open door. "I won't argue that point, milady."

"Milady? I hardly think so. Still, I shall save you from the approaching horde." She took his arm and continued toward the garden. "Shall we?"

He heaved a dramatic sigh of relief and placed his hand over her fingers at the crook of his arm. "I am forever in your debt."

Amy glanced over her shoulder as they stepped through the doors. Donetta and the masked children she led had stopped their approach and stared at them. "Not at all. It's my pleasure." She couldn't help but smile at Donetta as she and Jason stepped outside.

I'm too old to behave like this.

She bit her lip to stop the grin.

Outside, the evening air chilled her arms. Lamps lit the short footpath from the house, around a stone bench and back beneath the arbor. From the edge of the narrow porch, the entire yard came into view. Only one other couple strolled through the half-naked trees and bushes.

He stepped down onto the path and offered her his hand.

"Thank you." Leaves crunched beneath her shoes as she followed his footing. "I believe you're safe from the children, at least for the moment."

"I'm glad you changed your mind."

She ran her hands up her bare arms. "Consider it a debt paid for retrieving my receipt and samples the other day."

"So, you did recognize me." He chuckled as he removed his jacket and wrapped it around her shoulders.

The warmth of the coat and his act of kindness took her breath away. "Yes," she managed.

His white shirt stood in stark contrast to the darkness beyond the foot lamps. He paused in the center of the path. "Tell me more about yourself, Amy. Do you play the piano? Do you sing?"

"Oh, heavens no." Amy shook her head. "I do neither of those, to my mother's despair." Her words ran dry.

Say something.

"I have a garden...smaller than this. I draw animals."

"An artist then? Do you enjoy watercolors?"

"I've never tried paint."

"I have. I'm a dismal failure with a brush. The teacher ran me out of her class." His smile captivated her. Warm and mischievous, a grin inviting her to share his amusement.

"Compared to me, you're a classically trained artist."

Am I flirting? Who is this, Jason?

He tossed back his head and laughed. "Hardly. I'm better with numbers than with paintbrushes. I work as an accountant, and I apprentice as a solicitor. Not entirely impressive."

"Are you following in your father's footsteps?"

"Not at all." He shook his head.

A servant paused in the ballroom doorway, and his red livery caught Amy's attention. The uniformed servant surveyed the garden and then made a beeline for her and Jason.

"Excuse me, sir." The valet gave a short bow. "A gentleman wishes to speak with you. I've asked him to wait in the front parlor.

"To me? Can he not speak to me here?"

"He does not have an invitation, sir, or a mask." The valet withdrew a card from his pocket. "He gave me his card."

Jason took the card, read the name, then nodded to the servant. "Please provide Mr. Pierce with refreshments and tell him I will be there shortly."

"Yes, sir." The valet spun on his heel and marched from the garden

"I don't expect this to take long," Jason stated as they followed the valet toward the ballroom.

Amy removed his jacket from her shoulders as they stepped up to the garden doors. She folded it over her arm and handed it to Jason. "Here. You may need this."

He slipped into his jacket and entered the ballroom. "Do you see your parents?"

"Yes. Mother is in the dark blue dress." Amy took Jason's arm as they crossed the room.

He made a short bow to her parents and then turned to her. "I shall see you at dinner, if not before." He raised her gloved hand to his lips.

Her smile came with a blush as he winked and whispered, "Wish me luck." Then he turned and made his way through the dancers and disappeared into the foyer.

Chapter 14

Jason Harris

—

Jason pulled the ballroom door shut behind him and slipped off his mask. He could blame his annoyance with Otis, at least in part, on his delight in speaking with Amy Prescott. Her smile made his chest tighten in a most peculiar way. He would have much rather stayed in the garden and made her laugh one more time with his foolish banter than talk to his friend.

A short hallway across from the staircase led to the left wing of the house. The door to the morning parlor, used tonight to store coats and hats, stood open. He hurried inside.

Otis faced the windows, his hands folded behind his back. Dressed in black slacks and tails, he looked as though he intended to join the party. When the door closed, he spun and stared at Jason with furrowed brows, lined with impatience. "It took you long enough."

"It did what?" Jason approached Otis. Beyond the tall panes of glass, activity flourished along the lantern-lit drive. "As you may have surmised, we have guests. Can't this wait?"

"This is a once-in-a-lifetime opportunity. However, if you're not interested," Otis picked up his hat from the table, "I can show myself out."

"What is the matter with you? I've never seen you like this." Jason tossed his mask onto the empty sideboard. "You've got my attention. Tell me what's so important that it can't wait until morning."

Otis hesitated. His dark eyes scanned Jason from his oiled-back hair down to his boots and back up again. Then he lowered his eyes. "Father believes that despite Germany's decision to abandon the silver thaler, the U.S. silver market is poised to surge."

Jason poured a shot of scotch into two glasses and handed one to Otis. "I heard congress drafted a coinage act which proposes the U.S. shift to a gold standard. If that happens, the price of silver will collapse."

"Grant will never sign such a bill. The U.S. won't follow the Europeans."

"You're sure?" Jason took a sip and considered Otis. "Your father is certain about this information?"

Otis downed his shot and set the glass on the desk. "Silver and railroads are his best advice for your investments, but don't wait too long. Both are ready to jump in value, and then it will be too late. If you give me money tonight, P&P can purchase stock in your name when the market opens in the morning." His voice dropped to an urgent whisper, "It's your chance to get free from under your parents' thumb."

Jason shook his head. "But I am tied up tonight—"

"Then I must be on my way. You can stop by my father's office as your time permits, but you'll lose the opportunity I'm offering." Otis straightened his jacket and crossed the room toward the door.

"No. Wait here." Jason stopped Otis with his hand and held up one finger. "I'll get the cash." With a furtive glance at the empty foyer, he took the stairs two at a time and hurried to his bedroom.

He pulled a carved wooden box from beneath his bed and fished the key out of his nightstand. Inside were his savings from Dunham Accounting, five hundred dollars, and investment certificates in three separate silver mines.

Although his father urged him to deposit his money in the bank, Jason refused. Even though the argument for earning interest appealed to Jason, he also knew his father would monitor his account.

His cash remained locked under his bed.

Jason stuffed the money into one of his black socks, locked the box, and shoved it under the bed. He waited in the alcove above the foyer until the entrance was clear, then he rushed down the stairs and into the morning room.

Jason handed Otis the cash-filled sock. "You'd best be right about this. That's everything I've saved."

"You'll make your money back tenfold." Otis slipped the sock under his arm inside his jacket and winked.

Jason grabbed his mask and crossed the room, eager to return to the party and Amy. "On railroad bonds? I doubt it. Which bank holds those notes?" Jason asked over his shoulder as he exited the room and hallway, nodding to the servant who waited in the foyer.

"Jay Cooke and Company." Otis followed, setting his top hat in place.

"You're more than welcome to come in." Jason held out his hand to the ballroom entrance.

"Imagine your father's horror." Otis chuckled as the servant opened the entry door. "Thank you, but no. If I'm to see to your purchase when the market opens, I must depart."

Jason pulled on his mask. "Come by Barrister Hall's office tomorrow night. Bring my new bonds."

Otis tapped his hat and grinned at Jason's masked countenance. "I certainly will. Enjoy your evening." He strutted down the path to the drive, nodding to a few late arrivals as though he were nobility.

The attendant closed the door behind Otis.

Jason straightened his jacket and entered the ballroom, intent on continuing his conversation with the intriguing Miss Prescott. He nearly forgot his business with Otis, although the nagging impression he may have made a mistake stayed with him.

His mother confronted him as Jason edged onto the dance floor. "Donetta is here."

"I know, Mother. I saw her come in."

"And you snubbed her, in front of everyone, to walk outside with the Prescott girl."

"Ah...and where might that Prescott girl be now?" Jason whispered to his mother as he scanned the room.

"Jason! You will not embarrass me tonight."

"Never mind, I see her beside Father." He picked up his mother's hand and kissed her fingers. "Make my excuses to Donetta and her mother."

"There you are!"

As though mentioning their names had summoned the pair, Donetta and her mother halted in front of Jason. He stepped back, but the ladies followed, effectively pinning him against the wall.

Jason heaved a sigh of defeat. He viewed his desired destination with regret and caught Amy's furtive glance in his direction.

She searches for me.

Encouraged, Jason smiled at her, but she had already turned away.

"I'm glad to see you've returned to the party," Bethany stated. "Cal said he saw you when we came in. Donetta's been looking for you."

"Mother!" Donetta hissed, then dimpled her cheek at Jason. "Nathan told me you hoped to dance with me tonight."

Jason's gaze flicked to where Nathan, George Bisby, and Mary Nash conversed beside the nearest garden door.

Nathan raised his cup of punch in Jason's direction and whispered to George. Both men burst into laughter as they watched Jason.

Teeth clenched in annoyance, Jason smiled at Donetta. "And I do wish to dance."

At that moment, the refreshed musicians played the first few notes from one of the Strauss waltzes.

Jason bowed to Donetta and held out his hand. "Would you care to waltz, Miss Dunham?"

"Yes. Please." Donetta simpered and touched her fingertips to Jason's.

Resigned to fulfilling his duties as host, Jason took Donetta in his arms and stepped into the circle of dancers.

***

Amy Prescott

—

Amy kept her back to the dancers and tried to find interest in her father's conversation with Mr. Harris. The exquisite merchandise from the Orient, the market price of tea and silk, and the number of crewmen the new ship required would have been thought-provoking if her mind were not focused elsewhere.

Her mother nodded and smiled. A concerned look clouded her eyes whenever they rested on her father.

The music and dancing continued, first a quadrille, then a polka. In the relative silence before the next number, conversation in the room grew louder.

A flush along the back of her neck warned that Jason had returned to the ball. She peered over her shoulder, and their gazes met. Flustered to be caught gawking, she turned away. Hopefully, he would ask her to dance again or to walk in the garden. She had questions. How did the house staff recognize Jason? Why would they allow a solicitor into the Harris home and deliver a message to a masked guest during a party?

Who is Jason?

The musicians reclaimed their corner and struck up a waltz. Amy snuck another glance toward the entrance, but Jason had moved.

"Excuse me. Could I have this dance?"

Amy spun toward the deep voice and found a tall, dark-haired, masked stranger. "I...umm."

"It is Strauss. A lovely tune. Say you will." He held out his hand.

She shook her head. "I'm afraid—"

Jason twirled past her with Donetta in his arms.

"—I'd be delighted," escaped her lips along with a tenuous smile. She took the masked stranger's hand and rested her fingers lightly on his shoulder as they lurched onto the dance floor.

Much taller than her last partner, he lacked the sure touch and direction Jason provided while dancing. He stepped on her toes. Twice. Without apologizing. Finally, they achieved an equitable rhythm, and his attention lifted from their feet to her face. "So, you're the Spinster Prescott."

Amy blinked. "Excuse me?"

"You don't remember me?"

"I might if you weren't wearing a mask."

"Ah, yes, of course." He chuckled. "And it has been quite some time. You know me from primary school. I was a year ahead of you."

Amy studied him. "I'm sorry. I don't recall." Easily six feet tall, with dark hair and broad shoulders, whatever he may have looked like as a child of fourteen was nothing like the adult of twenty-something today.

"I watched you dance earlier with our host." He was baiting her—taunting her.

Amy arched an eyebrow. "Did you?"

"And I must warn you not to lose your head. Jason is promised to my sister."

Amy shrugged and shook her head. "Since I don't recognize you...."

"Donetta. It's rumored they will announce their engagement tonight."

Donetta Dunham's older brother! His name sat on the tip of her tongue. *Neville? Nigel? And he called Jason their host.*

Amy glanced at her parents, who remained beside Mr. Harris. As clear as a bell, she heard her mother call up the stairs, *'They have a son.'*

Jason Harris.

The music ended, and she stepped out of N. Dunham's arms, giving him a small curtsy. "Thank you."

"Perhaps we could dance again after supper?" he called as she hurried away.

"Or perhaps not," she muttered, dusting her gloved hands together. *This is what I expected from tonight—this, and the mockery from the young women upstairs.*

"Amy!"

Startled to hear her name called, she slowed and looked over her shoulder.

Jason hurried toward her as he dodged the dancers leaving the floor. When their eyes met, he tipped his head toward the garden and changed direction.

A remarkable case of butterflies erupted in Amy's stomach, despite discovering she'd been played for a fool. Curious about what Jason might have to say, she changed direction and made her way to the nearest garden door.

She shut the door behind her, cutting off the first few notes of a Lancers Quadrille.

Jason eased his door shut and grinned at her from across the patio. "We won't be alone for long." He took off his coat as he walked to her, dropping it over her shoulders, then guiding her along the short path. "After the Lancers will be the intermission and unmasking, then a light repast in the summer room." He pointed across the garden.

"This is your house," Amy stated with a hint of anger as she came to an abrupt halt.

Jason stepped in front of her and slid his mask to the top of his head. "My father's house, but yes. When did you guess who I was?" His smile was playful with delight that she finally knew his identity.

There he is! The man at the milliner's shop.

Anger boiled low in her chest at her own foolishness. "Donetta's brother told me when we danced."

Her back to the windows, light from the ballroom caressed Jason's face. "You danced with Nathan?" His brows rose.

"Nathan! That's his name. And yes." Amy moved back from his proximity. "He said you intend to announce your engagement to his sister this evening."

"He's mistaken." Jason stepped forward, a soft smile on his face. "I've no intention of becoming engaged to Donetta Dunham. Especially not now."

Amy caught her breath. "What does that mean?"

The tenderness in his eyes could mean anything. Couldn't it?

Her mouth suddenly dry, she moistened her lips with her tongue, catching his gaze.

"It means that although I would never agree to a betrothal with Miss Dunham—at any time—now that I've met you, I would find it difficult to court any other."

Chapter 15

Amy Prescott

—

"To court? Mr. Harris, I—"

"Please, continue to call me Jason."

Amy swallowed and nodded, never lowering her eyes. "Very well then, Jason, why would you want to court me, of all people?" She narrowed her eyes. "Is this some cruel jest to share with your friends?"

Jason's eyes widened. "What? Of course not."

"I know what they think of me. What they call me."

"I don't consider that lot in there my friends." He tipped his head toward the dancers inside. "Most are summer acquaintances whom I barely know." He ran his hand along his chin and then shook his head. "I work with Nathan at his father's shop. But from what I've seen and heard of his friends, they are cruel and petty beyond my understanding." A grin turned the corner of his lips up and deepened his dimples. "Besides, I have a mind and eyes in my head."

Amy nodded without speaking, her face suddenly warm beneath the mask, and walked past Jason further into the garden.

Jason took her elbow to steady her step in the semi-darkness.

Ahead of them, through the lighted windows of the adjacent wing, servants scurried to finish dressing the tables.

To their back, one of the ballroom doors opened, and music filled the garden for a moment.

"Summer acquaintances?" Amy held her skirt with one hand and clutched his coat together with the other. Steam from their breath circled their heads as they walked beneath the trees. "I've not heard that term before."

"I attended school in Europe for several years. Mother's family resides in London. While there, I came home every other summer."

Their path curled, and they passed beneath another arbor and toward another wall of glass doors.

"The years I remained in Boston, my cousin and I tutored from home."

Behind them, cheers and laughter erupted from the masquerade.

"Ah! They've taken off their masks," Jason remarked as they glanced back at the ballroom.

"You'll be looked for and missed."

"As will you." Jason shrugged. "We'll find them again at supper." His face in shadow, his voice tender in the darkness. "May I untie your mask?"

"If you like." Thankful that her voice didn't tremble, she began to turn, giving him access to the ribbons tied behind her head.

"Wait—don't turn," he whispered with a soft chuckle. "I want to see your lovely face. I can loosen the bow from behind." The gloved fingers of his other hand brushed soft against her cheek as he took the edge of her mask between his fingers.

As the mask lifted, cold air caressed her face. She blinked and looked around, no longer peering through eyeholes.

"Beautiful," Jason said. The white cloth over his knuckle brushed her face. "Happy Halloween, Miss Prescott." He shifted slightly, and light from the ballroom fell across his face.

"It's also my birthday," Amy exhaled the words, breathless at his closeness. *Why did I say that?*

He smiled. "Today?"

"Yes."

"Happy Birthday, my dear." He lifted her hand and kissed her gloved fingers. "Let's go in before you freeze and find where my mother has seated us." He guided her up the step and held the door.

Inside, Amy shivered as the warmth enveloped her.

Built on opposite wings of the grand house, tonight's dining area, like the ballroom, boasted glass doors that lead to the central garden. Round tables seating six or seven people each were evenly placed throughout. Small pumpkins, acorn squash, and colorful leaves decorated the center of seven dining tables.

Amy handed Jason his coat as the servants placed steaming dishes of food on the sideboard, then disappeared through a side door.

"A buffet?" Amy asked.

Jason put on his coat, adjusted his cuffs, and then took her hand. "A light repast. Many of the guests will leave after supper, but the musicians will return for several more sets." He led her around the tables to the far end of the room. "If I know Mother, she'll have us on the dais. The better to watch over her guests and make sure nothing goes amiss."

Tucked into the far corner of the room, a single table stood on a raised platform, one step above the floor.

Jason released Amy's hand and stepped onto the platform. He strolled around the table, studying the place settings.

"What are you looking at?"

"Mother always uses place cards to assign seating. If she doesn't control even the smallest part of her soirée, the affair will dissolve into utter chaos."

The drama he put into the statement made Amy chuckle.

Jason lifted his regard from the table cards and smiled. "Your family is at the host's table with mine, of course. I suspect my father had a word in deciding this. He hopes for a partnership with yours."

"I've heard."

Jason switched two of the cards as the main door opened and several unmasked guests entered. "Let's get our plates before a line forms."

Amy chose a small piece of cod in a cream sauce and a scoop of squash casserole.

Jason carried their plates to the upper table, then helped her up the step. He held her chair, and after she was seated, took his place beside her.

"There they are!" Rose Harris's voice carried, and the chatter in the room hushed.

Jason set down his fork and wiped his mouth with the napkin. "And there you are." He stood as his father assisted Rose and Amy's mother up the step.

"Have a seat, ladies. Robert and I will bring you a plate," Spencer said. "After being married this long, I know what she likes. Same for you, Robert?"

The two fathers chatted as they found the end of the buffet line.

Rose glowered at her son.

Margaret found her nameplate, and Jason held her chair as she took her seat. "This is lovely, Rose. I don't know how you manage all the details for such a wonderful party."

Jason pulled out Rose's chair. "Have a seat, Mother." His voice held a hint of victory.

Jason's rearrangement of the nameplates put him between Amy and Margaret, with Rose between Spencer and Robert.

Rose slid into her chair—her face flushed with ire. "We didn't know where you two had gone."

"We came to dinner, of course, through the garden." Jason rounded the table and seated himself across from his mother.

"You missed the unmasking," Rose persisted.

"And yet, we managed to unmask." Jason gave his mother a stiff smile. "Did you know today is Amy's birthday?" He lifted his fluted glass and wiggled the empty container at one of the waiters. "Champagne."

"Please, don't make a fuss," Amy pleaded.

"What a horrid day for a birthday," Rose complained to Margaret. "Jason, she's right. Women of a certain age don't like reminders they are aging."

"Nonsense, Mother." Jason motioned for the attendant to fill all the glasses. "Birthdays should always be celebrated."

Spencer and Robert returned with the plates as the waiter set the remaining bottle of champagne aside.

"What is this?" Spencer asked as he set down the plates.

"Today is Amy's birthday," Jason said, and rose to his feet. "And I propose a toast. To Amy. May you remember this birthday as one of the best, and may your next year be filled with delight and surprises." He touched the rim of his glass to hers. "Happy birthday."

"Hear, hear!" Spencer and Robert raised their glasses, and Margaret came to her feet. Rose followed with a soft, "hear, hear."

"Thank you very much. All of you." Amy set her glass down and motioned to the others to sit. "Please, be seated."

Her mother chuckled while everyone resumed their seats. "It's good to see you smile, dear, even if you are red as a beet."

Amy held chilled fingers to her cheek and closed her eyes.

Could someone die of embarrassment?

"Mr. Prescott, I spoke to your daughter about this earlier. I would ask your permission to call upon Amy."

Amy's eyes shot open, and she stared at Jason in disbelief.

"My goodness, this is a delightful surprise," Margaret said with a wide grin on her face.

"I would be happy to have you call upon my daughter." Robert Prescott rose and offered Jason his hand. "What do you say, Spencer?"

Jason's father chuckled. "I think it's a fine idea."

Jason's mother pressed her lips and looked down at her napkin. Her face pinched as though she'd swallowed something sour.

Amy's gaze finally returned to Jason. How could he have done this? In all honesty, he *had* broached the subject with her in the garden, but she thought it a cruel jest. That Jason intended to visit their home to spend time with her left her both excited and perplexed.

Jason beamed while he accepted their fathers' approval and took his seat.

"If you'll excuse me, I believe I'll visit the other tables." Rose set her napkin aside and came to her feet.

The men rose when she left the table.

Jason held his mother's hand as she stepped from the dais. "Have you finished?" He indicated Amy's napkin beside the plate.

"I have." Amy collected her gloves and mask. "After all, we began to eat before everyone else arrived."

"That's true. If you like, we can find out if the musicians are playing. I would very much enjoy a dance before the sated crowd descends."

"If you don't mind?" Amy asked her mother and father.

"Not at all." Margaret shook her head. "You have more energy than I do. Run along and enjoy the rest of your evening. We won't be staying much longer."

As Amy took Jason's hand and stood, screams erupted in the dining room. The open flame from a table candle had set one of the guests' sleeves on fire. The unfortunate girl stumbled backward onto the table behind her, waving her arm and shrieking.

Jason leapt from the dais. His coat already shrugged from his shoulders.

The other guests near the girl sprang to their feet and backed away, afraid their costumes would ignite as well.

"Mother?" Amy looked over her shoulder.

Margaret's eyes fluttered closed. Her arm bent at the elbow, her hand palm-up and her fingers extended. Then she clenched them into a fist, her lips moving in softly spoken prayer.

Across the dining room, Jason had reached the girl. His coat covered her torso on the ground. He spoke to her and her parents while they clutched each other's arms.

Donetta stood behind Jason, her hands resting on his shoulders as she gazed at the fallen young woman. She leaned over and whispered in Jason's ear and exchanged a smile with her dark-haired friend.

Jason nodded to whatever Donetta had asked and helped the injured girl to sit up.

Amy recognized her—the shy adolescent who had spoken to her upstairs, pointing her to the dressing room exit.

The girl peered up at her rescuer, her eyes soft with surprise, delight, and longing. Her lips parted in awe of Jason's nearness, then pressed tight as she swallowed several times.

Saved by such a handsome man, any girl's heart would skip a beat, but the young one positively glowed with what seemed evident to Amy.

The poor girl is infatuated with Jason.

Jason held her shoulders and scrutinized her arm while conferring with her parents. In moments, he helped her stand and gave the young woman over to the care of her mother, who exclaimed at her daughter's red arm and scorched sleeve.

Donetta glared when Jason strode past her without comment and headed straight for the raised table.

"Is she injured?" Spencer asked. He met his son in the aisle between tables.

"Surprisingly not." Jason handed his soiled jacket to one of the waiters with a nod. "Her gown is damaged, and the skin on her arm is red but not blackened nor blistered. The Colemans are taking her to their family physician to be safe." He took his gloves from the table then held his arm out to Amy. "Shall we?" He hesitated, "If you're not too upset."

"What I am is grateful your quick action saved her from injury." Amy inhaled a breath of relief and took Jason's arm. "She spoke with me upstairs."

"Lisbeth Coleman spoke to you?" Jason pointed toward the inside door. "She's painfully shy. In my experience, she hardly speaks at all."

Amy glanced back at her mother, but Margaret comforted Rose, who appeared on the verge of hysterics.

The dining room exit led to a short hallway that opened onto the foyer beneath the curved staircase.

A red-headed manservant hurried down the stairs with a jacket over his arm. "Mister Jason," he called. He shook out the coat and held it open.

"Excuse me," Jason murmured, then stepped to the servant and allowed him to slip the coat on over his shoulders. "Thank you, Patrick. You may discard the damaged jacket," he instructed while he arranged his sleeves.

"That's the odd thing, sir. I was told you put out flames with it, but the material isn't burned at all, only scuffed from ash."

Jason paused and exchanged a confused look with his manservant. "That is strange."

"It is certainly lucky, sir."

"For an unlucky happenstance, blessings abound. Lisbeth is uninjured, and my jacket only slightly soiled." He opened the ballroom door, and music spilled into the entry. "Add to that—the musicians have returned."

Chapter 16

Jason Harris

—

Jason escorted Amy across the empty ballroom floor to the musicians. A few older couples rested in the chairs along the wall, but most guests remained at supper.

The string quartet played a popular quadrille to an empty dance floor.

"Excuse me." Jason leaned down and spoke to the cellist, "Since there are not enough couples to complete a square, would you play a waltz for us instead?"

"Certainly, sir."

"Thank you." He turned back to his partner and watched Amy neaten her gloves. She didn't belong in a young girl's light-colored frock. Her rich auburn hair and dark eyes demanded a more vivid hue.

Why am I drawn to this woman?

Amy smoothed a wrinkle on her skirt and peered up with one of the sweetest smiles he'd ever encountered. "You asked them to play something for two?" Then she half-curtsied to her nonexistent corner.

The quartet finished the quadrille, then struck up the three-count beat of a waltz.

Jason walked in a circle around Amy, then bowed playfully, extending his hand. "Would you honor me with this dance, my lady?"

Amy dropped into a formal curtsy. "The honor would be mine, sir."

When she rose, he placed his right hand on her upper back and held his left one open before them.

She grinned up at him as she rested her arm on his, her hand on his shoulder. "We have the entire floor."

"Not for long."

"Then let us take advantage." She draped her fingers over his open palm, and they moved across the floor, her skirt flaring with each turn.

A laugh escaped her lips when Jason increased the length of their step until they whirled around the ballroom. He couldn't take his focus from her vibrant face and eyes.

"This is marvelous!" Amy laughed as they spun across the room in each other's arms. "But I'm afraid I'll fall."

"I won't let you fall." He slowed their pace to a more modest step.

Several groups had returned to the ballroom. Instead of joining the couple on the dance floor, they watched from the sidelines.

Jason slowed to a stop as the music ended, passed Amy under their joined hands, then bowed to his partner.

The guests who had watched the couple dance broke into applause.

Amy rose from her curtsy, eyes wide. A dark blush spread across her cheeks. "They watched us dance!"

Jason took her hand, wrapped her fingers around the inside of his arm, and strolled to the refreshment table. "They did, indeed." He nodded his thanks to the musicians, then picked up a glass of water. "Thirsty?"

"Thank you." Amy sipped the liquid then held the cool glass to her face. "You're comfortable being the center of attention." Her dark gaze rose to his.

Jason swallowed his mouthful of water, handed the glass to the refreshment attendant, then turned to survey the room. Two groups of four bowed and circled their corners. "I am. I've become used to it." He looked back at Amy and smiled. "But it's not a thing I desire."

"There you are, sweetheart," Margaret said as Amy's parents joined them at the refreshment table. "What a lovely waltz. I'm sorry we missed the beginning." Amy's mother clasped her hands in front of her heart. Her face beamed with joy for her daughter.

"Thank you," Jason replied with an easy smile while Amy cringed. "Amy didn't realize we'd acquired such an audience."

"It was positively beautiful," Margaret assured Amy. "I can't imagine where you learned to dance like that."

"Jason's the dancer," Amy stated. "You should dance with him, Mama. He's remarkable."

Jason held out his hand to Margaret, but she shook her head. "Maybe in my younger days, or even earlier this evening." Margaret tipped her head to Jason then turned to Amy. "We've come to get you. Your father is having the carriage brought around." Margaret touched Jason's sleeve. "Please tell your parents what a wonderful time we had this evening."

"I'm surprised they aren't with you." Jason searched the long room but failed to find his father's white hair. "They haven't left your side all evening."

"Your mother wasn't feeling well after the near-tragedy at dinner. Your father escorted her upstairs to rest," Robert said. "We had intended to wait until Spencer came down, but Margaret is tired, and I have to be at the warehouse in the morning."

"Of course. I understand." Jason walked with the Prescott family around the dancers as they made their way toward the foyer. "It has been my pleasure to meet you both and to see your daughter again."

"Again?" Margaret's brows rose. "You two met previously?" Her curious gaze went from Amy to Jason and back again

"In a way." The ballroom lights sparkled in Amy's eyes as she grinned at Jason, and they both laughed.

"We bumped into each other," Jason replied to Margaret. "Quite literally. I didn't know who she was."

Robert returned from the coatroom with their jackets and held Amy's as she slipped her arms into the sleeves. He did the same for Margaret. "I'll check on our carriage."

An elderly couple approached and waited to speak with Jason. "It has been a wonderful evening for me," he said to Margaret and Amy. "I intend to call on you soon. Perhaps this weekend?"

Amy studied Jason's eyes. "You may," she agreed with a nod. "I'd like that."

Robert stepped through the door. "The carriage is here."

"Goodbye, Jason. So nice to meet you. Please give our regards to your parents." Margaret took her husband's arm.

"Goodnight," Amy said and followed her parents out the door.

Jason released the air in his lungs as the attendant closed the door behind the Prescotts. Other guests waited to take their leave, and his duty warred with his desire to follow Amy Prescott to her carriage.

To the ends of the earth.

If he didn't know better, he'd think he was under a spell. He dismissed the foolish thought and turned to attend to his parents' other guests.

***

Amy Prescott

—

Her father moved forward to open the carriage door while Wrigley held the reins from the driver's perch.

Margaret held Amy's arm, and they followed Robert across the cobblestones to the vehicle. "Your young man is very nice."

"He's not mine." Amy winced. "And as nice as he appears, I'm not sure why he would want to call on me. I'm no one to him, and he's—well, he's rich, popular, and handsome."

"I agree. Jason is all of those things." Margaret nodded. "And it's obvious, at least to me, that he likes you, sweetheart, and he wants to get to know you better." Margaret stopped walking. "I'd hate to see you turn him away because you question his motives. You're a lovely young woman."

Amy pressed her lips and searched her mother's face. "He and I are from different worlds. I don't want—I can't do what you do."

"What *I* do?"

"Hide your true nature from Father. Deny your—" her voice dropped. "Deny your magic. Although you did save the evening with your quick action."

Margaret tightened her wool coat with her free hand and continued toward the carriage drawing Amy with her. "Your—Jason reacted as fast as I to the fire. What I did was perhaps unnecessary and came with great risk."

"There was no danger of being caught." Amy lowered her voice to a whisper, "No one saw you. And even if they had, who would connect a softly-spoken prayer to dousing the flames."

Robert held out his hand and helped his wife into the carriage. "There's one of my ladies, and here's the other. Up you go." He steadied Amy as she climbed into the rig then waved to Wrigley. "Take us home."

Amy folded her hands in her lap and watched the Harris home dwindle behind them.

"I certainly had an enjoyable and productive evening," Robert said. "Spencer Harris is agreeable to a joint venture sailing to the Orient." He rubbed his hands together. "With the Harris capital, the finish work on the newest ship can move forward."

When her mother didn't respond, Amy pulled her attention from the back window. "That sounds exciting."

"It is." Robert tossed his top hat onto the seat beside Amy and leaned back. "Not as exciting as your evening, I'd wager. A birthday toast from a striking young man, one who wishes to call on you." He grinned at Amy. "I may have to put aside money for a dowry after all."

"A dowry?" Amy exclaimed.

"How much were you considering?" Margaret sat up. "I had given up even thinking about grandchildren, but now—"

"Would you two please stop!" Amy demanded.

Robert and Margaret burst into laughter.

"I'm glad you're amused." Amy turned back to the window as her parents continued to chuckle. Every time she considered Jason coming to visit her at home, another burst of butterflies tickled her stomach.

She turned her thoughts instead to the girl who had caught fire at dinner. Were those the flames she had seen in the ballroom? The vision she and Jason had danced through was eerily like the portent she read in her father's future. Could Lisbeth Coleman's near-tragedy be the flames she foresaw in both instances?

Somehow, she didn't think so.

Chapter 17

Jason Harris

—

After a fitful night with little rest, Jason rose wearily on Friday morning and dressed for the workday with Patrick's assistance.

Downstairs, he stopped in the doorway of the morning room and shook his head.

I should have known.

Although a confrontation at some point was inevitable, his fatigue and the petty trap infuriated him, making his anger almost more than he could manage. With misgivings, he entered the room.

His mother waited in her dressing gown, perched on her usual chair, her fingers twined and clenched on the table. Her mood, dour, her face creased with grief. She muttered through pinched lips, "I hope you were pleased with your antics last night."

"I'm not sure what you mean." He took the chair across from her. His father's chair remained empty. Not an unusual occurrence, especially after such a late night.

Morgan set a plate of eggs and hash before him and poured a cup of hot tea.

"Thank you," Jason murmured.

"I'm speaking of your particular preference for the Spinster Prescott's company last night." She sniffed and held a hanky to her nose. "So very unbecoming of a host."

"My particular preference?" He gave his mother a hard smile. "I suppose I did." He stirred his eggs with the tines of his fork. "I'm afraid you'll have to stop calling her that, by the way."

"Why should I?" she bit out angrily.

"Because I intend to marry her." Jason hadn't realized until the words slipped from his mouth that he did indeed plan to marry Amylia Prescott. He took a bite of breakfast and chewed, running that realization and all it entailed through his mind.

His mother fanned her face and then gripped the hanky to her chest. "Oh! Jason!"

He swallowed, eyeing his mother. "I do wish you'd stop that. Father isn't here to be impressed."

Rose sat forward, all pretenses at illness gone. "Why do you treat me this way? Do you not care for your mother at all?"

Jason took his time chewing his second bite, then wiped his mouth. "This isn't about you." He cleaned his hands on the napkin, took another drink of his tea, and stood. "Your masquerade was a smashing success. You would have known that had you returned to the party to bid farewell to your guests and thank them for coming."

"I was too upset."

"Why? The evening went well." He leaned his knuckles on the table. "Lisbeth was uninjured despite catching herself on fire. Mr. Prescott agreed to Father's joint venture. Everyone, except you, had a marvelous time."

"You moved the nameplates. And then Donetta..." she let her voice fade and pouted her lips.

He straightened his suit jacket. "I had already told you I wouldn't marry Donetta Dunham." He turned and strode toward the door, speaking over his shoulder, "And while you are getting over that, make your peace with my decision to court Amy Prescott."

In the foyer, he shrugged on his overcoat, put on his hat and gloves, and picked up his cane in record time.

"Jason—"

He let the closing front door answer his mother.

He walked off his anger at an accelerated rate and arrived at the Dunham Accounting house earlier than expected. He paced outside the office until Mr. Dunham came to work and unlocked the door.

Inside, Jason stoked the little coal-burning stove that heated the work area then took his seat.

"How late can you stay this evening?" Mr. Dunham turned pages in a hard-bound ledger and then picked up a large envelope. "This package is from Majestic Freight. They need these shipping receipts separated and tallied by item and by ship, then included in the corresponding yearly ledger."

Jason took the package. "We can't complete the project today?"

"Not even if my son had come to the office on time and applied himself to helping you."

"What about help from the new man you hired?" Jason asked.

Mr. Dunham shook his head. "No. There's no budget or time to train him. This job requires someone already equipped to unravel this mess."

"I would gladly stay late, but Barrister Hall expects me after dinner."

"That's right. You work evenings for Keith." Calvary Dunham lowered himself into his chair. His gaze lifted to Jason. "What about this weekend? I'd be willing to pay extra for quick work on this account."

Jason opened his mouth to decline, then closed it. Courting would require flowers and gifts. And thanks to Otis, his funds were now tied up in railroad bonds. "I can be available to work this weekend."

"Good. I knew I could rely on you." He picked up two ledgers and the large envelope, then carried them to Jason's desk. "Tallied by Monday, first thing."

"Yes, sir."

Nathan arrived several minutes before noon. Blurry-eyed and groggy. "What time did you get here?"

"Earlier than your father."

Nathan shook his head and made a noise of disgust. "Your work ethic makes me look bad."

"You need no help in that regard."

Calvary Dunham cleared his throat and narrowed his eyes at his son. "Get to work, Nathan."

At noon, the other workers went to lunch, and Jason stepped out for a short break. He searched his pockets and found enough change for a meat pie from the local vendor. When he returned, Nathan didn't bother to look up but busied himself on another project for his father.

Late in the afternoon, Mr. Dunham rose from his desk and entered the back room.

Nathan leaned over and whispered to Jason, "Everyone is anxious to find out why you favored Spinster Prescott last night."

"Amy said you danced with her."

Nathan nodded. "She didn't remember me, but I don't mind." He tapped his pencil on his desk and grinned at Jason. "Maybe I could give her a little something to help her remember me next time."

"Leave her alone, Nathan."

Delight widened Nathan's grin into a broad smile. "Or what? Perhaps I'll stop by her house this weekend." A short burst of laughter escaped as he ducked his head, returning to his numbers, giggling to himself on and off the remainder of the afternoon.

At five, Jason closed the ledger he'd been working on and rubbed his eyes. Nathan had hurried out an hour ago, oblivious to his father's furious glare.

Jason gathered the separated piles of receipts and returned the organized mess to the envelope.

"Heading to Barrister Hall's now?" Mr. Dunham asked.

Jason set the Majestic Freight project on the corner of the large desk. "Yes. At least for a little while. If there is nothing he requires, I'll head home and to bed."

"You'll be here in the morning?"

"Yes, sir."

Outside, the day had turned bitter and dark. A sharp north wind blew across the city, threatening to topple Jason's hat. His long stride carried him to the barrister's small office, and he hurried inside.

Keith Hall looked up from the documents spread out across his desk. "Good. You're here. These are today's notes." He shoved the papers into an untidy stack and handed them to Jason. "Read through them and give me your perspective—especially on the cross-examination by Orland's council."

By nine o'clock, Jason's eyes burned, and his stomach growled incessantly. He'd finished the Benton versus Orland trial transcripts and now copied Barrister Hall's hastily made notes for Monday's court proceedings. He glanced at the door again and blinked his dry eyes.

Where was Otis?

"Let's call it a night, shall we?" The barrister closed the legal volume he'd been pursuing. "Did you finish straightening my ideas for Monday?"

"Yes." Jason stacked the paperwork with his most recent writing on top.

"Set them here." Hall indicated an empty portion of his desk. "I'll look over them this weekend."

Jason's stomach protested loudly as he placed the paperwork on the desk.

The barrister laughed. "Go home. I'll see you on Monday evening."

"Yes, sir."

Outside, the wind had calmed, but the night remained cold. Jason tugged his scarf up over his chin as he looked both ways down the street. He might find Otis at Revere's, but he didn't have a dime in his pocket, and he needed something to eat.

Otis will have to wait.

Chin tucked to his chest, Jason hurried up the hill. There were a few dollars tucked away in his bureau at home. He'd have to use that for spending cash until he could find Otis. Giving Otis his entire savings last night had been a foolish mistake, but he could sell a few of the newly purchased bonds back and re-establish at least some of his cash.

Jason had fully intended to call on Amy Prescott tomorrow and perhaps bring her a small gift to assure her of his regard, but visiting her would need to wait. At best, he could send her a letter of explanation and apology and set next Friday as the evening he would come to call.

Up ahead, under the streetlamp, a shadow shifted and resolved into a silhouette of a man.

Still leery from being followed last week, Jason slowed his pace. Although the hour was late, it certainly wasn't the middle of the night. To his surprise, a hansom cab waited for a fare on the cross street. If he'd had any money in his pocket, he would have turned around and purchased a ride.

As he approached the gentleman loitering on the corner, the individual glanced his way, then strode away into the shadows between the buildings.

It isn't the same man. It can't be.

When Jason passed the lamp post, he made a point of looking down both sides of the building on that corner. The man who had waited beneath the lamp had vanished.

Chapter 18

Amy Prescott

—

Amy tucked her nose into the scarf wrapped around her neck and shivered. Dressed in her oldest gown and gardening gloves, she removed the few remaining vegetables from the family garden. "That's the last of them." She laid the long stalk of Brussels sprouts on top of a basket of carrots and broccoli, then stood and dusted her skirt at the knees.

Peg lifted the basket. "I'll take this inside." The brisk north wind had colored the young maid's nose and cheeks cherry red.

"I'll be another moment." Beside the garden stood a burlap sack filled with rotting leaves. Amy emptied the bag of leaf mulch over the broccoli and carrot patch, spreading the decomposing foliage several inches thick. After that, she unlaced the stitches down the side of the burlap and arranged the opened sack over the rotting leaves, pinning the corners down with large rocks. She laid evergreen boughs over her cut-back rosemary and parsley to protect the crowns from ice and bitter winter winds.

Amy dusted her gloved hands together and emptied her thoughts, setting her purpose firmly in her mind. She placed one hand on the evergreen boughs and the other on the burlap.

"Lord and Lady, I pray to thee,
Bless and preserve these tender plants
Through winter's harsh season.
Replenish and restore the soil
For spring's fertile awakening.

Let my will be done."

Amy rose and looked toward the back of the houses adjacent to her own. Assured no one saw her whispering to the garden, she hurried inside.

The warmth of the kitchen enveloped her, and she shut the door on the gray, windy day outside. Steam from the bubbling pot on the stove filled the kitchen with the enticing scent of chicken soup. She shed her scarf and gloves and toed her shoes off near the door.

Peg and her mother sorted the garden items into piles. Some to be washed and added to the soup, and some stored in the basement.

"I'm going to change." Amy hurried through the kitchen toward the front stairs. "But I'll be back if you need help," she called over her shoulder.

Her mother laughed. "Too many cooks, darling. There's no rush."

Amy smiled, but she knew she had to keep busy.

Since she received the note from Jason on Saturday stating his regret at being too busy to call on her over the weekend, she'd kept herself in a whirl of activity. All the closets upstairs and the attic had been cleaned and organized. The dried herbs had been wrapped carefully and put away. The garden, which she'd neglected for her sketchpad and the absurd notion of learning to heal, was now picked clean and covered for the winter.

Tomorrow she would take her mother's suggestion and concentrate on producing a healing salve.

As Amy started up the stairs, a knock sounded at the front door. She looked down at her dirt-smudged skirt and stocking feet, then called toward the kitchen. "Peg?"

"Can you get that, sweetheart? I sent Peg to fetch onions from the basement," her mother replied from down the hall.

"Of course." Amy pushed a strand of hair from her face. "They'll assume I work here." She ran her hands down her clothing, and the dirt disappeared from the cloth leaving her dress old and worn but clean.

Earth-magic does have its benefits.

She opened the door, a pleasant smile pasted to her face, then halted in horror.

Nathan Dunham stared down at her. "Miss Prescott." One eyebrow rose, and his lips quirked in a quickly concealed grin. He tipped his hat and peered over his shoulder at the two young men who watched avidly from the nearby sidewalk.

"Mr. Dunham," Amy managed. "You've caught me at an unfortunate moment. How may I help you?"

"I see that. You've been...?"

"Preparing the garden for winter." Good manners dictated she invite the gentleman in out of the cold, but she didn't want to sit and chat with Nathan Dunham, tormenter from her childhood.

And what about his friends on the walk?

"If you're here for my father, you can find him at the harbor warehouse," Amy said hopefully.

"Uh, no. No, I'm here to speak with you, well—actually," Nathan held out a visiting card embellished with his name, "I intended to leave my card with your maid."

She took his card and looked from the gold print to his face. "Why would you—"

"I'd like to call on you, Miss Prescott, if that would be...acceptable." With a smirk, he touched the narrow brim of his top hat with his gloved fingers. "Good day, Miss Prescott." His friends' laughter floated back to her as he hurried from the front stoop to join them.

Amy shut the door and closed her eyes.

This is what comes from socializing. No doubt Jason and his summer friends find their jests at my expense amusing.

She tossed the calling card on the entrance table and stomped up the stairs. In her room, she removed the gardening gown and set it aside for Peg to clean and put away. With a casual wave of her hand over the clean material, the dirt smudges reappeared.

We must keep up appearances for the staff.

In a sudden surge of determination, Amy locked her door and pulled the curtains. Through the dim glow that slid through the slit in the draperies, she gathered her scrying bowl and a candle.

Seated on the floor in her oldest petticoat, she filled the shallow vessel until the water was about to overflow. "Please." Her drifted across the water, threatening to spill the contents—her prayer, too difficult to articulate.

In the depth of the bowl, shadows darted. A dark image formed and then resolved into the man she sought.

Anger and anxiety flared in his nostrils as he pounded on an unfamiliar door. She read his lips as he called her name. He took a step back and then threw his shoulder into the door. The expression on his face was a blend of rage-filled frustration, with an edge of fear in his eyes.

Amy held a hand to her chest to steady her breathing. In desperation, she searched the vision beyond Jason.

Where is he? Where does this take place?

She didn't recognize the walk or street behind him, and she couldn't see the doorway at all.

"No, no, no!" The vision sank into the boiling clouds beneath the water—but the clouds remained—churning with potential omens, a wellspring of knowledge if only she could interpret what they meant.

A light flickered behind the rolling vapor, then burst forth, so real and so close, Amy pulled her head back. Flames were her enemy, the uncontrollable element of passion and fury.

People moved beyond the flames, fleeing the danger. Between the smoke and the fire, she didn't recognize the individuals.

Are they on land or at sea?

She couldn't tell.

"Amy?" Her mother jiggled the door handle then knocked. "Who was at the door?"

Startled, Amy bumped the dish, spilling its contents and ending the vision. She moved the bowl to the dresser, and tossed her gardening gown over the spill, then freed the latch and opened the door a crack. "Nathan Dunham."

Her mother shook her head. "I'm not sure I know him. What did he want?"

Amy opened her bedroom door then stepped over the mess on the floor to reach the dressing gown in her wardrobe.

Margaret stood inside her room, waiting patiently.

"I know him from school. He has a sister, younger than me. She and I didn't get along." Amy pushed her arms into the robe. "As to what he wanted—" her voice fell, and she concentrated on tying the belt. With a sigh, she looked at her mother. "He wants to call on me."

"That's marvelous, isn't it?" Margaret shut the door then gestured to the desk lamp, and a flame rose, filling the darkened room with light.

Amy crossed her arms and leaned against the wall. "No, not really. I've no interest in Nathan Dunham, and he's not very nice."

Margaret studied her daughter and nodded. "I see. Well then, I hope you hear from Mr. Harris soon."

Chapter 19

Ayden MacKenna

—

The Tulls were forced to cancel their North Carolina trip to visit Dolly's sister, at least for now.

Travel by horse or mule proved impossible due to the equine flu epidemic. Stables around the city had closed until further notice.

Even the railway schedule and canal boat distributions were affected by the animals' illness. Steam locomotives couldn't obtain the coal deliveries they needed to run. Canal barges that required draft animals to tow them upriver couldn't operate .

The reliable streetcar shut down, and there were no hansom cabs to carry passengers inside the city. Commerce came to a standstill.

Merchandise from the ships, destined for the railway, was either unloaded and left on the dock or remained in the vessel's hold, clogging the shipping lanes as berths remained full.

Marion, Harry, and Ayden sat together at a table before the tavern opened. Dolly poured coffee into their cups then went to the back room to discuss supplies with Li Qiang.

"I don't know if your friend, Archie the tailor, will be able to take the suits back." Ayden set his cup down and looked across the table to Marion.

"Why would they be returned?" Marion blew on the dark, steaming liquid and took a sip. He hissed when the heat touched his tongue and set the cup down. "You still need them."

"But you're not leaving on your trip," Ayden argued.

"Maybe not today, but soon. Horse flu, like human flu, passes. In a few weeks, this delay will be a tale for Dolly to tell her sister." He glanced at his son and then back to Ayden. "I still need you to manage the tavern. Our delay in leaving will give you a few weeks of having me here to ask questions."

"Better you than me." Harry nudged Ayden's shoulder and went behind the bar to tidy up for the lunchtime patrons.

Saturdays could get busy, but it was hard to predict how today would go with the cabs and trolley shutdown.

Despite the transportation trouble, the tavern stayed full throughout the day, mostly with stranded ships' crews.

After sunset, the thin, dark-haired young man came in by himself and sat in the corner. He carried a large envelope which he placed on the table beside his drink.

Ayden poured a shot of whiskey for a dock worker and wiped a damp towel across the counter. He kept his eye on the young man—Otis—to see if his blond-haired friend from his foretelling would join him, but he did not. After an hour of watching Otis drink and open and close the envelope, Ayden decided to ask. He tapped Harry on the shoulder. "I'm going on break."

"You never take a break."

"I'll be over there." He pointed to the corner table where Otis sat, head down with his hand around his glass.

The tavern room remained full for the evening, and Ayden paused to speak with a few other regulars, asking after their family and especially their livestock. When he eventually stopped beside the table where Otis sat, he shook his head. "Not feeling well tonight, Mr. Pierce?"

"Call me Otis." He ran a finger beneath his nose and sniffed. "Mr. Pierce is my da."

"Can I sit?" Ayden pulled out a chair.

"Suit yourself." The thin young man took a deep gulp of beer.

"Are you waiting for your friend?"

"Jason?" Otis chuckled and shook his head. "I suppose." Then he shrugged. "I have the bonds I bought for him—my father bought, I mean, or most of them." He tapped the envelope with his finger. "Jase isn't going to be happy about it." He wiped his nose again. "Mr. Pierce *Senior* took a fifty percent retainer fee on the purchase." Red-rimmed eyes filled with anguish looked at Ayden. "I don't know what Jason will say. There was nothing I could do."

Ayden reached over and gripped the young man's wrist to comfort him. As he touched Otis, a flicker of movement on the tabletop caught his attention.

Not every table held a lantern, only those at the edge of the room where light from the chandelier didn't reach.

The flame grew, filling Ayden's sight until it was as though he stood inside the lamp.

Jason stumbled from a building in the *fire-vision*, supporting an older man with an arm around his shoulder.

Ayden recognized the building as the bank where he made daily deposits for Marion.

Close behind Jason came the young woman, Margaret's daughter. She assisted another man as she struggled to escape the burning building.

The vision pulled back, and Ayden realized it wasn't the flame of the lantern he looked through but the blaze that engulfed the buildings downtown. Boston burned—trapping these people in the fire.

Ayden leapt to his feet. His chair slid back and nearly toppled over. He caught it as he gulped a breath of air.

Otis gazed up at him with wide eyes. "Are you ill?" He pushed his empty glass across the table. "Send one of the girls back with another."

"You've had enough to drink. I'll send Glenda over to collect your tab, and then you should go home." He paused. "Where do you live? Beacon Hill?"

"Don't I wish."

"Don't go up the hill or into downtown." He strode away from Otis toward the bar and back room. "Harry, I need to go out." He tossed his vest toward the hook on the stockroom wall.

What I saw won't necessarily happen tonight.

But the urgency of the vision pounded at his temple, calling for an immediate response.

If it isn't happening now, it's about to happen.

In his room, he shrugged into his overcoat, grabbed his familiar derby, and slammed the door on his way out. In his peripheral vision, shadows separated and moved at the darkened end of the alley. One paced behind him, and the other ran in a different direction.

Not again. Not tonight.

He followed Broad Street to Summer Street, then climbed the low rise toward Beacon Hill. The bank he'd seen in the vision was off Kingston Street.

Long after sunset on a blustery Saturday night meant the commercial district was vacant. Silent. The cobblestone streets reflected in the light from the tall gaslit lamps at each intersection.

As he crossed Devonshire, a familiar figure stepped into the walkway in front of him and waited.

Ayden threw up his invisible *earth-shield* but didn't slow his pace. "I don't have time for your nonsense tonight, Gordon."

"You'll take the time." His hand rose, and a tendril of flame leapt from the streetlamp to his fingertips. "Besides, you're heading the wrong way, Mac. There's nothing up this hill that should interest you."

The rush of footsteps from behind was his only warning. A hard punch to his lower back staggered him with pain.

The shield warded only against magic, not physical contact. He swung his elbow backward, catching his assailant on the side of the head. He allowed his momentum to spin him around, and he gripped the man by his overcoat, shoving him toward Gordon.

Movement from the corner of his eye alerted him, and he ducked. The third man's swing flew over his head.

How many are there?

Ayden pressed his back to the masonry and held up his hands toward his attackers. Like Gordon, flames covered his palms and danced between his fingertips.

The four men's faces reflected in the firelight. Hesitant.

Gordon urged them on from behind. "Get him, damn you! You can handle one man, or are you all feeble?"

"Take a moment and consider how precious your life is," Ayden spoke to the men before him. "I've no desire to harm any of you." His gaze flashed to Gordon. "You're being misled about me."

Two of the men moved forward on either side of Ayden, unimpressed with his words of warning.

Ayden braced for their rush. One flaming hand raised toward each man. "I will tell you that I've learned magic not practiced here." His voice dropped to a whisper, "Violent, deadly magic."

The men paused.

"Do I have to do everything in this lousy coven?" Gordon yelled and pitched a fireball at Ayden. With a hard crack, the fire-wrapped cobblestone ricocheted from the magical shield and bounded down the street.

Glass shattered.

The attack stirred the two men to throw bolts of their own. Ice shards and stones propelled by magic bounced away as his assailants rushed forward.

Ayden raised one hand. His lips drew back in a snarl of rage, and he gripped his fist. Where fire once played across his palm, now water ran from his clenched fingers.

Both men halted in their rush forward and grabbed their throats. Water bubbled from their lips and their coughs gushed moisture onto the street.

"Look at me!" Ayden shouted at the men.

Both men, now on their knees, lifted their sight to Ayden.

He held one hand high engulfed with flames, the other gripped water running freely from his fist. He snarled, "Leave me be or die this night."

On their hands and knees, the two men bobbed their heads.

"Go!" Ayden opened his fist.

The men gasped and gulped air while they struggled to their feet.

"Leave. Now!"

The men dashed away, not bothering to retrieve their fallen hats.

Watching them go, Ayden took his eyes off Gordon. A mistake he would not typically make, but the sound and flicker of fire behind him distracted him. The sudden shock of his body taking Gordon's massive shoulder in his chest caused his head to rebound from the granite building behind him. Pain exploded in his skull and his gut as Gordon delivered several hard punches to his stomach.

"You'll not call them back," Gordon chanted as he struck again, punctuating his words with blows. "You'll not lead this coven. These are my people. My witches. Loyal to me."

Ayden blocked Gordon's swing toward his face and sunk his fist deep in the bully's gut. "I don't want your coven, Gordy."

Gordon's air whooshed out, but he lifted his fist, connecting it with Ayden's jaw. Had the hit been made with Gordon's full strength, Ayden knew his jaw would have broken. White dots flashed across his vision as he pushed Gordon back.

The two other witches had moved to either side of him, waiting their turn to throw magic or fists.

Ayden again set his back to the brick and raised his shield in time to repel stone pellets aimed at his head from one side. He lifted his fists to Gordon in a fighter's stance. "I've never tried to beat the hell out of someone while maintaining my shield and drowning their friends, but I'm up for the challenge." He stepped forward. "Let's try." Both clenched fingers ran with liquid as he swung his right fist at Gordon's face.

To either side of the fighters, the men gurgled and coughed.

Ayden's swing connected, and he stepped forward. "Come on, Gordy, you wanted to fight." He threw his other fist, but Gordon ducked, and it glanced off his arm. "Fight me, you son-of-a-bitch."

Already crouched to deflect Ayden's blow, Gordon dove forward and wrapped his arms around Ayden, driving him back against the building.

The coughing and gurgling to either side stopped when the blow disrupted Ayden's magic.

Ayden repeatedly struck Gordon on the side and the back, attempting to make the man release him. His breath became tight as the bully squeezed him, trying to crush his chest. As Ayden gasped, he inhaled smoke.

"Fire!"

Gordon's hold eased at the shout from his man.

Ayden shoved him back and looked up, blinking as ash and soot rained down from the building beside them.

One of Gordon's henchmen took off running toward the pier. The other stood beside him and Gordon as they watched the fire spread to the two adjacent buildings.

"Help me stop this." Ayden lifted his hands to the flames, but the inferno had taken a life of its own. No sooner would he quench one portion of the fire than two more would burst forward as though angry and hungry, starved for fuel.

Gordon had his hands up as well, sweat ran down his broad face, and he shook his head. "It's no use." He and glared at Ayden. "This is why I wanted you gone."

"I wasn't the one throwing fireballs."

"No, but you could be feeding this." Gordon shook his head as he walked backward. "You and your fire." He made a vulgar hand gesture at Ayden, then ran down the block, holding his hat to his head.

The fire had already jumped ahead several buildings. Fiery ash floated down the street, finding fuel on banners and brown autumn leaves.

Through the flames of memory, he saw Jason and Margaret's daughter help injured men from the bank.

With renewed determination, he ran up the hill into the flames that engulfed the financial district.

Chapter 20

Jason Harris

—

Jason rapped on the red door with his gloved knuckles and stood back. Behind him, the steep front steps led down to the dark cobbled street. He brushed at his jacket and straightened his hat.

One of the multi-story row houses, the Prescott home adjoined its neighbors on one side, with only a narrow walkway separation on the other. All faced with red brick, slight variations in character and paint trim made each home somewhat unique.

The journey from his home to Amy's had been strange, for even during chilly evenings, there were carriages and hansom cabs on The Hill. Tonight, however, Jason had encountered neither and little foot traffic, as though the entire town ground to a halt without the horses and mules.

Had the Harris stable not been filled with sick animals, Jason would have asked Riley to hitch up one of the carriages. If not from sheer laziness, then to allow him to take Amy for a ride later this evening.

As it was, he'd arrived later than he hoped, but Mr. Dunham had asked him to finish the ledger for Majestic Freight before he left and then paid him for his extra time both this week and last.

Because he rushed to arrive at Amy's on time, he hadn't stopped to purchase a present for her at the market. To call on a woman empty-handed was considered an impropriety, but he couldn't allow another evening to pass without calling on her. It had been entirely too long since he'd last seen Miss Prescott.

Almost ten days.

Footsteps sounded inside, and then a young woman wearing an apron answered the door. "May I help you?"

"Yes." Jason cleared his throat. "Jason Harris for Miss Prescott." He offered his card.

The maid glanced at the card then smiled at Jason. "I believe Miss Amy is expecting you. Please come in." With a polite nod, she backed away from the opening.

Jason removed his top hat and stepped into the entry, looking around.

"I'll take your hat and coat," the maid offered, then pointed to the adjacent seating area. "If you'd wait in there, I'll tell Miss Amy you're here."

The front parlor had a settee, a table, and two matching chairs, but the room, with its south-east facing window, and year-round light, housed many plants—potted ferns, colorful bushes, and even a large tree decorated the corners of the room.

"I'm glad you came."

Jason turned at Amy's voice and grinned at the excitement that radiated from her eyes. "I'd hoped to visit sooner."

"I read your note." Amy entered the room without dropping her gaze or giggling.

She's unique.

"I apologize for not bringing a gift. I ran late at work, and I didn't want you to think I wouldn't call."

Am I the one babbling?

"Never feel you must buy me gifts." She sat on the small couch. "Please, have a seat. Peg will bring refreshments."

The settee faced the window. Both houses and streetlights glittered up the hill, more numerous than the stars along the darkened skyline.

The maid returned with a tea service and a platter of small cakes. Their conversation lulled as she placed the tray on the table and poured two teas.

"Thank you, Peg. We won't need anything else." Amy smiled at the maid's wide grin.

"Enjoy your evening." The maid glanced at Jason, bobbed her head, then quickly left the room.

"Peg is more family than a servant," Amy explained. "Father has a few visitors, but he usually meets his clients at the warehouse on the dock. She's anxious to please."

"Your maid is friendly. Our staff is in terror of my mother. They never smile." Jason sipped his tea. "It's refreshing to be with happy people."

"We've never employed staff." Amy grinned. "Only Peg, who helps around the house with chores and occasionally acts as a housemaid, and Wrigley, who takes care of the buggy and equipment for our two horses."

"Are your horses ill? We've lost one and may lose another." Jason shook his head. "None of our animals can work."

"Father says the warehouse is full of goods he's unable to ship. This flu has been devastating for commerce, not to mention the loss of some beautiful animals." She put her cup and saucer on the table and turned to face him, although her eyes lingered on the window. "You asked about our horses. They were ill, but I treated them with an infusion of herbs to bring down their fever and settle their stomach and bowels. Wrigley tells me they are both doing much better."

"That's wonderful! You'll have to give me your recipe," Jason paused as Amy rose to her feet.

She pointed outside. "What is that?"

Above the hill, an orange glow silhouetted the horizon.

"I'm not sure." Jason stood as well.

Amy turned the lamp valve, and the light on her side of the settee went out. "Turn off the light," she instructed as she rounded the table and leaned against the sill for a better view.

The room went dark, and Jason joined her at the glass. "It looks like a fire."

"That's the financial district."

They waited silently while the radiance increased.

Amy gasped and gripped Jason's coat sleeve. "My father went to the bank." She looked at Jason, her eyes wide in alarm. "Your father's bank. He said they intended to review their partnership agreement."

"You're sure?" An occasional flame licked above the skyline. "There's no way to reach them."

"If we take the small buggy, we might." Amy ducked beneath a fern and spoke from the door, "I'll have Wrigley hitch up the cart."

"What's happening?" Margaret came to her feet as Amy and Jason rushed into the kitchen.

"There's a fire in the city. You can see it from here." Amy opened the back door. "We're taking the buggy to get father." She nodded at Jason. "Both of them."

Her mother's face paled. "Darling, you can't... deal with the fire. You know that. Besides, you don't know where the bank is."

"I don't plan to douse the fire." Amy glanced at Jason, then back to her mother. "I'll leave that to the fire department. I only want to get Father out of there."

"I know where the bank is, Mrs. Prescott. I'll keep Amy safe."

"I'm not sure you can," Margaret whispered, then hurried to the front of the house.

Jason followed Amy out back and across the yard.

She pounded on the carriage house door. "Wrigley? Are you in there?"

The door opened, and an older man glared first at Amy, then included Jason in his ire. "I am." He ran his thumb under his suspender. "What is it you want at this hour?"

"Rig one of the horses to the buggy." Amy moved past the servant into the carriage house.

"Now?" Wrigley followed her into the interior. "They're finally getting better."

"It can't be helped." She pulled a package from the carriage seat and stacked it on a shelf. "Hurry. There's a fire downtown. I need to reach Father before the fire worsens."

"A fire!" The servant plucked a driving halter from the wall.

Amy led one of the horses from its stall. "Jason, could you open the doors?"

With a nod, he unlatched the double doors and pushed them outward into an empty and dark alleyway.

Amy backed the gelding into position as Wrigley attached the breast and tie straps.

"I don't want you to go." Amy's mother stood in the carriage house doorway. "I want your father to come home safe, *but there is nothing you can do about the fire.*"

"Did you want to come with us then?" Amy challenged.

"I couldn't help with—this. It's too big." Margaret shook her head. "I'd only slow you down."

"I'm sorry, Mother." Amy climbed into the rigged carriage and took the reins. "We'll be back."

Jason pulled himself into the buggy as it jerked into motion. He looked back as he slid into the seat.

Amy's mother had followed the buggy into the alley. "Amy!"

Wrigley stood at the edge of the garage, shaking his head. "Let them go."

"Give me the reins," Jason said.

"Why?" Angry eyes filled with fear flashed at him.

"Because I know several ways to my father's bank." He held out his hands. "I won't turn back, I promise."

Amy pulled the straps, and they turned onto Beacon Street and raced along the Boston Common toward Park Street.

By the time Park Street's name changed to Winter Street, Jason had taken control of the horse, and flames danced steadily across the skyline. "My God, how did this happen?" Jason reined in, slowing the buggy, and then pulled hard to the right to miss a fire wagon in the center of the road.

A man stepped in front of the carriage and grabbed the gelding's harness.

Startled, the horse reared, but the man held firm to the harness and brought his front legs down. "Sorry, but I need to commandeer your horse."

"You can't!" Amy yelled, grabbing for the reins.

"This is the first horse we've seen. All the fire department horses are sick," a uniformed police officer spoke as he rounded the carriage. "Please step down and allow us to unhitch your animal."

Jason handed the officer one of his calling cards. "My name and address are on the back. We'll want the animal back," he squinted to read the officer's name tag in the semi-darkness, "Fire Chief Damrell."

The fire chief pocketed Jason's card. "If we live through this night, then yes, sir. I'll return the animal."

On the other side of the gelding, Amy continued to argue with the fireman. "No, no, no. We need the carriage and the horse to get my father."

Jason rounded the animal and took Amy's arm. "We have to let the horse go."

"What? Why?" She swiped at angry tears. "We need him."

"We don't. We're almost there." He pointed down the street toward a wall of fire. "The bank is near Kingston and Summer. We'll be fine."

They'd left the house in such a rush they'd forgotten their coats. In the chill night air, waves of heat washed over them as they hurried to the corner and down Kingston Street.

"There it is." Jason pointed, his arm around Amy's shoulders. He felt her shiver and took off his jacket, wrapping the warm garment around her.

The coat hung on Amy's smaller frame, but she pushed her arms into the jacket, buttoned the front, and shoved the sleeves up her wrists.

"The front doors will be locked. There's an employee entrance on the far side they would have used." Jason took Amy's hand and led her around the building.

"Why would they still be here? They have to be aware of the danger—of the fire?"

From the side near the employee door, he could see the back of the building. An explosion had blown the granite to fragments. A bent and broken gaslight lay in the alley.

"Why is there no fire here?" Amy asked.

"I don't know. Maybe the explosion blew the flames out temporarily. We need to hurry."

Flames crawled closer over the scorched frame of the building next door.

"Father?" Jason called as soon as they were inside the bank. Through a hole in the interior wall, he peered at the damage to the front of the bank. The explosion had devastated the lobby. Shards of window glass lay scattered across the marble tile, with the teller cage crushed beyond recognition.

The back room suffered worse damage. The plaster ceiling had come down, along with much of the framing on the second floor. Light from the flames next door illuminated the upper level with its wild flickering light.

"Father?" Jason called again and kicked a two-by-four out of their path.

"Jason?" His father's voice came from down the hallway.

"Careful." Jason steadied Amy as she stepped over a plaster mound, and they made their way toward the room at the end of the hallway. "We're coming!"

***

Amy Prescott

—

Amy gripped Jason's arm and ducked beneath a broken board. As she straightened, she looked up at the flickering light reflected through the hole in the ceiling. The flames were beyond her ability to control, but she could sense the weight of the structure above them.

Earth-skill.

The explosion had twisted the support beams, compromising the entire structure, and it teetered on the brink of collapse. They needed to get their fathers out immediately. Not knowing if the force of her thoughts and will could strengthen the entire building, she sent up a prayer to the goddess to help them then followed Jason.

When they reached the door, Jason twisted the knob and shoved, but it didn't budge. "It's jammed or blocked."

Amy pressed her palm against the door, wishing they could get through. "Papa? Are you in there?"

"Amy?" Her father's voice was weak and worried. "What are you doing here?"

Jason shoved against the door, and this time the hinges gave way.

Dust filled the dark room. The outside wall which would have held the window had collapsed and fallen inward. Broken lumber and stone piled against the large desk.

"He's trapped."

Until he spoke, Amy hadn't noticed Jason's father standing on the far side of the room.

"I tried to move the beam, but the rubble kept shifting. I thought the rest of the ceiling would come down on us." A gash across his forehead had covered half his face in blood. The other half, deathly white, was coated in masonry dust.

"Two of us can move it." Jason looked over the desk. "We're here, Mr. Prescott. We'll get you out."

"You should wait for help." Spencer's voice trembled with uncertainty.

"No one else is coming." Amy stepped over several pieces of rubble and put both hands against the thick timber that once spanned the room to the far wall. "They're busy with the fire."

"I told you I saw fire out the window," Robert's voice strengthened. "Right before the explosion."

"And the bank collapsed." Spencer limped across the room and reached for the end of the cross-member that pinned Robert. He nodded to his son.

The men strained to lift the heavy timber. Together they managed to shift it from across her father's hips.

Amy kept her hands on the beam, willing the structure above to hold firm. It didn't feel as though her prayers were anything more than requests sent to an absent Goddess. She could hardly sense water in the dry dust-soaked air in the room. With determination, she pressed her weight against the lumber, wishing with all her heart that she could do more.

Jason and Spencer shifted the beam, and Jason tossed chunks of masonry and broken boards from Robert's legs.

Spencer gripped Robert beneath his arms and pulled.

The support beam shifted.

Small pieces of debris and dust fell from above onto the heads of the two older men, and they cried out in pain.

Amy firmed her grip on the beam and pushed harder, determined the structure would hold for a few moments longer.

Spencer pulled again then fell back beside the desk, dragging Robert on top of him.

Jason rounded the furniture, ducked under the beam Amy held, and knelt beside her father. "Where are you injured, Mr. Prescott?"

Her father shook his head. "All over, but my leg is the worst."

Jason ran his hands along her father's torso, then felt down each leg. When he finished, he sat back on his heels. "Your kneecap is either broken, or the bone is displaced."

If only I could heal.

Amy swallowed, her throat dry and stinging with dust. "Can we carry him?"

"No." Jason shook his head. "My father is also injured. Mr. Prescott, you'll need to stand on your good leg," Jason gripped her father's hands and braced Robert's good foot against his boot. "One, two, three."

Robert cried out again as his injured leg moved, but his sound leg held his weight. He leaned heavily on Jason and looked up at his daughter.

"Amy," Jason mirrored her father's questioning look, "help your father. I'll get mine on his feet. We have to go."

With one last prayer for the structure above their heads to hold, Amy released the beam. She waited for half a heartbeat, then moved to her father and pulled his arm around her shoulder.

Robert tried to hop when Amy took a step but cringed in pain as his leg threatened to buckle beneath him. He shook his head. "I can't."

Amy wrapped her arms around his chest and held him upright.

"I need a cane or something to lean on. I can't put weight on my leg."

"There's an umbrella stand beside the door." Spencer pointed, then grunted as Jason pulled him upright. "Or there used to be."

Robert held the edge of the desk as Amy searched behind the door.

She returned with a shepherd's hook cane and handed it to her father. With one arm around his daughter, and the other holding the cane, they followed Jason and Spencer out the door and into the hallway.

They emerged from the side door and into complete despair. During the rescue, the fire had engulfed the block. The inferno sucked the air from Amy's chest.

"You should have left us to die," Robert whispered into Amy's hair.

She looked up, blinking moisture and defeat from her eyes. Bits of ash and cinders floated into the blackness, while on all sides, flames surged upward as though trying to steal the night sky.

Chapter 21

Ayden MacKenna

—

For anyone else, any normal human at least, the way would have been blocked by fire.

Ayden's thought squelched a narrow path in the inferno, and he walked through the blaze unharmed.

Tendrils of flame drew back as he passed, away from his presence, as he commanded.

How had the fire spread so fast?

Both pushed and drawn by the blaze, hot air rushed past, brushing against his trousers with near hurricane force. The was air so dry it was as though he had returned to the Thar Desert. Overhead, hot ash blew from one wooden rooftop to another, and the wind fanned new flames.

He passed into an area free from fire and halted. Across the diagonal stood a familiar landmark—the bank. The far side had collapsed due to some other catastrophe, for the fire had only begun to rise from its roof.

Ayden raised his hand, held the blaze at bay, and waited.

In moments, the side door opened, and Jason came outside. An older man clung to his shoulder. Behind him, the woman Ayden had seen in his vision emerged from the bank, supporting an injured man.

The small group paused when they cleared the building and gazed at the flames surrounding them in despair.

"Here!" Ayden raised his arm and stepped forward. "There's a way out, but you must hurry."

Their heads came up at his shout.

"Ayden?" Jason called as he and the man he helped limped forward.

"Hurry now, down that way." Ayden pointed through a tunnel of fire.

"Amy needs help with her father." Jason hesitated.

"I'll help her. Keep going until you are clear."

Amy and her father. Margaret's human husband and child.

Ayden took the cane and wrapped the man's arm around his shoulder. "Follow Jason," he spoke over the husband's head to Amy.

Amy nodded, and her pace quickened now that they shared the man's weight between them. Together, they carried Robert through to the other side.

Jason waited across the street with a crowd of bystanders. "We should go to the hospital," he called as Amy and Ayden approached.

"No." Amy's father shook his head.

The man leaning on Jason echoed his sentiments. "I agree with Robert. Home would be closer."

"You should have a surgeon look at your leg, at least," Jason recommended. He glanced between Amy and Robert.

"Move back. Everyone! Move back." A police officer pointed over the crowd's head. "Back, I say." Then he blew his whistle, to little effect.

More spectators were coming to watch the city burn.

"People, please—" a loud explosion down the block cut off his voice. The blast rose above the buildings, shooting a ball of fire and debris fifty feet into the air.

The crowd began to run.

"Wait." Ayden gripped Jason's arm before he could hurry away with the crowd. "Their panic is more dangerous than the fire, for the moment."

Jason nodded. "But we have injured. We can't stay here."

As the crowd thinned, Ayden tipped his head forward toward the next intersection. "Summer Street is too dangerous. They can't control the fire. Let's go down to the next one and circle around. We can head toward the Common and get you back to The Hill."

The man Jason assisted stood firm when Jason tried to move in the direction Ayden suggested. "Who are you, sir? Your timely rescue is most certainly appreciated, but I don't believe I know your name." The older man, half covered in blood, wobbled slightly.

Jason took a firmer grasp. "I know him," Jason stated. "Father, this is Ayden MacKenna. He works at Revere's Tavern. Mr. MacKenna, my father, Spencer Harris." Jason indicated Amy and her father. "This is Robert Prescott and his daughter Amy." Jason waved away burning ash that threatened to land on their heads. "Now, if we've finished with introductions, we need to move."

Ayden followed Jason and his father around the block and up a side street toward the big park.

Robert Prescott faded in and out of consciousness, groaning to be allowed to rest when awake.

Their burden slowed Ayden and Amy.

Jason and Spencer waited at the entrance to the Common.

A crowd, standing on the grass, watched and exclaimed as the flames spread.

Ayden, Amy, and Robert joined them.

"It's quicker for us to go through the Common," Jason stated. "But I don't want to leave you."

"I'll see they get home safe," Ayden assured him. "Your father needs care too."

"We will be fine. Please don't worry." She gripped Jason's arm with her free hand. "Thank you."

"We need to go, Son." Spencer staggered, and Jason held his father upright until he regained his balance.

"I'll come by your house tomorrow," Jason said over his shoulder as he and his father headed into the park.

"Which way?" Ayden asked over Robert's bowed head.

"North, along Tremont. We'll turn left on Park." She narrowed her eyes at him for a moment. "How do you know Jason?"

"I'm no danger to you." Ayden smiled as their gazes met. "Or your family. I work at a tavern Jason frequents with his friend, Otis Pierce. Do you know Otis?"

"No, I don't believe I do."

With most of the crowd behind them, they made good time. Several more groups of people brushed past them, exclaiming over the injured man between Amy and Ayden, but no one offered to help.

Robert was unconscious when Amy stopped in front of a home midway down the next block.

"I'll get help if you can hold him." She ducked from beneath her father's arm.

"Get the door. I'll carry your father inside." Ayden bent and took Robert's weight across his shoulders and lifted him. He hadn't carried this much weight since working his way home from India.

Amy hurried up the steps and held the door open. "Straight back to the dining room and lay him on the table. The light there is good, and I want to look at his leg."

Ayden gave Amy a nod of understanding and eased Robert through the narrow door, careful of his head, then headed down the long hallway.

"Amy? Is that you?" Margaret's voice hadn't changed. She emerged from a side room and halted, eyes wide, and smiled up at Ayden in confusion.

His heart thundered as he stood face-to-face with the woman he had once loved.

The woman I will always love.

The difference between the girl he remembered, and the reality of this woman left him speechless. The memory of his long-ago lover remained unchanged—her flesh unmarked by the passage of time.

No longer a girl, Margaret had grown into a beautiful, mature woman. The long brown hair that once flowed across their pillowcase now sparkled with streaks of gray, like his own. She wore it wound in a loose bun on top of her head like a crown of dark auburn and silver. Her face and figure had filled out to perfection, and except for the creases at their corners when she smiled, her eyes hadn't changed at all. Brown with dark lashes and arched brows, he had dreamed of those eyes night after night wanting only to see them again in this lifetime.

And here they are—with one distinct difference.

Those beloved eyes held no recognition, only startled surprise to find a stranger in her hallway, with her husband slung over his shoulder.

She doesn't remember me. Why would she?

"Yes, it's me." Amy edged between Ayden's burden and the hallway wall. "Father's injured." She tapped Ayden's arm. "The dining table is this way." Then she strode forward.

Her mother followed close behind her daughter. "What happened? How is he hurt?"

Ayden lowered Robert onto the table while Amy cleared the centerpiece. Margaret hurried to the far end of the table and eased her husband's back onto the hard surface.

Amy slipped a chair cushion beneath his head.

"We found him buried under debris inside the bank." Amy put her hands to either side of her father's head and closed her eyes. "I know his right knee is injured, but he keeps losing consciousness." A soft golden glow surrounded her hands and bled toward the injured man's head. "He may have taken a blow to the head."

Margaret's daughter is not a human child. She's a witch, like her mother and me.

"Amy!" Margaret grabbed her daughter's arm, breaking her concentration. The magical glow faded. "You should introduce your friend first, so I can thank him for his generous help and allow him to be on his way."

A deep flush crept up Amy's face from her chin to her hairline. She ran her hands down the skirt of her gown as though to wipe the magic glow from her fingers. "I'm sorry." She glanced up at Ayden through her lashes. "May I introduce Mr. Ayden MacKenna. He's an acquaintance of Jason's. He came to our rescue in the fire and helped me bring father home. Mr. MacKenna, this is my mother, Margaret Prescott."

The moment Amy said Ayden's name, Margaret paled, staggered back, and gripped the edge of the table. She shook her head slightly as in disbelief. Her wide eyes, darker than usual next to her pale skin, searched his. Her mouth opened, but no sound emerged.

***

Margaret Prescott

—

She hadn't focused on him, had she?

When the man carried Robert down the hall and laid him on the dining room table, her only thoughts were, '*Thank the Goddess, Amy is safe, and Robert is home.*'

She must not have looked at the man in the ash-covered jacket, or she would have recognized him. Wouldn't she?

Maybe not.

The man before her belonged to another lifetime. To that young girl so in love that even now, to hear his name and know she could reach out and touch his arm made her heart skip a beat.

Why did he come back?

Why did he leave?

She took a step back to catch her balance as her world tilted out of plumb.

Dear Goddess, Ayden MacKenna!

His dark curls had lightened over the years with touches of silver but remained thick and wild, in need of a trim.

Like always.

The hair at his temples and parts of his close-cropped beard on either side of his chin were white. In her memory, he was muscular but thin and hardly able to grow a beard. The man who stood before her had the broad chest *her* Ayden hadn't had time to acquire.

But his eyes.

She would never forget his eyes. Even creased with care lines, she would have known Ayden's brown flecked eyes.

She opened her mouth to speak—and he smiled.

Whatever she'd been about to say fled, and she clamped her mouth shut.

"You know Mr. MacKenna?" Amy asked, her voice, two parts concern, one part curiosity.

The smile faded from Ayden's face. "I'm sorry for my unexpected arrival in your home. I didn't mean to upset you."

"Mother?" Amy's voice rose in pitch, and she darted around the table to stand behind her mother.

"The fault is mine, Mr. MacKenna. It seems I've no more sense than to act as if I've seen a ghost." She found her balance and smiled at the man she'd assumed was long dead. "I'm sincerely grateful to you for bringing my husband and daughter home to me."

"It is my pleasure to serve you, Mrs. Prescott. As always." The smile was back as he searched her face as though she might have a hidden agenda or thoughts she wished to share. "I'll let you take care of your husband. I can find my way out."

There were things she desperately wanted to ask this man, like the details of his disappearance and where he'd been these past twenty-five years.

Oh, so many things.

But now was not the time.

"Thank you, Mr. MacKenna," Margaret murmured, she reached for Robert, but her gaze stayed locked with Ayden's.

He dipped his head, and then his footsteps echoed down the hallway, and the door closed.

"Mother?"

Margaret forced herself to smile at Amy and give her full attention to Robert. "Can you tell why he's still unconscious?"

The soft orange glow covered Amy's hands. She stood at the end of the table, her father's head between her palms. "His skull is whole, no cracks or indentations. There it is. There's a large bruise behind his ear and significant swelling."

"We should still have some ice."

Amy nodded, never opening her eyes.

Margaret hurried to the kitchen icebox. She used the icepick to splinter several hand-size shards into a towel then returned to the dining room.

Robert's eyes were open, and he held Amy's hand as they spoke softly.

"Here's the ice." Margaret passed the towel to her daughter, then took her husband's hand from Amy and kissed his forehead. "You terrified me." She smoothed back his hair. "I don't know what I would have done—"

"Shh Margaret. I'm not badly injured. A knock on the head and a twisted knee."

"I'll get bandages to wrap the knee," Amy said as she left the room.

"Did Amy tell you about the fire?"

"Not too much. You've been home but a few moments."

Robert held the ice-filled towel to his head. "It was as though we walked into Hades when we stepped out of the bank. I was sure we faced death."

Margaret shook her head in dismay. "You're home now."

"How did I get home? And Spencer? Where is he?"

"I don't know about Spencer. Jason and Amy left to find you, so I assume Spencer is with his son. As to how you got home, a Mr. MacKenna helped your daughter get you home."

"That's right." Robert closed his eyes. "He's an acquaintance of Spencer's son. I remember now. He led us out of the flames." His eyes opened slightly, and he gazed at Margaret. "He saved us all."

Margaret bit her lip and blinked away the tears that blurred her vision. "Thank goodness he was there for you." Her voice quivered, and she fell silent.

Surely the tears were for her husband and not for the man who had disappeared into thin air twenty-five years ago when she'd needed him most.

***

Ayden MacKenna

—

Ayden stood on the stone landing outside the Prescott home. He took several deep breaths and used a technique he learned in India to calm his heart and mind. Margaret had aged well, better than he had. A beautiful woman with a brave and talented daughter.

A witch daughter who uses earth-skills with ease.

Everything Gordon had told him was a lie. He opened his eyes and watched the orange glow of the skyline for several seconds. The air smelled of ash.

This fire could rage all night.

I can't stop these flames, but I can help keep the firemen safe and do so unobtrusively.

He hurried down the steps and retraced their path to the Common. The crowd of onlookers had continued to grow.

Once back on Summer Street, he edged close enough to a fire wagon to shift the spray where it would do the most good and shield the brave firefighters as they dared the flame to oust looters from the inferno—anything to keep his mind off Margaret.

Chapter 22

Jason Harris

—

Jason's father directed his son to help him up the stairs to his private study. After they entered the bookcase-lined room, he patted his son's shoulder. "Thank you for helping me upstairs without your mother seeing us." Spencer took off his coat and untied his neckerchief, tossing both ash-covered garments into a chair, then limped across the room to the sideboard. "Would you like a drink?"

"No. Not tonight." Jason eased toward the door. "I'm filthy and need to clean up." He held out his hands as proof. "Let me send Patrick up to help you undress and wash."

His father ignored him. "Have a seat, Son." Spencer set two short glasses of brandy on the table and moved his soiled coat and scarf to the sofa. He pointed to the second high-backed winged chair. "I said sit. We need to talk."

Jason hesitated. The only thing this horrible evening lacked was a heart-to-heart discussion with his father. Gripping his last shred of patience, he unbuttoned his jacket. "I don't see why this can't wait an hour." He lowered himself into the chair and looked at his father's face, still half covered in blood. "You said you'd hurt your back. Shouldn't you lie down?"

His father took a sip and then held the amber liquid up to the light. "Drink up."

"I never cared for brandy," Jason snapped. "You should remember that."

"It's a fine liquor. An expensive one, at least this bottle is." He raised a brow at Jason. "Your world is about to change substantially. You best have a taste of the good life while it still exists."

Jason picked up the glass and sipped. "What does that mean?"

"The bank—my bank—is gone." Spencer took another drink. "The investment I made toward becoming a partner is gone." His stare lifted to Jason and held. "I know you've stashed your earnings in that lockbox of yours. For the sake of your family, you need to turn your savings over to me."

Jason choked on the liquor and set the glass on the table between them. "I what?"

"I need the money you've hidden to bolster the household finances."

Jason rubbed his hands together and looked away from his father's fierce eyes. "I would help if I could."

"You can!" Spencer slammed his drink down on the table. "We ask very little of you."

"Listen to me." Jason stood, holding his father's glower. "The money is tied up in bonds."

"What kind of bonds? When?"

"I don't know precisely. The night of mother's masquerade, Otis came to the house—"

"Otis Pierce? That scoundrel! How could you be so foolish?"

Jason paced across the room. "His father had a line on an exceptional investment."

"What investment? Where are the certificates—the bonds?"

"Otis has them. I'll retrieve them tomorrow night."

"Your money is gone, you fool. If Otis had your documents, you would have had them by now." Spencer rubbed his face, then looked at his hand. "I'm filthy. Pull the cord. I need Patrick."

Jason tugged on a long velvet ribbon beside the fireplace, rounded the chairs, and walked to the door.

"Marry the Dunham girl immediately," his father stated somberly.

His father's stone-cold tone stopped Jason in his tracks.

"Bed her, and you can get your hands on her dowry."

Jason stared at the back of his father's head. "I won't marry Donetta. And even if I did, the money would be hers. I'd not take it from her and turn it over to you."

Spencer stood and turned. His lips pulled back in a snarl as he gripped the high-backed chair with both hands. He shoved it aside with such force the chair toppled and slid across the floor. "Damn it, boy. You'll do as I say!"

His father's show of anger fed Jason's determination. "I'll tell you what I told Mother, I intend to marry Amylia Prescott, and I do not need your permission to do so."

Patrick's footsteps echoed on the stairs, and Jason edged toward the hall.

"The Prescott woman doesn't seem as pliable as the Dunham girl, but she should have a sizeable dowry as well." Spencer nodded to himself, his eyes shifting back and forth as he pondered his options.

"Her dowry doesn't matter to me nor her pliability. She is simply the woman I love."

"Oh, for Christ's sake, get out of my sight." Spencer snatched up Jason's unfinished drink and downed the gulp of brandy. He drew his sleeve across his mouth and glared at his son. "You're pathetic. Worthless. No help at all to the family in our time of need."

Jason moved further into the hallway to allow Patrick to enter the study.

"Sir! Were you caught near the fire?" Patrick righted the chair and helped Spencer back into it. "Can I draw you a bath?"

"Yes. And pour me another brandy."

Jason fled down the hallway to his room. Anger lengthened his stride. Once there, he couldn't think what he'd come to retrieve. He spun several times, finally catching a glimpse of himself in the bureau mirror. Ash-covered curls ran riot over his head, a dirty golden-gray. His jacket and neckerchief were filthy.

I left my coat at Amy's house. Perhaps my hat is there and not lost.

Any reason to leave would suffice. Jason couldn't stay in this house one moment longer. In fact, the more he considered it, he most certainly needed to check on Amy's well-being. Did she get her father home safely? How badly had he been injured? While there, he could retrieve his coat.

Despite the hour, he slammed out of his room, down the stairs, and out the front door.

He could smell the smoke immediately. So heavy in the air that his first few breaths made him cough. He pulled a handkerchief from his pocket and held it over his nose and mouth. The fire still burned, and if the steady glow in the sky were any indication, the flames had spread.

***

Amy Prescott

—

Amy held a damp washcloth to her face and tipped her head back, pulling the pins from her smoke-scented hair. She and her mother had assessed her father's knee, using her magical *earth-sight* as cautiously as possible not to attract his or the servant's attention. Luckily, his leg bone must have slipped back into the knee joint on the journey home. From the amount of swelling, she would have never been able to maneuver it back into place. The blow to his head worried her more, but there was little she could do except bandage the bruise to cover her healing ointment.

Afterward, she'd returned to her room and shed her soiled skirt, short jacket, and blouse to turn over to Peg for cleaning. She stood in her underskirt and corset, eyes closed as the moisture on the cloth cooled her reddened skin. She ran her nails across her scalp as her thoughts moved from her father to Jason.

He's such a brave man. He never hesitated to rush in and help father.

Who else would have helped her? She could think of no one.

I hope he and his father made it home safely.

She dropped the washcloth in the water and turned the valve to lower the flame in the lamp. The silk dressing gown Peg had laid out across the bed felt smooth on her arms as she slipped it on and tied the belt. Her window faced southeast, like the parlor below her room. Visible from the higher vantage, flames flared and fell across the spreading orange glow.

This is horrible, dear Goddess.

The number of people rushing to the Common to watch the fire had slowed to a trickle, and the street below, two blocks from the park, was empty. Her gaze rose again to the spreading fire.

Perhaps Mother has the skill to pass water to the roof and dampen the shingles. I'll have to suggest it.

When she looked down again, Jason stood on the walk before her house. He rubbed his arms with his bare hands and stomped his feet when he stopped on the sidewalk.

Why was he out in the night without his overcoat and hat?

And then she remembered—his coat hung in the guest closet downstairs.

Both Peg and Wrigley were helping her mother settle her father in their bedroom. They had decided to bathe him upstairs rather than in the bathroom near the kitchen.

Amy waved when Jason looked up.

He waved back and grinned.

It felt traitorous to experience such joy in her heart with such devastation happening less than a mile away. But she couldn't help it. She held up her index finger, hoping he understood she would come down and not ring the front bell.

There wasn't time to put her dress back on or re-pin her hair. Besides, Peg was otherwise occupied. The dressing gown would have to do. Amy giggled at her presumption as she hurried down the stairs on bare feet. She pulled the door open a crack and peered out. "Hello."

"Good evening." Jason blew his breath on his hands then slid them beneath his arms. "I wanted to make sure you reached home safely and ask how your father fared."

"He's doing well. Please, come in before you freeze."

"Thank you." Jason entered, followed by the scent of smoke. His brows lifted when he saw her satin cover. "I didn't realize you'd already retired." Jason's face flushed. "It must be later than I thought."

"I wasn't in bed." Suddenly self-conscious, she pulled her robe closed at her neck and moved past the stairs to the guest closet. "Your coat is here. We should have thought to take them when we rushed off with the carriage." She handed him his overcoat and hat.

"Thank you." He folded the coat over his arm and held his hat. "I was going to walk back to Summer Street and see if the carriage is still there, and if possible, find your gelding."

"That's kind of you, but I don't think they'd let you take the horse, and without it, there'd be no way to get the carriage home."

"You're right." He placed the hat on his tangled curls. "If your groom has time tomorrow, I could come by and help him pull it home."

"I'm sure Wrigley would appreciate that." She didn't want him to leave. Not yet. "If you'd like, I could give you the rest of the infusion that helped our horses. They are fully recovered and don't need any more."

"That would be wonderful," he said as he put his coat on.

Amy pulled a spare jacket from the closet and pulled it on over her robe. "This way."

Most of the downstairs lights had been turned off, probably by Peg, who had a room upstairs, next to Amy's.

A small light burned in the kitchen, allowing Amy to see her gardening shoes beside the door. She pushed her feet into the flats and then went outside, across the garden path to the garage. She looked over her shoulder and found Jason right behind her. "Wrigley has an attached apartment there." She pointed to the door at the end of the building. "But it's separated from the garage." She lifted the latch and stepped inside.

The small enclosure smelled of hay, leather, and horses, an improvement from the cold smoke scent outside. Amy struck a match and lit an oil lamp on one of the worktables near the door.

Jason ducked beneath a leather strap hung from the low rafters. Gear and tools dangled from the tidy racks along the wall. "We have a stable at home but store the rigs elsewhere." He passed through the tack area to the horse stalls, where a curious head stretched into the passage. "You're friendly, aren't you, boy?"

The horse nudged his hand with his nose.

"He's hoping for treats. His name is Hob."

"I have nothing for you, Hob." Jason scratched his ears. "I'm impressed with how healthy he is. Was he sick at all? We've lost one horse to the flu, and the rest are down on their side."

"This helped both of our horses." She set a jar of light green liquid on the workbench beside the empty stall. "Add a one-half cup to a gallon of water if they are drinking on their own. Your hostler may need to tube-feed them this liquid until they regain their feet. If they are timid about eating, encourage them by adding molasses or salt to their oats."

Jason nodded and turned to the empty stall across from Hob. He rested his arms on the wooden gate. "I'll find your other horse tomorrow and bring him home. If they still need him, I'll get the name of the firehouse responsible for him."

Amy moved to stand beside Jason as he peered over the stall door into the clean area. She took a breath to settle her nerves. "Thank you." She looked up at him from the corner of her eye and smiled. "Not only for checking on Homer but for all you did for my father and me today. Not many people would rush into a collapsing building in the middle of a fire."

"You give me more credit than I deserve. After all, my father was in there too." He turned to face her, taking her shoulders in his hands. "Do you know how unusual you are? How magnificent? How brave?"

"Me?" Her palms caressed the lapel of his coat. "I'll admit to being different, but magnificent?" Her grin widened, and she shook her head. "That I've never heard."

His hands slid from her shoulders down her back, urging her closer, and she stepped into his embrace, tipping her head back to hold his gaze.

"You're hearing it now. From me." His head lowered toward hers. "I'd like to kiss you," he murmured.

Her stomach filled with nervous flutters. "You would?" Amy's gaze rose from his lips to his eyes. By the light of the oil lamp, they reflected light blue, almost white, his pupils large and dark, mesmerizing. "I confess I've never kissed a man. I'm not entirely sure how to go about it."

He smiled and hooked a long strand of dark hair behind her ear. "You appear to excel at everything you attempt, Miss Prescott." His eyes closed, and he lowered his mouth to hers. His lips, soft and warm, caressed her closed mouth, then his eyes opened, and he raised his head slightly. "Relax your jaw and lips." He urged her lips apart with the pad of his thumb. "That's it. Now, close your eyes."

Obedient to his instruction, her lashes fluttered closed. This time, when his mouth touched hers, his lips moved slowly, expertly coaxing her to participate in the kiss. As his arms tightened around her back, she snuggled closer and twined her arms around his neck, tipping her head sideways to meet his mouth more thoroughly.

Jason groaned and pulled his lips from hers. He kissed the side of her mouth, and then trailed hot kisses down her throat. "You—are a—very—fast—learner—my—dear," his murmured words interspersed with kisses.

Amy arched her back to give him better access to her long neck. "I've never felt anything like this." The flutters in her stomach had dropped well below her midsection.

Her jacket and silk gown slipped from one shoulder as Jason kissed his way back up her throat.

"I've never met anyone like you." His words tickled her ear.

"No?"

His mouth covered hers as his palm lifted her breast, and his thumb caressed her nipple.

What magic is this?

Her body surged forward into his, seeking something to satisfy the primal urge inside her—the pressure built into a crescendo of need.

Jason's other hand pressed gently on her lower back, pulling her body tight to his. "Amy." He broke the kiss, lifting his head. "We should stop."

"Not yet." She leaned against him, pulling his lips back to her open mouth.

With a groan, Jason lifted her rump onto the workbench, then stepped between her legs. He pressed his hardness into the fluttering need between her legs.

Oh, Goddess!

Unsure what to do, only knowing she needed something more, Amy wrapped her legs around Jason's hips and pulled their bodies tight together.

He gasped and lifted his lips from hers, holding her shoulders. "If we keep on, I won't be able to stop," he whispered, raw and breathless. "I never meant for our kiss to go this far."

Amy gulped air and leaned her head against Jason's chest, letting her legs drop to either side of his hips and swing above the floor. His heart hammered in time with hers. "I'm sorry," she whispered, emotion tightening her throat. "I don't know what came over me."

He held her from his chest and looked into her eyes as a tear escaped. His warm hands cupped her face while his thumb wiped the tear from her cheek. "Passion. It overcame us both. In a moment, I would have taken you on the hay beside Homer's stall. You are everything I want, Miss Prescott. Beautiful. Brave. Passionate." He exhaled a heavy sigh and pulled her coat over her bare shoulder. "And I have very little to offer such a prize as yourself."

Amy blinked and slid off the bench to her feet, capturing the horse flu solution before the large jar fell to the floor. "What do you mean?"

The door to the tack room opened, and Wrigley looked inside. "Oh, hello. I saw the light under the door and thought I'd left it burning."

Amy held up the container. "We came to fetch the horse solution for Mr. Harris's stable."

Wrigley nodded and smiled at Jason. "The medicine that Miss Amy fixed up will set your animals back on their feet." He winked at Amy. "Turn out the light when you leave. I'm going to bed."

"Is father settled?" Amy handed Jason the large jar.

"Yes. Your father's been bathed and doctored and is comfortable in bed. Your mother is taking good care of him."

"Thank you," Amy pushed her tangled hair back from her face and tightened her jacket.

Wrigley closed the door.

They listened as he hummed a happy tune to himself and chuckled several times before the door to his area closed.

"Do you think he knows what we were doing?" Amy asked, then looked up at Jason.

Jason grinned. "He knew." He bent his head and captured her lips in a quick kiss. "But he doesn't appear unhappy about it, does he? Don't worry."

She followed him to the door. "You're leaving?" The scent of smoke stung her nostrils as she followed Jason outside.

"I should leave while your honor is still intact." As though he couldn't help himself, he gave her another quick kiss. "At least most of it. I'll come by when I've located your horse." He hesitated as though he wished to kiss her again, and then his face broke into a joyous smile. "Goodnight, Miss Prescott." Instead of mounting the steps to the back door, he walked the narrow path to the side gate. He turned once more to gaze at her, then tipped his head and closed the wooden gate behind him.

Chapter 23

Jason Harris

—

When he reached home, he skirted the main house and headed for the barn. Unsure of the hour, he was pleased to find light still glimmered from the stable's front window.

As he opened the door, the rank odor of vomit mixed with horse dung made him gag. He pulled his handkerchief from his pocket and held the smoke-scented cloth over his face. "Riley?"

"Back here."

Jason followed the voice to the last stall on the left.

The door stood open, and the red-headed Irishman sat on the floor with a downed horse. The horse's head rested in the groom's lap. Tears filled the man's eyes as he shook his head. "I don't think I can stand to watch another die."

"You may not have to." Jason held up the jar of green liquid. "This is from a friend. She used it on her animals, and they recovered."

"I'd try anything." He wiped his nose, and gently moved the horse's head to the side, then gained his feet. "Add it to their water?"

"Yes. One-half cup per gallon. My friend also said to tube-feed the diluted mixture to horses that refuse to drink."

"Thank ye, sir." Riley hurried toward the front of the stable with the jar wrapped in his arms.

Jason left through the back exit, his sympathy and admiration with Riley. Taking care of so many sick animals wasn't a job he could do half as well as the

Irishman. Jason walked up the hill to the side door and shoved his hands into his overcoat pockets. He removed his hand along with the pocket contents.

What's this?

He stopped beside the wall and stared at the packet. He turned it over once and then opened it. Mr. Dunham had paid him in cash, handing him the envelope as he left the office tonight. In his rush to see Amy, he'd forgotten he had it.

Jason stuffed the money back in his pocket and tried to find some sign of dawn. It had to be morning. No night could last this long. The only light in the sky was the fire's reflection on the growing bank of smoke in the air. The ominous orange glow colored the ground where he stood.

Instead of taking the servants' stairs up to his room, he decided to take the backway to the kitchen. His stomach rumbled its approval.

Callie, the cook, pulled a loaf of bread from the oven and rested it on a wooden cutting board. "Mr. Jason! You're up early." The woman narrowed her eyes at him as she cleaned her hands on her apron. "Or ye haven't been to bed."

"It's been a long night." He reached for the hot bread.

Callie slapped his hand away. "Ye'll burn yourself. Here." She pulled a roasted chicken from the icebox, shaved to the bone on one side, but the other was crisped and untouched. "And I've bread from yesterday." She placed a crock of butter and several thick slices of bread at his elbow. "Take your hat and coat off before you eat," she instructed, then turned her back and continued with her baking chores.

Jason folded his coat on the bench beside him and set his hat on top. He was famished now that the smell of chicken and bread had replaced the smell of smoke and horse vomit. He spread the butter with the rounded butter knife and ate it with the chicken without pause for ten minutes.

Callie put a beaker of watered ale on the table then continued with her morning routine.

Sated, Jason pushed the plate to the side and rested his head on his arm. "I'll only be a moment. I need to find a horse."

A consistent nudge against Jason's shoulder woke him, and he squinted up at Callie. "Yes?"

"Ye said ye needed to find a horse an hour ago. Your parents are in the morning parlor waiting for breakfast. Do ye intend to join them?" She held a wooden spoon, the instrument of the nudges he'd felt.

"Heavens, no!" He ran his fingers through his hair and sat up, blinking.

Patrick hefted a tray and smiled as he walked across the kitchen.

"You didn't see me, Patrick." Jason pointed at the servant. "Do you understand?"

"Yes, sir." Patrick chuckled and backed through the kitchen door.

Jason growled and rubbed his hand across the stubble on his chin, then came to his feet. "I stopped in earlier, had a bite to eat, and left." He raised a brow at Callie. "If anyone asks."

"Aye, if they ask." She tucked a brown curl beneath her cap and turned her freckled face back to the stove. "Might ye be home for dinner?"

"I might." He put on his top hat and lifted his overcoat, feeling for the envelope in the pocket. "Is the fire out?" He slipped his arms into the jacket and rounded the cook's table.

"No, it still burns. I heard it reached the docks," Callie said over her shoulder.

Jason pulled the outside door closed and buttoned his jacket against the cold. Smoke filled the air and burned his eyes. "Lord have mercy."

How will I find the Prescotts' horse?

He searched for his handkerchief as he coughed. Stained from last night, it smelled of smoke but kept the ash floating in the air like snow out of his mouth and nostrils. He trudged up the hill toward the park.

The crowds from last night were gone. In the middle of the Common, a man hurried past him, clutching two small paintings and a woman's fur-trimmed coat.

Looters? The carriage!

One hand holding the stained cloth to his nose and mouth, Jason pulled the top hat from his head with the other and ran. He knew where they'd had to abandon the vehicle. He never gave any thought to someone stealing it or taking parts from the little rig.

He turned the corner onto Winter Street and raced toward Summer. At Washington, where Winter Street changed its name to Summer, he stumbled to a stop. With a sinking heart, he knew he'd lost the carriage.

Hot cinders floated in the air, and although the flames had moved north and east across the commercial district and to the docks, this area still smoldered. Smoking rubble blocked the road. The corner where the fireman had commandeered Amy's horse was no more.

Not ready to give up, Jason turned right on Washington, away from the fire, and ran down the long block cutting over to Chauncy at Bedford. The smoke in the air suffocated him, stealing his breath. Head down, he leaned against a building, coughing, and panting. When he looked up, two realizations struck him.

First, this area must have been evacuated, for even on a Sunday morning, there should have been people on the street attending the nearby church.

And second, a man sat on the curb, legs in the street with his head down—not far from the Prescotts' carriage.

Jason staggered onto the cobblestones, determined to get to the carriage. As he neared the man, he looked up.

His face, streaked dark with ash, and his clothes scorched where hot embers had landed; Ayden MacKenna looked demented with exhaustion.

"Have you been here all night?" Jason came to a halt before Ayden. "You look like hell."

Ayden chuckled, glanced up again at Jason, then gave a full-throated laugh. Holding his side, he lay on the walking path wheezing as he laughed.

"What's so funny?" Jason smiled.

"I can't look worse than you." Ayden wiped the moisture from his eye. "Did you get your father home?"

"He's there. Worried about his money and how much this fire will cost him." Jason sat beside Ayden on the curb. "He wants me to marry Donetta Dunham, take her dowry and give it to him."

"I don't know her." Ayden shook his head. His eyelids lowered with exhaustion.

Jason stared over his shoulder. "But I've set my mind to marry Amy Prescott."

Ayden's eyes opened, and he focused on Jason as he sat up. "You want to marry Margaret's daughter?"

"You know the Prescotts?"

Ayden shook his head. "Yes and no. I met your Amy last night for the first time, but her mother I've known since...." His gaze focused away from Jason. "Well, I knew her many years ago when I lived in Boston."

"Huh." Jason stared at Ayden, then pointed to the rig. "That's her carriage."

"This?" Ayden's head swung toward the vehicle. "How did it get here?"

"Amy's horses weren't sick. We brought the carriage last night to take our fathers home, but the fire department took the horse."

Ayden nodded. "I imagine they did."

"I came to retrieve the buggy and see if I could find her horse."

"I haven't seen any horses. The firemen are pulling the water trucks into place by hand." He looked back to Jason, his eyes red-rimmed from smoke and his face smeared with soot and sweat. "Most of the new fire hoses don't fit their pumps. They might as well be using a wet blanket to fight the flames."

The men sat side by side in silence for several moments, both watching the smoke roll into the sky.

"I want to take the carriage back to Amy." Jason's gaze met Ayden's. "I could use your help."

Ayden hung his head for a moment in exhaustion, then eyed the rig. The shaft tips rested on the cobblestone street. Slowly, he nodded and struggled to his feet. "I'll help you. I've sat too long as it is, and I've become stiff." Hands on his hips, he looked at the plumes of smoke filling the sky. "I hear it's reached the docks."

Jason stood beside him, sharing his view of the devastation. "Do you think it burned Revere's?"

"I couldn't say." He lifted his arms and stretched his back, then bent at the waist to grip the buggy shaft. "After we return the rig to Margaret, we can find out and look for your horse along the way."

They rounded the corner and retraced Jason's mad dash back to Washington Street, moving away from the fire. Even the slight change in grade made pulling the buggy much harder.

"Your friend, Otis, was in Revere's earlier last night looking for you." A furrow between Ayden's ash-stained brows showed his battle with exhaustion.

Jason couldn't find the breath in the smoky air to reply or question Ayden about Otis—and he had many questions.

Did Otis have the bonds? Why had he waited so long to give them to me?

Instead of asking, Jason lowered his head and pulled with all his strength to keep up with the larger man. As they turned onto Winter Street, Jason waved for Ayden to stop. "Let me tie this around my face. I can't breathe."

Ayden nodded, lowered the shaft, and coughed into his bent arm.

Jason folded the smoke-soiled cloth into a triangle and tied the ends behind his head, tucking the other end into his dirty neckerchief. He nodded to Ayden, and they both picked up their pole and tugged the carriage forward.

They passed Amy's street and turned into the alleyway behind the houses.

"Here!" Jason's smoke-roughened voice cracked, and they slowed to a stop.

As they lowered the shafts, the wide carriage house door swung open. Wrigley stared at them, his eyes bugging in surprise. "Where's Homer?"

Jason pulled the stained cloth from his face and shoved it into his pocket beside the envelope. "The firemen still have him. I'll look for him next."

Wrigley nodded, then pointed further down the alley. "Pull the rig forward and then back it in. The shaft stands are against the far wall." He changed the direction of his finger, indicating a "T" stand against the garage wall, then returned to the workroom in the front of the carriage house.

After the wagon was inside the garage, Jason ducked beneath the resting shafts and rubbed his hands against his slacks. "We're leaving, Wrigley," he called. Close and lock the door. People have lost their minds in the smoke."

Wrigley reappeared and handed each man a damp cloth. "For your hands and face." He watched Jason clean his face and then grinned. "Now that I can see who you are, would you like to speak with Miss Amy?"

Jason's face heated under the coachman's knowing stare. "Not this time, Wrigley. I'm in no condition to call on Miss Prescott."

"You don't look much worse than you did last night. She didn't seem to mind." The thin older man's chuckle turned into a snort as he took the towels back. "I'll tell her you brought the carriage and asked about her." He winked at Jason.

"Thank you." Jason stepped into the alleyway alongside Ayden. "Remember to lock up."

"I heard ye the first time."

The larger entrance to the carriage house closed. The metal snick of the bolt sliding home came through the wooden door.

"What happened last night?"

Jason shook his head. "Which way?" He walked past Ayden, stopping at the end of the alley to watch the heavy clouds of smoke roll into the sky. "Back the way we came?"

"No." Ayden pointed as he came to a halt beside Jason. "North. I've been south along the firebreak to the pier. We can't get to Revere's that way yet—if the tavern still stands."

They set out in silence.

Exhaustion ran the length of Jason's body, from the ever-present smoke-induced headache to the soles of his tired feet. He glanced at Ayden and saw the same ragged fatigue on the older man's face. "You mentioned Otis earlier."

For a moment, Ayden's brow pinched in confusion, and then he gave Jason a nod. "That's right—your friend. He was looking for you before the fire."

"Did he say what he wanted?"

Ayden tipped his head, and his gaze met Jason's. "He had an envelope for you. I don't remember much more." His hand scrubbed at his forehead. "I haven't slept since then, and the details are—well, all I remember is he seemed upset."

Jason's stomach dropped when they paused near the top of the hill. Devastation spread below them for as far as they could see, the horizon hidden in a foul smoky haze. Smoke rose from areas of burning debris near at hand, but firefighters had beaten down much of the fire to smoldering rubble. Firemen with shovels crossed the desolation as a horseless water wagon pumped water along the fire line.

"I find this bizarre in the most horrid sense of the word." Jason lifted his hand and rested his wrist on his damp brow. "How could this have happened? How can so much of the city just—be gone?"

They followed Park Street past the church and turned left on State. At Broad Street, they rounded the corner and headed toward the harbor.

Ayden tapped Jason's arm. "I think Revere's still stands. We've done what little we could."

They worked their way around a water wagon and headed down the hill, southeast toward the wharf. Beyond Revere's, arcs of water soared from ships along the river, pumping a continuous stream of liquid onto the burning port and city.

Several of the tables from the tavern were outside along the edge of the street. Glenda, the waitress, hurried out the door with a tray of clean bowls while Li Qiang served a seasoned vegetable broth to hungry firefighters. Many sat on the curb or the docks as they took a well-deserved rest from fighting the fire.

Harry paused on the step into Revere's and looked at Ayden and Jason. "Get yourselves a bowl of soup and come sit inside. There are empty tables." He tipped his head toward the firefighters. "They say they need to remain outside and stay acclimated to the cold." He shivered, and without waiting for a response, hurried inside.

Ayden got in line behind a tired fireman, and Jason followed. Once they had their soup bowls filled, they went inside the tavern.

The men sat at an empty table to the right of the doorway, adjacent to the tables Glenda served.

Ayden waved back when she held up her hand to them.

Jason put his hat on the empty chair beside him and tasted the soup. Steaming hot with an unusual spicy flavor, he closed his eyes for a moment to appreciate the taste and then continued to eat with renewed enthusiasm.

"Even now, they watch me," Ayden commented, then indicated a table in the corner with his spoon. "I'm too tired to confront them." He lowered his head to his meal.

Jason followed the direction of Ayden's spoon to the table across the room. "Who are they?"

Two individuals with dark overcoats sat across the room. The man facing their table caught Jason's gaze, then quickly lowered his head and spoke to his companion.

"They belong to a secret society. Many years ago, my family and I were members. This bunch is unhappy with my return to Boston, although, for the life of me, I can't figure out why."

"A secret society? I've heard of those." Jason took another sip of soup and eyed the society members.

The smaller of the two turned his head and peered over his shoulder at Jason.

Jason choked and dropped his spoon to reach for his napkin. "Good Lord!" He rose to his feet, coughing.

The last time he'd seen Lisbeth Coleman, she'd been escorted from his mother's masquerade by her parents in need of medical attention for her burned arm. Jason would be the first to admit, he didn't know her well, but he certainly knew her well enough to recognize her from across the room, even wearing men's attire.

Jason blinked tears from his eyes as Ayden rose to pound him on the back.

"Lisb—" The spicy burning sensation in his lungs cut short Jason's call, and another bout of coughing shook his frame.

Lisbeth rose from her chair. Alarm lifted her brows and widened her light-colored eyes. She snatched the top hat from the table and pulled it low over her blonde hair as she spun toward the door and fled the tavern.

Her companion stood rooted on the far side of their table, glaring at Ayden and Jason.

"Did you know the man who left?" Ayden asked.

"That wasn't a man," Jason gasped, shook his head, and cleared his throat. "She's a young woman named Lisbeth Coleman. Didn't you see the tall blonde girl? Our mothers are friends."

***

Ayden MacKenna

—

Ayden looked from Jason to the coven member across the room.

Surely, he wouldn't use magic and attack in such a public place?

He stepped forward, putting himself between the hostile stranger and Jason.

It never hurt to be prepared for whatever may happen.

The man approached and stopped in the middle of the tavern. "We hold you responsible," his low voice meant to reach no further than Ayden's ears.

"Your actions—*your people*—were the instigators." Ayden shook his head then shrugged. "All you had to do was leave me be."

"You don't recognize me, do you, Mac?" He placed a rounded bowler on his bald head. "A few pounds and a few years, and you look right through me. Then again, it's not like you took much notice of me when we were younger."

Ayden blinked and narrowed his eyes. "I've been two days without sleep, and smoke has blurred my vision, but I recognize you now, Milty."

"Don't call me that. My name is Milton." The witch sniffed and spit on the floor at Ayden's feet. "You never should have come back."

He's trying to draw you out—make you react.

And Goddess, how Ayden wanted to react.

As a kid, Milton Kohler had been Gordon's shadow. Twenty-five years and fifty pounds later, Milton finally found the bully in himself.

"You should leave," Ayden replied, never dropping his eyes.

"What's the trouble here?" Harry asked as he sat a tray of clean bowls on a nearby table and wiped his hands on his apron. "Do you need a hand, Ayden?"

"No. My friend is on his way out." Ayden indicated the door.

Milton leveled a glare at all three men, then walked to the door, threw it open, and stalked out.

"A friend, you say?" Harry lifted the tray and headed out the open door.

Ayden didn't answer. Fatigue clawed at him, demanding he close his eyes and rest. Even more than hunger, his head felt faint, and his scalp tingled with exhaustion.

Jason eyed him with concern when Ayden turned and rested his palms on the table. "I know you have questions about the people who are watching me and about your friend Otis, but I'm not fit company, nor can I put a coherent thought together. I need to rest."

"Can I help you get home?" Jason took up his hat, prepared to leave.

"I *am* home." Ayden tipped his head toward the bar. "I have a room in the back, and I think I can manage to make it to my bed without falling over." He offered his hand to Jason and was pleased with Jason's quick and firm handshake. "Enjoy the rest of your meal in peace. You should get some rest yourself."

"I will. I have a few more places and people to check on. Then I'll go over the hill and find my bed too."

With a half-hearted wave, Ayden lurched to the stockroom door beside the bar and into the back room.

They could use my help feeding the firemen.

I can't be everything to everyone. I need to rest.

Milton and Gordon's coven could come back while I sleep. They blame me for the fire.

That he could remedy, at least for the moment. He closed the inside door to his small room and bolted it, then checked the back exit. The alleyway was empty.

Ayden flipped the blanket up and reached under the bed, searching for a moment until his fingers touched the woven bag. He eased himself onto the floor beside the cot, breathing deeply to clear his head. Had he ever been this tired? This sleep-deprived?

On that nightmare ship bound for India.

Searching through the bag by touch alone, he found the chain to the locket.

A regular warding spell to the sacred points and asking the Goddess to wake him should anyone approach would be best, but he didn't have the stamina to stand, much less remember the proper prayers.

Despite Magi Rakesh's disapproval, the amulet had been a gift from the Fire-Priest Gravâratav for Ayden's many years of service. Ayden didn't trust the entity inside the magical stone completely—the tiny captive *elemental* bound to do its master's bidding—but he needed someone to watch over him while he slept.

He slipped the heavy necklace around his neck and lifted the red stone at the end of the chain, netted and bound inside woven wire strands. Weighing the amulet in his hand, he watched the flicker of light inside the stone dart back and forth. A living entity. An *elemental*—bound to serve him.

He gripped the stone in his hand, feeling its warmth. "Caz, come forth and do my bidding."

The tiny spark of light imprisoned in the stone zipped through Ayden's fingers and danced along the edge of the table. From where Ayden sat, and through blurred and tired eyes, it looked like nothing more than a candle flame. However, Ayden knew the sprite's true form. Dark and bent, as though the blaze had left only an animated cinder, the *fire-sprite* danced with unflagging energy.

"Sit on the candlewick and watch while I sleep. Should anyone approach, these doors—" Ayden pointed to both the inside and the outside door, "—wake me. Gently."

Ayden levered himself onto the cot and watched the sprite dance on the candlewick. "Remember, a gentle touch on my hand will wake me. No need to set my shirt on fire again."

The flame sputtered as though laughing, then disappeared when Ayden closed his eyes.

His last thought was of the alley behind Margaret's house. He thought he might have been there before, but it felt like a dream or a vision. Then exhaustion claimed him.

Chapter 24

Jason Harris

—

Jason's stare shifted from Ayden's departing figure to the tavern's front door. He picked up his soup and finished it off, drinking directly from the bowl, then snatched up his hat and hurried to the exit.

Outside, he looked in both directions, but Lisbeth and her companion were gone.

Their lunch break ended, the firemen gathered their equipment and walked up the hill in the direction Jason and Ayden had come down. The department names on their gear came from as far away as New Hampshire.

North of Revere's, black smoke continued to billow into the overcast sky, giving daylight the shaded aspect of twilight.

Harry approached the stoop, carrying the deep soup pot.

Jason opened and stood to the side as he held the door for Harry.

"Thank you."

"You're welcome." Jason nodded.

Glenda hurried through the opening behind Harry with a tub of dirty bowls and spoons. She dipped her head and blushed.

Jason smiled at Glenda and shut the door behind the waitress to keep the chill breeze from the tavern.

The air smelled of smoke, dead fish, and fuel oil. Where the fire had burned to the channel, men picked their way across the rubble and around skeletons of buildings, searching through what remained of the damaged structures.

Setting his hat firmly in place, he buttoned his coat and headed south, across the blackened area. He stayed on the street, away from the men with shovels. He didn't want to consider why they searched. Ahead, near the cross street, another group of men posed for photographs in front of the charred remains of a building.

Head down, Jason walked steadily into the winter wind.

He had a horse to find.

And people he needed to check on.

Jason followed the line of destruction uphill until he stood adjacent to the street where Barrister Hall once had an office. His gut clenched, and he swallowed several times to hold back tears. His city lay in ruins. Ash floated above the devastated financial district.

He had to pray Keith Hall had not been at his office Saturday night.

Further up the hill, he turned left and found Dunham Accounting. The street and office were deserted but still standing. He didn't pause but continued up the road.

Not far from where he'd found Ayden, he rounded a corner and came face-to-face with an ash-covered man leading Homer south into a residential neighborhood.

"You found him." Jason reached for the makeshift halter, but the man jerked the rein away.

"What do you mean? This horse is mine." He cast a furtive look over his shoulder. "Get out of my way."

"No." Jason blocked his path. "That horse belongs to the Prescott family, and I intend to return Homer to them."

The man looked behind him again, then swung his fist, glancing off Jason's cheekbone before connecting with his nose.

Pain erupted as his head flew back. Jason stumbled but regained his footing.

The shrill blast of a whistle rang out from behind the man.

Jason wiped the blood from his lips with the back of his gloved hand. He threw his shoulders into the stranger's midsection as the thief broke into a run, knocking him from his feet.

Both men went down.

The thief punched and kicked but couldn't land more than a few glancing blows.

Jason held tight—his arms wrapped around the man as his nose continued to throb. The sharp trill of the whistle grew louder in his ears.

A firm grip on his shoulder pulled Jason from the horse thief. "That's enough, I say!"

Yanked up and thrown aside by strong hands, Jason's back hit hard against a lamp post.

Another fireman restrained the horse thief against the building across the way.

"This horse is under my care until I locate the owners," the fire captain stated. He looked first at Jason, then at the other man while his men restrained the combatants. "If I thought I could find a police officer right now, I'd have you both arrested for looting and thievery."

Jason's nose continued to bleed. He pulled the yellowed handkerchief from his pocket and held it to his face. "I've been lookin' for the Prescotts' horse all day. Then this fellow says it's his and hits me in the nose."

"It's my horse," the thief protested. "And he attacked me first." The man pointed a filthy finger at Jason.

"I don't have time for this," the captain complained. He indicated the thief. "I watched you untie the horse and sneak away from our water truck." He turned to Jason. "You, I don't know. What's your name?"

"Jason Harris." He dabbed his nose, flipped the blood-stained cloth over, and pressed it back against his nose. "The horse belon's to the Prescotts of Beacon Hill. I intend to return it."

The fireman shrugged. "I don't know whose horse it is. But I do know who commandeered the animal."

"So do I." Jason nodded.

The fireman paused long enough to give the other man a chance to speak, but he only glared at the men restraining him. The fire captain then turned to Jason. "Who took the horse?"

"Fire Chief Damrell," he said without hesitation. Last night, he took the horse from us not far from here, and I gave him my card. He should have known how to contact me."

"That's correct, and Damrell did mention misplacing the card as well." The captain motioned to the lieutenant holding Homer's makeshift halter. "Give the man his horse, and let's get back to work."

"Wait a minute!" the thief protested.

"I hear another word from you, and I'll have the lieutenant tie you to the water wagon." The captain's voice shook with anger. "And if I catch sight of you again, I'll do exactly that then turn you in as a looter."

Jason took the reins with one hand and held the bloody handkerchief to his nose with the other. "Thank you, captain."

The firemen had already turned away from the excitement and hurried back to their wagon.

***

Amy Prescott

—

Wrigley knocked on her father's bedroom door before lunch to tell them Jason and his friend had returned the carriage.

Amy stood from her seat beside the bed. "Are they in the morning room or still in the garage?"

Wrigley chuckled and held up his hands. "They've already gone. Your young man said he would see you after he reclaimed Homer."

Her mother rounded the end of the bed. "And the friend who accompanied him? Was he the same friend who helped Robert home last night?" Margaret's eyes shone brightly with interest.

"I'm afraid I didn't see the man last night."

"He's tall with thick silver and black hair." Her mother glanced at her husband, asleep on his bed, and stepped closer to the coachman.

Wrigley shook his head. "I'm sorry, ma'am," he whispered. "Both men were filthy, covered with ash and whatnot. I didn't give Mr. Harris's friend much of a look."

Why would Mother ask about him? Who was Ayden MacKenna to her?

She would have asked her mother who he was over lunch, except her mother had taken a tray up to father's room. Amy ate in the kitchen with Peg. They spoke mainly about the fire, how far Peg had heard it had spread, and how many out-of-state fire departments had rushed to help put out the blaze.

Back in her room, a single ray of sunlight broke through the smoky, cloud-filled sky. A mosaic of grays with glimmers of white formed the perfect backdrop to the leafless tree across the street. The momentary splendor from Amy's bedroom window filled her heart with a ray of hope before the clouds closed again.

A sign from the Goddess. Perhaps the worst has passed.

Amy's father still rested comfortably in his room for now but would be chomping at the bit to return to work tomorrow. However, over and above her legitimate concern for his well-being, she worried her mother had begun acting peculiar.

She let the curtain fall closed. There was clean water in her room, refreshed by Peg that morning. Amy fought the urge to lock her bedroom door and light a candle.

Her most recent sketchpad lay open on her bed. The drawing was incomplete, but it held a remarkable likeness to Mr. Jason Harris. She gazed at the unfinished portrait.

Have I fallen in love?

A soft tap sounded at Amy's bedroom door, and she flipped the sketchpad closed. "Yes?"

Peg eased the door open far enough to lean in and cast a bright smile at Amy. "Wrigley asked me to find you. Your friend is waiting in the carriage house and would like a word with you."

The usual flutters that accompanied thoughts of Jason Harris tickled Amy's chest, and she held her fingers over her lips to stop her smile. "Tell him I'll be right down."

"I will." Peg grinned as her head disappeared and the door shut.

Amy bent to look in the dressing table mirror and pushed stray strands into place beneath the lavender ribbon that held her long auburn curls to the back of her head, and then she pinched both cheeks.

"Oh, for goodness sakes. What am I doing?" She took a deep breath, straightened her gown, and hurried down the stairs behind Peg. "Never mind, Peg. I'm on my way."

Outside, the heavy scent of smoke had lessened, but there remained a bitter chill in the breeze. Amy rubbed her arms as she crossed to the carriage house and hurried inside.

I should have put on a wrap.

Lanterns hung from both sides of Homer's stall filling the small area with light.

Wrigley had his head down, checking the gelding for injuries while cleaning thick ash from the horse's coat with a brush. "Tell me where you found him again?"

"Not far from where they took him from us. A looter had him. I stopped the man and told him that wasn't his horse." Jason's voice came from beyond the stables, near the carriage. "Which led to the disagreement."

Amy stepped closer to the stalls, pulled forward by the familiar disembodied voice.

He leaned against the carriage, head tipped back, holding one of Wrigley's grooming linens to his face.

"Did he break it?" Wrigley asked, never looking up from his grooming.

"I don't think so. Only bloodied it." He shifted the towel and groaned, then continued, "That was about the time the fire captain came running down the street. It appears Homer was his to watch until they could find the owner."

"How did he decide to let you have the horse?"

"He asked who took the horse from us originally, and of course, the thief didn't know. As soon as I mentioned Fire Chief Damrell, he handed Homer to me and chased the other man off."

Jason's jacket and slacks were smudged and covered with ash. His once black top hat lay on the ground beside his dirty boots, stained beyond repair.

Amy's chest tightened, and she blinked burning tears from her eyes. While she bathed and slept and ate, Jason had brought back their carriage and fought to bring her beloved Homer home.

"Are you sure you're well?" she stepped forward into the light from the stall.

"Jumpin' Jehoshaphat!" Wrigley came to his feet. "You 'bout scared the devil out of me."

Amy ignored Wrigley. Her gaze sought and found Jason's as he lowered the bloody towel.

"I'm not ill, only very tired." His eyes, lined red with irritation, weren't bruised. However, the thief's blow might have glanced off his cheekbone. Jason's skin below his eye had split and bled.

"Your cheek's bleeding."

"It is?" He lifted his fingers to his face.

Amy captured his hand. "Allow me. Your hands are none too clean." She took the towel and blotted the drops from his face. "This cut needs to be cleaned and bandaged. Come inside."

"I can't." Jason shook his head and pulled her hand back, drawing her closer. "I'm too wretched filthy to set foot in your mother's house. I need to go home."

"You'll not leave without allowing me to bandage this cut."

"Might as well give it up," Wrigley called from the stall. "You'll not dissuade her. The sooner you let her tend your wound, the sooner you'll be on your way."

"Sit here, in the light." Amy pointed to a white-painted chair across from Homer's stall. "There are bandages and salve in the workroom. I'll be right back."

She found clean linen and a jar of her homemade ointment, then wet a towel at the pump in the yard and wrung the excess moisture onto the ground. Wishing she had time to heat the water properly, she hurried back to Jason, damp cloth in one hand and a jar of her salve in the other.

She placed the jar on the workbench near the chair and eyed Jason's cut cheek and face. In the moments she'd been gone, his head had fallen back against the side of the stall. The rise and fall of his chest told her he slept. She stepped back, hesitant to wake him.

"He's been all over town today. When he walked that other fellow home earlier, they circled north of the fire. They had to skirt Washington Street and go all the way to State to get around it."

"The fire burned across the city to the docks?" Amy glanced back at Jason, but he continued to sleep. "What about Father's warehouse? Did that burn as well?"

"I don't know." Wrigley shook his head and leaned his arms on the stall door. "You know, Mr. Harris got into a fight over Homer because of you. He wanted to impress you and bring your animal home."

Fine silt of gray ash covered Jason's face and hair, except where blood had run from the cut on his cheek. Blood from his nose had dried across his lips and chin. His mouth gaped open slightly as he slept.

"My prince," Amy whispered and then flushed when Wrigley chuckled. "Jason," she said louder and touched his shoulder.

His red-rimmed eyes opened, and his ice-blue eyes met hers. "Hmm?"

"I'm going to clean your face and put ointment on your cut." She waited for a response, and when there was none, she whispered, "Are you awake?"

Jason's lips quirked, but his eyes remained closed. "I am. You may proceed."

Taking care not to pull open the tear, Amy cleaned the skin beneath his eye and wiped the soot and blood from his face. She gently applied the salve to the cut, then capped the Mason jar and set it on the bench. "Not much doctoring needed. The cut had already closed."

Blue eyes reappeared, and Jason smiled at her. "You have a delicate touch." He rose from the chair slowly, bent to pick up his ruined top hat from the floor, and put it on his head. "I need a bath and rest in that order. I should head home."

"I understand." Amy followed him through the work area and paused with him inside the door. "Will you go to work tomorrow?"

Jason's brows rose as he shrugged. "If Mr. Dunham will open the doors, I will. This weekend has seen such devastation."

"When—" Amy pressed her lips and tucked her chin as her cheeks warmed.

"When will I see you next?" Jason lifted her chin with his fingers and placed a soft kiss on her lips. "As soon as possible. I'll send word when I can visit, or we can meet." He clasped the top button on his overcoat and reached for the door, then paused, his hand on the latch. "How well do you know Lisbeth Coleman?"

Amy shook her head. "Not well. I met her for the first time at your masquerade. I believe our fathers know each other through business." Concern for the young woman made her search his face in the dim light. "Was she injured in the fire?"

"Not at all. I didn't mean to alarm you." He lifted her chilled fingers with his warm hand. "I saw her today. She appeared well." He kissed her fingers. "You should go inside and get warm."

He opened the door, and a gust of wind swirled past him and pressed her skirt against her legs. "I shall. And no more fights for you tonight."

Jason squeezed her fingers. "I shall go straight home, Miss Prescott." He followed her to the back door. "I'll send word as soon as I know when we can be together."

"I shall look forward to hearing from you."

He made an awkward bow and grabbed his hat before it tumbled from his head and laughed. "That is indeed good to know."

His laughter warmed her heart as he slipped through the side gate.

***

Jason Harris

—

Late, because of another morning argument with his parents, Jason opened the front door of Dunham Accounting and stepped inside.

Nathan glanced up from his ledger and grinned, then lowered his head.

"It's good to see you could make it, Mr. Harris." Mr. Dunham spoke without looking up from his work. "I'd begun to worry you were one of the weekend casualties."

"No, sir. My father required a word with me this morning." He leaned his *épée* against the wall, hung up his jacket, an old one, but clean, and set his father's old bowler on the hook beside it. Then he wove his way through the desks to his usual seat beside Nathan.

"Young men should take time to consult with their fathers. There is no shame in that."

Jason nodded at Mr. Dunham as he took his seat.

"I've had to put several of our projects on hold. I'm unsure if our clients wish us to continue or are even still in business after this weekend. As such, you will be released today at noon and may return in the morning. I will try to ascertain our clients' status this afternoon." Mr. Dunham did not raise his head from the notation he made in the ledger before him.

The three men in the front whispered to each other for a moment, then returned to their tasks.

Jason opened his register and emptied an envelope of receipts onto his work desk.

"It appears we have a free afternoon," Nathan spoke low out of the side of his mouth, never lifting his scrutiny from his pencil as it notated sums.

"It's just as well. I need to check on Barrister Hall at the courthouse and then try to find a gift for Amy."

"A gift?" Nathan's eyebrow raised, and his gaze slid from his work to Jason's face. "What kind of gift?"

"The kind that would mean something. I intend to marry Amy, and I want to present her with a proper present when I ask her and obtain her father's permission."

"You're a dolt."

They worked in silence for close to an hour before Nathan whispered, "When do you plan to see her?"

"I told her I'd send word when we can meet. I'd go today, but I must find Barrister Hall and Otis Pierce. I don't know how either fared during the fire."

"Otis Pierce," Nathan scoffed. "Why someone with your family connections insists on marrying Spinster Prescott and associating with gutter rats like Pierce—"

"Don't judge me," Jason glared at the dark-haired young man, "and mind your tongue."

Nathan chuckled, and both men fell silent.

At noon, Mr. Dunham closed his journal loudly, drawing the room's attention. "Be here tomorrow morning at eight o'clock sharp." He looked at his son and Jason. "I should know then who will be staying and how much work we have for the week."

Jason tidied his desk and, ignoring Nathan, took his coat and hat, nodded to Mr. Dunham, and left the office.

The air held the taint of smoke, and he knew a few fires continued to burn, but for the most part, firefighters had subdued the wretched flames.

The courthouse felt like an empty funeral parlor as he entered through the big front doors. Without the usual crowd in the main corridor, his shoes echoed down an empty hallway. A notice posted on the docket near the courtrooms notified jurors and barristers that hearings today would be rescheduled.

Raised voices down the hall drew his attention, and he stepped back from the board.

Barrister Hall barreled around the corner, his leather case under one arm. When he caught sight of Jason, his lowered, angry brow rose in delight.

"Jason! What a pleasant surprise to find you here." The thin, white-haired attorney stopped beside the docket and adjusted his spectacles as he looked Jason over. "You seem fit. How did your family fare this weekend?"

"Everyone is safe," Jason replied. His relief at finding Keith in one piece set his mind at rest. "My father's bank was a casualty, however. He is quite worried about the disaster's effects on the economy."

"Oh, no doubt. But rebuilding should bring in jobs and goods. Insurers won't be pleased, of course, but then they never are. What brings you to the courthouse today?"

"Quite honestly, *you* did. I hoped to find word of you and to be certain you endured the fire." He lowered his voice. "I'm sorry about your office."

Barrister Hall nodded and shifted his brief bag to the other arm. "Thank you, but there was nothing there I cannot replace. Books and paper. I'm sure it went up in a whoosh." He narrowed his eyes. "Since the court is postponed, but several judges are here, you should take your exam."

"Today? But I haven't prepared."

"I doubt you need further preparation. You've read Blackstone's Commentaries cover to cover several times this year." He motioned for Jason to follow and set off down another hallway. He knocked briefly on a closed door, then grinned at Jason, turned the knob, and walked in.

"Judge Brown, do you have a moment?"

Jason followed Barrister Hall into the judge's private chambers.

Judge Brown's wire-rimmed spectacles magnified his blue eyes. He rose from the seat and extended his hand across the desk to Keith Hall. "Good to see you, Keith. I hope all is well with you." The judge had removed his jacket and rolled up his sleeves. His robe hung on the wall behind him, and several volumes of books lay open on his desk.

Barrister Hall took his hand and nodded. "I'm well, Garrett. Thank you." He released the judge and gestured to Jason. "This is the young man I told you about. He's been my apprentice for several years now, Jason Harris." He put a hand on Jason's shoulder and held his arm out to the judge. "Jason, this is a long-time friend of mine, Judge Garrett Brown."

"I've heard great things about you, son." Judge Brown walked around his desk and took Jason's hand. The judge had on tweed slacks and a matching vest. A gold pocket watch chain hung from the waistcoat pocket.

"Thank you, sir."

The judge looked up at the attorney. "What can I do for you, counselor?"

"I thought, since we find ourselves with time on our hands this afternoon, it might be possible for Jason to take the Bar Examination."

"The Bar for Mr. Harris?" Judge Brown squinted at Jason through his glasses. "I don't know why not. I have another young man coming in shortly to do the same thing."

"I'm afraid I don't have the funds to take the exam today." Panic tightened Jason's chest, and he clenched his fists.

"It would be my pleasure to shoulder the cost of the examination," Keith Hall said. "After all, I've benefited from your labor for quite some time."

"And if I fail?" Jason whispered to Keith.

"I have every confidence you know this material, perhaps even better than I do myself." He leaned back and considered Jason. "I'll tell you what. If you pass, I'll pay the cost, and if you don't, you can continue to work for me as I rebuild my office."

"You won't find a better bargain than that," Judge Brown interjected. He withdrew two envelopes bearing the Massachusetts State Seal and pencils from his desk drawer. "Follow me." He led Jason and Barrister Hall into the adjoining courtroom, filled with empty chairs. He placed one envelope and pencil on the prosecutor's table and one on the defendant's. "The other applicant will join us shortly. Please, have a seat."

With trepidation, Jason removed his jacket and borrowed hat.

Keith Hall handed him his calling card. "This is my address. Not the posh neighborhood you're used to, but I call it home. I'll be working out of my house until I can find another space for the office. Please come any evening you would like to work or pay a visit."

"Thank you."

As Keith Hall left the courtroom, Judge Brown looked at his watch and took his seat behind the bench. "You may begin, Mr. Harris."

Chapter 25

Ayden MacKenna

—

The sting of a flame on his hand woke him. The slant of the smoke-filtered light through the small window was the same as when he went to sleep.

Have I slept at all?

Ayden lay still for a moment, acclimating himself to the sounds outside his small room and watching the tiny *fire-elemental* dance on the candlewick.

The tiny gremlin would lift one leg and then the other, a twist of ash in constant motion inside a candle flame. A useless bit of clever animation, or was it more? Even after all his time spent in the deserts of India and Persia, the elemental creatures found there confounded him.

Trapped as this one was in a magical prison, bound by *earth-magic*, did it long to be free? Did it resent his master, as Ayden had resented his, or did it only know enough to follow simple commands finding contentment in safety and service?

I may never know.

The scuff of a shoe in the storeroom broke his musing and set Ayden in motion. He gripped the red stone, lifted it from his chest, and held it toward the dancing flame. "Return."

In less than a blink, the flicker of light shot into the stone, flashing as though a bit of starlight were trapped in the gem.

"Ayden?" Harry called through the door and tapped on the wood. "Are you here?"

Ayden rose and unbolted the door and looked out at the bartender. "I am. What do you need?"

Harry moved back as he looked Ayden up and down. "First off, I thought to check if you were still alive. No one has seen you for over twenty-four hours."

"Twenty-four hours?" Ayden ran a hand through his hair. "I didn't realize I'd slept that long."

"What's more, there's a woman out front asking for you." Harry's inspection took in Ayden's clothing, and he raised one brow. "But you may want to wash up a bit first. She looks like a lady."

Ayden lifted his filthy collar and grimaced over his shoulder at his dirty bedding. "Damn." His hand ran across the two-day growth of stubble on his chin, and he turned his gaze to Harry. "A young lady with yellow hair, wearing trousers?"

Harry shook his head and made a face that said he thought Ayden sounded ridiculous. "No."

"Is she a dark-haired young woman not raven-haired but auburn?"

"How many women are you expecting?" Harry exclaimed. "And no. Not a young woman at all, more your age. Well dressed, with a pleasing face." He stepped back and smiled at Ayden. "Should I tell her you were hoping for one of the younger ladies?"

Margaret!

"No." Ayden closed the door in Harry's face, then opened it again. "Tell her I'll be a moment longer. I need to wash up and change my attire."

"I should hope so—"

"I need a shave."

"I'm not sure she'll wait that long."

"Tell her twenty minutes at the most. I'll be right out." Ayden shut the door and pulled the chain from the amulet he still gripped in his fist over his head. He shoved the trinket back into the bag and slid it under his bed, then turned to the water on his dresser.

He eyed his reflection critically in the small mirror tacked to the wall.

What could Margaret possibly want?

Dressed in his new suit, his freshly washed hair slicked back, and his new beard growth cleaned from his neck and upper cheeks, Ayden entered the tavern's main room.

Margaret sat at the table furthest away from the window, sipping a cup of tea. She spotted him immediately and set her cup in the saucer and smiled.

"Hello, Margaret." He sat in the chair beside her, both angled toward the tavern entrance. "What a surprise. It's good to see you." His smooth, pleasant tone masked a torrent of emotions. This woman loved and belonged to another man, a man whose life he saved. And yet, the thought of her lips and her dark, smiling eyes had kept him alive and yearning for Boston most of his adult life. Regardless of what she meant to someone else, she still meant the world to him.

Her smile faltered as she studied the bottom of her teacup. "I wanted to make sure you were well and to thank you again for bringing Robert home."

"My pleasure." Ayden forced a cordial smile. "I enjoyed meeting your daughter, although I wish it had been under better circumstances. She reminds me of you."

"That's funny." Margaret sipped from her cup then placed it on the saucer. "I see more of her father in her than I do myself."

"How is her father doing? Is Robert recovering from his injuries?"

"He is. Thank you for asking. He's home with Amy now. I can't stay too long, but there is something I needed to ask." Her gaze found his for a moment. "This is foolish."

"Nothing you ask will be foolish. I've been gone a long time, but it is still me. You can ask me anything."

Her eyes sought his, and she cleared her throat. "Why did you leave like you did, without a word? I thought we...." She shrugged one shoulder.

Ayden swallowed the tightness in his own throat before he spoke. He'd rehearsed this conversation in his mind a million times. Accusations and anger at her family would only hurt her, and she was as much a victim at this moment as he had been.

"I think the easiest explanation for what happened is I was abducted."

"Abducted?"

Ayden nodded. "I was thrown in the hold of a ship and indentured to a magician from India."

"How did they hold you? I mean, with your skills, couldn't you have escaped?"

"I would have thought as much myself, but a magical contract, sealed with my blood, stayed my magic. I did not sign willingly, mind you. I was unconscious when the contract was made." The last sentence ground between his teeth, and he looked away to shield her from his rage.

She touched his arm. "Oh, Ayden. I had no idea something like that could happen."

"Well, it did."

"Were others taken?"

"No. Only me. As soon as I could, I returned to find my parents and little Melvyn, only to discover they left Boston not long after I did. If they took a ship to find me, they failed."

"They didn't take a ship." Margaret pressed her lips. "After you disappeared, I went to your parents, but they didn't know what had happened to you either. They were devastated. I went by every couple of weeks that spring to make sure they were doing well." She paused and sipped her tea. When she spoke again, her voice was low and filled with pain. "But that summer, the Irish area on the North End was ravaged by cholera."

"Oh, no." Dread filled Ayden's chest.

"I'm sorry." A tear slipped from Margaret's eye. "Cholera took your mother in August of '49. After she passed, your father and brother left the area." Margaret touched the corner of her eyes with her napkin. "I don't know where they are now."

"Thank you for telling me." Ayden nodded and swallowed his pain. "I have other questions if you have the time."

"Certainly. Anything."

"What happened to the coven after I left? Where is your family?"

"I never joined the coven, as you know." They shared a sad smile. "Less than three months after your father left Boston, my mother and brothers did as well. After they had gone, she sold the farm and her house on Beacon Hill."

She hesitated, as if she wanted to say more, but thought better of it. Instead, she shrugged. "Mother took the twins and settled in Canada. I think. I haven't heard from them."

"They left you here alone?"

"No. I had married Robert—and we had our daughter."

Ayden's heart contracted.

Had I meant so little to her?

Less than a year after my disappearance, she married and began a family. "That was swift."

"Swift?"

"Your marriage. It's good you didn't mourn me for long. I'm glad you got on with your life." Agitated and angry, he shifted in his seat. Jealousy beyond words ate at his throat, and he pressed his lips together to still the bitterness.

Margaret's voice hissed with anger. "I mourned you more than you know. I needed you, and you had vanished. I'd known Robert all my life. He grew up next door to us. He was there when I needed—" She straightened in her seat. "Perhaps it was a mistake to come here."

"No. It was no mistake." As quickly as his anger had come, it washed away. He shook his head. "We both needed to say things, to clear the air so that we can go on from here."

"You're right." Margaret exhaled a heavy sigh. "It wasn't your fault you were gone." She nodded and reached for her small wrist bag that lay on the table. "I should go."

"One last question. I promise not to make you angry."

Margaret lifted her chin. "Go on."

"Do you know Lisbeth Coleman and her family?"

"I do. Lisbeth's father, Isaac, and my husband have had a working agreement for years. For almost as long as Robert and I have been married. Why do you ask?"

"Are you involved with the coven in any way?"

Margaret shook her head. "Not at all." She lowered her voice. "Why?"

"I've been approached by several of their current members. They want me to leave Boston and to stay away from you specifically."

"You're joking?"

"I wish I were. More than that, Jason was with me the other night in the tavern, and two of the coven members followed me inside. Jason recognized Lisbeth Coleman, disguised as a man."

"Lisbeth would never dress as a man, for heaven's sake. She's as timid as a church mouse. Honestly, Ayden! And here I was beginning to believe you."

"I have never lied to you, Margaret. I never will." The timbre of his voice was sad and serious.

Margaret rose slowly to her feet, her eyes never leaving his. Her face was somber with consideration. "If what you say is true, then what do you suggest?"

Ayden rose as Margaret did. "Be cautious. Keep your wits about you. Do you still practice at all?"

"Some."

"Then set a few wards that test for magic. I'm not suggesting you or your family are in any danger but forewarned is forearmed."

Margaret nodded and held her skirt as she rounded the table. "Oh, and I almost forgot. Robert would like to have you over for dinner sometime next week to properly thank you for your assistance the other night."

"I would be honored." Ayden dipped his head.

"I'll send an invitation once we set the date." She stared at him for several moments from across the table. Neither of them said a word. Then she offered him a sad smile. "It's been nice speaking with you, Ayden. Do take care."

***

Jason Harris

—

Jason answered the last question in the examination packet, set down his pencil, and scrutinized Judge Brown.

The judge had remained behind his raised desk most of the afternoon while the two hopeful candidates completed the test. Now the judge's eyes were closed, and a slight snore escaped his lips.

Jason scooped up the test sheets, tapped their ends on the desk, then carried them and his pencil to the bench. "Do I give this to you?"

"Finished already?" Judge Brown blinked and closed the book he held open in his lap. "Set it on the desk. Is your name on it?"

"It is." Jason put the pencil on the top of the test. "When will I learn the results?"

"I'll look these over this week as time permits. I'll put a note on the docket in the lobby after I have the test scores." He reopened the book in his lap and returned to reading.

Dismissed, Jason gathered his coat and hat, glanced at the other applicant busily writing an answer to one of the questions, then exited the courtroom through the doors at the back. He followed the empty hallway to the front of the courthouse and down the steps.

Although the air still held the odor of ash, not every breath burned his lungs.

Not far from the courthouse, he paused at the windows of a shop that carried dry goods and ready-made textiles such as gloves, stockings, collars, and hats.

A gift like that would be too impersonal.

Across the narrow street, the jeweler had already closed shop. The store's windows were boarded against looting, even though this area didn't receive much damage from the fire or thieves.

I don't have enough money for gold and gemstones, even though it's what she deserves.

His lack of funds brought Otis to mind, and his steps turned toward the Pierce and Peabody Investment Firm. Both Otis's family home and his father's office were on the shabbier side of town and spared the devastation of the fire in the commercial district.

As he made his way down the narrow street toward P&P Investments, he recognized the thin, dark-haired man who came out of the office door.

Otis straightened his top hat on the landing and looked around. His chin came up when he spotted Jason, and he narrowed his eyes warily. "I was coming to find you." He stepped to the walkway in front of Jason. "What happened to your other coat and hat?" he exclaimed.

"There was a fire."

Otis rolled his eyes. "And your coat and hat burned as well as the city?"

"They are being cleaned, if that is possible, from the condition they were in." Jason tucked his walking stick under his arm and glared at Otis. "Where have *you* been?"

"Since the fire?" Otis turned and strolled down the hill toward the waterfront.

"No. Since my mother's masquerade." Jason kept pace beside him. "Where are my bonds?"

"I have them."

"With you? I need them."

They turned onto the harbor road, and Otis stopped outside a chowder house. "Have you had dinner?" He opened the door. "My treat. We can have a seat and discuss your bonds like civilized men."

Jason took a breath and stared at Otis.

Whatever he's up to, it isn't good.

Reluctantly, Jason nodded once and followed Otis into the eatery.

The waitress came to the table and smiled at Otis. "The usual?"

"Yes. And one for my friend."

The waitress raised her brows and gave Jason a big smile. "Right away."

"The women always smile at you," Otis grumbled.

"Forget the waitress. Give me the bonds."

Otis looked from the departing server to Jason. "Before I do, you need to know my father took his fees out of the amount. He thought it would be best to take the entire retainer up front."

Jason leaned over the table and hissed, "Fees? You never said anything about retainers or fees."

"I know. I thought since you are my friend, he would take that into consideration."

"Give me the bonds," Jason insisted.

"Here you go." The waitress set two bowls of white chowder in front of the men. "Enjoy." The bell on the front door called her away from their table.

Jason pushed the food aside and placed his hand palm up on the table between them. "Now."

Otis pulled a large, folded envelope out of his inside coat pocket and set it in Jason's hand.

Jason opened the flap and glanced through the contents. "Half?" Disbelief and anger coursed through him, and he struggled against the urge to throttle his red-faced friend. "I trusted you with everything I had. All my savings." He looked through the bonds again. "What are these worth now?"

"Now?"

"Yes." He spoke through clenched teeth, "If I cash them right now, what are they worth?"

"You might get their face value, two hundred and fifty dollars, but probably not. The market will be volatile for a while because of the fire. Your best decision would be to hold on to them for at least a year."

"A year?" Jason's voice rose, disturbing the diners at the next table. He lowered his voice. "You and your father have stolen half my savings, and now you tell me to wait a year? What are these? Railroad bonds?"

"Yes, and good ones too. Northern Pacific bonds through Cooke & Company out of Pennsylvania." He opened his mouth to say more, then suddenly closed it and tucked his chin.

"Spit it out." Jason put the envelope in his jacket.

Otis took a spoonful of chowder and shoved it in his mouth. "Mm?" He swallowed. "I don't know what you mean?"

"I know how you act when you have a secret. What aren't you telling me?"

"It's good news." Otis attempted to smile, but only one side of his mouth lifted, then he took a long minute to blow on his hot chowder.

"We were able to secure a loan on your behalf. With this additional capital invested wisely in railroad bonds, their future revenue should more than make up for any fee or retainer." Otis looked up from his meal.

Dumbfounded with horror, Jason could only shake his head. "You what?" he managed to whisper.

Otis remained silent. Sitting back, he wiped his mouth with the napkin.

"I'm sure I misheard you, *my friend*. Did you say you secured a loan *in my name?*"

Otis nodded briskly. "Yes, but well—I didn't. Pierce and Peabody made the loan to you."

"That would be impossible since I didn't sign a note of repayment or agree to this farce."

Otis's eyes widened as he stared at his friend.

Jason could feel the heat around his collar. He glanced down at the ache in his hand and saw he had gripped the edge of the table, so hard his knuckles were white. "There is no loan."

"There is. The promissory note holds your signature. My father signed as a witness." Otis couldn't look Jason in the eyes and dropped his gaze to his half-eaten chowder. "I'm sorry. I can see this doesn't come as good news, but with the bonds those funds purchased, you stand to make double that much back. Ten thousand dollars in bond notes will yield a fortune in two years."

Jason couldn't speak. He took several short, halting breaths but couldn't get enough air to fill his lungs. "How," he whispered. "How do you know what my signature even looks like?"

"I—" Otis swallowed and began again. "I paid your bill at Revere's the night before your mother's masquerade. I discovered the running tab you signed in my pocket a few days later."

Jason reached across the table and grabbed Otis by the jacket. "You've planned this since Halloween?" His other hand joined his first, and he pulled Otis to his feet. "How could you do this to me?" His voice rose, and he shook Otis, uncaring that tears rolled down the traitor's cheeks.

"Here now! Stop that nonsense this instance!"

A sharp rap to the side of his head turned Jason's attention to the waitress.

She wielded a wooden spoon in defense of her regular patron. "Let him go and get out." She lifted the spoon.

Jason plucked it from her hand and threw it to the floor. "And where are these ten thousand dollars' worth of bonds? In your father's safe?" He kicked his chair back and picked up his walking cane. He struggled with the urge to pull the blade and have done with Otis.

The bastard.

He turned and glared at the people in the chowder house who watched them.

He pointed at Otis. "We're not done with this." He turned from the table and slammed out the door stomping away with no destination in mind. He had to get away from Otis before he said or did something he couldn't take back.

"I don't know why you're so upset," Otis called behind him. "You're not out any money and look to make a small fortune when the bonds mature."

Jason refused to turn around or slow his pace.

"You'll thank me then!"

Chapter 26

Jason Harris

—

Jason drew his watch from its pocket and checked the time. The morning hours were passing too slowly for him.

The accounting house would close again at noon today. Three of Dunham's clients lost property in the fire and canceled their future work orders. What work remained wasn't due to the clients until next week.

Despite the shortened wages, which he sorely needed, thoughts of Amy had him anxious to be out and on with his day. On his way home last night, he passed a street vendor putting up her wares. She had several lovely handmade brooches and dozens of buttons but hurried to get off the street before sunset.

Today, he wanted to take his time and look over everything the old woman had to offer.

Perhaps she has something unusual and perfect for his future bride.

He grinned to himself and caught Nathan's knowing look. "What's that look for?"

Nathan shook his head. "Plans for this afternoon?" he whispered, sending a cautious look toward his father.

Calvary Dunham had his head down over his ledgers and paid his workers no mind. The three new employees who usually sat in front were absent this morning.

Jason nodded. "As soon as I leave here, I intend to go shopping. I've put aside a small amount to purchase Amy a betrothal gift."

"God's teeth! You're actually going to marry the spinster?" Nathan's exclamation turned into a chuckle. "With your looks and your father's influence, you could have any young woman you desired. Why settle for Amylia Prescott?"

Jason clenched his teeth at Nathan's irksome tone. "I agree that I can marry whomever I desire, but I don't see Amy as settling for someone less." He sat back in his chair and stared at his friend. "Even though you can't see the value in someone or something doesn't mean I cannot. I will be delighted should she consent to take my hand in marriage."

Nathan rolled his eyes. "I'm sure you know better than I what her value is." He turned back to his ledger. "It's a shame you can't see what you're getting before you pledge your life away."

"If by see you mean through Georgie's peephole, you can put that from your mind." He shut the journal firmly and snatched up the extra pencil. "Never," he enunciated.

Jason rose and approached Mr. Dunham's desk. "This ledger is balanced. Did you have more, sir?"

"No, not today." Nathan's father took the book and set it on a small stack of identical journals at the edge of his large desk. "I should have something more for you on Thursday. Would you be interested?"

"Yes, sir." Jason retrieved his hat, coat, and cane from the sidewall. "I'll see you Thursday morning." He hurried out without speaking to Nathan.

The smoke from the fire had cleared, but the dry scent of ash and burned wood still permeated the air. His path to the jewelry seller took him through the burned area near the docks. Teams of men worked to clear debris, while others posed for more photographs near ruins.

On the street where he had seen the jewelry vendor, a younger woman sold fresh meat and cheese-filled pierogies.

Jason approached the peddler with a disarming smile. "One, please." He pulled several small coins from his pocket and exchanged them for the hot treat. "I didn't see you here yesterday."

The young woman's olive complexion darkened, and she lowered her eyes with a shy smile. "This is a popular corner. Much foot traffic." She gestured in both directions down the street. "Sometimes Aunt Meira, with her trinkets and jewelry, gets here first."

Jason tasted the meat pie, and warm juice ran from the pierogi. He leaned forward to keep his jacket clean and pulled his handkerchief to wipe his chin. "These are delicious. Do you make them yourself?"

"No." The woman giggled at Jason, her hand over her mouth. "My mama makes these fresh every morning."

"And your aunt, when you sell at this corner, where does she take her cart?" He took another taste, mindful of the thick, savory gravy.

"Down two blocks that way, near a small park."

"Thank you." He popped the last bit of pierogi into his mouth, wiped his hands, and tipped his hat to the young woman.

Jason hurried in the direction she pointed. Across from a neighborhood park, he found the trinket vendor. She displayed earrings and brooches, along with several clutch purses, cleverly ornamented with colorful stones. Scarves and shawls draped over the cart handle presented an array of colors, and at the far end, the woman sat on a stool working diligently on her latest offering.

Nothing displayed would be right for Amy. The gift had to be both personal and affordable. And although Aunt Meira's work was detailed and lovely, he couldn't remember seeing Amy wear a scarf or elaborate earrings.

Jason circled the cart and stopped beside the woman, watching her work. She wielded a pair of small pliers, bending a heavier silver wire into a clasp connecting a round locket with a milky-white stone in the middle and a book chain necklace of etched silver squares.

"Is this your work?" Jason asked.

"My son is the silversmith now, although this is my design." She chuckled and winked at Jason, then returned her attention to her work. "He created the locket and set the stone. The only thing these old hands can do now is put the pieces together."

"What stone is that?"

"This is a moonstone. Treasured by the Romans and thought to contain mystical qualities. This beautiful white stone opens the heart when given as a gift during courtship." She grinned at Jason and attached the next silver square of the chain. "Your young lady would find this quite lovely."

Jason nodded, mesmerized, as she skillfully twisted the silver wire, connecting the small squares of the book chain. "I've never seen anything like this."

She attached the last segment and made an elegant hook with her hand tool. She placed the locket and chain on a square of blue velvet. "The ornament opens to hide a small treasure." She ran her nail between the edges and flicked the metal circle apart to display the hidden cavity. "You'll not find another like it in the city."

"How much do you want for it?" He closed the locket and picked up the piece. It felt surprisingly light in his grip, and the silver attachments smooth as he caressed the metalwork with his fingertips.

"Five dollars," the old woman said.

"I'd pay less than half that for a locket at Sweeny's up the street." He ran his thumb over the white stone. "I'll give you two."

"Three dollars."

"Done." Jason withdrew his wallet from his inside pocket. "Do you have a box for it?"

"Never store silver in a box." She swept up the blue velvet cover and pulled a drawstring, capturing the necklace inside the pouch. "The moonstone you give your beloved will allow her to find the light in the darkness." She held the bag out of Jason's reach. "It is a water stone, potent protection for travelers on the sea and sought for magical rituals for both love and divination."

"Yes. I will let her know."

The old woman grinned. "You'll not recall a thing I've said once you receive her kiss in thanks for this token of your affection." She closed her eyes, covering the velvet bag with her hand, and murmured, her lips moving silently as though in prayer. Then her dark eyes opened, shining with an inner glow. "I've blessed the moonstone and silver. May this token of affection bring love and light to your loved one." She held up the bag.

Jason took the present. "Thank you." The locket was perfect, and he was confident Amy would love it, but the old woman's conversation left him uneasy. He hurried back the way he had come.

I'll give it to her tonight.

Now that he'd found the right present, he couldn't wait to see the delight in Amy's eyes when she opened the gift. He would leave the necklace in the velvet bag but wanted a small container for her to unwrap. Callie, the cook, would be able to help him find the right box and paper.

His pace quickened as he skirted the destruction of the financial district.

***

Amy Prescott

—

Amy slipped the marker between the pages and set the book on the night-stand. She watched the steady rise and fall of her father's chest as he slept. How he could fall asleep as she read Jules Verne perplexed her. Verne's writing inspired her imagination more than any of Jane Austen's books. Next time she'd slip in a few chapters of Shelly's horror fantasy and see if that caught his attention.

She chuckled to herself as she closed the door to her parents' room. By tomorrow her father would be up and around despite her mother's insistence he should rest and recover. No doubt anxious to check on his dockside ware-house and walk the deck of any of his ships in port. He owned three, and one of them was either preparing to set sail or expected to return, keeping her father at the harbor most days.

She straightened the sleeve on her day dress, a light green satin material with dark green accents down the bodice and arms, as well as the double ruffle and drape. This morning, Peg had pulled her hair back on both sides with sharp pronged combs decorated with sparkling green stones. She al-lowed Amy's auburn tresses to wave down her back. Limp curls were the best she could do, a flat wave of brownish red, nothing like Jason's riot of golden curls.

She stopped at the top of the stairs as the mantle clock in the dining room chimed three. She closed her eyes and imagined a little girl with Jason's curls and her own brown eyes. A vision? No. A dream and longing, perhaps.

But what about my magic?

The magic she couldn't use except to garden and make salve?

I swore never to hide who I am or lie to my husband.

Suddenly, having a green thumb and making ointments didn't feel like a lie. Amy's mother could light all the candles in a room with a thought. That was magic you could see and would need explaining.

Does sensing the moisture in garden manure even qualify as magic?

Confused by self-doubt, she lowered herself to the reading bench at the top of the steps. Shelves lined the sides of the tiny alcove filled with all her favorite characters. Light from the window made reading in the morning an enjoyable pastime. Even past noon, the book nook remained well-lit and cozy.

Frost coated the inside pane and glittered with tiny prismatic colors through the frozen moisture. With a mischievous grin, she wrote a large capital J on the window then encircled the letter with a heart. An un-Amy-like giggle escaped her lips, and she ran her hand over the glass, turning the frozen moisture to liquid, erasing her artwork.

Beyond the glass, a blue sky finally showed over Boston as cold northern winds scoured the city clear of smoke. Across the way, an unfamiliar man loitered along the walk. A thick scarf pulled up to his hat on either side as his breath hung in the chill air as frozen vapor.

Down the street, a familiar figure caught her eye. Nathan Dunham strode directly to her house and proceeded up the walk to the door.

"Oh, Goddess! What could he want?" Amy murmured.

A sharp rap at the door echoed up the stairs to the nook, and Peg's light step sounded as she crossed the hall to the door.

Amy peered around the edge of the nook to see down the stairs to the entry, but she couldn't make out their words.

Whatever Nathan said convinced Peg to let him in. As they disappeared down the hall, their muffled conversation receded into the parlor. Then Peg hurried up the stairs.

"What did he say?" Amy rose when Peg's gaze met hers.

"That he's here on behalf of Mr. Harris." Concern etched Peg's face, and she wrung her hands. "I could tell him you are busy with your father and ask him to leave a note." Her voice lowered. "I know you don't care for Mr. Dunham, but he said it was urgent."

Amy squeezed the maid's arm in reassurance. "I'll speak with him."

Nathan stood before the window, hands behind his back as though he stood on the deck of a ship. His trousers and frock coat were made of fine wool and dyed dark brown. He'd tossed his overcoat and top hat on the settee rather than allow Peg to hang them up. Whatever Nathan Dunham wanted, he intended to be here only a short while.

"Mr. Dunham." Amy entered the room and greeted her unwelcome guest with a slight nod of her head. "How may I assist you?"

"Miss Prescott. It is good to see you again. I wish it were under better circumstances, however." He turned and offered a sad smile. "There has been an incident."

"I'm not sure I know what you mean."

Nathan shook his head. "Jason and I were released from work at my father's office early today. He hurried away on some errand, and I followed shortly thereafter." He looked up from his hands and took a deep breath. "On my way home, I found Jason, beaten and bloody by the park. I took him to the nearest place to get help, a friend of mine not far from here. He asked for you." He paced over to his coat. "I am here to escort you to him. Should you choose to go to his aid."

"Yes. Of course." She turned and called up the stairs, "Peg?"

"Yes, miss?" Peg looked over the railing.

"Would you bring down my medicine bag? It's in father's room." Then she crossed the foyer to the coats. "Which injury is the most critical?"

Nathan followed her as he shrugged on his coat, his top hat perched precariously on his head. "I'm not sure. He took a beating."

Amy buttoned up her heavy walking jacket and pulled her winter bonnet from the shelf. She quickly tied the warm velvet beneath her chin and wrapped the long ends around her neck, tucking them in her jacket. "Thank you." She took the bag from Peg. "Please tell mother I've gone with Nathan Dunham. Jason's injured."

Peg's eyes widened, and she nodded. "I will."

Nathan followed Amy out the door and down the walk. She stopped beneath a bare-limbed tree and looked in one direction, then the other. "Which way?"

Across the street, the individual she'd spotted from the reading nook paused his pacing and stared at the couple.

"It's not far." Nathan held out an arm. "He awaits you at the Bisby home."

***

Jason Harris

—

Jason cradled the weight of the velvet bag in his pocket. His eager step carried him up the hill toward the Common and home.

The day had begun with bitter cold, and the relentless north wind continued to blow well into the afternoon. The temperature kept most folks inside and off the street.

I was lucky the jewelry vendor was still selling.

Her business had to have been slow today.

He lifted his head and squinted into the wind as he neared the cross street. Movement on the next block caught his attention.

A man with a top hat and greatcoat stared directly at him, the scarf around his neck wrapped high over his ears.

Now that he knew, it was apparent to Jason who this person had always been.

Lisbeth Coleman dressed as a man.

The notion that one of the Brahmin debutantes would flaunt convention in such an unacceptable way was only slightly less surprising than Ayden's conviction that she belonged to a secret society who spied on the man at Revere's Tavern.

Lisbeth motioned Jason forward with her gloved hand, then stepped into a thick growth of leafless shrubbery between two houses.

Jason followed her down a slender path through the bushes to a hidden garden behind the house. "Lisbeth, stop! Why are you dressed in men's clothes and following me?"

She looked up at him with a solemn, steady expression on her face—no coy laughter or blushing. "I'm not following you, well only once from Revere's. But that doesn't matter—"

"It matters! What would your father say?"

"My father's the one who assigned me to watch Ayden MacKenna. I only followed you the first night I saw you there because...." A rosy blush colored her face.

"Your *father* sent you? Has he some part in Ayden's 'secret society' nonsense?"

"Secret society?" Lisbeth's eyes widened, and she nodded. "But it's true. Mr. MacKenna's family were active members in the cov—society, as well as Margaret Prescott's family before she wed. Of course, this happened well before the Colemans moved to Boston." She waved her hand. "It's all ancient history, but what is important now—"

"Then you admit you are spying on Mr. MacKenna?" Although he understood her words, the content of her message made no sense.

"Not anymore." She glanced away. "Once you recognized me, father had no choice but to remove me from the tavern. Now I watch the Prescott home instead."

Jason exhaled heavily in frustration. "Lisbeth, I don't understand why anyone needs watching or why you, of all people, would dress as a man and follow strangers through the night."

"Jason!" She grabbed his arm and gave him a shake. "Nathan Dunham was at the Prescott home not an hour ago. Amy left with him. Now, I know how you feel about Miss Prescott, and it was made clear to me that regardless of my feelings for you, those within the— um, society may never become betrothed to those without the society. Amylia's mother left the order before she married, and her daughter shows no sign that she can— um, would be welcomed into it." She paused in her tirade then pushed him back. "I want you to be happy, and I think your Miss Prescott may be in danger. I've seen the ugly side of Nathan Dunham and his sister."

"Amy would never leave with Nathan." Jason's heart thundered with a sudden rush of adrenaline. "Where could they have gone?"

"I followed them," Lisbeth admitted in a hushed voice. "They went into a house on Beacon Street."

"The Bisby house." Panic coursed through his veins. "Thank you, Lisbeth." He grabbed the tall, thin woman and kissed her forehead, knocking her top hat to the ground. "I am forever in your debt." He turned and ran.

"Tell no one we spoke!" Lisbeth's words followed his footsteps up the empty street.

Chapter 27

Amy Prescott

—

The house Nathan led Amy to wasn't far. It was a long block down and one block over, facing the Common. He strode before her up the walk and opened the door, gesturing for her to enter.

Amy paused before going in and studied the entrance.

Have I seen this doorway somewhere? Why is this familiar?

"Please, proceed. We don't want to keep Jason waiting."

Amy glanced back at the peculiar look of excitement on Nathan's face and hesitated. "Jason is here?"

"Step inside, Miss Prescott. The temperature is dreadful. We don't want to put a chill on the house." He moved forward, crowding her from behind.

Amy clutched her medicine satchel and crossed the threshold. Warm air greeted her and the sound of voices. Her eyes had no time to adjust to the dark entryway, and she moved blindly into the house.

Nathan followed her inside, closed the door, and slid the deadbolt lock shut.

"Why is there no light?" Amy asked.

Across the room, a light flared and illuminated several people who stared or grinned at Amy.

"Who are they?" She gripped her bag with both hands addressing Nathan.

Nathan shed his coat and hat, hanging them on pegs in the entry. "You know everyone here. There in the back is my sister, Donetta, and this is George Bisby. Surely you remember him."

George lifted his hand when Nathan mentioned his name.

"Next to Georgie is John Davis. He was at the Harris masquerade with his family. Perhaps you remember Michael Kent, Bruce Delinger, and Kip Rogers from school. Kip was your year, I believe."

John's grin seemed overeager and a bit deranged. The others shuffled their feet and averted their eyes.

She nodded at John and the others, then turned to Nathan. "Yes, of course. But why are they here? Where is Jason?"

"Set your bag down and let me take your coat and hat."

Her gut told her to leave. These boys were up to no good, and she'd never trusted Donetta. But if Jason needed her assistance, she didn't want to leave him in their hands either. She put the bag at her feet and untied her hat. "I want to see Jason immediately."

"Of course, you do." Nathan hung her outerwear on pegs next to his jacket and smiled with delight at Amy. "Unfortunately, he isn't here."

"Then, where is he?" Amy demanded. She reached for her coat.

Nathan pushed forward, forcing Amy back into the entry hall where the others waited. He shrugged. "He may be at home or the courthouse with his barrister friend."

"Then why did you bring me here?" Unwilling to move further into the house, she put her back to the wall.

"To aid Mr. Harris, of course, although not in the way you thought." Nathan sneered and moved closer. "You see, I've been acquainted with Mr. Harris for quite some time and have come to know his peculiar preference in women. Most recently, his infatuation with you, Miss Prescott. Unfortunately, you are not his type. He enjoys women with vast sexual experience, and you, my dear, are the virginal and dried-up Spinster Prescott." He winked at the other men. "But I think we can rectify your lack of knowledge."

"You intend to help her?" Donetta pushed her way through the half-circle of men and confronted her brother. "She stole my betrothed!" Thin lips pulled back in a snarl, Donetta pointed at her rival. "I want to see her ruined for what she did to me."

"I stole no one from you." Amy matched Donetta's glare with one of her own. "Jason makes his own choices. As do I." She scoured the men who watched with her livid glare. "And I choose to leave. Now." The boys didn't frighten her. She'd taken their measure as Nathan had introduced them. Only one, besides Nathan, showed any interest in whatever nonsense the older Dunham had planned.

"Let her go." George Bisby's voice quivered, and he flushed at Nathan's hot stare.

"Let—her—go?" Nathan yelled at George. "After all the trouble of getting her here?"

"Georgie's right." The shortest young man with sandy-brown hair shared a quick look with George. "Peeping is one thing. This—" he held his arm out toward Amy, "—this is something entirely different. I'll take no part in violating this woman."

Violating?

Her already poor opinion of the Dunham siblings diminished even further. She inched along the hallway wall toward the entry as the men argued.

One of the young men standing beside George shook his head. A deep blush colored his face, and he turned his back. "No," he muttered and walked away.

"But you have to!" Donetta wailed in her obnoxious, high-pitched whine. She swung toward Amy, her ringlets bouncing in ire. "I hate you," she seethed, her tiny hands arched into claws.

Amy shook her head at Donetta. "I've done nothing to you." She edged closer to the door. "Jason and I are truly sorry for any hurt our affection for each other may have caused—"

Donetta screamed in rage and leapt at Amy, latching onto her hair with her thin fingers and yanking her head to one side, pulling her into the room.

Both women cried out in pain as Amy's green stone comb fell to the floor, the sharp prongs glittering with blood.

Amy snatched the comb from the tile and held the bloodied prongs toward Donetta and Nathan. "Do not come near me again. Either of you!"

Blood ran from the back of Donetta's hand down her fingers and trickled onto the floor in crimson droplets. She held her wrist with her other hand as she threw her head back and wailed her brother's name.

Nathan looked from his sister's injury to Amy, his voice low and threatening. "What have you done?" He stepped in front of Donetta, never taking his eyes from Amy.

A loud pounding against the front door caused him to stop and glance toward the sound.

Jason's angry voice echoed through the foyer and hallway. "Georgie, open this door!"

Nathan shook his head as Georgie moved forward. "Are you frightened of Jason Harris?' he scoffed. "Leave it locked. We haven't begun to defile this little flower."

"But—" A loud thump on the door cut Georgie short, then his eyes widened, and he yelled, "Not my mother's door!"

Another blow shook the door. And another. A loud crack sounded as the deadbolt split from the casing. The door flew open, shattering the wall plaster behind it.

Jason stepped through the opening, his razor-sharp *épée* blade in one hand. The hardwood cover of the walking cane held as a baton in the other.

The cold outside air engulfed Amy as Jason's heated gaze raked her from head to foot. "Gather your things," he instructed in a low, angry voice. "Then get behind me."

Amy tucked the bloodied comb into her pocket, picked up her medicine bag with one hand, and plucked her coat and hat from the pegs with the other. Once Jason stood between her and the other men, she slipped her arms into her overcoat.

Jason looked from side to side as he glared at each of the watchers in the hallway. "Tell me who injured Amy, so I know who to kill first." When he moved forward, everyone except the Dunham siblings moved back.

"She injured me," Donetta cried and held out her hand as evidence.

"You don't want to fight me, Jason," Nathan warned, pushing his sister to one side. "You won't win."

"At this moment, I would indeed win. I have no doubt."

Amy couldn't see his face, but Jason's low chuckle sent a shiver down her back.

"I urge you to try me, Nathan. Please. I will gut you like the slimy snake you've always been." Jason whirled his blade expertly and inched forward. "Come on!" he yelled.

The men at the back of the small group turned and ran.

Georgie squeezed past Nathan. His hands held out in supplication to Jason. "Please stop. You've caused enough damage. Take Miss Prescott and go."

"Go?" Jason ground out between clenched teeth. "You want me to leave, after what you had planned? Don't deny anything—I can read your face like a damned open book."

Amy pulled on her hat and took a firm grip on her bag. "I want to go," she said softly. "Now."

"I agree," Jason spoke over his shoulder. "Miss Prescott is your salvation, more than you know or deserve." He pointed the tip of his blade at Georgie. "Your private shows are done. I'll speak with your father immediately upon their return." The aim of the sword lifted to Nathan's chin when the larger man approached. "Stop right there."

"We were only helping you out, my friend." He smiled over Jason's head at Amy. "I know how much you like your lady friend at Revere's. What is her name?" His grin widened. "Molly?"

Near Nathan, Donetta stood fuming. The blood no longer ran down her fingers, although she continued to hold her hand as though she'd broken her wrist. "You can't do this to me." She leaned around her brother, her face puckered and filled with hate. "You can't leave with her. You were promised to me."

"An empty promise between our mothers," Jason replied softly. "Besides, you've had a hand in this all along, and yes, I can quite easily walk away from you."

"I'm leaving." Amy tucked the long velvet ties to her hat into the neck of her coat. She took several steps before she realized her knees were shaking. Her stomach rolled with nausea, and she thought she might fall.

Jason's arm wrapped around her waist, and his hand gently guided her elbow forward. "I've got you." He kept pace with her as they hurried down the walkway. His small *épée* sword once again secured inside the walking cane. The handle hooked over his arm. "Let me take your bag."

"No. I can carry it." She stopped walking and pulled away from Jason. "I'm well. I don't—" Her voice broke, and she cleared her throat, blinking rapidly to fight back the tears. "I can manage on my own." She raised her gaze to Jason's, and a tear trickled down her cheek.

He reached for the bag anyway, and she let him take it. He wrapped his arm around her back and pulled her close to his chest.

Amy rested her forehead against his shoulder. Her breath hiccupped once, then her composure broke, and she sobbed against his chest. "I wasn't frightened." She shook her head as she spoke into his jacket. "Not really. I was angry, but I knew you would come. I knew you would find me."

"Shh. You're safe." He rubbed his hand across her back then offered her his handkerchief. "Let's get you home and warm."

***

Jason Harris

—

All-consuming rage followed fast on the heels of the unabated terror which had left him drained. He kept his arm around Amy's shoulders as much to comfort himself as to reassure her.

She is safe.

His view of the world had forever shifted. What concerned this woman now consumed him and his need to see to her safety.

She will only be beyond their reach when she wears my name.

Nathan and his friends were only a small part of the Brahmin youth. The worst part. And in all honesty, the other young men at Georgie's today would be more honorable and decent if not for Nathan Dunham's influence.

Across the street, a man wearing a familiar top hat loitered, pausing his pace to watch Jason escort Amy up to her front steps. He touched the rim of his cover, tipping it slightly to Jason, then turned on his heel and walked in the other direction.

Jason opened the door to Amy's home and ushered her inside. He helped her with her coat and hat then returned her bag to her.

"Thank you." Her demeanor had calmed.

She handled the entire situation more calmly than I did. Perhaps she had no notion of what they intended for her.

"You're welcome." He tugged his glove off and ran his knuckles over her rosy chilled cheek. "I'm relieved beyond measure that you were not hurt. Why on earth would you leave the safety of your home to go with Nathan Dunham?"

"He told me you were injured and had asked for my care." She held up the bag of medicines, then placed it on the floor beside the table. "I went with him to help you."

"Mr. Harris!" Margaret called over the rail then hurried down the steps. "Peg told us you were wounded." She looked from Jason to Amy, then exclaimed at the bloodstains on Amy's skirt. "How badly are you hurt?"

"It's not my blood, nor your daughter's," Jason assured her.

Amy took her mother's hands and held them until Margaret looked into her eyes. "It was only another cruel joke. Jason was never injured."

"But the blood—"

Amy withdrew the comb from her pocket and displayed the stained prongs to her mother. "Donetta Dunham was there with her brother. She became angry, believing Jason favors me over her."

"She's not wrong." Jason smiled at Amy's immediate blush.

"She pulled my hair and was cut by the sharp comb. This blood is Donetta's."

"I dare say your lovely comb has exacted an act of well-deserved revenge." She took the object from Amy and studied the dried stains. "May I keep this?"

"Of course."

"Mr. Harris, would you care to stay for tea?" Margaret wrapped the comb in a handkerchief and returned both to the pocket of her gown.

"I would love to stay, but I cannot." He gave Mrs. Prescott a short bow. "Another time, perhaps."

"Dinner on Saturday then, and I won't allow you to bow out. I intend to send Wrigley with an invitation for Mr. MacKenna. Saturday is Robert's birthday, and I want everyone here to share the day with us."

"I shall put your dinner party in my calendar. What time?"

"Five o'clock, but feel free to stop by beforehand, if you like." Margaret gave Jason a slight wink, then leaned in and kissed her daughter's cheek. "I'm glad you are both well." Margaret passed between the two, leaving a slight scent of lavender, and climbed the stairs. "Goodbye, Mr. Harris," she called over her shoulder.

Jason shared a grin with Amy, then lifted her fingers and kissed the back of her hand. "I would caution you not to go about on your own for a few days. If I can't accompany you, have Wrigley drive you or take Peg."

"I'm not so foolish as to fall for the same type of trick again."

"I know that, and so does Nathan." He ducked his head and captured her lips in a brief kiss. "I will see you Saturday afternoon."

Before he could move back, Amy wrapped her arms around his waist and pressed her head against his chest. "Thank you." She looked up, and her dark eyes swam in unshed tears. "I've never had someone defend me as soundly as you did—as you have." She wiped at her cheeks and chuckled. "How did you know where to find me?"

"Ah, that." He tucked the crown of her head beneath his chin. "I received word you'd left your home in Nathan's company. That alone told me where you'd gone."

"It did?" She pulled back. Her brow creased in confusion.

"I work with Nathan. I talk about you. He talks about Georgie's house. But enough of that." He placed her at arm's length. "I must depart. I hope you have a pleasant evening, Miss Prescott."

Amy leaned against the open door as he put his hat on his head and began down the walk. "And you, Mr. Harris."

On his way home, he discovered the forgotten necklace in his pocket.

I'll ask Callie to wrap it and then give it to Amy on Saturday.

He checked on the stable before he went into the house. All the horses were standing in their stalls, and Riley, the stableman, was fast asleep in his bunk.

Inside his father's house, the servants were setting the table for dinner. Jason asked Patrick to have Callie make him a tray and bring it to his bedroom after his parents were served. "If my parents ask about me, tell them I wasn't feeling well and took dinner upstairs."

"Yes, sir," Patrick replied with an understanding look.

In his room, Jason hung up his frock coat and slipped off his shoes. Morgan must have stoked the fire. With appreciation, Jason stretched out in the chair that faced the flame.

If Mr. Dunham released them early again tomorrow, he would go to the courthouse to check if Judge Brown had posted the examination results. Perhaps Barrister Hall had established a new office and needed a helping hand in the evenings. Anything to keep him away from this house and make the time until Saturday pass quicker.

Chapter 28

Jason Harris

—

He'd avoided his parents long enough.

After the horrifying event with Nathan yesterday, it was clear he had a duty to set the record straight regarding the Dunham family, more specifically, the two children.

Wondering how he would be able to face and work with Nathan this morning, Jason hurried down the stairs to breakfast. He found only his mother in her dressing gown in the morning room, reading the newspaper and drinking tea.

"Where's Father?" Jason took the seat across from his mother and nodded to Patrick to pour his tea.

"He had an early appointment with the insurers. They never want to pay the full amount of the claim, but I think this time they will." She turned the page without looking up.

"That's good then. Father's investment in the bank was insured. Or is this about the bank itself?"

"The partners are all at the meeting. If funds are released, they intend to rebuild immediately."

She never looked up.

Jason sat in silence as she nibbled a sweet bun and sipped tea. He waved off the bread basket Patrick offered and instead plucked an apple from the bowl of fruit in the center of the table. "I'll see you tonight."

His mother made no response.

He pondered his mother's odd mood as he walked to Dunham Accounting. Her dismissive behavior was strikingly out of character. He'd expected more browbeating over Donetta.

Surprised to find the lights on and the door unlocked at the accounting house, Jason hurried inside out of the cold morning air.

Mr. Dunham sat at his desk in the empty office, reviewing a tally of numbers.

"Good morning." Jason put his outerwear up and approached Mr. Dunham's desk. "Did you receive word on the delayed projects?"

"Please. Have a seat." Mr. Dunham placed his pencil on the desk and gestured to a chair in the front row. "I came early to speak with you before the others arrive."

An empty feeling churned low in Jason's stomach as he lowered himself to the indicated seat. "Yes?"

"I've had a distressing report regarding your behavior toward my daughter and several serious threats made against my son. In fact, Donetta bears an injury done by your hand that will forever mark her." His furious gaze rose to pierce Jason. His voice lowered to an angry hiss, "I wanted to call the police and have you charged with assault, but my daughter, with her soft heart and misplaced affection for you, begged me to reconsider. However," he leaned forward, fists bearing his weight pressed against his desk as he rose from his chair. "I do not have to tolerate your company in my shop. You are summarily dismissed. Take everything that belongs to you from your desk and leave the premises. Do not think to approach me or anyone in my family again."

Jason blinked and shook his head slightly. "Sir! I would never—"

"I found it hard to believe myself having thought you a decent young man, acceptable in every way for my lovely daughter. Luckily, you showed your true nature in time." He broke eye contact and glared red-faced at the tally on his desk. "Good day to you, Mr. Harris. There is nothing more to say."

Stunned, Jason rose and walked to his desk. He'd never kept personal items in the cubby beneath the writing surface, but he ran his hand in the empty hollow anyway. At the open closet, Jason pulled on his overcoat and hat. In a daze, he paused at the door and looked back at Mr. Dunham. "I never hurt your daughter, sir. I never touched her."

Mr. Dunham made a dismissive gesture with his hand, never looking up from his desk.

Outside, the morning appeared unchanged, but the foundation of Jason's world had shifted. Mr. Dunham would never believe him over his son and daughter, and even if Jason offered witnesses, Donetta's injury could only be explained by implicating Amy.

Nathan found a convenient way to alter the truth and hide his disgusting plan.

To place Amy at Georgie's house, of her own volition, might cast aspersions on her good name.

I could never do that to clear my reputation, even if Amy didn't care.

He walked like a man set adrift, lost in his inner turmoil. Directionless. He gazed unseeing on the roadway before his feet. When he raised his head, he stood before the courthouse.

A sigh of resignation escaped as he mounted the steps to the door.

Could the day get worse?

Bracing himself for disappointment, he made his way through a group of people to the public board. Tacked to the top of the board was a notice that candidates seeking their scores for the Boston bar examination were to see Judge Garrett Brown.

The courtroom where he had taken his test had an early trial in progress. Two doors down, he spied Judge Brown in his chamber, reading a document behind his desk.

Jason knocked on the door. "Pardon me, Judge Brown. I've come for my examination results."

The judge peered at Jason over his spectacles, then the light of recognition lit his face. "Mr. Harris, Barrister Hall's young friend. Please come in."

Jason slid through the partially opened door.

Judge Brown rose and extended his hand. "Please have a seat."

"I don't want to take up too much of your time."

"You won't." He opened one drawer, then another. "I have them right here. Somewhere. Here they are." The judge held up a stack of envelopes, then shuffled through them, pulling out two. "Here you are, Mr. Harris. Your test results. There is also an envelope for Mr. Hall. If you would be so kind as to see that he gets it, I'd be most appreciative."

"Certainly, sir. Thank you, sir." Jason left the chamber as Judge Brown returned to his work. Outside the room, he opened the envelope in the busy hallway and slid the paper out of the packet. He quickly scanned the examination result, a slow grin spreading across his face.

"I can practice law." His statement drew a few amused looks, and he pushed the report back into the envelope.

Do I want to be a solicitor or a barrister?

Counsel clients on the law or try cases before a judge and jury?

He'd talk to Barrister Hall about those choices when he delivered the envelope from Judge Brown.

Outside the courthouse, he considered going to Barrister Hall's house to tell him the good news and deliver Judge Brown's envelope, but instead, he turned toward home.

As he entered his home, his parents' angry voices echoed down from the second-floor landing. He held the front door and glanced at Patrick, who stood near the hall to the kitchen.

Patrick ducked his head and disappeared into Callie's domain.

Curious.

It wasn't that his parents never fought; they often did, but to display such emotion in front of the staff was rare. He tried to get the gist of what could have upset them, tipping his head and snatching at words.

"...not in my house!" his father stated.

"This isn't about you. I'll never be able to face my dear friends," his mother sobbed.

His father's red face appeared above the upstairs railing. "You're home."

The suddenly calm tone didn't fool Jason.

This is about me.

"Just now," Jason replied and pulled the door closed.

"Your mother and I must speak with you." His father's visage disappeared. His parents lowered voices reached him as he climbed the stairs, still wearing his outer vestments. He followed the sound of their conversation into his mother's sitting room.

His mother turned her head as he entered, but not before he glimpsed her swollen eyes and splotched face. She looked to the fire that crackled on the hearth and held a handkerchief to her mouth.

Pressed hard together, his father's lips formed a stern white line across his face. His white-gold hair, usually so carefully groomed, rioted haphazardly as he raked his hand through his curls. "We have received word this afternoon of your shameful antics last night at the Bisby residence." He turned and paced away from Jason.

"Father, I—"

His father spun and flung his hand out in anger. He swept a ceramic urn from the nearby table, shattering the delicately painted treasure against the wall. He rounded on Jason. "I have not given you leave to speak, boy!"

His mother uttered a short squawk of dismay then fell silent. Her gaze darted from her husband to her son.

Jason lifted his chin and braced himself for blows. His father had not raised a hand to Jason in years, long before his school days in Europe, but the look in Spencer's eyes brought back vivid recollections of those painful encounters.

I am no longer that child. Never again.

"But I shall speak, nevertheless. What happened at the Bisby's—"

"Is a disgrace!" his father screamed.

"Is a lie," Jason shouted back. "Whatever you heard has been twisted—"

"Donetta is disfigured *by your blade*. Are your whores not enough for you anymore? Now you need to attack genteel-bred young women and force yourself upon them as well?" Another figurine smashed against the fireplace stones.

A chill crept up his spine and held at the back of his neck. He squared his shoulders and cleared his throat. "There was an altercation at the Bisby house yesterday," he said with a calm, reasoned voice. "There were several people there when I arrived, including Donetta and her brother, Nathan."

Spencer held out his hand toward Jason and nodded to his wife. "What did I tell you?"

"I did not injure Donetta. That happened before I arrived. I did draw my blade in defense of another, however." Jason glanced at his mother, then returned to his father's skeptical eyes.

"And who, pray tell, was that?" Spencer crossed his arms and rocked back on his heels as though he'd heard this story a thousand times.

"I won't reveal her name without her permission. However, this woman came to the Bisby house because of a charade created by Nathan Dunham."

"The same Nathan Dunham who you threatened with your little sword?" Spencer charged forward, shaking his finger at the épée in Jason's hand. "Or is that a lie as well?" With a swift move, he snatched the cane from Jason and threw it directly into the fireplace flames. "I should have done that long ago."

His mother yelped as hot ash and sparks flew into the room. She jumped up from her chair, brushing at a cinder from her gown. Weeping, she turned to Jason. "Bethany Dunham has withdrawn her proposal for you to marry her lovely daughter in fear for Donetta's safety. You are no longer allowed in their home." She covered her face with the white lace-lined cloth. "And neither are we!" she wailed as her voice broke, and she sobbed deeply into the handkerchief.

Spencer put his arm around Rose and glared at his son. "I want you out of this house today. You've whored and taken advantage of our generosity and good name for far too long."

Jason blinked, pulling his gaze from the fire that eagerly licked and darkened the wood on his walking cane. "As you wish."

There's nothing to be gained by arguing. They've already made up their minds.

He strode down the hallway to his room to find Patrick waiting beside his bedroom door. "I'll be leaving immediately. Find Morgan and bring my large trunk from storage. Please ask Riley to ready a carriage. He'll need to drive me to my new—location."

Inside his room, he pulled his suits from the wardrobe and opened his bureau, stacking underclothes, handkerchiefs, and sundry items on the bed. From the lockbox beneath his bed, he withdrew his silver stock certificates and the envelope from Otis containing the Northern Railroad bonds. He slipped both into his inside pocket beside Judge Brown's letter for Barrister Hall.

On his bedside table sat a gift box wrapped with silver paper. Callie must have had Patrick place it in his room this morning.

Jason picked up the treasure he'd purchased for Amy. Blue ribbons adorned the silver paper and held the wrapping tight to the small box.

Jobless and homeless, how can I ask for her hand now?

The small container fit snugly in his overcoat pocket with his other valuables. With renewed determination, he packed the items from the top of the bureau—his comb and shaving items—into a small leather bag.

"Is this the one you wanted?" Patrick asked as he and Morgan set the large trunk in the hallway.

"That's the one." Jason tossed the leather bag onto the bed beside his underclothes then raked his hand through his hair as he looked around the room. "What else?"

"Shoes. Boots. Gloves. Umbrella. Your top hat and other jacket have been cleaned." Patrick spoke as he cleared the bed, folding items into the trunk.

"I'll gather your things downstairs," Morgan spoke from the hall. "And ask Riley to pull the small carriage around front."

"Thank you." Jason gathered the few adornment items he owned. Two pairs of cufflinks and a second watch chain. He dropped them in his suit pocket.

Patrick closed the trunk and bent to lift the heavy luggage.

"Hold on. Let me help."

"But Sir—" Patrick began to argue.

"No more 'Sir' nonsense either. I'm no longer part of this family." He lifted one end of the trunk. "You no longer work for me."

Patrick smiled and lifted his end. "Not for money, perhaps."

They sat the trunk on the foyer floor as Morgan came through the door. "Riley has the carriage ready. I put your other items on the seat." He gave Patrick a nod. "We'll strap this to the footman's perch in back."

"I'll be right out," Jason told them and turned down the hall to the kitchen.

Callie waited for him near the kitchen entrance. "Did you find her present?" She held out a bag of baked goods. "Blueberry muffins. I know they're your favorite."

"Thank you." Jason took the bag. "I found her gift." He patted his bulging pocket. "I'd thought to give the necklace to her when I propose, but I've nothing to offer a wife now." He glanced down the hall toward the staircase.

"Aye, you do." Callie bunched up her freckled nose and grinned. "You have a strong arm and a big heart. Don't make the woman who loves you wait. And if there's a need to wait, decide on the waitin' together."

"You are wise beyond your years." Jason kissed Callie's cheek. "Goodbye, Callie."

"Let us know where you will be," she dropped her voice to a whisper, "and if you need a cook."

"I'll send word." Jason found a smile for the young cook then strode to the door. He forced himself not to look up at the banister railing.

I don't care if they watch me leave.

Jason shut the door a bit harder than necessary. He showed Riley the envelope with Barrister Hall's address. "Take me here first. I need to deliver this message."

"I know the area," Riley replied.

Returning the envelope to his vest pocket, he climbed into the small buggy. Morgan had stacked his newer overcoat, top hat, and umbrella on the seat across from him and had not even forgotten his raincoat.

Jason lifted the shade as they pulled away from the residence and shook his head. He'd have chosen to leave his parents' home differently, but it was past time to go. A room at Revere's would suffice until he found a job and a place to live. Tomorrow, Jason would cash the railroad bonds Otis had secured for him. That would give him enough to get by for a time if he was thrifty.

He shut the shade and stared at his small pile of belongings as he struggled to control his anger. His father's oft-used argument that at least Calvary Dunham had a son who worked for him was countered in Jason's mind by the thought that at least Nathan had a father who believed him, even when he told lies.

Both to my detriment.

If he were honest, he was angrier over the loss of his cane than the loss of his parents.

The sharp tap of Riley's knuckles against the side of the carriage brought Jason out of his reverie. The rig slowed to a stop as Jason checked to ensure he still had Barrister Hall's letter from Judge Brown. His thoughts were scattered and at loose ends, as though there was something important he had forgotten. He scrubbed his hand over his face and let himself out of the rig.

"I'll be right back," he told Riley as he settled his hat, then crossed the road to Keith's home. This neighborhood wasn't the safest, and he thought again of his smooth cherrywood *épée* cane.

An overwhelming sense of familiarity assailed him as he stood in front of Keith's address. Curiously, he scanned the lane. At the end of the winding block, in the direction of the pier, he could see the front stoop of Pierce and Peabody Investments and the shingle that read 'P&P Investments.'

Marvelous neighborhood.

Loose and broken steps led to a peeling green door with a rusted knocker in the center. Jason rapped three times, then brushed the rust dust from his gloves.

"Coming," Keith called from inside. The door opened, and Barrister Hall, in a three-piece suit with his white hair unbrushed, opened his eyes wide. "This is a pleasant surprise." He stepped aside. "Please, come in."

"Thank you, but I can't." Jason indicated Riley and the carriage waiting across the street. "I need to make arrangements for tonight, but I wanted to deliver this to you from Judge Brown." He handed Keith the envelope.

The barrister tucked the correspondence into his pocket unopened. His eyes narrowed as he studied the carriage. "Arrangements for tonight? Is that your trunk strapped to the back of your rig?"

"It is. I'm currently without residence." Jason shuffled his feet, aware of the scrutiny of the older man. "I thought to take a room at Revere's Tavern. I know a man who works there."

"Nonsense!" Keith proclaimed. "I bought this two-story green monstrosity two years ago intending to spruce it up and rent the apartment upstairs." He looked out the door, craning his neck to see the dirty upstairs windows. "It needs a bit of love, I won't lie, but you can stay until you find a place of your own." He grinned at Jason. "Interested? Would you like to see it first?"

"Yes, and yes." Jason motioned to Riley he would be a moment longer, then followed Barrister Hall inside.

The home of a bachelor, books, and newspapers littered the sofa and the tables in the parlor. Although not as worn down as the front door would have him believe, the entire place needed a good cleaning with a mop and broom.

Jason followed Keith up the dusty narrow stairs past the staircase wall, devoid of family photographs or paintings.

The barrister opened the door at the top of the staircase and allowed it to swing wide. "You can lock this access to ensure your privacy. There's an outside entrance from the small kitchen and a staircase down to the backyard."

Jason followed him into the upstairs apartment. The bare floors needed sweeping, the windows cleaned, and a fresh coat of paint would brighten the interior. From the top of the steps, he could view the living area, which faced the street with bay windows. He paused at the narrow galley kitchen that boasted a small gas stove, an icebox, a sink, and at the far end, the rear exit.

Jason crossed the kitchen, unbolted the door, and turned the knob, but the wood was stuck.

"Won't it open?" Keith asked from behind.

"No." Jason stepped back.

"Give it a good yank."

He jerked on the door, and it begrudgingly gave way. Cold air and a few snowflakes blew past him as he looked down the exterior stairs leading to a gravel path that rounded the side of the house. The wooden steps would need to be replaced and painted, but the handrail seemed sturdy as he shook it.

Returning inside, he forced the door closed and threw the bolt.

"Not ideal, I know." Keith apologized.

Jason opened the bedroom door. A small stack of books sat in the middle of the empty room. At the back, two tall windows would light the place nicely on a sunnier day when cleaned.

Keith picked up the books, blew the dust from the top, and waved his hand in the cloud. "I'll take this downstairs."

Even though the apartment needed a week's worth of cleaning, along with furnishings, the first young sprouts of hope took root in Jason's heart.

A place of my own.

I'll need to clean now, then find a bed for tonight.

The decision to take Barrister Hall's offer already made, he hurried down the steps.

Keith waited for him near the door. "Do you want to stay?"

"I do." Jason reached out and shook the attorney's hand soundly. "I'll have Riley help me with the trunk."

"Wonderful! I'd hoped you would." Keith released his hand. "I have cleaning supplies and an unused cot and mattress you can use until you find something better."

"Thank you," Jason called over his shoulder as he signaled to Riley. "I'm staying here." He hurried across the street. "Help me take the trunk inside."

"Certainly." Riley stepped down from the front seat. "Is this a friend of yours then?"

"It is." Jason took one of the side handles, and they hoisted the trunk from its resting platform. "But if my parents ask, you dropped me at Revere's."

"It's where we told Patrick you were going anyway." Riley shrugged and shared a grin with Jason. "Who's to say you won't end up at Revere's Tavern by tonight?"

Chapter 29

Ayden MacKenna

—

The coven hadn't given up trying to intimidate him. Even after the attack they staged before the fire, and their part in the horror that followed. From how Milton acted when confronted, they blamed Ayden for everything.

He placed the tiny *elemental*, Caz, on the candlewick before he slept each night in case Gordon or other coven members thought to approach his door. It was quicker than casting a ward, and Ayden had developed sympathy for the little bound *elemental*. It brightened his evening to watch Caz dance along the blackened wick with such joy to be released, even for a few hours, from his prison.

He banked the coals in his small stove and sat back, watching the low flame flicker through the open door.

Within the flames, his younger brother, Melvyn, laughed at him before sticking out his tongue and running into their house. He'd not been much older than a toddler.

I wonder what became of him.

He tried to see his current image in the flame, but just as viewing Margaret had been taken from him when he was in India, Melvyn's image remained elusive.

He must be across the sea. But where?

Ayden rubbed his eyes and shut the stove's door.

Caz had ceased his jubilant dance and sat, hunched like a small cinder-gnome on the wick.

"Wake me if someone approaches," he told the small *elemental,* then turned down the bedside lamp and rolled onto his side, pulling the cover over his shoulders.

His dreams became nightmares—endless searches through tunnels of fire he couldn't control, pursuing phantoms through the smoke and embers, calling out, repeatedly, sometimes for Margaret, sometimes for Amy or his mother, their faces both distant and close in the haze.

He woke to a sharp tap on his door.

On the table, Caz slept. His steady flame was small and constant.

"Some guardian you are," Ayden muttered at the silent cinder.

The tap sounded again at the door to the stockroom.

"Yes?" Ayden called as he sat up and rubbed his face.

What time is it? Have I overslept?

"It's me. Molly," a soft feminine voice replied. "A footman named Wrigley dropped off an invitation. Do you want me to slip it under your door?" She sounded amused.

"Yes. Thank you."

He lifted his watch from the nightstand and peered at the dial.

Ten 'til noon.

He'd managed on less sleep than this. Perhaps the constant running in his dreams left him exhausted each morning.

"There you go," Molly called before her footsteps faded as she returned to the tavern.

He stared at the small white envelope on the floor near the door. Of course, it would be from Margaret inviting him to dinner to thank him for saving her husband. Ayden closed his eyes and exhaled, shaking his head.

After all her family did to me, why do I still care so much for Margaret? A happily married woman with a grown daughter. Can I sit across the table from her loving husband and smile?

He rose from his resting place and splashed water on his face, dried it with a hand towel, and tossed the damp cloth across the room, waking Caz, causing him to jump and flutter.

Ayden picked up the amulet from the bedside table and held it out to the tiny *fire-elemental.* "Return."

Caz leapt from the candlewick and disappeared into the red gem. Light from inside the stone fluttered for several moments before it settled into a steady, dim glow.

Ayden slipped the amulet into his pocket and bent to retrieve the envelope. "Let's see what Margaret has to say."

His name, penciled on the front of the envelope in block letters, did not strike him as coming from a woman's hand. The invitation inside was written in the same handwriting that addressed the envelope.

Dear Mr. MacKenna:

Please accept my invitation to celebrate the day of my birth, this Saturday, November 16th.

Had it not been for you, this celebration with my family would not have been possible.

Dinner will be served at six o'clock. I look forward to seeing you again.

With courteous regards,

Robert Prescott

Ayden tossed the invitation onto his bed. What would the coven think of the budding friendship between him and the Prescott family?

It might terrify them enough for Ayden to discover what their harassment was all about. Who was pulling Gordon and Milton's strings? He tried but couldn't recall who had been the coven leader when he had fallen in love with Margaret James. An older man, but then when you were nineteen, everyone over thirty seemed old.

I wonder who runs the coven now? Who gives Milton and Gordon and Lisbeth their orders to watch me?

***

Margaret Prescott

—

Margaret stood at the book nook window, watching the gently falling snow swirl and melt before it changed to tiny droplets leaving ever-changing rings in the puddles on the ground. She would have hoped for better weather to mark Robert's birthday celebration. Had they not expected guests, it wouldn't have mattered, but Jason Harris would be here shortly—and Ayden.

She'd changed her mind a half-dozen times about inviting Ayden into her home. For all the years that had passed, her feelings for him were still too strong, the pain fresh every time she looked into his eyes.

Robert had decided for her, insisting Mr. MacKenna be here to celebrate a birthday Robert otherwise would have missed.

As though her thoughts conjured him, her husband limped from his bedroom and came to a halt behind her. "What are you doing, my dear?"

"Watching the snow."

"It's snowing?" He pressed forward, holding her shoulders to see out the window. "It looks like rain."

"Hmm. Yes, it does."

"Are you coming down?" He gripped the rail and eased his injured knee down one step and then another, pausing to look back when she didn't answer. "Maggie, are you ill?"

"Not at all. Only a bit nervous, I suppose."

"About Mr. MacKenna?" Robert tipped his head like he always did when he studied her face as though trying to read her thoughts. "Was he the one you told me about when we were children?"

"We were older than children, Rob."

"Were we?" He chuckled and took another few steps. "Then tonight should be interesting."

"You're a strange man, Robert Prescott."

"I've been called worse." He reached the bottom of the staircase and looked up at his wife. "You look especially lovely tonight—in case you were worried."

"Why would I be worried?"

"Why indeed?" He chuckled and continued down the short hallway calling out to Amy, "Who has a birthday hug for their father?"

Margaret smiled and lifted her eyes to the view outside the window. Robert was right. The snow had changed to rain.

***

Ayden MacKenna

—

The path from Revere's Tavern to the Prescott home had become a familiar trail. Up the slight incline to near the top of Beacon Hill, past the Common, down a block and over. Along the residential street, a young woman dressed in a man's overcoat and top hat would have given any other man pause, but then again, anyone else would have seen only the *glamour* she cast—a tall, broad-shouldered man pacing along the walkway.

Her magical enchantment was a good one, and if Jason hadn't caught her unaware at the tavern and called her by name, Ayden may not have given the individual another thought.

He tipped his hat and murmured, "Miss Coleman," as he passed, without pausing to see if his recognition startled her or if she then hurried away to report his approach to Margaret Prescott's home. He turned at the Prescotts' address and rapped his gloved knuckles against the door.

The light rain settled on his shoulders and dripped slowly from the brim of his hat while he waited.

"Good evening, Mr. MacKenna." The young housemaid smiled as she opened and stepped back to allow him to enter. "Let me take your things."

"Thank you." He let the garment slip from his shoulders, then plucked a wrapped package from the pocket. "Mr. Prescott's present." He winked at the maid.

She chuckled as she took his coat and hat. "I'll put these in the kitchen to dry. The family is in the parlor." She indicated the room as she passed on her way to the kitchen. "Can I bring you something to drink?" She paused at the kitchen entrance and looked back for his reply.

"I'll have water with dinner."

She nodded, swishing her skirts into the kitchen.

Three sets of eyes focused on him as he stepped into the room. "Good evening and happy birthday." He held out the small package to Robert.

Robert stood and shook Ayden's hand, then took the package. "You shouldn't have gotten me a gift. This may be my celebration, but you made it possible."

"Nonsense." Ayden unbuttoned his jacket and sat in a high-backed chair that faced the settee and table. "Your daughter and Mr. Harris were the brave ones, running into a burning building. I only helped Miss Prescott get you home."

"Please, call me Amy." The young woman looked lovely tonight. Anticipation sparkled in her eyes like stars.

"Only if you return the favor and call me Ayden." His gaze naturally slid to her mother. "Mrs. Prescott," he nodded in greeting.

"Please," she replied, as she sat forward and placed her wine glass on the table, "you've known me too long to sit behind formality. Comfortable or not, you will address me a Margaret." She flashed a glance at her husband. "Rob calls me Maggie." She grinned at her startled daughter. "Amylia calls me Mother, but I would not approve of that from you."

Robert chuckled as he resumed his seat. "You never disappoint, Maggie."

"Mother!" Amy exclaimed, eyes wide as she stared at her mother.

Margaret shrugged her shoulders and lifted a hand toward Amy. "As I said."

"Margaret it is." Ayden tipped his head in defeat as a knock sounded at the front door.

Amy stood, but Margaret put a hand on her arm. "Allow Peg to show him in."

Ayden and Robert shared an amused look before Ayden composed his face and watched the door.

Peg walked past the parlor door carrying the new guest's coat and hat, and then Jason stepped into the room. The humidity outside had given riot to the young man's golden curls, but it was the look in his eyes as he sought and found Amy that tightened Ayden's chest.

I remember being that young and in love.

He cast a glance at Margaret and caught her looking at him. A blush warmed her cheeks.

She remembers too.

Both he and Robert rose and shook Jason's hand.

Jason greeted Ayden first, and then Robert, offering him a wrapped gift. "Happy birthday, sir."

" I certainly didn't mean for everyone to bring presents," Robert protested, taking the wrapped package. "However, it is thoughtful of you both."

"You should open it." Jason took the empty chair beside the settee.

Robert looked at Margaret, and she nodded. "There's time before dinner if you'd like. They're your presents, after all."

Robert grinned, displaying the eagerness of a child. "Ayden's first."

Inside the box, a pair of silver cufflinks were arranged to show the etched face of the jewelry—flames.

Ayden's face heated as Robert's astonished gaze rose to meet his. "The design seemed humorously ironic at the time. However, they now appear to be in poor taste."

"Dear man, you jest!" Robert handed the box to his wife. "I'm a man of irony and humorously poor taste myself. I love them. Thank you very much."

He lifted Jason's gift. "It feels like a book."

Jason grinned as Robert tore off the wrapping.

"Gulliver's Travels. I haven't read this in many years. Thank you."

"I hope you enjoy it. Swift's satire on the human condition crouched in fantasy has always been a favorite of mine."

"I'm a fan of Jules Verne, so this will be a wonderful read." He paged through the book, stopping on the first few pages. "Is this your copy?"

"Not anymore. Now it is yours." Jason's smile faltered. "I hope you don't mind. I've had it since I was in France. As you can see, it's kept me company on many a night."

"No, no. Not at all. I'm surprised you'd be willing to part with it."

"Dinner is served," Peg announced from the doorway.

Jason rose and held out his hand to Amy. He tucked her fingers around his arm, and the young couple followed Peg down the hall to the dining room.

Margaret stood and reached out to help Robert. "Don't put your weight on it."

"I'll be fine, Maggie." Robert came to his feet, supporting himself with the back of the chair.

"Hmph." Margaret rustled her skirt around the table. "No fool like an old one, Rob. Give me your arm."

The friendly banter between Margaret and her husband both amused Ayden and made him sad. He'd dreamed of growing old with Margaret, of raising a child and sharing their lives—everything Robert had.

Margaret's husband is a fine man, a good father, likable and generous. I should be happy for her.

He followed Mr. and Mrs. Prescott into the dining room.

Ribbons and letters cut out of paper proclaiming Happy Birthday decorated Robert's high-backed chair.

"Peg, you truly do everything. How would we ever get along without you?" Robert gave the housemaid a sincere smile and tipped his head.

"It's the least I can do for making me part of your family," Peg replied, then scurried into the kitchen as the tea kettle whistled.

When everyone settled around the table, Robert cleared his throat. "I want to thank Mr. MacKenna," he held up his hand and smiled, "Ayden—and Jason, for being here to celebrate the forty-fifth anniversary of my birth and for their very thoughtful presents."

Peg entered from the kitchen, set Robert's and Margaret's plate in front of them, and then returned. In short order, everyone had their dinner of duck, sliced fried potatoes, and boiled carrots. Peg placed the teapot in the center of the table. "Enjoy your dinner."

Ayden ate sparingly, even though the duck was cooked to perfection, always aware of Margaret's presence at his elbow.

"I've been convalescing all week and haven't a decent story to tell." Robert crossed his fork and knife over the bones on his plate. "Jason, how was your week?"

"Eventful." He glanced around the table. "I learned on Wednesday that I had passed the Boston State Bar Examination."

"Congratulations!" Robert exclaimed.

"That's wonderful news." Margaret lifted her wine glass to Jason.

"Do you plan to remain with Dunham Accounting?" Robert asked.

"No." Jason shook his head. "My last day with them was also on Wednesday."

A quick but meaningful look passed between Jason, Amy, and Margaret.

"An eventful day." Ayden set his napkin beside his plate.

"And I moved into an apartment above Barrister Hall's residence. I'll be working with him, not only with his clients but helping him manage the property and find new offices." He shook his head. "His office was destroyed in the fire.

"We're still working out the details. I'm more than an apprentice, but less than a partner. Either way, I've been cleaning and trying to furnish the apartment so that it feels more like home."

"Here we are," Peg said as she carried the two-tiered cake to the table. She had decorated the white cream frosting with dried fruit and nuts. "Happy birthday, Mr. Prescott." Peg set the cake in front of Robert and handed him the cake knife. "I'll be right back with some small plates."

Robert rose and grimaced, holding the edge of the table for support.

"Your leg?" Margaret asked from across the table.

"Yes. It seems I've used it a bit more than I should today." He sliced the cake as Peg brought the plates. After the first cut, he handed the knife to Peg. "If you could finish. I need to sit." He eased himself down into the chair and smiled at his guests. "My leg is sound. It only aches from use. Please, have a piece of my birthday cake."

"This is delicious," Jason commented. "Did your maid cook it? Our cook at home makes such treats, but nothing as light and tasty as this."

"Peg and I baked it this morning," Margaret explained. "This cake turned out well, but we've had a few less than positive baking ventures in the past.

Amy giggled. "The blueberry tarts?"

"We agreed never to mention those, remember?" Margaret chuckled. Her face became serious as Wrigley hesitated near the kitchen door, then crossed the dining room to whisper in her ear. Her gaze moved from her husband to Ayden, then she nodded to Wrigley. "I'll be right there."

Wrigley gave a slight nod and withdrew.

"It seems there is a... solicitor that wishes to speak with me." Margaret placed her napkin by the plate with her half-eaten cake.

"I'll go with you." Robert made to rise, then gasped and fell back onto his seat.

"No, dear. You rest. Perhaps Jason and Amy will help you climb the stairs." Margaret offered Ayden a tense smile. "If Ayden would accompany me to meet with this fellow, I'm sure we can see to whatever he wants and send him on his way."

"Certainly," Ayden replied and rose to hold Margaret's chair as she came to her feet.

"Take care of your father," Margaret said, then led Ayden into the kitchen.

Near the back door, Ayden slipped his greatcoat and hat and Margaret a wool shawl from the hooks and strode outside.

A light showed through the small window beside the entrance to the coach house. Ayden had only seen the back side of the building when he and Jason had returned the rig after the fire.

Twenty-five years ago, my world revolved around the small, attached apartment.

Margaret opened the door, and they made their way through what appeared to be Wrigley's workroom. A harness was laid out on a workbench, and leather straps hung from the rafters.

Beyond the work area, the passage narrowed past two horse stalls, built side by side.

A man waited beyond the livestock, near the carriage. He wore a black-caped overcoat and top hat, which made his blond-white hair shine.

Wrigley leaned against the wall across from the stalls, arms crossed.

Margaret stopped as soon as she saw the man, then moved forward with a measured pace. "Mr. Coleman. I'm surprised to find you waiting in the coach house. Wrigley said you were a solicitor. You should have come to the front door. We had cake for Robert's birthday. You would have been welcome to join us."

The tall, white-haired man tipped his hat to Margaret, but his eyes focused on Ayden. "Congratulations to your husband. However, this is not a social call, Mrs. Prescott. I've come on coven business."

"Coven?" Margaret shook her head and glanced in confusion between the three tense men. "Did I hear you correctly? Did you say *coven* business?"

The tall, thin man in black nodded. "Yes. Although both your families are no longer in the area, and you have separated yourself from our company since your marriage to an unskilled, the coven remains."

"And your position with the coven?" Ayden edged forward to stand beside Margaret.

"I am the High Priest of the Coleman Coven." Isaac Coleman grinned. "A title I assumed over fifteen years ago."

"I see." Ayden took another step forward, partially shielding Margaret from the strange witch. "Your underlings have made more than a nuisance of themselves over the last few weeks. They are constantly on my doorstep. I'd go as far as to say they caused the recent fire."

On the other side of Margaret, Wrigley pushed away from the wall and faced Coleman.

"Ah, Mr. MacKenna. And I heard it was you who was at fault."

"A gang of your coven members attacked me."

"A misunderstanding, I assure you. However, because of the party you host this evening, Mrs. Prescott, it is incumbent on me to inform you that the Coleman Coven will accept no rival covens in our city."

"You think Margaret and I have formed a rival coven?" Ayden's voice rose along with anger.

"There are now enough witches gathered this evening under your roof," Mr. Coleman spoke to Margaret, ignoring Ayden, "to form a rival coven."

"We're having a birthday party," Margaret stressed. She grasped Ayden's arm, effectively holding him back.

"High priest or not, this man's an idiot," Wrigley grumbled dismissively. "In my day, a High Priest was smart. Intimidating." He blew through his lips, making a sound of disgust.

"I'll take no disrespect from a common stable hand," Coleman raised his hand.

Wrigley flicked his wrist, and a wall of air shoved Coleman against the carriage. "As I said, you're a damned idiot." He spat at Coleman's feet. "There's been three witches living here for nigh-on twenty years. I'm not sure why one more has your dander up."

"Wrigley," Margaret's voice pulled the servant back to her side.

The coven priest relaxed and exhaled as the invisible barrier released. "You'll regret that," he muttered to Wrigley as he straightened his shoulder cape.

"Oh, hush." Red-faced, Margaret marched forward and poked the tall man with her finger. "I'm ashamed to have ever considered you my friend, Isaac Coleman. You've hidden your true self, pretending to be a member of the Brahmin. The deceitful act of using your daughter at the Harris Masquerade is beyond the pale. What was the point of setting her gown on fire?"

"To see if you had truly given up your magic." He raised his hand to shove her finger from his chest but hesitated and calmed his voice instead. "We discovered you had not."

"Don't test me, Isaac. I may not use the power I inherited, but I promise you, I am every bit as strong as my mother ever was." Margaret stomped her foot, and the ground rumbled.

Both horses neighed nervously and poked their heads from their stalls.

Wrigley smiled and crossed his arms.

"Perhaps this would be a good time for you to apologize to Mrs. Prescott for interrupting her dinner party and take your leave." Ayden mirrored Wrigley's stance.

"I won't tolerate a rival coven." Coleman adjusted his top hat. "There will be repercussions if you continue."

"There is no rival coven, you badger, only the one in your head." Wrigley grasped a leather strap from the wall. "Besides, I need not use my magic to whip your hide." He laughed and snapped the strip, making the end crack loudly.

"Enough." Margaret chastised with her tone. "Your poor daughter, to have grown up with such a covetous and envious father."

"At least my daughter has magic," Isaac sneered.

"At least my daughter has a father she can be proud of," Margaret replied. "Please leave. You are not welcome in my home or on my property. Do not come here again."

The three of them watched in silence as Isaac Coleman turned and marched out of the carriage house.

"He'll be back," Wrigley muttered.

"I'm surprised he knew about Amy's skills. She keeps her magic well hidden." Ayden watched Isaac Coleman pause in the alleyway as two men emerged from the shadows to speak with him.

"Coleman doesn't know about Amy," Margaret told him as Wrigley exclaimed, "Amy has magic?"

Margaret nodded and turned to Wrigley. "She doesn't have full powers, but yes, she has shown some skill."

"Who did you mean by the third in the house then?" Ayden asked.

Margaret and Wrigley shared a glance then Wrigley spoke. "I meant my niece, Peg. I took her in after her parents passed. Margaret was good enough to give us a home."

"You could have lived in the house and been part of the family," Margaret told Wrigley.

"Hush, now Maggie. We are part of your family, and we know that. We do our part, is all."

"However, I do wish you hadn't told him there were already three witches in the house. I don't think he knew about Peg. Now he does," Margaret scolded.

Wrigley nodded solemnly. "That's true. But I can't take it back now."

Ayden closed the garage doors and lowered the drop bar latch. "So, in reality, there's five of us to frighten High Priest Coleman and his thugs."

"More than enough for a rival coven apparently," Margaret quipped.

"He'll be back," Ayden echoed Wrigley's warning as he rounded the carriage and stopped beside Margaret.

"He won't. He's a coward. He may have great influence within his small group, but the Prescotts belong to the Boston Brahmin. He won't want to lose that connection by pricking my anger more than he already has."

Ayden followed Margaret toward the house, but in the middle of the backyard, he stopped.

Margaret looked back at him. "Are you coming in?"

"No." he shook his head. "I'm too angry to fool anyone inside. Please tell your husband that I had to return to the tavern."

"Do you want me to rig up the carriage? It might not be safe to walk tonight." Wrigley leaned against the wall of the carriage house. "His little coven fellows will be milling about."

"They won't bother me, at least not directly. The bullies tried it before and failed." He gazed down into Margaret's eyes. "But I am afraid he'll come after you."

"Don't be. We are more than capable of defending ourselves against Isaac Coleman and his ilk." Margaret ran her fingers up Ayden's arm, then dropped her hand abruptly and stepped back. "Goodnight, Ayden. Thank you for coming."

"Goodnight, Maggie." He waited until the back door closed, then he turned to Wrigley. "You've known Margaret a long time?"

Wrigley nodded. "Since she was a young girl. I knew your folks too when we were all part of Brown's Coven."

Ayden moved closer and lowered his voice. "Then you know what happened to me?"

"Not more than what I heard. You ran off. Broke that little girl's heart." He tipped his head toward the house. "Your family hoped you'd come home, but in the end, they left as well." He shook his head and leaned forward. "You want to fill me in on the missing details?"

"Not tonight, Wrigley." Ayden held out his hand to the driver. "Keep an eye on our girl."

"It's what I've always done." Wrigley shook Ayden's hand. "Just don't disappear again."

Chapter 30

Jason Harris

—

Amy closed the door to her father's room and gave Jason a sweet smile. "Thank you for helping him up the stairs."

"My pleasure." He followed her down the hall. "Could you tell if he reinjured his knee?"

"I don't think so, but he'll have to take his recovery a little slower." Amy reached for the stair rail and then backed up.

"Is your father up there?" Margaret's voice preceded her up the stairs.

"He laid down but said he wasn't ready to sleep yet."

Margaret strode past Amy and addressed Jason, "I'm sorry for such an abrupt ending to Robert's dinner party." She took his hand. "Thank you for the gift. I know he'll enjoy reading it." Margaret's kind words reflected none of the warmth he had come to associate with Amy's mother. Preoccupation clouded her usually sharp eyes.

"You're certainly welcome," Jason assured her and would have said more, but she hastened into her husband's room and closed the door.

"I wonder what happened with the solicitor." Amy's puzzled gaze lingered on her father's door.

"We could ask Ayden," Jason suggested.

Downstairs, no one waited in the parlor or dining room.

In the kitchen, Peg labored at the sink, washing the last of the dishes.

"Where's Mr. MacKenna?" Amy asked, clearly puzzled.

"I don't know." Peg shrugged and set a cleaned pot on the stove to dry. "He didn't come in with your mother."

"How odd. I thought Mr. MacKenna would have said goodbye." Amy opened the back door and hurried outside. "Wrigley will know what's happening."

"Oh!" Peg pointed at the coat pegs behind the door. "Grab her wrap. She never remembers it."

Jason took a soft wool cloak and followed Amy out and across the small yard. He could see his breath, but without a hint of a breeze, the cold night was not unbearable.

Amy knocked at Wrigley's door as Jason wrapped the cloak around her shoulders.

The scrape of furniture against the wood floor came from inside, followed by a swear word. The door swung open, and Amy stumbled back into Jason.

Wrigley glared at them while he rubbed his shin. "And what can I do for you two this lovely evening?"

Amy held onto Jason's arm. "Is Mr. MacKenna with you?"

"No," he said as he stood upright. "As far as I know, he went in the house."

"He's not inside. Peg told us mother came in alone."

"Then he went home." Wrigley shrugged. "Why get me out of bed?"

"You're right. I apologize." Amy's face flushed, and she drew the wool cape around her. "It's only—Mother appeared out of sorts when I spoke to her upstairs. Did the solicitor say something to offend her?"

"I couldn't say. You'll have to ask your mother." Wrigley lifted his gaze from Amy to Jason and arched one shaggy brow. "If you wait for the right moment, Mr. Harris, you'll find it has passed you by." He gave Jason a faint nod. "Take care on your walk home tonight." Wrigley's tone held more than simple contempt for the chilly weather. "There's a devil's moon on the rise."

"Wrigley—" Amy began, but the coachman held up one finger.

"I can't tell you what I don't know. Now, goodnight to you both." He closed the door.

Amy blinked at the closed door, then shrugged and turned to Jason. "Well, I've made a fool of myself."

"Not at all." Jason put his arm around her and walked to the middle of the yard. "Your mother was definitely preoccupied." He glanced over their shoulders at the light in Wrigley's window and saw the curtain move.

"What did Wrigley mean about waiting for the right moment?" Amy looked up at Jason from the corner of her eye.

Jason faced Amy and took her hand. "When Peg took my overcoat this evening, she noticed I'd left the gifts in the pockets. She gave both presents to me before I entered the parlor. I must assume she told your coachman about one of them."

Amy's brows drew together. "You gave Father a single present, the book."

"That's true. I still have this one." He withdrew the box wrapped in silver paper from his pocket and held it up. His heartbeat drummed in his ears as he lowered himself to one knee.

Amy's eyes widened, and her free hand fluttered to her chest.

"You've captivated me from the moment we bumped into each other on the street, Miss Prescott. And when I held you in my arms while we danced, I realized how much I wanted to get to know you better. After you risked your life at my side to save our fathers, I had no doubt."

"Jason," his name was a breathless whisper on her lips as she took the silver box.

"Please say you'll consent to be my wife. I love you, Amy. Accept this gift as a token of the love I carry for you in my heart."

She pulled her hand from his and wiped tears from her cheeks. "I want to say yes. I sincerely wish I could." A sob caught her words, and she covered her mouth for a moment.

Jason rose and held her shoulders as she caught her breath. Her response left an ache in his gut.

Bad things come in threes.

He never thought Amy would be the third ache in his string of bad luck. He looked up to blink the moisture from his eyes. "You should go in. You'll catch a chill." His throat tightened, and he could say no more. It was time to leave.

Amy grabbed his sleeve as he moved toward the gate. "Wait. You misunderstand." She held the present to her chest, and love-light gleamed through tearful eyes. "There are—many things you don't know about me. I..." She hesitated and fell silent.

Jason rested his hand on her shoulders and cleared his throat. "We will have a lifetime to uncover each other's secrets. At least say you'll consider becoming my bride."

Amy sniffed and smiled up at him. "Come inside, and I'll open your present."

***

Amy Prescott

—

Amy hung her cloak on a hook by the door and shivered, then took a seat at the small kitchen table where Wrigley and Peg ate their meals. A small gas lantern burned low in the center of the table.

"Peg must have gone to bed." Amy's gaze stayed on him as he sat across from her.

"Well, open it," Jason urged with a laugh.

Amy bit her lower lip. "I don't want to tear the paper," she teased.

"Tear it." He reached for the box. "Here, I'll tear it."

Amy lifted it out of his reach and laughed. "I can do it." She untied the ribbon and pulled the box free of the paper. Inside the container, she found a soft velvet bag.

"It's in there," Jason urged.

"I know." Amy chuckled and pulled the jewelry from the pouch. The silver glistened, and the moonstone took on the colors of fire from the lamp. "Oh, Jason—this is gorgeous!" Her fingers explored the silver squares linked to form the book chain necklace, then she lifted the locket and ran her thumb over the stone.

This gem was blessed. I feel the charm.

"Where did you find such a treasure?"

"A street vendor I discovered not far from the courthouse. Her silver jewelry is handmade, one of a kind. The locket opens. You could put a picture or a flower from your garden inside."

Amy used her nail to open the locket. "Or a ringlet of hair."

"Hair?" Jason grinned in confusion. "Whose hair?"

"Why yours, of course." Amy rose from the stool, leaving the locket open on the table, and searched a cabinet drawer. She returned with a small pair of scissors and a spool of black thread. "I'll only take a tiny lock from underneath if you have no objection." She cut a six-inch string from the bobbin and twisted the strand into a small slipknot.

"By all means. Take whatever you need." Jason pulled one of his curls straight and tried to look at it, crossing his eyes.

"You're such a clown." She poked his shoulder and laughed. "Turn your head so your hair faces the light. That's it." She slipped a length of black thread around a slender curl and pulled the knot tight. A quick snip with the tiny shears, and she held a golden ringlet on her palm. "You'll never miss it."

He ran his hand through his hair. "I needed a trim."

"You still need a trim." Amy arranged the clipping, a curl length of her little finger, inside the locket. Then she snapped it closed. "Would you hook this for me?" She pulled the delicate hook from the eyelet, turned her back to Jason, and held the ends of the necklace at her shoulders.

"Certainly." Jason rose and swept her dark hair to one side.

Amy shivered as his warm hands caressed her neck when he took the hook and eyelet from her fingers. His lips slid along her hairline as the cool silver weight settled around her neck, and the locket lowered to rest below her collarbone.

"You smell like flowers," he whispered, trailing a soft kiss from beneath her ear to the edge of her gown. "And taste like heaven."

Amy's eyes closed, and she leaned against Jason's chest. "You make me tremble." She caught her breath as his low chuckle sounded in her ear.

"That's good to know." His arms held her close, and his lips rested against her temple. "Now, tell me you'll marry me."

She turned within the circle of his arms and pressed her palm to the side of his face. "I want to say yes. I truly do."

"Then say it." Ice blue eyes and a riot of golden curls reflected the light of the low flame—the legendary Harris beauty.

She almost said yes.

Almost.

Then she remembered the sadness in her mother's eyes and the care she used to hide the magical skills Amy could never hope to have. She'd sworn she wouldn't do that to herself or to the man she loved.

Then, in the back of her mind, Nathan's insidious voice whispered, *'Jason likes women with more experience than a spinster like you. What was her name? Molly?'*

A shudder racked her frame. "I fear I'm not the type of woman you want." Her hand moved from his face to his shoulder, turning her head away from the desire in his eyes. "I've no experience with romance, much less physical love...." She couldn't go on. To be this close to your heart's desire and yet to lack the single thing to make it come true.

With magic, I'm only half-skilled. With love, I have no skill or knowledge at all.

"Why would you think—" Jason shook his head. "Nathan," he uttered with disgust.

Startled, Amy looked up.

"Nathan said those things and lied to hurt you," Jason whispered.

"And Molly—was she a lie too?"

Jason dropped his hands from her shoulders and turned away. "Molly is a real woman, but she means nothing to me." He glanced back, catching her gaze. "I don't love her. I've never loved her."

"But she's real." It wasn't that she didn't believe Jason. It was her cursed imagination that put an unknown woman in the arms of the man she loved. Her chest ached.

Anger flared in Jason's face as he turned. "You said I didn't know everything about you, and that is true. I don't need to know every thought you've had or every emotion you've ever felt. I only need to look inside myself to know how I feel about you. Who you were a year ago doesn't matter to me today. Who you'll be a year from now is so much more important."

"I understand." Amy nodded.

"But you won't say yes."

She shook her head. "Not yet. Give me more time." Her arms lifted to reach behind her neck and unclasp the necklace.

Jason stopped her. "The gift is yours, no matter what you decide. It would suit only you, and I've no heart to return it." He lifted his coat from the hook, pushing his arms into the sleeves, then picked up his top hat. "Will you see me out?"

"Of course." Amy followed Jason to the front door.

In the entryway, he turned to her and took a deep breath, capturing her gaze with his. "I don't intend to pressure you. You deserve time to consider a proposal of marriage." He put his hat on his curls and took her hand. "But while you consider all you know and don't know about me, believe in your heart how much I've come to admire you. How I cherish your company and look forward to the time I spend with you." He lifted her hand to his lips and kissed her chilled fingers. "I've fallen hopelessly in love with you, Amylia Harris. I'm besotted. Simply bewitched."

Amy didn't trust herself to speak. Tears were dangerously close, and she didn't want them to spoil the moment. Instead, she slipped her arms inside his overcoat and hugged him close, her ear to his chest.

He folded his arms around her in a gentle hug.

They stood in a silent embrace while she untangled her emotions. Dry-eyed, she moved away from Jason and offered him a genuine smile. "Thank you for the locket. It is beautiful and a gift I shall always treasure."

"You're most welcome." He opened the front door and stepped onto the stoop. "Give your parents my regards. I'll stop by next week if that is acceptable to you. Oh, and here—" He pulled a calling card with his name from his pocket. "I've written my new address on the back should you need to send me a note."

Amy took the card. "Thank you. You are always welcome here." She tucked the card in her skirt pocket. "I'll look forward to your visit."

He offered a smile and then strode down the walk to the street, his hands in his overcoat pockets.

Where's his cane?

She waited for him to turn around and look back, but he never did. With a weight around her heart, she closed the door and meandered through the downstairs, turning off the lights while lost in thoughts of the evening. As she put her foot on the stair, her mother's soft voice drifted down to her.

"I'm surprised Jason left so early." Margaret closed the book in her hands and sat forward on the reading bench.

Amy didn't respond until she reached the top step, then she crossed her arms and heaved a sigh. "I'm afraid he's unhappy with me."

"Whatever for?"

Amy touched the silver necklace, sliding the pads of her fingers along the intricate flat links and then lifting the locket to inspect the moonstone. "He proposed we wed and gave me this as a token of his affection."

Margaret came to her feet, her scrutiny on the stone. "Does he know what this stone means?"

"No." Amy smiled at her mother. "I'm sure he doesn't. A street vendor sold it to him. It is blessed."

"May I?" At Amy's nod, Margaret held the locket within her palms. "Feminine energy with both sensual and healing facets. It resonates with love and light."

"And it's beautiful," Amy said, taking the treasure back and placing it against the bare skin above her neckline.

"Then you're betrothed."

"No."

"No? You surprise me. I thought this young man was the one for you."

"I think he is. I mean, I hope he is." Amy worried her hands together and then held one out toward her bedroom door. "Come to my room. I need to speak with you." She glanced over her shoulder. "Without unexpected interruption."

Margaret nodded and followed Amy into her room.

Amy closed the door and leaned her back against it.

Margaret found a seat at the dressing table and gazed at her daughter. "What troubles you, darling?"

"I don't know how to do it—how *you* do it" Rubbing her arms, she moved to the bed. "You've kept your magic hidden from Father for years." She picked up her drawing books and stacked them on the nightstand, then flounced onto the mattress. "Who does that betray, your true nature or Father's trust? I don't know if I could live like that."

Margaret's eyes widened as Amy spoke. "What makes you think Robert doesn't know, on some level at least, that I have skills other people do not?" She leaned forward. "Remember, I grew up with Robert. He was my childhood playmate and oldest friend. I would never lie to him."

She held up one finger to silence Amy's comment. "However, marriage is not meant to rend your innermost secrets from your soul. Both parties deserve the privacy of their thoughts and respect given to each other's past. What you choose to share is up to you and does not need to be laid bare before you become betrothed." She leaned back and smiled. "Ask me again after twenty years of marriage if you share every thought, secret, and emotion in your soul with your husband."

"To keep my true nature hidden from Jason would not be a betrayal?"

"You have a green thumb and use your *earth-sight* to help others. You are prescient, and on occasion, use divination to find your way. Keeping those abilities to yourself is no betrayal of the man you love." Margaret shook her head. "Don't let it keep you from finding happiness."

Amy pressed her lips. Everything her mother said made sense. "You told father about your skills?"

"No. We never speak of it, although I'm confident Robert knows—or at least suspects. There are certain truths about himself that he holds close to his heart as well. We don't discuss them, but I know just the same. Respect, trust, and love are all a part of marriage." Margaret tipped her head as she studied Amy. "I can read your face. What else is on your mind?"

"There's another woman."

"Are you sure? The only young woman I've heard associated with Jason's name besides yourself is Donetta Dunham. Is that who you mean?"

Amy shook her head. "No. Her name is Molly. He sees her at Revere's."

Margaret blinked. Her mouth opened to speak and then snapped shut.

"Do you know something?" Amy asked.

"What I know I hesitate to speak. Well brought up, young women don't speak of...." Margaret waved her hand as though to finish the sentence. "Who told you about this, Molly?"

"Nathan Dunham. He said Jason prefers women with more experience like Molly at Revere's."

"Amy, I'm sure this Molly is a genuinely nice girl, although I believe she is a good ten years older than you. She's a slattern who works at Revere's."

"You've seen her?"

"When I went there to speak with Mr. MacKenna. Yes, I spoke with her." She narrowed her eyes at Amy. "Darling, do you know what a slattern is?"

Amy considered the question and then slowly shook her head. "A tavern worker?"

"No." Margaret chuckled. "They don't serve beer. She's a prostitute, dear. Many men, husbands and otherwise, purchase their services. For some wives, a prostitute is a blessing."

Amy stared at her mother, her mind spinning.

A prostitute!

"I don't know what to think. Jason pays this woman, Molly, to... to fornicate with him?"

"It's not at all unusual and certainly not something to stop you from becoming betrothed. If the thought of Jason having relations with another woman bothers you after you wed, you could ask him to be more discreet or to stop visiting her altogether."

Shock and relief are a strange mix of emotions.

Amy shook her head. "It never occurred to me he would pay a prostitute."

Margaret stood and straightened her skirt. "He probably wouldn't need to, but your young man is a gentleman and would never press an innocent young girl to dishonor herself to satisfy his physical desires." She shrugged. "If there's nothing else, I'm off to bed."

Amy nodded. "We can talk more later. Goodnight, Mother."

After the door closed, Amy glanced out the window at the empty street, then wandered across the room and picked up her sketchpad.

A prostitute. But what did they do? Rut like animals?

Her lack of information stretched before her, an abyss of ignorance, and a desire for knowledge.

Chapter 31

Jason Harris

—

The law books and case files not destroyed in the downtown fire sat stacked near a makeshift bookshelf in what had been Barrister Hall's spare bedroom at the front of the house. Along with an old desk Keith purchased from a neighbor, Keith and Jason had a working office in the barrister's home.

After thoroughly cleaning his new apartment, Keith helped Jason move the spare bed, nightstand, and bureau upstairs. The living area and the tiny kitchen remained empty. Jason had neither the heart nor the resources to furnish the unused rooms.

He hadn't sought out his parents, nor had they him, as far as he knew. Had Jason been forced to live on the street and beg for shelter, they would not have known or cared.

Nor had he returned to the Prescott home seeking Amy's company. Certain he would press her for an answer if he did, he decided to stay away.

She'll let me know when she's made up her mind.

But he did hate waiting.

Fortunately, rearranging the house to prepare Keith's office and cleaning his new quarters had kept him busy all week. However, his patience was near an end.

If I haven't heard from her by Saturday, I'll visit the charming Miss Prescott.

Hopefully, she'll have had enough time to consider his proposal and come to a decision. Not that he had anything to offer.

He paged through the case file Keith gave him to review, a lawsuit involving the theft of firearms between neighbors.

Downstairs, Keith continued work on his temporary office. His efforts echoed through the open door at the foot of the stairs. It sounded as though he were pounding nails into a section of the floorboards that refused to lie flat.

Jason turned the page in the file and read the sworn testimony of the plaintiff. The affidavit proceeded to tell a tale of deception and greed on the part of his neighbor, the accused.

"Jason?" Keith called up the stairs and through the apartment's open door.

"Yes?" Jason turned to the next page of the testimony.

"There's a man at the door who wishes to speak to you."

Jason dropped the file on the end of the bed and rose.

A guest?

Riley knew where he was if his parents found a bit of concern for their offspring or needed him. And he'd given a card with his address to Amy.

He expected neither to call on him.

Tucking the tail of his shirt into his trousers, he straightened his vest and hurried downstairs.

The Prescotts' coachman stood inside the front door in his heavy coat and cap. He held out an envelope with hands gloved in rough leather. "Miss Amy sends her regards and would like for you to call on her." Wrigley shuffled his feet, clearly uneasy in a messenger role.

"She does?" Jason took the envelope and slid his finger under the flap. "What does this say?"

"How should I know?" Wrigley grumbled. "Is this your new place?" He looked around the corner into the office, where Keith pulled books from a box and arranged them on the shelves.

"It is," Jason scanned the short note.

My Dearest Jason,

Please call on me at your earliest convenience. I have an answer to the question you asked.

Yours Truly,

Amy

"I've lived in worse," Wrigley said.

"It could be argued you live in a shed right now." Jason looked up from the letter with a grin and met Wrigley's hard stare. "You know I jest."

"I know it, and what is all well and good for a man would not be fit for a lady." Wrigley peered up the staircase. "Is there a nice view from the second floor?"

"Would you like to come upstairs and—"

"Don't mind if I do." Wrigley moved past Jason. His heavy boots clumped up the wooden stairs.

Jason chuckled and followed the coachman up the stairs.

"Not much for decorating, are you?" Wrigley stood at the bowed front windows. "I can see where the city burned. You'll be able to watch them rebuild."

"I hope to find a place of my own soon."

Wrigley glanced at the small kitchen.

"That door leads to an outside staircase." Jason followed the driver to the bedroom.

"Hmph." Fists on his hips, holding his overcoat back, Wrigley stared at the bed. "Children grow up so fast. Well, there's nothing to be done about it." He spun and stared at Jason. "When can I tell Miss Amy to expect your visit?"

Jason lifted the letter. "This evening?"

"After dinner?"

"Yes. That would—"

"I'll let her know." Wrigley paused on the staircase and looked over his shoulder at Jason. "You'll be good to the lass should she acquiesce?" His grin widened. "I wouldn't want to have to burn you alive." He winked and gave a guttural laugh as he continued down the stairs. "You know I jest." He paused after he opened the door and smiled up at Jason, who watched from the stairs. "Seven o'clock then?"

"Um. Yes. Seven would be fine."

Keith looked out of the office as the front door closed. "A craftsman?"

"The Prescotts' coachman. He's something of a character."

"So I gather." Kevin dusted a bookend and then looked up at Jason on the stair. "Did we pass inspection?"

"I suppose." Jason slowly descended the staircase. "It's hard to tell."

"I'm sure we did." Keith returned to the bookshelf and set the bookend in place. "It will be nice to have a woman living here. They always make a house feel more like home somehow."

Jason hesitated on the last step, unsure if he'd heard Keith correctly. "Do you mean to say you wouldn't mind if, after Amy and I wed, we lived upstairs?"

Keith gave him a wink and grinned. "I mean to say just that."

"I don't know how much I could pay you. My income is practically non-existent at this moment."

"Your portion of work will pick up," Keith assured him. He pulled more books from a box and placed them on the shelf. "Once we settle with the insurance company, we'll have funds to find a new office space." He paused and looked around the room. "Then again, this isn't too bad. We're not far from the courthouse. This room would be your office as the solicitor. I would work at court." He smiled at Jason, his thick white hair sticking up haphazardly around his head. "I think this will work out quite well indeed."

"You're sure?"

He returned to carefully unpacking his beloved law books. "I'm positive. Now, go get ready to visit your young lady and her family."

Upstairs, Jason changed into a clean shirt and then pulled the envelope containing the railroad bonds from beneath his mattress. He would surrender the bonds for their current value. Hopefully, he would acquire enough cash for a small bride's gift, with enough left over to furnish the apartment as Amy saw fit.

He called farewell to Keith as he pulled on his overcoat and hat and closed the door behind him.

A few houses down, the office of P&P Investments drew him like a beacon. In addition to surrendering the bonds in his pocket, he intended to ask about the illegal loan made in his name. He'd let other things push Pierce's unethical behavior from his mind, but now was the time to cash these bonds and straighten out this other nonsense.

The door rang an overhead bell as Jason stepped inside.

The home's original entrance had been expanded to span the entire width of the house and hold the P&P office. There were two work areas. The smaller, on his left, faced the west window. Its chair pushed close to the desk with several folders stacked on top. The larger table sat in the middle of the room and faced the front door. Behind the larger workspace, tall bookshelves lined the wall from the right wall to a door which undoubtedly led to the Pierce's living space. To Jason's right, a small guest area sat in the corner close to the east window. Two chairs and a small couch formed an open waiting room.

Otis Pierce Senior had his back to the door as he returned a ledger to a high shelf. "Be right with you." He sounded much like his son.

Jason removed his hat and waited. He'd never met Otis's father, although he'd heard his friend's tales of an overbearing parent and experienced the man's unethical business dealings firsthand.

"I'm sorry about the wait. How may I assist you?" Mr. Pierce spoke before he turned. When his gaze found Jason, his eyebrows lifted. "Mr. Harris. How good to finally meet you." He rounded the desk and extended his hand. "O.J. speaks very highly of you."

"Mr. Pierce." Jason took his hand. "It is good to meet you as well. I've meant to come to your office and speak with you."

"Please, have a seat. Could I offer you something to drink? I have water, tea, or brandy."

"Nothing. Thank you." Jason sat across the desk from Mr. Pierce. "I've never heard Otis called O.J." He pulled the envelope holding the bonds from his coat pocket.

"His mother called him that when he was a baby. She liked O.J. better than Junior, I suppose." He chuckled and rubbed his palms together. "What have you there?"

Jason tossed the envelope across the desk. "Bonds. Worth half of the money I gave Otis to invest. He failed to mention your exorbitant upfront fee."

Mr. Pierce opened the envelope and quickly sifted through the bonds. "O.J. was unaware of the fee at that time. He's aware of them now." He placed the envelope on the desk. "How may I help you today?"

"A couple of things. First, I want to surrender these bonds." He held up his hand to forestall Mr. Pierce's argument. "I understand you will pay no interest on the short time I've held them, but I find I need the cash now more than I'll need the interest later. I plan to marry soon."

Mr. Pierce nodded. "I see."

"I trust the large fee will cover any minor penalty or inconvenience caused by surrendering these documents." Jason matched the older man's now brittle smile.

"Of course." He withdrew a pen stand with ink from a drawer and set it on the desk. "Please sign at the bottom of each certificate releasing your claim." Mr. Pierce rose. "I'll get your cash." He opened the door to the back of the house and disappeared.

Jason dipped the nib in the well and signed each twenty-five-dollar bond, spreading the documents across the desk to allow his signature to dry.

Moments later, Mr. Pierce returned. "On a normal business transaction of this type, handled outside of the Boston Exchange or a bank, it's standard for the client to send word they wish to relinquish their paper for cash. Luckily, I have enough to cover this transaction on hand, although it will leave me short for the remainder of the day."

"Apologies for not knowing your rules." Jason held out his hand.

Mr. Pierce counted out two hundred dollars in paper and fifty in coined currency.

"Thank you." Jason folded the bills, slid them into his trouser pocket, and dropped the coins into an inner compartment of his overcoat.

"Now to my second reason for coming in today." He resumed his seat and leaned forward, elbows resting on Otis Pierce's desk. "I understand you've made a loan for a substantial sum in my name."

"That's true. It's part of our service, a portion of what your initial service fee obtained for you. Our ability to act on your behalf—to supply funds in your name and purchase exclusive stocks and bonds—is available only to select clients."

"I see. And how do I benefit from these services?" Jason clenched and unclenched his gloved fist on the desktop. "Your tactics are dishonest. Your ethics abhorrent."

"You only say this because your father is a banker—bound by rules and regulations. With me, however, you will earn much more than by diligently saving and scraping along with a banker."

"How so?"

Mr. Pierce turned and pulled a thick binder from the bookshelves behind him. "These are registered Northern Pacific Railroad bonds, purchased in your name with the funds loaned to you by P&P Investments." He opened the binder, flipped through a few pages, and spun the book for Jason to view. "Numbered bonds, registered to you, purchased from Jay Cooke and Company. These pay seven percent interest over ten years with a guarantee offered by Cooke and Company." He grinned. "This rate is only available to Cooke's junior partners, of which I am one."

"And the terms of the loan?"

"Repayment with interest when the bonds mature. The interest rate is three percent. You make money for doing nothing."

"Not for nothing. My earnings remain less than the fee you charged."

"If you double your investment, you will earn twice as much. In fact, today only, I can offer you an even lower interest rate for the entire sum." Mr. Pierce's smile widened. "You lose nothing and stand to gain back all and more." He pulled a contract from the back of the bond binder. "Here it is in black and white." He took the pen from Jason's hand, scratched out the interest rate of three percent and wrote in two, then initialed the change." He handed Jason the pen back. "Look over the contract and then add your signature to the bottom of the last page."

Jason paged through the note to the back. The signature line was blank. "Otis told me you forged my signature."

"O.J. is young. He doesn't understand how we do business. Forging your signature on this document would be illegal."

"Then how did you make the loan?"

"I made the loan on your behalf based on your status as a select client. We've already discussed this." Pierce pressed his lips, and impatience glittered in his dark eyes. "Do you need me to explain it again?"

"No." Numbers and percentages danced through Jason's mind. The figures Pierce boasted added up. He had money in his pocket to furnish a home for Amy and an investment that would pay off nicely in ten years.

"Did you want to double your investment?"

"Of course, but I'm not sure a loan of this size would be a good idea."

"Nonsense! All you need to do is change the loan amount and add your signature." Otis tapped his finger on the signature line. "I'll send a telegraph to Cooke and Company to issue the additional bonds in your name today."

Jason read the last page. "Let me think this over. I'll come back after supper and let you know my decision." He flipped to the front of the document and scanned it again. "How do you offer such low interest rates?"

"The bonds fully secure this loan. Our unsecured loans are offered at a rate of twenty percent, interest due quarterly." He winked as he gathered the document from Jason. "You see why this is such an outstanding offer." He set the note aside and rose with his hand out. "I'm glad to have met you, Mr. Harris, and it is certainly my pleasure to do business with you."

Jason shook his hand and then took up his hat. "And you. Thank you for your time."

"Certainly, Mr. Harris, and congratulations on your engagement."

Jason pulled the door closed behind him. The evening had fallen across the city. Lights flickered on along the street as city dwellers moved from office or shop to home.

He buttoned his overcoat as he walked toward the pier, his thoughts on Mr. Pierce's offer and his upcoming evening with Amy. His stomach grumbled, and he grinned. Dinner at Revere's would satisfy his hunger, and after that, he would walk through the blackened city to his sweetheart's house.

***

Amy Prescott

—

Wrigley sat at the small kitchen table, finishing his supper as Peg dried dinner dishes at the kitchen sink.

Amy perched on the edge of her seat across from Wrigley and prayed for patience. Her prayer went unanswered. "Tell me again what Jason said." Amy folded her hands on the table and willed herself to be still.

Wrigley swallowed a spoonful of chowder and lifted an eyebrow at Amy. "I already told ye. He said yes."

"Yes, he would come by soon, or yes, he would be here after dinner?"

"I told him to come to the house after dinner, and he said yes. That's all I know." He scooped another spoonful into his mouth.

"Then where could he be?"

The clock on the mantel in the dining room struck nine times.

Amy shook her head and rose to her feet. "He's changed his mind."

Peg laughed and laid the cloth on the counter to dry. "He'll come to you. If not tonight, then tomorrow. He hasn't changed his mind any more than you have."

The knock at the door set all the depressed and stilled butterflies in her stomach into motion.

"I'll get it," Peg said, lifting the apron over her head.

Amy ignored Peg and spun on her heel to race across the house to the entrance. She smoothed her hair and straightened her skirt, then opened the door.

Has he been in a fight?

Jason's coat and hair were disheveled. His hat sat oddly to one side of his head, and he wobbled a bit from one side to the other. "I'm sorry I'm late," his words slurred slightly.

When he grinned, she knew. "You're drunk!"

"No. I've had a few drinks, it's true. I'm not so drunk that I couldn't find my way to your door."

"But not sober enough to be on time."

"They wouldn't let me leave. The men kept buying me drinks, and the women—" He rolled his eyes and chuckled. "May I come in?" Red and white smudges of women's cosmetics marred the shoulder and collar of Jason's suit coat.

"I'm not sure." She stepped out on the stoop and pulled the door slightly closed behind her. "Where have you been?"

"I went to Revere's for dinner." He put his hand against the brick, and the weaving stopped. "I supped with Ayden MacKenna and the lad who works behind the bar. I shouldn't have told them, but I did. That's how everything started."

"Told them what?" Amy crossed her arms. The night air was crisp and chilled her shoulders.

"How I'd asked you to be my wife, and although you hadn't given me an answer yet, I thought you might say yes. That's when the toasting began."

"I see. And the women?"

The front door opened, and her mother looked from one to the other. "What on earth are you two doing out in the cold. Come inside so we can shut the door."

After Jason hung his coat in the closet beneath the stairs, Amy led him to the parlor.

Peg walked in with a tea service and frosted sugar cookies. "Let it steep for a moment before you pour." She smiled at Jason, and her grin widened as she looked at Amy. "If you need anything...."

"Thank you," Amy said to Peg. Her regard shifted to Jason. "Late or not, I'm glad you came." She held her skirt as she sat on the settee then patted the cushion beside her. "Please, have a seat and a cup of tea."

Jason settled beside her, but his hand stilled hers above the tea service. "I'm heartsick at being late. You're more important to me than the next toast or endless congratulations. When I realized the time, I left straight away. Please forgive me." He took her hand in his.

How are his hands so warm and mine so cold?

His lateness didn't matter. How often had Amy's father come home late from the warehouse or drunk from a night spent with friends? "Of course, you're forgiven."

Jason kissed her fingers, then smiled, never taking his gaze from her face. "Tell me your answer, my darling. Will you consent to be my wife?"

Her answer to Jason was simple, and honestly, she knew it all along. "Yes."

Chapter 32

Amy Prescott

—

August 1, 1873

Amy and Peg had altered her mother's ivory gown to fit Amy's narrower waist and slender figure. They added a ruffle of rose satin at the bottom to lengthen the hem, a matching dust ruffle to her petticoat, and a gathered rose satin bell to the three-quarter length sleeves. The results delighted them both.

The beautiful gown lay draped across Amy's bed.

Dressed in only her chemise, drawers, and corset, Amy sat at her dressing table as Peg put the final additions on her hair.

"I want to leave it long in back," Peg spoke around the hairpins held in her teeth. "The curls are holding well."

Amy's gaze met Peg's in the mirror. "Whatever you think is best, only nothing too elaborate."

"Trust me. Your hair will be lovely." Peg pinned both sides of the hair back, allowing Amy's curled locks to drape over her shoulders. "I think a few curls in front." Using a pick, she pulled loose tendrils from the hairline. After folding the hair length in curling paper, she captured the end with the hot curling tong and rolled the iron up the paper to within an inch of Amy's forehead. Repeating the process, she created several ringlets. "We'll put the veil on after you've dressed." Finished with the iron, she returned it to the holder and doused the flame on the oil lamp heater.

A knock sounded, and her mother entered the room, closing the door behind her. "Something new." She held out a flat white box to her daughter.

Amy took the present and opened the box, revealing a silver and pearl tiara with matching earrings. "This is beautiful. Thank you, Mother." She put the open box on the dressing table and kissed her mother's cheek. "I love you."

Her mother hugged her shoulders. "And I love you, darling." When they separated, Margaret smiled at Peg. "Let's get our bride dressed."

Peg and Margaret slipped the light linen underskirt over Amy's head, followed by her mother's original cage crinoline and two very full petticoats. Finally, the lengthened bridal skirt settled over the underclothes, and Peg fastened the binding in back. Peg lifted Amy's hair as Margaret held the bodice jacket for Amy's arms, then moved around in front to secure the long row of bone buttons.

"Have a seat, and I'll button up your shoes while Peg puts on your headpiece."

Peg lifted the sheer veil and draped it over Amy's hair and secured the tiara through the netting. Then she reached over and lifted the front of the lace curtain, folding it back over the jeweled headpiece. "Your earrings and your necklace next, then your gloves."

Amy clipped the pearls to her ears and handed the locket up to Peg. "Can you latch this?"

"Of course. We should have thought to put this on before the veil."

Margaret lifted the back of the mantle and Amy's hair as Peg slipped the hook into the eyelet on the book chain.

Amy settled the precious gift from Jason on the front of her jacket. She steadied her breath as she pulled on her long gloves.

It was time.

Her father waited at the foot of the stairs in his formal cut jacket. He pulled on his white gloves and held his arm to Amy.

One hand on her skirt, the other on her father's arm, Amy held up her chin and battled waves of both joy and misgivings. But she had no desire to turn back.

She and Jason had decided to have a small wedding service. Although she thought at first an outdoor wedding would be unusual and perfect, the weather that summer had been unpredictable. When Jason suggested the courthouse, Amy had reluctantly agreed.

The Prescotts' carriage waited for the bride at the end of the front walk. Sitting in the high seat, Wrigley patted the top of his hat and turned left to right to show off his new black suit as Amy approached.

At the carriage, Amy grinned up at the family coachman. "You are quite dashing, Wrigley."

"And you're a lovely bride, Miss Amy," Wrigley replied.

Her father assisted her into the vehicle, then Peg and her mother before he climbed aboard and closed the door. He grinned at Amy. "You look beautiful, but your color is a little high. How are you feeling?"

"Stop teasing your daughter, Robert," Margaret admonished. "Her color is rosy, as it should be. She looks lovely."

Amy looked to Peg. "Am I blotched and red?"

"You're not." Peg took her hand. "They're having fun with you. Do you want your veil down?"

"Yes. Please." Veil down, she looked out the carriage window and managed her nerves.

A busy Saturday, the streets between the Prescott home and the courthouse thronged with people. Often, Wrigley had to slow their pace or stop to allow cross traffic to decrease. Also, being Saturday, the courthouse would have customarily been empty.

Today, however, Amy would say her vows to Jason before a judge in front of close friends and family. For her, that amounted to perfect.

Although Jason swore he never wanted a large church wedding with his parents' Boston Brahmins friends in attendance, she worried. The estrangement between Jason and his parents continued unresolved. And though her family had invited them to attend their son's wedding, their coachman, Riley, had returned their unopened invitation.

When the carriage stopped in front of the courthouse, a stranger opened the door and smiled at the occupants. "Hello, and congratulations on your wedding day. My name is Harry Tull. Mr. MacKenna asked me to remain with your carriage, so your coachman could attend the ceremony." He placed the step block on the ground and stood back as her father exited the vehicle.

"Robert Prescott," her father said, shaking the young man's hand. "Very thoughtful of you and Mr. MacKenna." He called up to Wrigley, "Tie off the reins for the moment. This young man will see to the rig while we're inside." He turned to the occupants and helped her mother out, followed by Peg. He braced his hands on the sides of the carriage door and smiled in at Amy. "I didn't mean to make you angry. You're the loveliest bride I've ever seen. Your young man will be properly impressed."

Amy placed her gloved hand in his and stepped from the carriage. It was warm beneath her layers of clothing. Bright sunshine bathed the day in its golden light as the sounds of new construction echoed from a few blocks over.

The stone steps of the courthouse and the tall white columns were her next task.

One step at a time.

Her father wrapped her fingers around his arm and walked beside her.

Beyond the columns waited Ayden MacKenna. He was dressed, like her father, in a formal black tailcoat, and his smile took in the Prescott bridal party. "Good afternoon. Beautiful day for a wedding."

"Mr. MacKenna," Amy acknowledged Ayden. "It is good to see you. Both Jason and I welcome your presence on our special day."

"I am pleased to have been invited." He held open the tall front door. "The groom and the best man are inside." Ayden leaned toward Margaret. "The judge is someone we know or used to know—Garrett Brown."

Amy and Robert entered the cool interior of the courthouse.

Her mother's reply was lost as Margaret and Ayden fell back to speak with Wrigley.

"Do you know the judge?" Amy asked her father and then looked over her shoulder to Peg.

Her father shook his head. "Never heard of him. Must be a friend from their childhood together."

Amy raised a brow at Peg, but the maid shook her head. "I don't know any judges, or anyone named Brown."

They stopped before the closed courtroom doors. There would be no music or flowers—no guests wishing the couple happiness. But the people Amy loved would be there, and that was what mattered to her. She hoped Jason wouldn't be disappointed not having a spectacular Boston Brahmins' wedding with all his mother's friends.

Ayden rested his hand on the doorknob. "I'll escort your mother to her seat. Wrigley and Peg can follow us in." He grinned at Peg. "Jason and his best man, Keith Hall, are at the front of the courtroom with Judge Brown."

"That's where Peg should stand too," Amy said.

Peg nodded and chuckled. "Yes, I remember."

"Give us a few minutes to be seated. Then your father will escort you to Jason."

"Oh wait! I almost forgot." Margaret opened her large bag and removed two floral smudge bundles bound with ribbons and lace. The scent of rose and lavender escaped from her purse, and the fresh aroma filled the air. "These are for you girls." She handed one to Peg, and the larger bouquet bound with white and rose ribbons that matched the rose accents on her dress, to Amy. She turned to Ayden. "Now I'm ready." She took Ayden's arm, and they passed through the door.

Several moments later, Peg took her uncle's arm, and with a last smile of encouragement at Amy, they entered the courtroom.

Her father put his hand over her cold fingers that gripped his jacket. "I remember when I first saw you in your mother's arms. I never thought I'd have a child." He patted her hand softly. "You've been a blessing to me every single day of your life. You make me proud."

Amy blinked, thankful the veil hid the emotion that welled in her eyes. "I love you, Papa." She sniffed, and Robert pulled a handkerchief from his pocket.

"Your mother gave me this before we left the house. I'm sure she meant it for you."

Amy took the embroidered cotton handkerchief and dabbed her eyes. As tears cleared from her sinus, the floral scent from the smudge bouquet made her smile.

How lucky I am to have parents who allowed me to look forward without regret.

"They should be ready for us," her father said and opened the door.

Someone, Amy suspected her mother and Peg, had tied roses and white ribbons from each chair lining the aisle she would walk.

Judge Brown waited beyond the gallery divider in front of his raised bench in his official black robe.

Jason stood on the right, with Keith Hall beside him.

Peg to the left beside Judge Brown and Amy's mother came to her feet in the first row.

On the right side of the aisle, Jason's mother and father rose.

"Spencer told me they were coming," her father confided to Amy in a whisper.

"You knew?" Amy glanced at her father.

"Yes, but it was to be a surprise. Spencer asked me not to speak of their plans."

Amy's gaze settled on Jason's as they passed the first row and then the railing.

Her father shook Jason's hand and then turned to his daughter. Blinking tears from his eyes, he carefully lifted the veil and folded the lacy mesh away from her face. "You'll always be my little girl, you know." He kissed the top of her head and then placed her hand in Jason's before taking his seat beside Margaret.

Amy hardly noticed. When Jason smiled, her heart constricted with the pure joy of holding this man's hand.

Peg's light touch on her arm drew her attention from her groom. "Give me your flowers and your glove."

"Yes." Amy handed her smudge bouquet to her maid of honor and unbuttoned her left glove, slipping the lower part from her hand. She gave that to Peg before she faced the judge.

"Miss Prescott." Judge Brown tipped his head, looking over his wire-frame spectacles. Lines creased from his blue eyes when he smiled. "Since this will be a simple ceremony, and because of the busy schedule yesterday in the courtroom, I apologize for not providing time for a rehearsal, but I promise, all will go well. You will take with you a memory of this day to cherish for a lifetime." He looked up and spoke to the room. "Please be seated."

"We, the family and friends of this young couple, are here today to see Amy and Jason join hands and be bound together by their love as husband and wife. And although my duties as an official of the Commonwealth of Massachusetts are secular, I have given much thought to how I can make this ceremony one that will give everyone in attendance a loving and cherished memory." He held out his hand. "If I may have the rings."

Peg and Keith placed two rings in Judge Brown's hand and then moved back to either side of Jason and Amy.

"Rings have been given as promises and sureties since early times. They are a circle. Magical and never-ending, never changing. A ring has no beginning and no end. Like the circle, true love itself is infinite. It goes on, defying boundaries and restrictions. It flourishes and blooms both in the light and in the dark. Love is a gift we give, not only to each other but to ourselves, and an honor we bestow from the bottom of our hearts and souls.

"Today, we ask the infinite light of the divine to shine upon this union and allow me to offer a blessing to this ceremony and to the rings I hold.

"Bless this marriage with the gifts of the east. Bring this young couple a lifetime of bright beginnings that renew each day with the sun's rising, give them a communication of the heart, mind, body, and soul.

"Bless this marriage with gifts of the south. Provide them richness in their souls, a light in their hearts—the heat of passion, and the warmth and comfort of a loving home.

"Bless this marriage with gifts of the west. Show them the soft and pure cleansing of a rainstorm, the rushing excitement of a raging river, and the way to a commitment as deep as the ocean itself.

"Bless this marriage with gifts of the north. Allow them to build a solid foundation for their lives, abundance, and growth of their home, and the stability they will find by holding one another at the end of the day."

Amy swallowed and fought the urge to glance over her shoulder at Ayden and her mother to confirm her suspicions about Judge Brown. The blessings were beautiful and everything she would have wanted—still, they were not something a magistrate of the court would say.

She looked at Jason, and their eyes met.

His smile of confidence and happiness dispelled any concern about his approval.

"However," Judge Brown continued, "no ceremony can create your marriage; only you can do that—through love and patience; through dedication and perseverance; through talking and listening, helping and supporting and believing in each other. Through tenderness and laughter, through learning to forgive, learning to appreciate your differences, and by learning to make the important things matter and to let go of the rest. All this ceremony can do is to witness and affirm the choice you make to stand together as husband and wife."

He held out his hand, palm up, displaying the two rings, one gold, and the other one silver. "Jason, please take the ring you chose for Amy. Do you promise to show Amy your honor and fidelity, to share her laughter and joy, to support and stand by her in times of difficulty, to dream and hope together with her, and to spend each day loving her more than the day before?"

Jason slid the silver ring onto her finger. "I do."

"Amy, please take the ring you chose for Jason. Do you promise to show Jason your honor and fidelity, to share his hopes and dreams, to laugh with him and share endless days of joy, to stand side by side with him in times of trouble, and to spend each day loving him more than the day before?"

"Yes, I do." Amy put the gold ring on Jason's finger.

"Your vows are spoken. Your promises to one another are made. Now, if you would take each other's left hands, holding your rings close. Over your left hands, take each other's right hand."

Peg unwound a long white ribbon from the bride's bouquet and offered it to the judge.

Judge Brown took the ribbon. He smiled at Amy and Jason as he wrapped the shimmering band around the bride and groom's wrists, binding them together loosely, then he tied a knot. "This ribbon is a symbol of your life, your love, and the eternal connection the two of you have made with one another. This connection is not formed by this simple ribbon or even the knots that bind your hands. They are formed instead by your vows, your souls, and your two hearts, now bound together as one.

"By the power of your love and commitment, and the power vested in me by the Commonwealth of Massachusetts, I pronounce you husband and wife. You may kiss the bride."

Jason's lips brushed hers in a chaste kiss, but his eyes held fire as he lifted his head and gazed into hers.

Judge Brown unwound the ribbon without untying the knot and spoke to the small gathering, "May I present Mr. and Mrs. Jason Harris."

As the small gathering clapped with enthusiasm, Judge Brown directed Amy and Jason to the attorney tables, where three copies of the marriage license were laid out. "Signatures from the bride and groom and both witnesses on each copy, please."

***

Jason Harris

—

Jason signed his name on the marriage license with a flourish, then handed Amy the pen. As he stepped away from the table, he glanced over at his parents and met his father's gaze. His parents had entered the courtroom right before Amy's family. There had been no opportunity to speak with them. Hell, he hadn't spoken with them in months. Shock at seeing them at his wedding would have been understating his reaction.

"I'm going to speak to my father," Jason whispered.

Amy nodded. "I'll be a moment longer."

Jason held out his hand as he approached Spencer. "I'm glad you decided to come."

Spencer hesitated, looking from Jason's extended hand to his face. He spoke in a whisper to his son, "Your father-in-law spoke of attending this wedding during our last meeting. I didn't think it wise not to attend. After all, you have married the daughter of my partner in this China venture."

Jason withdrew his hand. "And you, mother. I see you've worn your second-best brooch, or is it your third-best?"

"I don't understand why you didn't have your wedding ceremony in a church," she hissed at him, then smiled politely at Margaret across the aisle. "How do I explain your behavior to my friends?"

"As best you can, I suppose. Good day to you both." He returned to his bride as she handed Judge Brown the pen.

"I would have joined you to say hello." Amy peered around Jason's shoulder and smiled at her new in-laws. "I was surprised to see them."

"Don't bother. My parents are not here for you and me. I doubt they'll join us for dinner."

"Why do you say that?" Amy redirected her smile to Jason.

"The brooch my mother is wearing." He shook his head and slipped his arm around his wife's shoulders. "I'll explain later."

Judge Brown gathered the newly signed documents, "Excuse me. Let me get these out of our way," and placed them on his raised Judge's bench.

"The service was beautiful," Amy told him. "Perfect, in fact. Thank you."

"My pleasure," he remarked over his shoulder. Then gave his attention to the couple. "I didn't connect your family name with your mother. I only knew her before she married and became Margaret Prescott."

"You knew my mother?"

"Yes," Judge Brown nodded. "And Mr. MacKenna, but it was long ago. I thought they'd both left Boston. Imagine my surprise when they walked in today."

Jason blinked at the judge's comment and studied Ayden and Amy's mother.

Were they all involved in the mysterious secret society back in the '40s? Was that their connection?

"Everyone!" Robert Prescott raised his hand and spoke to the entire room. "I've made reservations for a celebratory dinner at Parker House. Everyone is welcome."

"I'm afraid we will be unable to join you," Spencer shook Robert's hand then touched his wife's back, directing her to the door at the back of the courtroom. "We have another engagement."

"Another time then, Spencer. Good to see you today." Robert clapped his free hand on Spencer's shoulder.

My father must love that.

Jason followed Amy through the courtroom divider and stepped aside to allow the judge to join them.

Robert spoke to Wrigley and Peg, "Will you dine with us?" Then smiled at Judge Brown. "My wife tells me she knew you before we wed. Please share a meal with us and renew your acquaintance."

"I'd be delighted." Judge Brown shook hands with Ayden. "You were younger than Jason the last time I saw you."

Ayden grinned. "And you weren't quite as gray, Garrett."

"You've got some gray as well, I see." Judge Brown pointed to Ayden's thick hair.

Ayden chuckled. "Twenty-five years will age a man."

Wrigley leaned in and spoke into Robert's ear.

"That's fine. Come back for us in two hours." Robert nodded to the coachman.

"Keith, do you intend to join us?" Jason inquired as his witness escorted Peg from the front of the courtroom.

"Certainly." Keith gave Peg's fingers on his arm a light pat. "With such a lovely dinner companion, how could I refuse? But I can't stay late. I have plans for the evening." He winked at Jason.

Jason grasped Amy's hand. "Then let us proceed." He escorted his wife to the back of the courtroom, noticing his parents had already disappeared.

"Jason is in a rush, it seems," Ayden chuckled.

Garrett walked beside Ayden. "Wouldn't you be?"

Jason and Amy exchanged a smile.

Amy's cheeks had become rosy with the banter behind them. "I've never dined at the Parker House. Have you?"

"Yes. I've attended social functions there with my parents when I was younger. Both the restaurant and hotel are top-notch. If you like, I could ask if there's a room available for us tonight."

Amy shook her head. "No. I want to go home. To our home." Her face colored. "I've looked forward to being there with you."

Across the street at the restaurant, a table for eight sparkled with dinnerware and candles. Although the reservation was for ten guests, The Parker House accommodated the wedding party.

Jason held Amy's chair then sat beside her. The circular table allowed everyone to take part in the conversation.

Robert asked their server to provide champagne flutes for everyone and chill a second bottle at the table. Once glasses were in hand, Robert came to his feet. "I want to thank each of you for being here today and tonight.

"When Amy told us she wished to have a small wedding, with only close friends and family in attendance, I admit I was dismayed. Like all fathers, I suppose, I had dreamed of the day I would walk my beautiful daughter down the aisle of a large church filled with familiar faces.

"However, the ceremony could not have been more beautiful," he lifted his glass toward Judge Brown, "and the courtroom a perfect venue for my new son. Most of all, I know the good wishes from everyone were sincere and heartfelt."

He turned his glass toward Jason and Amy. "To my daughter, Amy, and her husband, Jason. May happiness and joy be with you, always."

Everyone lifted their glass, chanting, "Here, here."

As Robert sat, Keith Hall rose and grinned at Jason. "As best man, I'd like to propose a toast to Jason and Amy.

"As it says in Corinthians 13:7: *'Love never gives up, never loses faith, is always hopeful and endures through every circumstance.'* Those are wise words to remember. I also wish to offer this: your happiness together does not come to you for having found the perfect person, but by learning to see an imperfect person perfectly." He raised his glass. "To love."

"To love," the voices around the table echoed.

The waiter brought bread and took their orders, returning with separate drink orders.

"We'll have to catch up some time," Garrett said to Ayden. "The last I heard; you'd taken a ship to parts unknown."

"That's not entirely false, as far as rumors go. That tale, however, will need to be for another time." Ayden winked at Jason and grinned at Garrett. "Let's say I've recently returned from overseas. I'd hoped to find my family, but I've had no luck."

"Your father came to me not long after you departed, sure there had to be foul play involved with your disappearance. Of course, I couldn't tell him what had become of you. I don't have the skill to gather that...type of information. I don't believe I saw your parents again after that."

Ayden shook his head, his eyes on the half glass of whiskey in his hand. "My mother passed later that same summer—I discovered. My father and brother left the area soon after."

"I'm sorry for that."

"What about you, Garrett?" Margaret leaned forward. "I lost track of you, of everyone really, after Amy was born and my family moved north."

"After the loss of two of the most talented families from our—group, it was time for me to step aside as leader. Since my background was in law, I returned to the bar and worked my way up to the bench."

"My family's departure wasn't your fault," Margaret responded.

"Nor was mine," Ayden added. "By the way, I met your replacement the other night. I was unimpressed." He downed the remains of his drink then lifted it to the waiter for a refill.

Jason followed the conversation with interest. They spoke of the secret society Lisbeth belonged to; he was sure of it.

"But you're biased," Garrett chuckled.

"What group did you lead?" Robert asked. "Certainly not the Brahmins. I would have known you and Ayden both before now."

Garrett grinned at Ayden and Margaret. "I was the head of a minimal social circle, similar to a card club, I suppose. We were much smaller and less influential than the Boston Brahmins."

"That explains how all of you know each other—from an old social club?" Robert sipped his champagne.

"Essentially," Ayden replied as the restaurant staff brought their orders to the table.

The conversation quieted while they ate. The restaurant had filled with guests while they talked, and the buzz of voices, along with the clink of china and glassware, filled the silence at their table.

Finally, Jason set his knife and fork across his plate and patted his lips with his napkin. When he glanced at Amy, he found her watching him. "Is your dinner satisfactory?"

She lifted her fork with a small piece of chicken on the tines. "Delicious."

"If you don't mind, I'd like to leave when you finish. The others can stay and reminisce."

Amy grinned and looked at him from the corner of her eye. "I don't mind." Then her cheeks darkened.

Jason's breath caught and desire, suppressed with formalities until now, surged through his blood.

Soon, she will be in my arms as my wife.

Garrett placed his napkin beside his plate. "This was an excellent meal. Thank you, Mr. Prescott, for inviting me to dine with you."

"The pleasure is ours, and please, call me Robert."

"Of course." Garrett scanned the table, his eyes lighting on each of them. "I can't remember when I have shared such a wonderful time with good friends. I must thank you for that as well. I don't seem to get out as much as I should."

"Speaking of socializing," Keith pushed his plate away, "I was going to go by The Union Club tonight. I could use some company. Perhaps we could find a game of euchre."

"Euchre?" Ayden asked.

"The latest craze in trump. Easy to learn," Garrett informed Ayden, then to Keith, "I'd love to join you."

"I'll go if only to watch and learn." Ayden finished his drink and waved off the waiter, ready to refill his glass.

"I told Wrigley we'd be done by seven, although I expect he'll already be waiting." Robert snapped shut his pocket watch and signaled for the tab.

The three single gentlemen rose to their feet.

"Then we'll be off." Keith pulled his hat check tab from his pocket. "Congratulations again on your lovely wedding. Don't look for me to be back at the house before noon tomorrow." He winked at Jason and turned to Robert. "Thank you, sir, for the fine meal."

"Not at all." Robert rose and shook Keith's hand. "It has been a pleasure to meet you."

"Madam, Miss." Keith bowed to Margaret and Peg, smiled at the newlyweds again, then headed for the hat check.

Garrett and Ayden made their goodbyes and followed Keith to retrieve their garments.

"We will be leaving as well." Jason stopped their waiter. "Could you hold one of the cabs for us?"

"Yes, sir." The young man hurried to the entrance and stepped outside.

Amy and her mother were hugging when he turned back to the table. Whatever they were whispering made Amy blush.

"This is rather awkward," Robert said as they shook hands. "I'd wish you a good evening, but I know what that entails, and I admit I have mixed feelings."

Both men chuckled.

"Then I shall wish you a good evening and thank you for dinner."

"Certainly, son. Anytime."

"Your veil?" Jason asked Amy as he retrieved his top hat from the cloakroom.

"No. Peg will take it home—umm. Peg will return the veil and my flowers later this week." Amy took his arm as they left the restaurant and crossed the walk to the cab.

The cabbie held Amy's hand as she ascended the step to the carriage, and Jason followed her in. Moments later, the rig jerked into motion and moved down the street.

From the happy chatter in the restaurant to the silence in the carriage, Jason struggled to find something witty or charming to say to ease the sudden tension. He licked his lips and swallowed.

Amy kept her attention directed out the window, her silhouette dark against the passing streetlights.

"The breeze feels good," she stated. Her eyes closed, and she lifted her chin a fraction.

"Breeze?" he echoed and immediately felt like a dolt. Amy, his virgin bride, appeared light-hearted and cool as a cucumber while he struggled to make simple conversation.

A virgin.

There lay the issue. Jason knew what the evening would bring, and although Amy may have some idea of what would transpire, she had never experienced the act.

I've always been a willing student, never an experienced teacher.

A first for him as well. A pleasurable task at which he must excel.

I want to open this gift for Amy, unwrap the pleasure we will share in each other's arms.

He allowed his gaze to linger on his bride and reined in his raging desire.

Chapter 33

Amy Harris

—

The movement of night air through the carriage window cooled the perspiration on her face. She closed her eyes and took a deep breath of air. Hot. Humid.

Her senses were alive with anticipation and an unrelenting fear of the unknown. Of course, she knew what tonight would bring, in a vague sort of way. Even her complete understanding of animal reproduction didn't give precise enough details on what to expect.

Jason's palm covered her hand, resting on the seat between them. "Your hand is cold."

His was hot.

She shifted her shoulders to unstick the fabric from her back.

How can my fingers be icy when the heat of the carriage is overwhelming?

"A touch of nerves, I suspect." Amy chuckled self-consciously and dislodged Jason's hand to tug the handkerchief from her sleeve and blot her face. "I like Judge Brown very much. Do you work with him often?"

"Never." Jason shook his head. "He and I first met the day I took the bar and again when I asked him about using his courtroom for our wedding."

Amy lifted her chin to the slight breeze and closed her eyes.

"We could have stayed the night at the hotel. I could have the driver turn around if you like."

Startled, Amy looked at Jason. "No. I want to spend tonight in your home."

"Our home." He lifted her hand and touched his mouth to her chilled fingers.

"Yes." She closed her eyes again, this time focusing on the soft pressure of his lips. The night air lifted the loose tendrils from her neck. "Ah." She shivered then smiled at Jason. "You gave me a chill."

"That's good." He chuckled and enfolded her hand in his.

They shared the remainder of the ride in companionable silence.

When the cab came to a standstill in front of Jason's building, nerves took wing in her chest.

Is this fear or anticipation?

The carriage door opened, and the driver helped her down the step. Jason followed her out of the vehicle and paid the driver as Amy walked around the cab to the walkway. Both floors boasted a bay window, like the adjacent buildings. The homes on either side had lights beyond the curtained windows.

As the hansom cab pulled away, Jason took her elbow. "Welcome home, Mrs. Harris."

Amy smiled and accompanied Jason to the front door.

Unlocking the latch with a key from his pocket, he let the door swing open into darkness. "One day, I shall carry you over the threshold of our own home, but until then, this will have to do."

"You're going to carry me inside?"

"I'm fairly certain it was in the contract. The groom carries the bride."

Laughter bubbled up, and she covered her mouth with her hand. "Oh, Jason."

"Hold your petticoat, Mrs. Harris," Jason advised as he picked her up in his arms.

One hand pressed down on the bell of her skirt to prevent it from rising over her head, while the other wrapped around Jason's neck. Her merriment echoed down the street and filled the house as they moved inside.

Once in the house, he lowered her feet and shut the door. "Up the stairs as well?"

"No." Amy backed onto the first step on the staircase, her hand held in front of her, laughter still threatened. "These are steep, and I'm heavier than I look."

"I think I should try at least." He grinned and tossed his top hat toward the entry table. "I'm stronger than I look."

Another peal of glee escaped as she gripped her skirt, turned, and raced up the steps. She reached the top before she realized Jason had remained at the foot of the steps.

His eyes shone with happiness and emotion as he looked up at her, loosening his neckerchief. "Would you like water or wine? I have both in the kitchen for us."

"Water, please."

Jason bowed. "One moment, madam, and I shall join you."

When he left the entry, she paced into the darkened front room. She struck a match and turned the key on the wall sconce and lit the mantel. Where moments before the last rays of the sunset had colored the city sky through the window, she now saw her reflection. She straightened.

I've seen this before.

Mesmerized, she walked toward her image. Her gown swayed across the room with her steps—the heat of the upstairs room oppressive after the hot August day.

Movement in the reflection behind her drew Amy's attention.

Jason set a carafe of water and two glasses on the table. Their gazes met in the window's mirror as he moved closer and caressed her arm, then his head dropped, and his lips warmed on the side of her neck.

Her eyes fluttered closed, and her head fell back against his shoulder. "I've dreamed of this."

His soft chuckle teased the wisps of hair at her throat and made her shiver. "As have I." He released her and turned off the light.

The last rays of sunlight had softened to a shimmer of gold along the horizon.

"We need whatever breeze we can catch more than we need light." He lifted the bottom divided pane of both angled windows then took her hand. "Come. I'll open the bedroom window. Sometimes, I can get a cross breeze."

Light from the tall streetlamps illuminated the room enough for her to see shapes and avoid tripping.

Jason led her past the door at the top of the stairs and into the bedroom.

When he released her hand, she stopped. No outside light penetrated the inky blackness of the bedroom until Jason drew back the drapery, and his silhouette shown against the city lights.

As he cranked open the casement window, the slightest breath of air passed her cheek before the room became still again. Sweat trickled between her breast, and she wiped the perspiration from her brow with the back of her hand. "We forgot the water."

"Sit on the bed and allow me to fetch it."

Even though she could see the outline of the narrow bed, she took his hand and let him lead her to it.

"I'll return in a moment."

While he was in the other room, Amy pulled off her gloves and slipped her locket and earrings inside, then laid them across a low bench at the foot of the bed. Her corset didn't allow her to bend enough to reach her shoes, so instead, she unbuttoned the high collar on the bodice and pulled the pins from her hair.

"Here." Jason's voice was soft and filled with tenderness as he handed her the water. He guided her hand to the glass.

"Thank you." The cool water refreshed her mouth and throat. She swallowed and held the glass out to Jason. Her eyes had adjusted to the darkness, and although she couldn't see his face, she could see his shape before her.

He took the glass from her hand and set the container on the dresser. "Let me unbutton your shoes." He lifted her foot without waiting for her to speak.

She fell back on her elbows and rested her head against the wall. As the low boot came off, she groaned. "That feels marvelous."

The footwear dropped to the floor, and he ran his thumb firmly down the arch of her foot.

She groaned again. Eyes closed, she smiled as the other boot came off.

"Stockings?" His hands slid up her silk hose and untied the ribbons below her knees. The fine material slid easily over her calf from first one foot and then the other.

The heavy air cooled on her damp toes, and she wriggled them.

"Give me your hands, and I'll help you up. Undressing you will be easier if you stand."

Amy raised her arms, and the springy crinoline bell lifted her skirt and petticoats from her legs.

Jason took her hands and pulled her to her feet. "There's the tiniest trace of air moving through the apartment."

"I don't feel anything."

"You'll feel it once we get your clothes off."

Thankful for the darkness, if only to hide her hot cheeks, Amy reached out when he released her hands, expecting to feel Jason's jacket. Instead, her palms pressed against his naked chest. "I'm sorry."

Jason caught her hands as she pulled away and returned them to his upper body. "Don't be sorry," his voice soft in the dark. "I want you to touch me." His fingers worked the buttons of her bodice, quick and sure, and opened the garment. "I certainly intend to touch you."

The night breeze cooled the damp camisole as her fingers spread across Jason's chest, careful not to press inward with her sight for fear the glow of magic would shine bright in the darkness.

He wrapped his arms around her, beneath her bodice, and pulled her to his chest. "I'm going to kiss you now."

Her head tipped back in anticipation as her eyelids closed. She slid her fingers up his neck and into his hair, urging his lips to meet hers. What began as a tender kiss of affection transformed into a passionate embrace.

They no longer needed to hide their passion for one another.

No one would interfere.

Their lips lingered together as Jason pushed her bodice from her shoulders.

Lips still touching, Amy pulled her arms from the sleeves and tossed the garment onto the growing pile of clothes on the bench.

Jason unbuttoned her camisole, and that too landed in the collection at the end of the bed. "Crinolette or hoop?"

"Crinoline," Amy replied.

"That makes everything easier." He slipped the button on her silk skirt, then the two petticoats, and finally the crinoline. As he pulled the waistbands forward, the skirt and ruffled slips collapsed at her feet. A tug on the tie at her waist and the drawers followed the skirts to the floor.

Suddenly clad in only her knee-length chemise and corset, the light breeze from the open window touched her damp flesh, and she gasped. "Wait."

"Wait?" Jason's lips captured hers again as his skillful fingers unhooked the front of the corset. Releasing her from its binding, he tossed it aside.

She pulled her head back and turned her away. "This is too fast. I can't—"

He gently turned her face and bumped her nose with his. "We'll take the good parts much, much slower." His open mouth brushed hers. "Ever so slow." He tasted her top lip and then her bottom one. "I promise." He bent, lifted her out of the circle of clothing, and stepped forward.

"My skirt?" Amy asked.

Jason laid her on the bed. "Slid beneath the bed. Safe and out of the way." His hand glided over her knee and along her outer thigh to her hip.

Amy gasped. Without thought, she grabbed his wrist, then released him. "I'm sorry," she whispered.

"I understand." He sat on the edge of the bed and heaved a deep sigh. "You're not used to being touched so intimately, and as you've pointed out, my anticipation is forging ahead of my good sense." He found her hand and brought it to his lips. "But we have all night. There's no rush. And I want you to like this." He touched the tip of his tongue to the center of her palm. "I want you to like this very much."

***

Jason Harris

—

He folded her fingers closed and kissed her knuckles. "I love you, my dear." From the blackness beside him, Amy whispered, "I love you, too."

"And you trust me?"

"Yes."

Jason nodded. "That's good. I intend to keep your trust and earn your passion." His lips and teeth nibbled on her knuckles as he considered their situation. "Let's try something. Here, rise on your knees." Jason stood and held her hands to balance her, but their hands, slick with sweat, slipped, and she wobbled. "Turn around and brace your hands on the wall."

"Like this?" Her long cotton shift remained the only material between him and the length of her body. Her knees were wide to help steady her on the narrow bed.

Jason swallowed.

Take it slow.

"Yes. Perfect. Let me free your chemise from beneath your knees."

Amy rocked to release the cloth. "Now what?"

"I touch you." He quickly discarded his remaining clothes and eased his weight onto the bed behind her. His palms rested lightly on the chemise covering her hips. "You may tell me to stop at any time." He ran his hands down to her knees, then up, inside the chemise to her hips. Her body coated with a thin layer of moisture from the heat made her skin slick to the touch.

She inhaled sharply.

He ran his hands up her back to her neck, then down to her waist. As his mouth caressed her neck, his palms rode up her flat stomach and lifted her breast, bearing their weight in his hands. "You are perfect." He brushed her nipples, already pebbled with arousal from his touch.

Her head fell back against his shoulder, and she moaned. "I had no idea it would feel like this."

His left hand spanned the distance between her breasts, touching the hardened tips with a gentle motion, while his right hand followed the slight curve of her belly and stroked the soft hair between her legs. "I know."

She tensed.

We have plenty of time.

Jason ran his hand down Amy's leg and up the back of her thigh to her buttocks. His fingers brushed between her legs from behind, then gripped her bottom firmly and kneaded, pulling away from her center.

Her gasp turned into a low chuckle, and she turned her head, capturing his mouth with her own and wrapping her arm behind his head, arching her back.

Jason's erection quivered. Knowing he could last all night did nothing to quench his desire for Amy. Her beauty. Her gentle yet fierce nature. Her honesty and gentle spirit. All his, for as long as they both lived.

Their kiss deepened, and he slipped his fingers inside her, only far enough to wet the tips and circle them with slow deliberation around her pleasure center.

Amy gasped, bucking involuntarily into his hand.

"Let's dispense with the chemise." He lifted the garment over her head and pulled it from her lifted arms, tossing it behind him on to the floor. "There's a slight breeze through the house."

"I can feel it." With one hand braced against the wall, Amy twisted toward the back window and lifted her hair from her neck.

The scent of honeysuckle and summer rose drifted in on the night air and mixed with the trace of musk from his fingertips. "Lay with me, Amy." Her mouth captured his as he lifted her hips and lowered them both to the bed. "I need to make love to my wife."

Her back on the bed, Amy wrapped her arms around Jason's neck. "I thought we were doing that."

"Ah, my love." His lips touched hers, tasting the wine from dinner. "We have only begun. I suspect we shall see the morning before we sleep."

Chapter 34

Jason Harris

—

September 1873

Jason admired his enthusiastic wife from the top of the stairs as she tied the bonnet's ribbon beneath her chin and selected a light-colored parasol from the stand beside the open door.

"They're here, sweetheart," Amy called. She waited for him in a pool of morning sunshine that splashed across the tile and brightened the entrance.

"I see that." Jason hurried down to her and waved out the entrance to Wrigley.

Margaret and Peg waved back at him in response through the open carriage windows. The women planned to complete their shopping before the market became crowded and then retire to Margaret's house that afternoon for tea. Tonight, Margaret and Robert would host a family evening.

"Remember, dinner is at eight o'clock." Excitement danced in Amy's eyes as she tucked a strand of hair beneath her bonnet and grinned up at Jason.

"I'll be there by seven." He kissed her cheek. "Have fun."

"See you tonight." Amy waved to her mother and hurried down the walk to the carriage, a skip in her step.

Jason's smile lingered after he closed the door. He'd finally attained everything he wanted, married to a remarkable woman that he loved beyond reason, living away from his parents' tyrannical rule, and achieving the title of attorney-at-law. He picked up his business card from the desk and ran his thumb over the letters, Jason S. Harris, Esquire.

The clock in the foyer struck nine. Jason's first client would arrive soon, and he had a busy morning scheduled.

Early in the afternoon, he escorted his last client of the day to the front door. "I'll have the document filed with the county clerk this afternoon, sir."

The thin man put his hat over his balding head and extended a fragile hand to Jason. "Thank you, Mr. Harris." The elderly man navigated the steps to the walk, leaning heavily on his cane.

Jason rested his shoulder against the frame of the open door and inhaled deeply, unwilling to return inside. The sky, dark blue and cloudless, hovered above maple trees draped in early autumn's golden gown. The year had nearly come full circle since the day he bumped into Amy on the street, a turning point in his life.

A life I shall pour my heart and soul into for the rest of my days.

As he straightened to return to his desk, he caught a glimpse of Keith rushing down the street.

Keith never ran. At least Jason had never seen him doing so. The barrister hurried when late for a trial, but Keith's brisk but even-paced tread was the most Jason had ever witnessed.

Until now.

Coat flapping, hat in hand, Keith's silver hair bounced with each stride. When he spotted Jason in the doorway, he waved and walked, heel to toe, even faster, if that were possible.

As he turned up their stone walkway, he tried to speak, then shook his head and bent at the waist, hands on his knees and his head down.

Alarmed, Jason stepped down from the landing and gripped Keith's arm. "Are you ill?"

Keith shook his head. "I've news," he gasped as he caught his breath.

"Well, come inside and sit, have a glass of water and tell me your news." Jason helped steady him up the step then followed his friend inside.

Keith sprawled at the kitchen table; his long legs stretched out for a moment, then curled again, his head down.

"Are you certain you're well?" Jason set a glass of lukewarm water on the table and lowered himself to the chair across from the barrister.

Keith nodded, looking up and catching Jason's gaze with his own. "Trading was stopped on the New York Stock Exchange this morning." He pulled a folded newspaper from his frock pocket. "A big bank out of Philadelphia failed. I don't know the name —"

"Jay Cooke and Company," Jason whispered as he unfolded the newsprint and pressed it flat to the table.

"That's the one." Keith picked up the glass and sipped. "Other banks have begun to tumble." He leaned his back against the wall. "Another spike, driven into the heart of this city. This failure will affect your father—affect all of us."

Jason blinked. "I know." The lines of text blurred for a moment then came into sharp focus as he skimmed the newspaper's front page.

Jay Cooke and Company, as exclusive bond agent for the Northern Pacific Railroad, had become overextended. Unable to market enough railroad bonds to cover their investment in the railway, they now owned seventy-five percent of the NPRR, a railroad already heavily in debt.

Two days ago, the bank's situation became public knowledge. Investors withdrew funds at an alarming rate and created a run on Jay Cooke and Company, collapsing the bank.

As of this morning, the panic had grown to such an extent the New York Stock Exchange discontinued trading until the uproar could die down. Smaller banks without vast reserves were caught in the panic.

Jason tried to swallow, but his mouth and throat were too dry.

He held ten thousand dollars' worth of Northern Pacific Railroad bonds that now had no value.

Worse, he owed ten thousand dollars to Pierce and Peabody for the unethical loan to purchase those bonds.

An unsecured loan to an unscrupulous bastard.

"Worried about your father?" Keith pushed the half-full glass toward Jason.

"What?" Jason licked his lips. His gaze lifted from the water to Keith. "My father. Yes." He sipped from the glass then returned it to the table as he stood. "I should check on him." Dazed with disbelief, Jason automatically grabbed his hat as he stepped from their door.

At the edge of the street, he glanced to his right.

His father's new bank stood up the hill in that direction. Rebuilt with insurance money from the fire, the cost for both goods and labor had been exorbitant.

Jason had learned of these facts through conversations with Amy's father.

Although Robert Prescott had to have known of Jason's estrangement with his parents, Amy's father never mentioned that awkward situation. Robert did, however, frequently speak about his shipping venture with Spencer Harris and Spencer's excitement at his bank's grand reopening.

Father doesn't have vast reserves.

Still contemplating his destination from the road's edge, Jason looked left.

Down the block at the Pierce and Peabody offices, Otis Senior had to be devastated. The news of the Jay Cooke collapse would be a significant setback for his business. Undoubtedly, Jason wasn't the only fool to buy into the railroad bond scheme.

Best not go there.

His feet carried him away from Otis Pierce and toward his father's bank. If the bank remained open by some slim chance, perhaps his father would save Jason from the unsecured loan predicament.

A half-block away from the small bank, Jason halted.

Two dozen men with raised fists yelled angrily at each other and pounded on the bank's locked door.

One gentleman ripped the notice from the door and held it high in the air. "It says closed until further notice!" he yelled.

A groundswell of angry replies met this announcement. Glass shattered as a rock sailed through the front windows.

Jason turned away. Some of those men might recognize him, and being torn to bits by an angry mob in place of his father would help no one.

What can I do?

Dread clouded his mind. Otis would come for Jason, sooner or later, or the mysterious Peabody would. His father would never help him with that debt, even if he had the means, and by the look of the scene behind him, Spencer would be desperate to save himself.

Deep in thought, Jason turned the corner away from the angry mob and kept his head down. His pace quickened as he crossed the Common. At the end of the block that held the Prescott home, he stopped.

Along with Peg and Margaret, Amy waited beside the carriage as Wrigley removed packages secured on the top of the rig. One by one, Wrigley handed the parcels to the laughing women who hurried inside with their treasures.

Jason couldn't remember ever seeing Wrigley smile like that.

As the carriage pulled away, movement across the road caught Jason's attention. A man wearing a gray top hat stopped to examine a display of late-blooming roses and then continued down the block and around the corner.

Little Lisbeth Coleman and the bizarre secret society still watched the Prescott home. How did I ever mistake her for a man?

Jason ran a hand over his face, returning his thoughts to his current concern.

Could this latest financial disaster be as bad as '69?

The gold manipulation scandal had rocked the Grant administration and forced dozens of brokerage firms into bankruptcy.

Would this crisis be worse?

And what could he do about the sum he allegedly owed P&P?

Jason hadn't spoken to his parents since the wedding nearly two months ago, but he knew his father's advice would be to take whatever cash Jason needed from Amy's dowry.

Jason squeezed his eyes shut and spun on his heel.

No!

Amy's bridal gift from her father is hers. I won't involve her in my financial catastrophe.

He caught a hansom back to his apartment. There was time for him to compose himself, tidy his clothing up, and then take another cab back to the Prescotts' for dinner.

When he stepped down from the cab, he glanced down the street toward Pierce and Peabody's office. The P&P shingle no longer hung from the decorative iron bracket attached to the covered porch.

As the cab pulled away, a sharp object jabbed painfully into his back.

"Mr. Harris," Otis Pierce Senior's voice grated in his ear. "I hoped I might catch you at home. It has been a very rough week for banking and investments in general. I believe we have several things to discuss."

Jason stiffened.

Would Pierce dare press a knife to my back in broad daylight? A gun?

He glared over his shoulder into the older man's face. "I have plans for this evening, sir, and I need time to prepare. We can set an appointment for tomorrow."

Another poke. Harder this time—intended to move Jason down the street toward the P&P office.

Not a sharp point...a gun then, or a cane.

"Unfortunately, I must insist. The sooner we come to an understanding the better, for us both." Pierce shoved again.

Jason stumbled forward, then acquiesced. "An understanding then, but quickly. I have to be somewhere else in two hours."

"I understand. You're a busy man. An important man." Pierce marched Jason down the hill and into the P&P office. "Have a seat." Pierce rounded the large desk and placed the walking cane on the edge of the polished desktop. "We have a problem."

The P&P office hadn't changed since Jason's last visit, but Otis Senior looked vastly different. Gone was the well-groomed brokerage owner. This man needed both a bath and a shave. Stubble from at least two days' growth covered his cheeks while wrinkles and stains marred his clothes. More telling was the anger and desperation that seeped from his eyes.

"And what problem is that?"

"The money you owe me." Pierce sank into his chair and folded his fingers together on the desk. "More precisely, the interest on the money you owe me that comes due at the end of this month."

"What interest? What money do I owe you?" Rage and trepidation filled Jason's chest, and his lungs ached for air. "I gave your son five hundred dollars to make a special stock purchase which I cashed months ago. The rest of this imaginary debt is in your head."

"Twenty thousand dollars' worth of stock purchased in your name says differently, Mr. Harris."

"Twenty? I never signed a note or lending agreement whatsoever." Jason leaned forward and pounded his finger on the desktop. "I owe you *nothing*."

"My documents speak differently on the matter." The older man's grin chilled Jason. "I have your signature on *two* notes for ten thousand dollars each, with an addendum directing me to act on your behalf as your broker for Northern Pacific Railroad stock purchased through Jay Cooke and Company. I could give you the dates if you like."

"The dates wouldn't matter because the signatures don't exist. If they do, they're forgeries."

"Now, now. Anyone can see the signatures are yours, why they're an exact match. How would you prove they are not? Besides, I have a witness."

"Impossible." Jason clenched and unclenched his fists. The sound of a footstep outside the entry warned him, and he stepped aside as the door swung open.

Taller than Jason by a handspan and heavier than Otis Senior, a hatless swarthy-skinned man stood in the doorway. Beardless, with dark almond-shaped eyes and heavy black brows, the newcomer grinned at Jason, showing two rotted teeth.

"I don't believe you've met my associate, Mr. Edwardo Guerra Peabody."

Peabody pulled his hand from his pocket and flipped open a butterfly knife with skill, flashing it forward and back until the blade extended firmly from his hand. His grin widened, and he picked at his fingernails with the point.

"My associate handles the less dignified aspects of our business."

"Forgery or perjury?"

"He's a man of many trades." Pierce's smile widened. "Today, he's the head of our collections team."

Jason eased to his left, never taking his gaze from the man with the knife. He put the guest chair between himself and Peabody. "Even if I owed you this obscene amount of money—"

"You do."

Jason glanced at Pierce. "I haven't the means to repay a loan of this size even if it were an honest debt."

"Only the interest is due."

"What's due doesn't matter. What's due is a fabrication by you." Jason's angry retort silenced as Peabody flipped his blade around, the sound clicking through the air as it opened and shut.

"Mr. Peabody likes to use his knife." Pierce pulled a cigar from a humidor on his desk. "I normally can't allow that, of course, especially on our good clients. What he does in the alleyway behind brothels is his business." Pierce clipped the end of the cigar and struck a match. "Women are his specialty." Pierce snickered and looked Jason in the eye. "I hear you have a new wife." He held the flame to the stogie and puffed several times until the end of the tobacco glowed. "Do you like your wife, Mr. Harris?"

Horror and disbelief choked Jason's reply before it could escape his throat. Pierce grinned through a cloud of white smoke.

Peabody played with his knife, the snick, snick, chink a counterpoint to the man's silent stare.

"My wife has nothing to do with this. You won't touch her." Jason tore his gaze from Peabody's threatening display and pointed at Pierce. "If Amy is harmed in any way, I will kill you."

"There's no threat to your wife, Mr. Harris. In fact, both your wife's well-being and your father's reputation are perfectly safe." Pierce's smug face held the threat even though he denied the accusation. "I'm not even going to ask you for funds you don't have."

"What then?"

"A little business on the side. A fine young man such as you should have no difficulty performing a few tasks in place of an interest payment."

"Interest I don't owe on a loan I never agreed to."

"You would have taken the returns quick enough, I'm certain." Pierce blew a mouthful of smoke at the ceiling. "Information is worth its weight in gold or interest payments, and you are wonderfully placed to provide me with what I need to know.

"You're a trusted attorney with access to documents and testimony not available to the public. Your father is a banker, and at this crucial time, his insight could make or break a poor brokerage firm like mine.

"Then there's your father-in-law—a successful cargo merchant with a small fleet of ships, importing goods from around the world. Advance knowledge of what he will unload could allow a man to set the market, so to speak."

Pierce glanced from the smoke spreading across the ceiling and into Jason's eyes. "We'll be in touch, Mr. Harris. Of that, you can be certain. Have a pleasant evening."

Peabody chuckled and stepped away from the door, his hand and blade in constant motion.

"I won't be intimidated," Jason warned as he crossed the room to the entrance.

"You will, and you are." Pierce puffed, the ember glowing, and looked Jason up and down as though sizing him up. "You'll be a good lad and do as you're told. See if you don't." Pierce brushed the ash into a tray on the desk. "Oh, and one last thing."

Peabody flipped the knife into his pocket and moved forward, a small club in his other hand. The thug thrust the black baton deep into Jason's gut.

Jason's breath whooshed out, and he doubled over. His knees and hands hit the hardwood floor as pain exploded in his diaphragm. He struggled to inhale, but a low-pitched gurgle was the most he could manage.

"Get him up," Pierce snickered. "He has somewhere to be."

Jason blinked at Pierce through watering eyes. "Bastard," he whispered.

Peabody gripped him beneath his arm and pulled him to his feet. A hard shove sent Jason reeling out of the exit.

The peeling blue door slammed shut while Jason fought to keep his balance on the narrow stoop. Bent at the waist and holding the pain in his abdomen, he struggled to take a full breath of air.

His hat lay in the empty flowerbed, and Jason grimaced as he reached for the topper. His arm wrapped around his stomach; he made his way up the block to his house.

At home, he found a note Keith had left on the entry table. In the barrister's clear handwriting, the message stated he would be out for the evening.

Probably at his social club with Judge Brown.

Keith also noted that Jason had received a letter from Colorado, delivered by Riley.

Jason glanced at his name on the front of the envelope penned by his cousin's hand but didn't pick it up. He couldn't read or attempt to care about Nichole's broken heart right now.

What the hell am I going to do?

Chapter 35

Amy Harris

—

April 1874

Amy bent to pluck a weed from her mother's garden then straightened. With a hand on the small of her back, she stretched and groaned as her spine popped softly. The cauliflower, spinach, and broccoli were already beginning to sprout. She closed her eyes and allowed the sunlight to fall across her face.

Springtime at last.

Her first winter as a married woman had been both joyous and trying. The delicate bond between her and Jason had grown stronger during the cold months and long nights.

Her skin still tingled with thoughts of last night's surrender. Jason had changed his gentle arousal of her from his fingertips to his tongue. Although shocked at first, the sensation had quickly quieted her half-hearted protest and sent her spiraling to new heights of desire.

Joyous indeed.

"Lower your bonnet, dear heart. The sunshine has turned your face pink." Margaret paced past her daughter and entered the carriage house storeroom.

Amy only caught sight of her mother's dress as she disappeared into the work area. "I've finished with the garden," she called to the now empty doorway. "I'm going inside."

"I'll be right in," her mother replied from inside the storeroom. "Will you be returning home or staying for supper?"

"Home." Amy pulled the gardening gloves from her hands and leaned against the open doorframe. "I am supposed to wait for Jason to fetch me, but it's such a beautiful day."

Margaret returned with a small leather punch and hammer. "I'll ask Wrigley to hitch Hob or Homer. Either he or Peg can see you home."

"I'd rather walk. I don't need a nursemaid."

Margaret halted her stride to the back door and stared at Amy. "We've all been given strict instructions not to allow you to go about on your own." She raised one brow at her daughter. "I, for one, do not want to receive another talking to from your husband."

"He is ridiculous. I've walked around here since I was a child." Amy held the door for her mother then followed her inside.

"Do you have any idea what Jason's afraid of?" Margaret set the tools on the counter.

"No. Jason only says he couldn't live with himself should something happen to me."

"Do you think it's tied to that incident with Donetta and Nathan Dunham?"

Amy shrugged as she pulled the gardening bonnet from her head and hung it from a peg behind the door. "I don't know. I've even tried to scry for possible dangers or, well, anything. I see nothing perilous." She tipped her head at Margaret's tools. "What are those for?"

"Your father." Her mother chuckled. "He needs his leather belt let out an inch. He claims he doesn't, but I know it pinches him when he sits."

"That's Peg's cooking." Amy laughed. "I think Jason has lost weight eating mine."

"You're always welcome to stay for supper, you know. Peg makes enough for you both." She dropped her voice and winked at Amy. "I think that's part of the problem." Her hand patted the hole punch. "Robert tries to finish it all."

Amy laughed. "Poor father. A victim of overabundance."

"Overindulgence, you mean." Margaret glanced out the kitchen window, then waved. "There's Wrigley." She looked at her daughter. "Can I send the last of the winter vegetables home with you?" She tipped her head at a wicker basket of beets, carrots, and squash on the floor.

Amy nodded. "Of course, if you won't allow me to walk."

"And try your husband's wrath? I think not."

"Did you need me?" Wrigley opened the door and spoke into the kitchen without entering.

"Could you see Mrs. Harris home?" Her mother grinned mischievously at her.

"Of course." He chuckled as Amy rolled her eyes. "I'll hitch the carriage."

Amy released an exasperated sigh. "I'll get my shawl."

Margaret chuckled. "I'll wrap up a few of Peg's biscuits for you to take as well. Heaven forbid your father discovers these before dinner."

Amy withdrew her shawl from the front closet and twirled it around her shoulders as the front door opened.

"I'm glad I caught you still here." Robert smiled in greeting and hugged his daughter.

"Only barely. Wrigley is preparing the carriage." Amy took her father's arm as they walked through the house to the kitchen. "You know I'm not allowed to be out by myself any longer."

"Margaret doesn't go out by herself anymore either." Robert patted her hand. "Times are not what they were even six months ago. Too many unemployed vagrants on the street are looking for mischief."

"That doesn't make it easier to tolerate," her mother chimed in and hugged her daughter. "Wrigley should be ready for you, and the basket is in the coach. Have a nice evening and invite your husband for supper this weekend. Mr. MacKenna will be here as well. We'll have a lovely time."

"I will, mother."

"Oh, wait! I almost forgot." Robert pulled a crumpled letter from his pocket. "I met with Spencer this morning, and he gave me this to pass on to Jason."

Amy took the letter. "This doesn't appear to be his cousin's hand."

"No," Robert agreed. "Spencer told me he recognized his brother's handwriting."

Amy slipped the letter into her handbag. "I'll see he gets it."

Jason's coddling put a strain on their marriage, despite her father's defense of his actions. Instead of feeling cossetted and protected, she felt imprisoned and obstructed.

She hugged her mother goodbye one last time and hurried through the carriage house to the back street. As she climbed into the carriage, she promised herself she'd talk to Jason again tonight about his overprotective behavior.

The coddling must stop.

***

Jason Harris

—

The Pierce and Peabody door was locked.

Jason peered up and down the street, knocked again, and waited.

He'd received strict instructions to have the jury roster for the Stanley versus Massachusetts case delivered to Otis Pierce no later than noon today, or there would be hell to pay.

These payments to hell have become never-ending.

He pulled out his watch and noted the time.

Ten 'til noon. Where could Pierce be?

The paper with the names of the jurors burned a hole in his jacket. If caught with this privileged information, it would mean trouble. Then again, the seated jury would be common knowledge by tomorrow. This information would only be worth something to somebody today.

If that someone intended to tamper with a juror.

Pierce would be fully capable of threatening or cajoling a juror or two to influence the outcome of a trial.

I wonder if Stanley is a friend or a foe of Pierce's?

He circled the house, but the curtains were drawn. There didn't appear to be anyone home. He hesitated and glanced around again, then withdrew the envelope from his pocket, slipping the list of names beneath the back door. With hunched shoulders, he hurried back to the street and up the hill to Barrister Hall's home.

Surprised to find the door unlocked and Keith at home in the middle of the day, Jason paused in the opening to the front office and shoved the house key back into his pocket. "You're home. Did something happen at the courthouse?"

Keith leaned back in his chair, his fingers steepled beneath his bushy white eyebrows as he studied Jason. "A delay in the proceedings. I have to return by three." He indicated one of the guest chairs. "Please, have a seat. There's something we need to discuss."

He has discovered what I've been doing.

Sudden panic made Jason light-headed, and he swallowed. Crossing to the guest chair, he lowered himself slowly to the seat. "Is something wrong?"

Keith scratched his nose and nodded. His hair bobbed around his face. "Unfortunately, there is."

Jason waited in silence, his back stiff as though braced for a blow; he closed his eyes and sent up a silent prayer.

"I know you're aware that most, if not all, of the factories have either closed their doors or released workers. You've seen the results of the poor economy and job losses yourself. Few people have the means to pay for our services." He shook his head and stared at the desktop. "My income has been reduced by half, yet my bills and mortgage remain the same." His apologetic gaze met Jason's. "As much as I enjoy having you and your lovely wife occupying the rooms upstairs, I need to lease that space to a paying tenant."

Jason blinked. "I...um."

"I don't intend to put you out on the street, of course. You'll need time to obtain new lodging. However, I will advertise the space immediately and can hopefully lease to new tenants before the end of May."

Jason's thoughts scattered. Keith's unexpected request left him both relieved and speechless. Where would they go?

Keith rose from his chair. "You have some time to consider your options and speak with your wife." He shrugged on his coat and picked up his top hat from the desk, running his fingers around the brim. "I'm sorry to put you in such a position. I hope there are no hard feelings."

"I'm not upset with you." Jason held out his hand to Keith. "You've' been beyond generous allowing Amy and me to stay in your unrented apartment. There is nothing in my heart but gratitude."

Keith released his hand. "I best get back. Court resumes soon."

Jason followed Keith to the front stoop, then stood behind the closed door. One hand scrubbed his face while the other rested on his hip.

My family will never consider helping us.

Perhaps, for a short time, they could stay at Amy's parents' home. Although he hated to contemplate that course of action, he'd already looked for work in several accounting firms to bring in extra money. At every job he applied for, fifty other men put in applications as well. At a few places, the line of men seeking employment for a single opening stretched out the door and around the corner.

He'd never seen times like these. Even his stock in the three silver mines wouldn't secure a room for more than a few months at the Revere's, and he couldn't ask Amy to live there.

***

Amy Harris

—

Amy found the front door unlocked and directed Wrigley up the stairs with the basket. "Set that on the counter in the kitchen, please." She wouldn't have been able to walk home with the vegetables, which they needed, and now regretted her anger at Jason. Not that he didn't deserve it sometimes. He coddled her, and it would have to stop.

"Is that you?" Jason called down the stairs. He waited for Wrigley to reach the top before he started down.

Amy hung up her shawl and pulled off her gloves. "It's me. Mother sent the last of the fall garden home to us along with several biscuits. I could heat last night's stew for dinner."

"I'm not sure how much is left. Keith was home for lunch today."

"He was?" She pulled the envelope from her purse. "Isn't that unusual?"

"It is, but he wanted to speak with me." Jason took the envelope. "What's this?"

"Father gave it to me. He had a meeting with your father and promised to get this to you." She followed Jason into the office. "Your father said he thought it was his brother's handwriting."

Jason nodded and slowly lowered himself into the big chair behind the desk while he read the letter. "This is from Uncle Quincy."

Amy sat in the guest chair. "Is something wrong?"

Wrigley came down the stairs and paused at the office door. "I'm heading home."

"Thank you," Amy said.

"It is never a bother." Wrigley nodded toward Jason. "That must be interesting reading."

Jason raised his hand. "All right. Goodbye." He never looked up.

Wrigley chuckled and grinned at Amy's raised brow. "I'll see myself out."

Jason finished reading the letter, blinked up at Amy, then began to reread it.

"What does it say?"

"Uncle Quincy says his ranch is doing quite well." Jason grinned at Amy. "So well, in fact, he feels it's time to separate his accounts from his neighbor's and retain a solicitor. To those ends, he would like my help."

"That is wonderful! Who manages them now?" Amy leaned forward.

"He doesn't say, and Nichole has never spoken of her father's business to me." He handed her the letter and waited while she read it. "What do you think?"

Amy quickly scanned the note. "He wants us to move there." She lifted her gaze from the paper. "To live with him in Colorado."

Jason nodded. "I know this is sudden and completely unexpected, but it comes at a good time for me." He gestured with his arm. "There's no work here. I've searched." He swallowed and glanced down at his hands. "Here, my family won't acknowledge me. At least in Colorado, I'll have my cousin and Uncle Quincy and work I know I can do."

Amy finished reading the letter, folded the paper, and handed it back to Jason. "It sounds as though you've already made up your mind."

"I have, but it's not only my decision. I'm asking what you think."

"I'll be leaving my family—my mother."

"I know it's a lot to consider, but there's something else you need to know." He stuffed the letter into his pocket. "Keith has asked us to move by the beginning of the month. Work is slow, and although I know he can pick up public defender cases, the hardship cases don't pay well. He needs to rent our apartment to make his house payment."

"I didn't know." Amy blinked in surprise and sat back. "I'd offer the use of my dowry, but it isn't cash."

"I know it's not, and I wouldn't let you use that anyway. That ship is yours, and someday it will turn a substantial profit."

"I could ask my parents for money." Her face lightened. "I know they wouldn't mind."

Jason took her hands. "Your parents would do anything for you. I know that. But Amy, this economy is hurting your father too. Money is tight for everyone, and whether he speaks of it or not to you and your mother, sales of his imported goods must have fallen off."

The last ray of hope extinguished in Amy's heart. Leaving her home and family would be the most difficult thing she'd ever done, but for the first time in a long while, there was a spark of light in Jason's eyes. An eagerness to strike out, like his uncle had, and find something new.

Slowly she nodded her head. "All right, yes, but only if you promise not to hover over me every moment as though I might break."

"Of course, I promise." Jason jumped to his feet, drawing her up to him. "Thank you, my love." He caught her up in a hug, lifting her off her feet and twirling her around in the small space. "This will be the best thing for us to do. A way to begin anew, in a new place."

"We can tell my parents at dinner this weekend."

"I'll sell my stock in the silver mines. It's not worth much, but it should be enough for two tickets to Denver." He set her on her feet. "After I know our arrival date, I'll send a telegram to Uncle Quincy."

A thousand things she needed to do raced through her head. What would she bring? What would they need to leave behind? "Our furniture?"

"Keith can have it. He can rent the apartment furnished. The ranch will have everything we need, and you'll get to know Nichole. I'm certain you'll love her as I do."

"How soon, Jason? When will we leave?"

"As soon as possible, I should imagine. Next week?"

"Next week! I'm not sure that's enough time for all I have to accomplish."

"What is that? We pack our clothing and personal treasures, my books, and your drawings and recipes. I'm certain Uncle Quincy will be suitably impressed with your skills at gardening and producing your healing salves." Jason threw out his arms in excitement. "It will be wonderful."

Amy stepped back, watching her husband act like a child at Christmas. "If you are certain this is what we must do and that it must be done quickly, I'll make every effort to be ready."

"I'm sorry," Jason lowered his arms, his expression turned serious. He ran his hands up her arms then pulled her close in a gentle embrace. "What is it you need to do before we can leave?"

Amy sniffed and wrapped her arms around her husband, enjoying the feel of his shirt against her cheek. "I must find a way to say goodbye."

Chapter 36

Ayden MacKenna

—

His shoulder braced against the wall; Ayden gazed out of the rain-splattered train terminal window. A passing shower had muddied the street and drop-off area in front of the terminal building, and people tiptoed around puddles carrying umbrellas to ward off the last few drops of moisture.

After the devastating fire and Robert's birthday party, Ayden became close friends with the Prescotts, especially Amy's husband, Jason. Sharing lunches, laughter, and sometimes even fatherly advice with the fellow had given Ayden a kinship he would always cherish. The friendship of the newlyweds gave Ayden a piece of the life he'd missed, and in doing so, lit a warm fire in his heart for the young couple. He was sad to see them leave.

Ayden studied the large clock on the wall above the ticket counters then the departure times. The next train would leave in less than an hour.

I'll wait another thirty minutes, then assume I misheard the station.

With eight train stations in the Boston area, it was a challenge to keep them straight. Still, he was positive he'd heard Jason mention the B&A Railroad. He walked a circuit around the passenger area then glanced again out of the window.

Wrigley sat on the high seat of the Prescotts' carriage. He'd stopped as close to the entrance as he could manage. Several rigs waited for passengers directly in front of the station doors. As the carriage door swung open, Wrigley handed the large umbrella down to Robert.

Amy's father held the canopy above Margaret and Peg as they wove their way between carriages and around puddles into the station.

Ayden navigated past an excited fair-haired family keeping his sight on the Prescotts as they came into the terminal.

Once the women were inside, Robert searched through the window to find Wrigley as the rain picked up again.

"Hurry, Robert," Margaret called. "Wrigley will drown before he gets to the station livery." She brushed the front of her skirt and mumbled, "We have more than one umbrella. I don't know why we never bring more."

Robert dashed back outside into the rainstorm.

"Mr. MacKenna," Peg greeted Ayden as he approached. "Have Jason and Amy arrived?"

"I haven't seen them." He smiled at the young woman and looked at Amy's teary eyed mother. "Hello, Margaret."

"Ayden." Margaret wiped her cheek with the back of her hand. "It's a pleasure to see you again."

Peg pointed across the terminal to the ticket counter. "They have pamphlets at the counter with routes and schedules. I'm going to get one."

Margaret gave her approval and returned her attention to Ayden. "It is kind of you to see the children off on their big adventure."

"Not at all. They've become like family." He tipped his head to the side and considered her dark eyes. "I understand why you're upset. I know Amy will miss you too."

"Ah, well as to that." Margaret blinked and touched the edge of the handkerchief to her eye. "I'm trying to keep my head up for Amy's sake. It may be for the best they are leaving Boston." She glanced up at Ayden. "Isaac Coleman and his damned coven put my back up. I want my daughter as far away from their influence as she can get. I don't trust him or his supporters."

"They continue to follow me," Ayden spoke softly. "And I agree, Amy and Jason would be safer away from them."

"There's more." She averted her eyes. "If it comes to defending our home—and I'm afraid it might—Wrigley and Peg would inevitably display their power." She looked at Ayden from the corner of her eye, then looked away. Her face flushed. "Amy doesn't know they're witches."

"You must jest. Amy grew up with them." Ayden lowered his voice when he spied Peg returning with several brochures. "How much have you kept from your daughter?"

Margaret closed her eyes and sighed, her voice soft and filled with regret. "More than just this. More than you know."

Still reading the travel pamphlets, Peg came to a halt beside Margaret. "I admit I'm envious of Amy." She grinned at Ayden and Margaret. "I'd like to travel someday." Her brows rose as her gaze shifted out the window. "They're here, and oh! Look at the rainbow."

The rain had stopped for the moment, and the late day sun broke through the clouds to display a full spectrum of color outside the train station windows.

Beyond the waiting buggies, Robert helped Amy from the wagon as Jason and Wrigley conferred with Riley, who held the reins. After a brief discussion, Robert escorted Amy around the traffic to the terminal entrance while the three men continued down the street with the young couple's luggage.

***

Jason Harris

—

"We'll drop these at the luggage car," Jason instructed Riley while they waited for Amy to clear the wagon with her father.

She glanced back and smiled as she held her skirt from the muddy ground with one hand and clutched her father's arm with the other. They made their way through several waiting carriages and disappeared in the crowd near the terminal entrance.

Riley shook the reins and guided the horses past the waiting cabbies to a sign beside the terminal that read BAGGAGE CAR. He reined in behind a similar wagon and waited beneath a wide canopy while porters unloaded trunks and hat boxes.

"Did my parents know where you were going?" Jason asked as he watched the baggage removed from the wagon in front of them.

How things had changed.

There had been days when his father's comments and his mother's constant interference in his life made him yearn to get away from them, and now that he was leaving, their cold disinterest cut him to the quick.

"Your father did. I don't speak to your mother often."

Jason nodded at the groom. "Then he knows I'm leaving Boston."

Did I wrong them so terribly not to warrant a goodbye?

Riley nodded, then shrugged. "It's not for me to say what your father knows. He wasn't surprised when I asked for time away from his service today. He asked if it was on your behalf, and I told him it was."

"Then he may not know."

"He spends a good deal of time in your father-in-law's company. I can think of no reason your wife's father might consider your move a secret." Riley raised an eyebrow. "He knows."

The wagon ahead of them pulled away from the porters, and Riley guided the team forward at a slow pace.

A muscular man in a blue uniform, and red whiskers, stood in front of a tall rack of metal tickets. He wrote quickly on a small pad of paper, then lifted his regard. "Next."

Wrigley tossed back the rain tarp, hopped into the wagon bed, and wrestled with the trunks.

The luggage attendant's gaze settled on Jason. "The name of the traveling party, sir."

Jason hopped from the seat. "Mr. and Mrs. Jason Harris."

Two young porters in blue unloaded the trunks as quickly as Wrigley could shove them to the back of the wagon.

"How many items for baggage?"

"The four large steamer trunks there." Jason pointed, then took a smaller wicker basket from Wrigley. "We'll keep this with us."

"And your final destination?"

"Denver."

The porter selected a metal ticket from the rack behind him with DNVR23 etched into the surface. He handed it to Jason. "You'll change trains several times before you reach your destination. Your luggage will transfer as well but will not be available to you until you retrieve it in Denver. You'll need the ticket to claim your luggage." He made a note in his log and indicated the X on the paperwork where Jason would sign.

Jason took the thin board from the porter and read the line.

Harris – 4 steamers – DNVR23 X_____

With a flourish, Jason signed his name and took the ticket. "Thank you."

"You'll be asked to sign again when you retrieve your trunks."

"I understand." Jason slipped the metal ticket into his pocket, then reached up and shook Riley's hand. "Take care of yourself and thank you for all you've done for Amy and me."

"You're welcome. Take care of your pretty wife. I hear there are still wild Indians where you're going."

"Nichole hasn't mentioned any in her letters, and I'm sure she would have if she'd seen one."

Riley chuckled. "Tell your cousin I said hello, although I doubt she'd remember me."

"I'll remind her." Jason waved as Riley pulled away.

The wagon moved forward from beneath the shelter as the rain returned in full force.

Wrigley opened the umbrella and waited near the edge of the baggage canopy.

Jason hurried past their steamer trunks and around the young porter who marked DNVR23 on the top of each trunk in yellow chalk.

"You best keep those dry," Jason commented.

Wrigley held the umbrella over both their heads, and the men dashed for the entrance.

Inside, people filled the terminal building. On the far side of the crowd, Jason could see the rail cars filling with passengers.

"Jason!"

The shout brought Jason to his toes, and he looked over the heads around him in search of the caller.

Ayden's hand waved above the crowd.

He took a step closer and recognized Amy's parents beside Ayden.

Then he caught sight of Amy.

Her red-rimmed eyes met his briefly above the handkerchief she held to her nose. Then she averted her gaze and turned a shoulder to his approach.

"Damn," Jason swore under his breath. This move from Boston needed to happen to protect them both. Uncle Quincy's invitation was a deliverance from the crushing unemployment and P&P's ever-increasing demands. But he never wanted to make Amy cry.

"She'll be all right," Wrigley spoke in his ear. "She told Peg and her mother she was excited to go west."

Jason contemplated the leathered older servant. "She did?"

Wrigley nodded and shook out the umbrella to collapse it. "Encourage her to look forward. Don't let her wave goodbye for too long."

***

Amy Harris

—

Amy wiped her face and blinked the remaining tears from her eyes. When she turned back to her husband, he had made his way through the crowd of passengers and well-wishers to the family.

Amy cleared her throat and offered Jason a tentative smile. "I told them they shouldn't come to the station, but they wouldn't listen."

"I couldn't let you go without seeing you one last time." Margaret pulled her daughter close and whispered, "Be brave and look for me in your special dreams. I'll hold you in my heart until we see each other again, sweetheart."

"I love you, Mother." Amy clutched her mother again, then eased out of her arms.

"Unfortunately, we've arrived too late to visit properly. Had I known you would be here, we would have come earlier." Jason handed Amy the basket he'd brought from the wagon.

"Nonsense. We've only come to see you off." Robert held out his hand and shook Jason's. "God's speed."

Margaret leaned forward and kissed Jason on both cheeks.

"All aboard!" The conductor called.

Passengers pressed forward.

Amy hugged Peg. "Try not to feed Papa so much, only a slice of his favorite cake from me now and then. Make sure Wrigley takes care of himself. I'll miss you both."

"I will." Peg lifted a lock of Amy's hair. "I'll think of you when I look in the mirror. All the wonderful conversations we had while I brushed your hair. I'll miss you too." She sniffed.

Then Amy stood before the man who had raised her. The rim of his eyes turned red in their silence. "I love you, Father."

"And I love you, my girl." It was all he could say as the time had run out. Jason took her hand.

Amy held to her father's grip for as long as she could, then she turned to go with Jason and had to let go.

"Write to me," her mother instructed.

"I will," Amy called back. "As soon as we get there."

The conductor took their tickets and told Jason where to find their seats.

Amy put her basket and purse beneath one of the seats and removed her bonnet. She lowered herself to the cushioned bench beside the window that looked out over the passenger area.

Her sadness at leaving warred in her heart with the excitement of a new beginning in her life—a new chapter for her and her husband.

Jason sat across from her, stowed his hat beneath the bench seat, and took her hand.

***

Jason Harris

—

Jason held his wife's hand while she searched for her family in the rapidly emptying terminal.

"There they are!" Amy pointed. "Beyond the crowd not far from the entrance."

"I see them." Jason waved with Amy, and although he continued to stare out the window, the faces in the terminal blurred. The horror that haunted him would soon be left behind to become a fading memory. A reprieve from the effects of the devastating fire, the outrageous lies told by a young woman he could never marry, his parents' abandonment, and the dishonest debt to a swindler. Perhaps his anger at so much loss would be made tolerable by time and distance.

At least for now.

Wrigley's suggestion to keep Amy looking forward to new possibilities would not only benefit her but him as well.

It was a moment before he realized Amy had begun to cry again. He switched seats to sit beside her and wrapped his arms around her.

Her head fell against his chest as her shoulders shook.

"You know, it's been years since I've seen Uncle Quincy. My father was always the stodgy banker, and his brother the daring adventurer. After Uncle Quincy married, he went west to seek his fortune and left his wife and daughter at our house."

"I remember you telling me that." Amy looked up.

"When he sent for Aunt Emily and Nichole, my cousin was heartbroken. She was preparing for her Brahmin debut when Father put a stop to it and told them they were to leave for Denver immediately." He brushed his thumb across Amy's cheek. "Do you remember my cousin? Did you know her in school?

"Not really. I knew *of* her." Amy cleared her throat and dried her eyes. "Isn't she five years younger than you?"

Jason nodded. "Even so, we look very much alike."

The train jerked, and they both turned to the window. The whistle sang its warning and final farewell to Boston, and the remaining people in the terminal disappeared behind a cloud of steam. When the air cleared, Amy's family was nowhere in sight.

As the train slowly picked up speed, the station was left behind as the tracks wound slowly through the city toward the end of the first leg of their trip in Albany, New York.

"I look forward to meeting her and your uncle."

"This will be a fresh start in a part of the country I never thought to see."

"Nor did I." Her smile brightened his heart, and the love shining from her eyes soothed his regret at her tears.

"I love you, my dear—profoundly."

"Profoundly?" she chuckled.

"To the deepest part of my heart—a love beyond measure."

Her laughter caught the attention of an older couple who were seated nearby, and she quieted. "I love you too, Mr. Harris. I believe our future is bright."

"With you as my shining star, how could it be otherwise?"

A Sneak Peek at Passage

They go west seeking peace—but love is not simple, and neither is family. When Nichole slips between memory and madness, Jason makes a choice that threatens everything he holds dear.

—

The Soul of the Witch Saga continues in Book 3:
Passage

Chapter 1

Elsewhere, far from Boston and the Colorado ranch, another thread of the story begins.

— ✧ —

Courtney Veau

—

Present-day — Denver, Colorado

Courtney rested her shoulder against the wall beside the second-floor window and looked down on the street below. The diverse Denver neighborhood had a mix of historic homes and new development. The buildings and trees along the block cast tall shadows across the pavement and foretold the approach of evening. Two helmeted bicyclists coasted past parked cars, then passed from view.

A small sigh escaped her lips, and she raised her gaze to the darkening eastern horizon. She waited for the first star to appear. Her thoughts jumped between her two great unresolved questions—why was she still here; and would he come again tonight?

Dust from the heavy tattered draperies tickled her nose as she peered between their panels. The curtains blocked the light from the passing day and left the small apartment behind her in semi-darkness. Her possessions were few. An inflatable mattress shoved into the corner by the closet. Beside the bed sat a small folding table, which held her laptop and cell phone. A sleeping bag, comforter, and pillow were thrown haphazardly across the mattress, and at the foot of the makeshift bed was a large flashlight. Her suitcase laid open in the closet with her few remaining clean clothes inside; the dirty ones were tossed behind the closet door.

The long shadows faded into twilight. She'd found what she came for—proof this house existed. There was no longer a reason to stay; and yet, just the possibility she might hear his voice again kept her waiting one more day.

Outside her window, the night took final possession of the evening. A few porch lights came on down the block. Headlights swung around the corner as a car turned onto the street and illuminated the pavement. The headlights winked off, and a car door slammed.

Behind her, the room took on a familiar chill. She turned from the window and pressed her back against the drapes as the echo of boots pounded up the back stairs. She gasped when he raced into the room, vaguely luminescent in the darkness. He was dressed in denim trousers and cotton shirt, with a silk scarf tied loosely around his neck.

Where's his hat?

Had he lost it in the race up the stairs? That wide-brimmed cowboy hat was such a part of him he seemed naked without it. His hair had come loose from its binding, and he shoved it out of his eyes with a familiar movement. She stood close enough to read the emotion play across his face, a mixture of fear and bewilderment. His breath was labored, and his anxiety tangible as he stopped and looked right at her. Her mouth fell open, and her heart tightened in her chest.

Does he see me?

He took a hesitant step in her direction. "Nichole?" his voice filled with horror, he whispered her name from another life.

"Yes, Merril! It's me." Courtney stepped toward the specter.

His head turned. His attention called away from her open arms. "Oh, sweet Jesus." Merril fell to his knees and reached for something no longer there. "Nicki, please don't go. Stay with me."

"Merril, I'm here." She ached for him and for herself, but her plea went unheard.

Sobs shook his broad shoulders.

Her heart clenched to witness his despair. She longed to comfort him, to assure him she was there, but could not. In defeat, she sank to her knees beside the grieving apparition.

"Nicki, don't leave me. Look at me—" His hushed voice, choked and broken.

"I'm right here, my love," she whispered, but the room grew warm, and Merril Shilo faded back into the past. Courtney hung her head in the darkness and fought back tears.

One question was answered, at least for now.

* * *

Two Weeks Earlier—Fort Worth, Texas

Courtney stirred. A medicinal antiseptic smell assaulted her nose while the muted beep and whir of machines slipped into her dream like an old memory.

"Miss Veau? Can you hear me, hon? Wake up, Courtney."

Courtney blinked gummy eyes and tried to focus on the speaker, but brightness obscured her vision. She closed them again as pain lanced across her brow.

"Courtney, open your eyes, please."

Icy fingers slipped beneath hers, and a cold palm rubbed the back of her hand.

"You need to wake up now."

She squinted at the dark-haired nurse and struggled to make sense of her surroundings.

Sudden realization hit, and her adrenaline surged. Beside her bed, the silent monitor sounded an alarm as her heart rate accelerated—she was back. She was Courtney Veau again.

What happened?

She didn't want to be Courtney Veau—not now! Not when everyone she loved knew her as Nichole Harris. *Had* known her, she realized. They wouldn't be alive anymore.

A gasp escaped her lips when the nurse came into focus and ended in a choked cough.

"Take it easy, darlin'. You're going to be just fine," the woman comforted in a slow southern drawl. She silenced the alarm and dimmed the overhead light. "Your throat is sore from the intubation tube. They had you on a ventilator when you first came in. Would you like a bit of ice to suck on?"

Courtney disagreed vehemently that things were going to be just fine. That she was here—at this place in time, and in this body—told her everything was lost. She tried to raise her hand, but plastic straps held her arm tight to the bed.

"Wha?" Courtney grimaced as her voice broke.

The nurse held the small cup of ice chips to her lips, and a few pieces of frozen moisture fell into her mouth. Delicious coolness trickled down Courtney's raw throat, and she moaned at the icy sensation.

"That should help. My name is Vicki. I'll be your nurse until they move you to a room. You gave us quite a scare this morning."

"What happened? Where... Why am I strap...strapped down?" Courtney croaked through her scratched throat. Tears seeped from the corner of her eyes into her hairline. She took a trembling breath and tried to focus on the here and now.

Vicki held the cup to Courtney's lips and tapped a few more chips into her mouth.

"You were brought to JPS by ambulance early this morning. You were in a car accident. We had a difficult time getting you stabilized—then you fought us each time you woke. That's why you're restrained." Vicki offered a few more ice chips and dabbed Courtney's watering eyes with a tissue. "Who is Merril?"

Courtney choked on the icy fluid in her throat.

"Easy now, darlin'. Here, let's set you up." Vicki raised the head of the bed. "I only ask because you called his name while you were waking. Admissions have been here twice asking for a person to contact about your condition. Is Merril a friend or family member?"

Hearing his name nearly broke Courtney. She longed to wail her grief to the entire ICU, but she had grown up aware of her family's notoriety and had learned to be inconspicuous. Instead, she swallowed back her tears and struggled to control her grief. "Merril's not, I mean he's... You won't be able to contact him." A sob escaped her throat.

Vicki eyed her with concern, then pulled two tissues and wiped the tears from Courtney's face. "Are you all right, darlin'?"

"Yeah," Courtney murmured without conviction.

"I hope so. If you promise to stay calm, I'll remove these restraints." Vicki didn't wait for an answer before she unlatched the straps.

"What else is wrong with me?" Courtney's right hand trembled.

Vicki removed the last restraint from Courtney's leg and set it aside. Then, she rolled the bedside tray within Courtney's reach. "The initial diagnosis is a TBI—traumatic brain injury—but that hasn't been confirmed yet." She set the cup of ice on the tray. "The TBI is the immediate concern, of course. That, along with deep bruises on your left side and leg as well as cuts on your face and scalp."

The arrival of a new patient in the ER drew Vicki away from Courtney's bedside.

Courtney slid the cup from the hinged lid and flipped back the tray-top to reveal a mirror. Her breath caught as she studied her reflection. The room seemed unsteady, and Courtney watched the blood drain from the face in the mirror.

The left side of her face was showered with small cuts. Her left iris swam in a pool of red, and she could see the beginning of a black eye in the dark puffy lid. Two of the cuts on her forehead were taped shut, and the entire left side of her face was swollen, giving her a lopsided, grotesque appearance.

Her mouth fell open as she looked past the injuries and studied the face beneath. The dark brown eyes and fine brown hair were familiar but wrong. The last time she looked in a mirror she'd seen the reflection of Nichole Harris's blonde hair and blue eyes. Courtney searched for a possible explanation but failed when the ache in her heart became too great. Nichole Harris felt more real and alive to her than Courtney Veau ever had.

She let the lid fall shut and clenched her jaw to control the tears, but it was no use. Despair welled inside her, and inconsolable sobs shook her frame.

Vicki glanced in as she passed Courtney's room. "What's the matter, hon? Are you in pain?"

"No, no," Courtney muttered. More sobs erupted as memories overwhelmed her. "I shouldn't be here," she gasped. "I would go back if I could, but I don't know how." Bitter tears closed her throat, and she coughed, trying to catch her breath.

"You need to calm yourself down, sugar, or you're going to make yourself sick." Vicki shoved a few tissues into Courtney's hand.

Courtney gulped down her tears and caught her breath several times, trying to even out her breathing. When the sharp rush of emotion passed, it left a dull, empty ache.

"I am going to have the doctor speak to you." Vicki set the box of tissues in Courtney's lap, then hurried out of the room.

Courtney held a tissue to her face. The love of her life, the very beat of her heart, was either a dream or a man long dead. The pain in her chest crawled up her throat, and her tenuous grip on reality threatened to shatter.

The ICU became busy, and she was left alone with her memories. She looked up from the damp tissues twisted in her hands when Vicki approached with an orderly.

"You've been assigned a room, hon," Vicki informed her. She helped Courtney move to the narrow gurney. "The doctor and an admission clerk will be up to see you. Don't forget these." Vicki set a clear plastic tote filled with Courtney's belongings on the transfer bed.

The orderly pushed her out through a set of double doors and into the elevator. As they passed the nurses' station on the third floor, a nurse picked up her chart from the foot of the rolling bed and followed them into the room. The thin, gray-haired woman reviewed her chart as the orderly assisted Courtney into her new bed. He put her tote in a small closet, and then pushed the gurney from the room.

"Lunch will be up in a few minutes." The nurse wrote her name—Rhonda—on the marker board by the door then slid Courtney's chart into a plastic chart holder. "How do you feel, Courtney? Any pain?"

Courtney shook her head and dabbed at the moisture on her face.

"Then, why the tears?" The short-haired nurse leaned against the sink counter, crossed her arms and looked with disapproval at Courtney.

Through watery eyes, Courtney peered at the nurse. She'd never met this woman before, although she recognized the tone of her voice and attitude. Rhonda knew who her father had been and wasn't pleased to have his daughter as a patient.

Courtney matched the older woman's glare and twisted the crisp white sheets in her hands. She would offer no explanation for her grief. Anxiety wound itself into a tight fist inside her stomach and sat clenched beneath her broken heart.

She hated when people recognized her—hated it with a passion built on years of unrelenting notoriety. Strangers made assumptions about her, and it was always hurtful. Whether they were fans or skeptics of her father, it was never pleasant to be recognized.

Rhonda's smile tightened, and she lifted one shoulder in a partial shrug. "Fine. Don't tell me. I'm sure it would be—" She cleared her throat and stood away from the counter as the doctor pulled the chart from the holder at the door.

"Hello, Miss Veau, I'm Doctor Chambers." The short, balding doctor glanced dismissively at Rhonda, then continued to Courtney's bedside as he paged through her chart. "You were in a car accident this morning and were admitted through the ER. Do you remember the accident?" He paused and looked up from the chart for Courtney's answer.

Courtney watched Rhonda scurry from the room before she looked at Dr. Chambers. "No, I don't."

The doctor nodded and returned his attention to the chart. "You had a CT scan and blood work upon admission. Your brain scan was clear. There's no indication of a TBI, and you have no illegal substances in your blood." Dr. Chambers smiled at his small jest and closed the file. "However, from the description of the accident, I believe you're lucky to be alive." He pulled the penlight from the pocket of his coat. "Let's take a look at how you're doing, shall we?"

The doctor tested her eyes and reflexes and then requested she stand to check her balance. He inspected the deep bruising along her left leg and hip while muttering to himself under his breath. When he was done, he assisted her back into the bed and helped arrange the covers.

"I must say again, you are extremely lucky, young lady. If it were possible, I'd say your father was watching after you." Dr. Chambers listened to her lungs, and then hung the stethoscope around his neck.

Courtney's eyes widened. "You know who my father was?"

He didn't act star-struck or hateful.

"Oh, yes. My wife was a big fan. We used to watch his show on television. I know it has been some years since he passed but allow me to say how sorry I am for your loss."

Courtney bowed her head and blinked away the tears, touched by his sincere sympathy. "Thank you," she whispered then gulped back a sob.

"Is there something else going on, Miss Veau? Something that upsets you? Both the paramedics and the ER nurse noted your...odd behavior. I would like to help if I can." He waited while Courtney mopped her face and blew her nose.

"I'm sorry for crying like this." Courtney added more tissue to the pile on her bed. Dr. Chambers lifted the trash receptacle, and she cleared the used tissues.

"That's quite all right, you've been through a traumatic event. However, considering these notes, I need to ask, is there someone abusive in your life? A boyfriend perhaps?" Dr. Chambers stepped back and rested his hip against the counter.

Courtney shook her head. "No. There's no one. Certainly no one abusive."

"The report says you struggled and fought in the ambulance and the ER before you were fully awake. Anything you tell me will be kept in confidence, but please, allow me to help you."

Courtney turned away. She stammered as she searched for the right explanation. "I...experienced something after the car accident...before I woke up in the emergency room. It was so real." She shook her head and blinked moisture from her eyes.

"Something that frightened you?" Dr. Chambers flipped back a few pages. "The first responders did perform CPR." His gaze rose to meet Courtney's. "You may have had an NDE. I'm no expert, but a classic near-death experience is normally associated with pleasant, even peaceful sensations."

"It wasn't like that. What I experienced was different. It lasted much longer. I was somewhere and someone else for days. I can't explain how—and it doesn't make sense—but I know it happened." Her voice trembled and the emotion she struggled to contain broke free.

"Okay, Miss Veau, it's all right. I'm going to order some medication that will help get you over the emotional hump, so to speak. I'll also refer you to a doctor who works with patients who have encountered something similar." Dr. Chambers patted her shoulder, then offered her the wastebasket again.

Courtney deposited her latest round of tissue casualties. "Thank you."

"We'll keep you a few days under observation, but you should be able to go home by the end of the week." The doctor slid the chart into the door. "Get some rest, Miss Veau."

She closed her eyes, lay back and willed her tears to stop. She would never see Merril again, and the stranglehold of grief that knowledge created would not let go. What's more—Merril was not the only loved one ripped from her life. Amy was gone, Nichole's friend and confidant, as well as Jason, Nichole's cousin. Alive yesterday, and yet dead for more than a hundred years.

The line between then and now blurred. She opened her eyes and saw Rhonda pull a syringe from her IV line.

"Sweet dreams," Rhonda whispered in a sing-song voice and cast a cold glance over her shoulder at Courtney as she flipped the light switch off. Courtney could just make out her muttered "Freak" as she left the room.

Chapter 2

Courtney Veau

Three days later, a knock at her door woke Courtney, and she opened her eyes enough to watch an orderly deliver the breakfast tray. Although a warming cover hid the food, she could smell eggs. For the first time since waking in the hospital, she felt hungry, and her stomach growled in anticipation.

The marker board by the door showed Debra was her nurse today. A dark-skinned young woman in gold scrubs came in, took her vitals, and then updated her chart. Debra was friendly and professional, a clear sign she'd never heard of Russell Veau.

After she finished breakfast, an admissions clerk entered her room. The middle-aged woman appeared annoyed at the unfinished paperwork. She presented Courtney with several forms attached to a clipboard and indicated which to complete, initial, or sign. Explanations done, she waved toward the door. "I'll wait outside."

Courtney could hear her chat with the nurses in the hallway as she completed the forms. She paused when she reached the emergency contact and bounced the pencil eraser off the form a couple of times. Finally, she wrote a name—Greta James.

Greta had been the trust attorney who administered her parents' estate after their death in the plane crash. Courtney's grandmother, Mary Curtis, had been awarded custody of their four-year-old daughter, and Greta sent them monthly support payments. The young attorney had been an occasional visitor to their home over the years. After Granny passed, Courtney had Greta apply to designate her as an emancipated minor. She hadn't spoken to Greta since the emancipation hearing, but there was no one else.

Courtney set the clipboard on the bedside tray and relaxed against the pillows, her gaze on the date at the top of the form, April 14. She'd been admitted to the hospital three days ago, but for her, time had become tangled.

Four days ago she'd been someone else. She remembered nothing of Nichole Harris's life before waking in her body, but the time spent in Nichole's
world haunted Courtney in glorious detail. She could hear the sounds of the
ranch; smell the dust in the air and the hay in the barn.

The first time she set eyes on Merril, a rush of emotion had swelled her
heart and overwhelmed her with confusion. She'd awakened with Nichole's
feelings but without Nichole's memories, and none of her own.

Courtney took a sip from her juice. Her emotions were less volatile today,
and she wondered if Dr. Chambers continued to prescribe anxiety medication.

I hope he did.

She could still feel the jagged edges of her broken heart. She closed her
eyes and conjured a vision of Merril as if he were in her room. His green eyes,
flecked with gold, would flash with concern to find her in a hospital bed. The
thought of his expressive eyes and sideways smile made her stomach flip. A
knock at the door jarred her from her daydream, and she opened her eyes to
find a tall, thin man standing in the doorway.

"Courtney Veau?" the man asked, with an easy professional smile. "My
name's Dr. Phelps. Dr. Chambers asked me to speak with you. May I come in?"

Instead of a hospital-white lab coat, he wore a brown corduroy sports
jacket with a computer bag slung over one shoulder. Dr. Phelps looked more
like a college professor with thinning brown hair and black-framed glasses.

Courtney hesitated a moment then replied, "Yes, of course."

Dr. Phelps tipped his head and entered the room. "Dr. Chambers told me
about your condition." He set his computer bag on the counter then took
a seat in the bedside chair. "I understand you required CPR at the accident
site. Dr. Chambers suspects you experienced a phenomenon we call NDE or
near-death experience, and it continues to upset you. Is this correct?" Dr.
Phelps peered at Courtney over the line in his bifocal lenses and waited for
her reply.

"I ... um ..." Courtney paused to gather her thoughts. "It wasn't the phenomenon that upset me." She shredded a tissue and turned away from his
penetrating gaze. "When I woke up and realized where I was—I knew the
people I loved were gone. Forever."

"Ah, yes, I see, I see." Dr. Phelps nodded and reset his glasses with his index
finger then regarded Courtney. "Miss Veau, your ordeal is not particularly

unusual. Many individuals who experience clinical death see loved ones or have visions of light. Most are not upset by it. In fact, most take comfort in these encounters."

"Do they ever relive past lives?" She looked up from the bits of tissue in her lap to Dr. Phelps.

Dr. Phelps blinked in surprise. "Well...the accounts of this phenomenon are many and varied. Entire books and studies have been written on this subject. Almost certainly, what happened to you would fall into one of the categories recounted by others."

"Do they ever become someone else?" Courtney tilted her head and held Dr. Phelps regard with her own.

Dr. Phelps blinked again. "Since what they encounter is thought to be caused by a hallucinogenic state, the result of oxygen deprivation, they could imagine they are."

"Oh, really?" Courtney's eyes narrowed. "So, you're saying I imagined it."

"I am not judging your incident by any means. The science behind this phenomenon is still uncertain and based on multiple theories, even though it has been documented for years in every culture of the world. I am simply giving you one possible explanation."

She studied the doctor in silence. Although she seethed with anger, his comment provoked an idea. She hadn't been in some distant undocumented past; she could find evidence her experience had been real.

Dr. Phelps nodded to himself and reached for his computer bag. "Dr. Chambers said you would be released today since your injuries are healing nicely and can be well managed at home." He opened his laptop and tapped briskly on the keyboard. "I would like to visit with you again at my office and have you recount your ordeal in more detail. Perhaps we can find a way to understand why this has upset you to such a degree."

"I already told you why it upset me," she replied immediately.

Dr. Phelps stopped typing and looked again at Courtney. "And why was that?"

Grief and frustration combined to make her statement sharper than intended. "Because I would rather be back there with him than here with you."

Dr. Phelps lowered his chin and observed Courtney over the top of his glasses. "And how would you return to him, Miss Veau?"

"I'm not a suicide risk if that's what you're implying, doctor." She clenched her jaw in aggravation.

Dr. Phelps held her stare for a moment, then turned back to his computer and tapped the keys a few more times. "I can't stay any longer today, but I can see you at ten o'clock tomorrow morning if that is agreeable. The sooner we discuss your experience, the better you will feel."

After he left, she played with his business card and read over the appointment time while she considered her research options.

Debra returned after lunch and confirmed her release, then took her vitals one last time. Moments later, a med-tech came to remove her IV.

Released from the IV tether, Courtney opened the closet and withdrew the clear tote with her personal items. She emptied the bag on the bed and set her shoes and purse to one side. She dressed while considering where to begin her search. A historical society seemed her best option.

She had just pulled on her jeans when she realized her shirt was missing. "Well, crap."

Debra entered the room with Courtney's discharge paperwork and gave Courtney a curious look. "Is something wrong?"

"I don't have a shirt." She sighed in exasperation and rested her hands on her hips.

"They would have cut it off in the ambulance." Debra set the paperwork on the counter and studied Courtney. "I have an old scrub top in my locker you could have," Debra offered with a generous smile. "I don't wear it anymore. Let me get it."

The nurse was out the door before Courtney could convey her gratitude and relief.

I'm alone now.

That realization hit hard, and she pressed her lips to still their quivering. There was no one she could call for help.

It's the same as before the accident. I'll just have to make do.

Courtney pulled her phone from her purse and turned it on. The happy tone assured her she had battery life. She pressed the contact number for her insurance agent while she waited in her bra for Debra to return. The agent transferred her to the claims department where she received a claim number. Next, she looked up a taxi company on her smartphone and pressed the link to call a cab. Technology made modern life convenient, but she hadn't missed it. Although to be honest, she'd had no memory of technology while she was Nichole...not until the end.

Courtney thanked the cab dispatcher and ended the call as Debra returned. She took the shirt from the nurse. "Thank you," she said and pulled the faded blue top over her head. Courtney listened to Debra read her release instructions while she tied her shoes.

"Your medication should be ready at the pharmacy you have listed. Follow up with Dr. Phelps as soon as possible."

"I have an appointment with him in the morning." Courtney placed her phone and earrings in her purse and slipped the bag over her shoulder.

"That's good." Debra made a note in Courtney's file and then indicated the wheelchair in the doorway. "Let's get you downstairs."

***

Courtney paced with her slow limp at the hospital entrance while she waited for the taxi. Once the cab arrived, she directed the driver to take her to a rental car company near the hospital. She gave the rental agent her insurance claim number and chose a compact car from the vehicles on the lot. A quick stop at the pharmacy to get her prescriptions, then Courtney drove the familiar road to her apartment.

As soon as she unlocked the door and stepped inside, she couldn't help but view the place with new eyes. It was small, but well-appointed with an updated kitchen and bath. Her two-year-old furniture looked showroom new and unused. There were no pictures of friends or family on the wall. She tossed her prescriptions and purse on the kitchen table and walked through the entire apartment, her gaze noticing every detail.

What a small, safe haven I've created for myself.

Its emptiness left a dull ache in her heart.

In her narrow hallway, she stopped her inspection and searched her heart for something positive. She had no family or loved ones, but she did have financial freedom. The trust fund from her parents' estate initially held a substantial amount and had supported Courtney and her grandmother for fifteen years. What remained in her account would see her through college, with a small sum left over for emergencies. It seemed a paltry thing compared to her empty life.

Her thoughts turned to her father. Russell Veau had been a gifted spiritualist and medium. He argued against the term *psychic*. He could not read minds or see into the future. His gift had been the ability to find lost souls and communicate with those who had passed from life. That had been the basis for his television show. He'd also been a philanthropist and worked pro-bono for individuals who needed his help. He'd worked with both state and local agencies to help find missing persons and had often been asked to locate lost or stolen children. The living soul was a beacon to her father. His gift of finding people bordered on magical; however, he was best remembered for his work with the dead.

Courtney had known very little about her father's philanthropy while growing up. Granny Curtis never spoke of it. It wasn't until she turned eighteen that his files, along with articles and newspaper clippings, came to her from Greta. There were boxes of records stacked in the back closet. She'd read through it all, speechless at what she learned. The most personal items—her father's journal and genealogy work—she kept in a box in her bedroom closet. She gravitated to it now and eased her stiff body to the floor. Courtney pulled the small box of mementos onto her lap with a disheartened sigh.

She closed her eyes and fought back the old emotion, the unfairness, and the self-pity. She couldn't miss her parents because she'd never known them, yet their lives and their loss had shaped her own. She shook her head to dispel those thoughts and opened her eyes.

She raised the lid of the box and shuffled through the photographs. There were some of herself as a baby with her mother, and one of her as a toddler, walking and holding her father's hand. There were several photographs of Granny Curtis and her, but they were not what she searched for, and she set them to the side.

She glanced at her father's notes. He'd traced their ancestry several generations but could never get further than Alexander and Catherine Veau. She read a postcard her father discovered during his search. Handwritten by Catherine, and addressed to Alexander, in the flowery cursive of the post-Civil War era, the ink was faded and barely legible. Catherine inquired when Alexander planned to return home from his visit to the capital and signed the card, *Forever yours, Catherine*. Courtney read the card and then set it aside, as well.

Her hands trembled as she picked up her father's journal. She held the book to her chest and spoke to her father through the tightness in her throat. "Daddy, something has happened. I don't...I'm not sure what to do." She swallowed and struggled to regain her composure. "I want to ask you what you thought...what you think I should do?"

She closed her eyes and collected her thoughts. Her father's journal pressed against her breast, expressing more eloquently within her mind the question she asked of her father.

What do I do now?

She lowered the diary and looked at the worn cover, then opened it randomly and read the first line at the top of the page. "*...an item of great significance was found inside the old home.*"

She sat in stillness, the book, open on her lap, as her finger tapped a slow beat against the faded ink. Day turned to dusk, and the apartment grew dark. Her thoughts were far away, reliving her time as Nichole. She remembered the places she went, and finally recalled the route they had taken to the house in Denver. Amy had driven the wagon westward into the city, turning the right at a diagonal thoroughfare and right again at a livery stable. What was the street name? Piper Street? Patch Street? Excitement fluttered in her stomach.

I'm going to find the house.

It took more than one try to get to her feet after sitting for so long. Her left leg and side were sore and stiff. She pulled herself onto the bed with her right arm and sat for a moment as a wave of dizziness swept over her. When it passed, she stood with one hand secure against the wall.

She crept into the kitchen and switched on the overhead light, and then tore open her prescriptions and swallowed one of each with a sip of water. Her backpack was in its usual spot beside the couch. She set it on the counter and slid her laptop from its pocket.

When the screen came to life, she typed in her password and navigated to her favorite map website. In moments, a satellite view of the Denver area appeared on her screen. She followed the highway west toward the city. Ignoring the northern sweep of I-70, she followed Colfax Avenue straight instead.

They'd ridden toward the mountains until they reached a diagonal cross street. Zooming into the area on the map, she saw City Park first—then she spotted the diagonal.

Park Avenue.

"Holy shit," she muttered as her finger traced Park Avenue northwest and turned right on Pence Street. If memory served, the house would be two blocks down on the left, but she'd only been there once.

She clicked the street view icon on the map program and moved the icon house by house down the street until she found it. A chill raced down her spine so sharp it took her breath away. The trees were overgrown and the neighborhood nothing as she remembered, but she was positive. That was her house.

Courtney Veau had never been to Denver. She and Granny Curtis never traveled outside of Texas, yet she knew the inside of that house. She remembered watching Amy walk to the front door and then stop to look up at the second floor. She knew there were narrow stairs at the back of the house that led from the kitchen to the second floor. It was as if she had been there only yesterday.

She bookmarked the page, sent two pages to the printer, and closed the laptop. Had she sat on the kitchen stool and stared at the photo of her house for over an hour? A moan escaped her lips when she stood and tried to stretch. A sharp pain in her side stopped her. She held still until it resolved to a dull ache. The printer ended its chunka-chunka sound, and she limped down the hall to retrieve her printouts.

She looked at the map and the photo of her house and shook her head in amazement.

Dr. Phelps is going to think I'm nuts.

But she didn't care. What happened to her had been real. He could scoff if he liked or add another chapter to his research.

She froze as a crazy idea took hold. Butterflies fluttered in her stomach, and her pulse raced. With a grin on her face, she opened her laptop and began another search.

———

The Soul of the Witch Saga continues in Book 3:

Passage

Also by

Soul of the Witch Saga

Prodigy – Book 1

Pyromancer – Book 2

Passage – Book 3

Prophecy – Book 4

Paradox – Book 5

Patriarch – Book 6

—

J.L.'s Timeless Quest

Aubrielle's Call

The Corsair's Tempest

Hawthorn and Mistletoe

—

The Hunter Chronicles

Hunter's Gamble

Hunter and Lily Graham

The Kid in Black

Penelope's Heart

All of these stories take place within the same shared universe.

About the Author

C. (Connie) Marie Bowen writes paranormal romance and historical fantasy set within a richly layered, persistent universe. Her award-winning novel *Passage* launched the *Soul of the Witch* series, introducing a world where magic, loyalty, and sacrifice intertwine.

Bowen's stories span multiple series, with characters crossing paths and timelines within the shared universe of the Soul of the Witch Saga. Figures such as Hunter from *The Hunter Chronicles* and J.L. from *The Timeless Quest* play meaningful roles within this interconnected world.

Born in Denver, Colorado, Bowen grew up with a love of ghost stories and storytelling. She now lives in the greater Chicagoland area with her husband and two rescue pets, Abigail and Rousseaux.

Visit https://www.cmariebowen.com to explore her connected series and learn more.

www.ingramcontent.com/pod-product-compliance
Lightning Source LLC
Chambersburg PA
CBHW060852250626
47159CB00008B/2707